More Praise for Robert B. Parker and Spenser!

"[Spenser is] tough, wisecracking, unafraid, lonely, unexpectedly literate—in many respects the very exemplar of the species."

—The New York Times

"The best writer of this kind of fiction in the business today."
—The New Republic

"Robert B. Parker has taken his place beside Dashiell Hammett, Raymond Chandler, and Ross Macdonald."
—The Boston Globe

"Spenser probably had more to do with changing the private eye from a coffin-chaser to a full-bodied human being than any other detective hero."

—The Chicago Sun-Times

ROBERT B. PARKER

A NEW COLLECTION OF THREE COMPLETE NOVELS

ROBERT B. PARKER

A NEW COLLECTION OF
THREE COMPLETE NOVELS

The Judas Goat

Looking for Rachel Wallace

Early Autumn

WINGS BOOKS
New York • Avenel, New Jersey

This omnibus was originally published in separate volumes under the titles:

The Judas Goat, copyright © 1978 by Robert B. Parker
Looking for Rachel Wallace, copyright © 1980 by Robert B. Parker
Early Autumn, copyright © 1981 by Robert B. Parker

This 1996 edition is published by Wings Books, a division of Random House Value Publishing, Inc., 40 Engelhard Avenue, Avenel, New Jersey 07001, by arrangement with Delacorte Press, an imprint of Dell Publishing, a division of Bantam Doubleday Dell Publishing Group, Inc.

Wings Books and colophon are trademarks of Random House Value Publishing, Inc.

Random House
New York • Toronto • London • Sydney • Auckland

Printed and bound in the United States of America

Library of Congress Cataloging-in-Publication Data

8   7   6   5   4   3   2   1

Contents

THE JUDAS GOAT

CHAPTER ONE

HUGH DIXON'S HOME sat on a hill in Weston and looked out over the low Massachusetts hills as if asphalt had not been invented yet. It was a big fieldstone house that looked like it ought to have vineyards, and the front entrance was porticoed. It didn't look like the kind of place where they have much truck with private cops, but you can't judge a house by its portico. I parked in the lower parking lot as befitted my social status and climbed the winding drive to the house. Birds sang. Somewhere out of sight on the grounds I could hear a hedge being clipped. The bell made the standard high-tone chime sound in the house when I pushed the button, and while I waited for a servant to let me in I checked my appearance reflected in the full-length windows on each side of the door. There was no way to tell, looking at me, that I only had $387 in the bank. Three-piece white linen suit, blue striped shirt, white silk tie and mahogany loafers with understated tassels that Gucci would have sold his soul for. Maybe Dixon could hire me to stand around and dress up the place. As long as I kept my coat buttoned you couldn't see the gun.

The servant who answered was Asian and male. He wore a white coat and black trousers. I gave him my card and he let me stand in the foyer while he went and showed it to someone. The floor of the foyer was polished stone, and

3

opened into a two-storied entry room with a balcony running around the second story and white plaster frieze around the ceiling. A grand piano sat in the middle of the room and an oil portrait of a stern person was on the wall over a sideboard.

The servant returned and I followed him through the house and out onto the terrace. A man with a huge torso was sitting in a wheel chair with a light gray blanket over his lap and legs. He had a big head and thick black hair with a lot of gray and no sideburns. His face was thick-featured with a big meaty nose and long earlobes. The servant said, "Mr. Dixon," and gestured me toward him. Dixon didn't move as I walked over to him. He stared out over the hills. There was no sign of a book or magazine. No indication of paperwork, portable radio, TV, just the hills to look at. In his lap was a yellow cat, asleep. There was nothing else on the terrace. No other furniture, not even a chair for me.

From this side of the house I couldn't hear the clippers anymore.

I said, "Mr. Dixon?"

He turned, just his head, the rest of him motionless, and looked at me.

"I'm Spenser," I said. "You wanted to talk to me about doing some work for you."

Full front, his face was accurate enough. It looked the way a face should, but it was like a skillful and uninspired sculpture. There was no motion in the face. No sense that blood flowed beneath it and thoughts evolved behind it. It was all surface, exact, detailed and dead.

Except the eyes. The eyes snarled with life and purpose, or something like that. I didn't know exactly what then. Now I do.

I stood. He looked. The cat slept. "How good are you, Spenser?"

"Depends on what you want me to be good at."

"How good are you at doing what you're told?"

"Mediocre," I said. "That's one reason I didn't last with the cops."

4

"How good are you at hanging in there when it's tough?"

"On a scale of ten, ten."

"If I hire you on for something will you quit in the middle?"

"Maybe. If, for instance, you bullshitted me when we started and I got in and found out I'd been bullshitted. I might pack it in on you."

"What will you do for twenty thousand dollars?"

"What are we going to do, Mr. Dixon, play twenty questions until I guess what you want to hire me for?"

"How much you think I weigh?" Dixon said.

"Two forty-five, two fifty," I said. "But I can't see under the blanket."

"I weigh one hundred eighty. My legs are like two strings on a balloon."

I didn't say anything.

He took an 8x10 matted photograph out from under the blanket and held it out to me. The cat awoke and jumped down, annoyed. I took the picture. It was a Bachrach photo of a handsome fortyish woman and two well-bred-looking girls in their late teens. Vassar maybe, or Smith. I started to hand it back to him. He shook his head, left once, right once. "No," he said, "you keep it."

"Your family?"

"Used to be, they got blown into hamburg by a bomb in a restaurant in London a year ago. I remember my daughter's left foot was on the floor next to me, not attached to the rest of her, just her foot, with her cork-soled shoe still on. I'd bought her the shoe that morning."

"I'm sorry" didn't have the right ring for a moment like that so I didn't try. I said, "That how you ended up in the chair?"

He nodded once down, once up. "I was in the hospital for nearly a year."

His voice was like his face, flat and accurate and un-human. There was a stillness in him that only his eyes denied.

"And I got something to do with this."

He nodded again. Once up, once down. "I want them found."

"The bombers?"

Nod.

"You know who they are?"

"No. The London police say it's probably a group called Liberty."

"Why would they blow you up?"

"Because we were where they threw the bomb. They did not know us, or care about us. They had other things to think about and they blew my entire family into garbage. I want them found."

"And that's all you know?"

"I know what they look like. I was awake through it all, and I lay there and looked at each of them and memorized their faces. I'd know every one of them the minute I saw them. That's all I could do. I was paralyzed and I couldn't move and I looked at them as they stood in the rubble and looked at what they'd done, and I memorized everything about them."

He took a manila folder out from under the blanket and gave it to me. "A Scotland Yard detective and an artist came with one of those drawing packs while I was in the hospital and we made these pictures and I gave them the descriptions."

In the folder were nine Identikit sketches of young people, eight men and a woman, and ten pages of typewritten descriptions.

"I had copies made," he said. "The pictures are pretty good. All of them."

"Do I keep these too?" I said.

"Yes."

"You want me to find these people?"

"Yes. I'll give you twenty-five hundred dollars a head, twenty-five thousand for the lot. And expenses."

"Dead or alive?"

"Either one."

"I don't do assassinations."

6

"I'm not asking you to do assassinations. But if you have to kill one or all of them, you still get paid. Either way. I just want them caught."

"And what?"

"And whatever you do with murderers. Brought to justice, punished. Jailed. Executed. That's not your problem. I want them found."

"Where do I start looking?"

"I don't know. I know what I've told you. I suppose you should start in London. That's where they killed us."

I don't think the pronoun was a mistake. He was mostly dead too.

"Okay. I'll need some money."

From his shirt pocket he took a card and held it out to me. I took it and read it. It said, "Jason Carroll, Attorney at Law." Classy. No address, just the name and title.

"He's at One Hundred Federal Street," Dixon said. "Go there and tell him how much you need."

"If I'm going to London I'll need a lot."

"Doesn't matter. You say. When can you go?"

"Fortunately I'm between cases," I said. "I can leave tomorrow."

He said, "I had you checked out. You're between cases a lot. Twenty thousand dollars is the biggest money you've ever seen. You've been minor league all your life."

"Why waste all that bread on a minor leaguer then?"

"Because you're the best I could get. You're tough, you won't cheat me, you'll stick. I heard that from my people. I also heard that sometimes you think you're Captain Midnight. Mostly that's why you stayed in the minors, I heard. For me that's good. A hungry Captain Midnight is just what I need."

"Sometimes I think I'm Hop Harrigan," I said.

"No matter. If I could do this myself I would. But I can't. So I've got to hire you."

"And sometimes you think you're Daddy Warbucks. Just so it's all straight between us. I'll find these people for you. I'm not only the best you can get. I'm the best there is.

But the things I won't do for money are one hell of a lot more numerous than the things I will do."

"Good. A little ego doesn't hurt. I don't care what you do or what your philosophy of life is or whether you're good or bad or if you wet the bed at night. All I care about is these nine people. I want them. Twenty-five hundred a head. Dead or alive. The ones you get alive I want to see. The ones you get dead, I want proof."

"Okay," I said. He didn't offer to shake hands. I didn't offer to salute. He was staring out at the hills again. The cat jumped back up in his lap. "And you want me to keep the picture of your family?" I said.

He didn't look at me. "Yes. Look at it every morning when you get up and remember that the people you're after blew them into mincemeat."

I nodded. He didn't see me. I don't think he saw anything. He looked at the hills. The cat was already asleep again in his lap. I found my way out.

CHAPTER TWO

THE SECRETARY in Jason Carroll's outer office had blond hair that looked real and a tan that looked all over. I speculated on the all-overness as she led me down the hall to Carroll. She was wearing a blue top and tight white pants.

Carroll got up from behind his chrome and onyx desk and came around to greet me. He was blond too, and tan, and slim in a double-breasted blue blazer and white trousers. They looked like a dance team. Sissy and Bobby.

"Glad to see you, Spenser. Come in. Sit down. Mr. Dixon told me you'd be stopping by." He had a firm and practiced handshake, and a Princeton class ring. I sat on a chrome couch with black leather cushions, near a picture window from which you could see a lot of the harbor and some of the railroad yards behind what was left of South Station. A stereo was playing something classical very softly.

"My office is on the second floor over a cigar store," I said.

"Do you like it there?" Carroll asked.

"It's closer to sea level," I said. "This is a little rarified for me."

There were oil paintings of horses on the office walls.

"Would you care for a drink," Carroll said.

"Beer would be good," I said.

"Would Coors be all right? I bring it back whenever I'm out west."

"Yeah, okay. Coors is okay for a domestic beer, I guess."

"I can give you Heineken's if you prefer. Light or dark."

"I'm kidding, Mr. Carroll, Coors would be swell. I can't usually tell one beer from another. As long as it's cold."

He touched an intercom switch and said, "Jan, could we have two Coors please." Then he leaned back in his high leather swivel chair, and folded his hands over his stomach and said, "How can I help?"

The blonde came in with two cans of beer and two chilled glasses on a small tray. She served me first, probably my Jack Nicholson smile, then her boss, and went out.

"Hugh Dixon has hired me to go to London and start looking for the people who killed his wife and daughters. I'll need five grand to start with and he said you'd give me what I need."

"Of course." He took a checkbook from the middle drawer of his desk and wrote a check.

"Will this be enough?"

"For now. If I want more will you send it?"

"As much as you need."

I drank a little Coors from the can. Rocky Mountain spring water. Zowie.

"Tell me a little about Hugh Dixon," I said.

"His financial position is extremely stable," Carroll said. "He has a great many financial interests all over the world. All of which he has acquired through his own efforts. He is a truly self-made man."

"I figured he could pay his bills. I was more interested in what kind of man he is."

"Very successful. Very successful. A real genius for business and finance. I don't think he had a great deal of formal education. I think he started as a cement finisher or something. Then he got a truck and then a backhoe, and by the time he was twenty-five he was on his way."

Carroll wasn't going to talk about Dixon, I guessed. He was just going to talk about his money.

"How did he make most of it? What sort of business?"

If you can't lick 'em, join 'em.

"Building trades at first, and then trucking, and now he has conglomerated so extensively that one cannot specify his business anymore."

"Those are tough trades," I said. "Candy asses do not flourish there."

Carroll looked a little pained. "Certainly not," he said. "Mr. Dixon is a very strong and resourceful man." Carroll sipped a little of his beer. He used the glass. His nails were manicured. His movements were languid and elegant. Breeding, I thought. Ivy League will do that for you. Probably went to Choate too.

"The terrible tragedy of his family . . ." Carroll couldn't find the words for a minute and settled for shaking his head. "They said he shouldn't be alive either. His injuries were so terrible. He should have died. It's miraculous, the doctors said."

"I think he had something to do," I said. "I think he wouldn't die because he had to get even."

"And for that he's hired you."

"Yeah."

"I will help all I can. I went to London when it . . . when he was injured. I know the police on the case and so forth. I can put you in touch with someone in Mr. Dixon's

London office who can help on the scene. I handle all of Mr. Dixon's affairs. Or at least many of them. Especially since the accident."

"Okay," I said. "Do this for me. Give me the name of the person who runs the office over there. Have them get me a hotel room. I'll fly over tonight."

"Do you have a passport?" Carroll looked doubtful.

"Yeah."

"I'll have Jan put you on a flight for London. Do you have a preference?"

"I don't care for biplanes."

"No, I suppose not. If it doesn't matter I'll have Jan arrange for flight fifty-five, Pan Am, leaves every night for London at eight. First class all right?"

"That'll be fine. How do you know there will be room?"

"Mr. Dixon's organization flies extensively. We have a somewhat special status with the airlines."

"I'll bet you do."

"Mr. Michael Flanders will meet you at Heathrow Airport tomorrow morning. He's from Mr. Dixon's London office and will be able to fill you in."

"I imagine you have a somewhat special status with Mr. Flanders."

"Why do you say so?"

"How do you know he'll be free tomorrow morning?"

"Oh, I see. Yes. Well, everyone in the organization knows how strongly Mr. Dixon feels about this business and everyone is ready to do anything necessary."

I finished my beer. Carroll took another sip of his. A man who sips beer is not trustworthy. He smiled at me, white teeth in perfect order, looked at his watch, two hands, nothing so gauche as a digital, and said, "Nearly noon. I expect you'll have some packing to do."

"Yeah. And maybe a few phone calls to the State Department and such."

He raised his eyebrows.

"I'm not going over to look at the *Beowulf* manuscript

11

in the British Museum. I gotta bring a gun. I need to know the rules on that."

"Oh, of course, I really don't know anything about that sort of thing."

"Yeah, that's why I'm going and you're not."

He flashed his perfect caps at me again. "The tickets will be at the Pan Am counter at Logan," he said. "I hope you have a good trip. And . . . I don't quite know what one says at such a time. Good hunting, I suppose, but that sounds awfully dramatic."

"Except when Trevor Howard says it," I said.

On the way out I gave Jan the thumbs-up gesture like in the old RAF movies. I think she was offended.

CHAPTER THREE

MY FIRST MOVE was to call the airline. They said I could bring a handgun as long as it was disassembled, packed in a suitcase and checked through. The ammunition had to be separate. Of course it couldn't be carried aboard.

"Okay if I chew gum when my ears pop?" I said.

"Certainly, sir."

"Thank you."

Next I called the British Consulate. They told me that if I were bringing in a shotgun there would be no problem. I could simply carry it in. No papers required.

"I had in mind a thirty-eight caliber Smith and Wesson revolver. A shotgun in a hip holster tends to chafe. And carry-ing it around London at high port seems a bit showy."

"Indeed. Well, for a handgun the regulations state that if you are properly licensed it will be held at customs until you have received authorization from the chief of police in the city or town of your visit. In this case, you say London?"

"Yes."

"Well, that is where you should apply. It is not permitted of course to bring in machine guns, submachine guns, automatic rifles or any weapon capable of firing a gas-disseminating missile."

"Oh, damn," I said.

Then I called Carroll back. "Have your man in London arrange a permit for me with the London cops." I gave him the serial number, the number of my Mass carry license and the number of my private detective license.

"They may be sticky about issuing this without your presence."

"If they are they are. I'll be there in the morning. Maybe Flanders can have softened them up at least. Don't you people have a somewhat special status with the London fuzz?"

"We will do what we can, Mr. Spenser," he said, and hung up.

A little abrupt for a guy with his breeding. I looked at my watch: 2:00. I looked out my office window. On Mass Avenue a thin old man with a goatee was walking a small old dog on a leash. Even from two stories up you could see the leash was new. Bright metal links and a red leather handle. The old man paused and rummaged through a little basket that was attached to a lamppost. The dog sat in that still patient way old dogs have, his short legs a little bowed.

I called Susan Silverman. She wasn't home. I called my answering service. There were no messages. I told them I was out of town on business. Didn't know when I'd be back. The girl at the other end took the news without a quiver.

I locked up the office and went home to pack. A suitcase, a flight bag and a garment bag for my other suit. I packed two boxes of .38 bullets in the suitcase. Took the cylinder out of the gun and packed it in two pieces in the flight bag along with the holster. By three-fifteen I was packed. I called Susan Silverman again. No answer.

There are people in the city of Boston who have

13

threatened to kill me. I don't like to walk around without a gun. So I took my spare, and stuck it in my belt at the small of my back. It was a Colt .357 Magnum with a four-inch barrel. I kept it around in case I was ever attacked by a finback whale, and it was heavy and uncomfortable under my coat as I took Carroll's check down to my bank and cashed it.

"Would you like this in traveler's checks, Mr. Spenser?"

"No. Plain money. If you have any English money I'd take that."

"I'm sorry. We could get you some perhaps Friday."

"No. Just give me the greenies. I'll change it over there."

"Are you sure you want to walk around with this amount in cash?"

"Yes. Look at my boyish face. Would someone mug me?"

"Well, you're quite a big man."

"But oh so gentle," I said.

Back in my apartment at quarter to four I called Susan Silverman again. No answer.

I got out the phone book and called the registrar's office at the Harvard Summer School.

"I'm trying to locate a student. Mrs. Silverman. She's taking a couple of courses there in counseling, I think."

There was some discussion of how difficult it would be to find a student like that without more information. They'd transfer me to the School of Education.

The School of Education offices were closing at four-thirty and it would be quite difficult to locate a student. Had I tried the registrar? Yes, I had. Perhaps someone in the Department of Counseling and Guidance could help me. She switched me there. Did I know the professor's name. No, I didn't. The course number? No. Well, it would be very difficult.

"Not as difficult as I will be if I have to come over there and kick a professor."

"I beg your pardon?"

14

"Just check the schedules. Tell me if there's a counseling course meeting at this hour or later. You must have schedules. Pretend this isn't a matter of life and death. Pretend I have a government grant to award. Pretend I'm Solomon Guggenheim."

"I believe that Solomon Guggenheim is dead," she said.

"Jesus Christ . . ."

"But I'll check," she said. "Hold the line, please." There was distant typing and vague movement at the other end of the line and in thirty seconds the secretary came back on.

"There's a class in Techniques of Counseling, Professor More, that meets from two-o-five to four fifty-five."

"Where is it?"

She told me. I hung up and headed for Harvard Square. It was four-twenty.

At four-forty I found a hydrant on Mass Avenue outside the Harvard Yard and parked in front of it. You could usually count on a hydrant. I asked a young woman in tennis shorts and hiking boots to direct me to Sever Hall and at four-fifty-six was waiting under a tree near the steps when Susan came out. She was wearing a blue madras jumpsuit with a big gold zipper, and carrying her books in a huge white canvas shoulder bag. She had a quality coming down the steps that she always had. She looked as if it were her building and she was strolling out to survey the grounds. I felt the jolt. I'd been looking at her for about three years now but every time I saw her I felt a kind of jolt, a body shock that was tangible. It made the muscles in my neck and shoulders tighten. She saw me and her face brightened and she smiled.

Two undergraduates eyed her covertly. The jumpsuit fitted her well. Her dark hair glistened in the sunshine and as she got close I could see my reflection in the opaque lenses of her big sunglasses. My white three-piece suit looked terrific.

She said to me, "I beg your pardon, are you a Greek multibillionaire shipping magnate and member of the international jet set?"

I said, "Yes, I am, would you care to marry me and live on my private island in great luxury?"

15

She said, "Yes, I would, but I'm committed to a small-time thug in Boston and first I'll have to shake him."

"It's not the thug I mind," I said. "It's the small-time."

She hooked her arm through mine and said, "You're big-time with me, kid."

As we walked through the Yard several students and faculty eyed Susan. I didn't blame them but looked hard at them anyway. It's good to keep in practice.

"Why are you here?" she said.

"I gotta go to England at eight tonight and I wanted some time to say goodbye."

"How long?"

"I don't know. Could be long. Could be some months. I can't tell."

"I will miss you," she said.

"We'll miss each other."

"Yes."

"I'm parked out on Mass Avenue."

"I parked at Everett Station and took the subway in. We can go to your apartment and I'll drive you to the airport in your car."

"Okay," I said. "But don't be so bossy. You know how I hate a bossy broad."

"Bossy?"

"Yeah."

"Did you have a plan for our farewell celebration?"

"Yeah."

"Forget it."

"Okay, boss."

She squeezed my arm and smiled. It was a stunner of a smile. There was something in it. Mischief was too weak a word. Evil too strong. But it was always there in the smile. Something that seemed to be saying, *You know what would be fun to do?*

I held the door for her and as she slid into my car the jumpsuit stretched tight and smooth over her thigh. I went around and got in and started the car.

16

"It strikes me," I said, "that if you were wearing under-wear beneath that jumpsuit it would show. It doesn't show."

"That's for me to know and you to find out, big fella."

"Oh, good," I said, "the celebration is back on."

CHAPTER FOUR

I FOUND OUT about the underwear, and some other things. Most of the other things I already knew, but it was a pleasure to be reminded. Afterward we lay on top of my bed, with the afternoon sun shining. Her body, strong, and a little damp from mutual exertion, glistened where the sun touched it.

"You are a strong and active person," I said.

"Regular exercise," she said. "And a positive attitude."

"I think you wrinkled my white linen suit."

"It would have wrinkled on the airplane anyway."

We got dressed and walked up Boylston Street and across the Prudential Center to a restaurant called St. Botolph. It was one of the zillion California-theme restaurants that had appeared in the wake of urban renewal like dandelions on a new seeded lawn. Tucked back of the Colonnade Hotel, it was brick and had hanging plants and relative informality where one could actually get a good meat loaf. Among other things.

I had the meat loaf and Susan had scallops Provençale. There wasn't much to say. I told her about the job.

"Bounty hunter," she said.

"Yeah, I guess so. Just like the movies."

"Do you have a plan?"

Her make-up was expert. Eye liner, eye shadow, color on the cheekbones, lipstick. She probably looked better at forty than she had at twenty. There were small lines at the corners of her eyes, and smile suggestions at the edges of her mouth that added to her face, gave it pattern and meaning.

"Same old plan I always have. I'll show up and mess around and see if I can get something stirring and see what happens. Maybe put an ad in the papers offering a big reward."

"A group like that? Do you think a reward could get one of them to turn another in?"

I shrugged. "Maybe. Maybe it would get them to make contact with me. One way or another. I have to have a contact. I need a Judas goat."

"Might they try to kill you if they know you're there?"

"Maybe. I plan to thwart them."

"And then you'll have your contact," Susan said.

"Yeah."

She shook her head. "This will not be a pleasant time for me."

"I know . . . I won't like it that much either."

"Maybe part of you won't. But you're having a grand adventure too. Tom Swift, Bounty Hunter. Part of you will have a wonderful time."

"That was truer before I knew you," I said. "Even bounty hunting is less fun without you."

"I think that's true. I appreciate it. I know that you are what you are. But if I lose you it will be chronic. It will be something I'll never completely get over."

"I'll come back," I said. "I won't die away from you."

"Oh, Jesus," she said, and her voice filled. She turned her head away.

My throat was very tight and my eyes burned. "I know the feeling," I said. "If I weren't such a tough manly bastard, I might come very close to sniffling a little myself."

She turned back toward me. Her eyes were very shiny, but her face was smooth and she said, "Well, maybe you, cupcake, but not me. I'm going to do one excerpt from my famous Miss Kitty impression and then we are going to laugh and chatter brightly till flight time." She put her hand on my forearm, and looked at me hard and leaned forward and said, "Be careful, Matt."

"A man's gotta do what he's gotta do, Kitty," I said. "Let's have a beer."

We were chatty and bright for the rest of the meal and the ride to the airport. Susan dropped me off at the International Terminal. I got out, unlocked the trunk, took out my luggage, put the .357 in the trunk, locked it and leaned into the car.

"I won't go in with you," she said. "Sitting and waiting in airports is too dismal. Send me a postcard. I'll be here when you come back."

I kissed her goodbye and hauled my luggage into the terminal.

The tickets were at the Pan Am desk as promised. I picked them up, checked my luggage through and went up to wait at the loading gate. It was a slow night at the International Terminal. I cleared the security check, found a seat near the boarding ramp and got out my book. I was working on a scholarly book that year. *Regeneration Through Violence,* by a guy named Richard Slotkin. A friend of Susan's had lent it to me to read because he wanted what he called "an untutored reaction from someone in the field." He was an English teacher at Tufts and could be excused that kind of talk. More or less.

I liked the book but I couldn't concentrate. Sitting alone at night in an airport is a lonely feeling. And waiting to fly away to another country, by yourself, on a nearly empty plane was very lonely. I half decided to turn around and call Susan and say come get me. I minded being alone more as I got older. Or was it just Susan. Either way. Ten years ago this would have been a great adventure. Now I wanted to run.

At eight-thirty we boarded. At eight-fifty we took off. By nine-fifteen I had my first beer from the stewardess and a bag of Smokehouse Almonds. I began to feel better. Tomorrow perhaps I could have dinner in Simpson's and maybe for lunch I could find a nice Indian restaurant. By ten I had drunk three beers and eaten perhaps half a pound of almonds. The flight was not crowded and the stewardess was attentive. Probably drawn by the elegance of my three-piece linen suit. Even wrinkled.

I read my book and ignored the movie and listened to the oldies but goodies channel on the headphones and had a few more beers, and my mood brightened some more. After midnight I stretched out across several seats and took a nap. When I woke up the stewardesses were serving coffee and rolls and the sun was shining in the windows.

We landed at Heathrow Airport outside of London at ten-fifty-five London time and I stumbled off the plane, stiff from sleeping on the seats. The coffee and rolls were sloshing around with the beer and Smokehouse Almonds.

For simple hodgepodge confusion and complicated extent, Heathrow Airport's name leads all the rest. I followed arrows and took Bus A and followed more arrows and finally found myself in the line at the passport window. The clerk looked at my passport, smiled and said, "Nice to see you, Mr. Spenser. Would you please step over to the security office, there."

"They've reported me. I'm to be arrested for excessive beer consumption on an international flight."

The clerk smiled and nodded toward the security office. "Right over there, please, sir."

I took my passport and went to the office. Inside was a security officer in uniform and a tall thin man, with long teeth, smoking a cigarette and wearing a dark green shirt with a brown tie.

"My name is Spenser," I said. "People at the passport desk sent me over."

The tall thin guy said, "Welcome to England, Spenser. I'm Michael Flanders."

We shook hands.

"Do you have baggage checks?"

I did.

"Let me have them, will you. I'll have your baggage taken care of."

He gave the checks to the security man, and steered

me out of the office with his hand on my elbow. We came out a different door and I realized we'd cleared customs. Flanders reached inside his tweed jacket and brought out an envelope with my name on it.

"Here," he said. "I was able to arrange this with the authorities this morning."

I opened the envelope. It was a gun permit.

"Not bad," I said.

We came out of the terminal building underneath one of the walkways that connects the second floors of everything at Heathrow. A black London cab was there and a porter was loading my luggage in while the security man watched.

"Not bad," I said.

Flanders smiled. "Nothing, really. Mr. Dixon's name has considerable sway here as it does in so many places." He gestured me into the cab, the driver came around and said something I didn't understand and we started off.

Flanders said to the cabbie, "Mayfair Hotel, if you would." And leaned back and lit another cigarette. His fingers were long and bony and stained with nicotine.

"We're putting you up in the Mayfair," he said to me. "It's a first-rate hotel and nicely located. I hope it will be satisfactory."

"Last case I was on," I said, "I slept two nights in a rented Pinto. I can make do okay in the Mayfair."

"Well, good," he said.

"You know why I'm here," I said.

"I do."

"What can you tell me?"

"Not very much, I'm afraid. Perhaps when we get you settled we can have lunch and talk about it. I imagine you'd like to freshen up a bit, get that suit off to the dry cleaners."

"Sure wrinkles on an airplane, doesn't it?"

"Indeed."

CHAPTER FIVE

THE MAYFAIR was a big flossy-looking hotel near Berkeley Square. Flanders paid the cabbie, turned the bags over to the hall porter and steered me to the desk. He didn't seem to have a lot of confidence in me. A hired thug from the provinces, can barely speak the language, no doubt. I checked my heel for a cow flap.

My room had a bed, a bureau, a blue wing chair, a small mahogany table and a white tiled bathroom. The window looked out over an airshaft into the building next door. Old-world charm. Flanders tipped the bell man, and checked his watch.

"One o'clock," he said. "Perhaps you'd like to take the afternoon and get settled, then we could have dinner and I could tell you what I know. Do you need money?"

"I have money, but I need pounds," I said.

"Yes," he said. "Of course. I'll have it changed for you." He took a big wallet from inside his jacket pocket. "Here's one hundred pounds," he said, "should you need it to hold you over."

"Thanks." I took my wallet out of my left hip pocket, and dug out $2500. "If you could change that for me, I'd appreciate it. Take out the hundred."

He looked at my wallet with some distaste. It was fat and slovenly.

"No need," he said. "Mr. Dixon's money, you know. He's been quite explicit about treating you well."

"So far so good," I said. "I won't tell him you got me a room on an airshaft."

"I am sorry about that," Flanders said. "It's peak season for touists, you know, and the notice was short."

"My lips are sealed," I said.

Flanders smiled tentatively. He wasn't sure if he was being kidded.

"Shall I come by for you, say six?"

"Six is good, but why not meet somewhere. I can find my way. If I get lost I'll ask a cop."

"Very well, would you care to try Simpson's-on-the-Strand? It's rather a London institution."

"Good, see you there at six-fifteen."

He gave me the address and departed. I unpacked and reassembled my gun, loaded it and put it on the night table.

Then I shaved, brushed my teeth and took a shower. I picked up the phone and asked the front desk to call me at five-thirty. Then I took a nap on the top of the spread. I missed Susan.

At five-forty-five, vigorous and alert, with a spring in my step and my revolver back in its hip holster, I strode out the main entrance of the Mayfair. I turned down Berkeley Street and headed for Piccadilly.

I had a city map that I'd bought in a shop in the hotel, and I'd been in London once before a few years back, before Susan, when I'd come for a week with Brenda Loring. I walked down Piccadilly, stopped at Fortnum and Mason and looked at the package food stuffs in the window. I was excited. I like cities and London was a city the way New York is a city. The fun it would be to stroll around Fortnum and Mason with Susan and buy some smoked quail's eggs or a jellied game hen or something imported from the Khyber Pass.

I moved on up into Piccadilly Circus, which was implacably ordinary, movie theaters and fast foods, turned right on Haymarket and walked on down to Trafalgar Square, Nelson and the lions, and the National Gallery and the goddamned pigeons. Kids were in competition to see who could accumulate the most pigeons on and around them. Walking up the Strand I passed a London cop walking peaceably along, hands behind his back, walkie-talkie in his hip pocket, the mike pinned to his lapel. His nightstick was artfully concealed in a deep and inconspicuous pocket.

As I walked I could feel an excited tight feeling in my stomach. I kept thinking of Samuel Johnson, and Shakespeare. "The old country," I thought. Which wasn't quite so. My family was Irish. But it was the ancestral home, anyway, for people who spoke English and could read it.

Simpson's was on the right, just past the Savoy Hotel. I wondered if they played "Stompin' at the Savoy" over the music in the elevators. Probably the wrong Savoy. I turned into Simpson's, which was oak paneled and high ceilinged, and spoke to the maître d'. The maître d' assigned a subordinate to take me to Flanders, who rose as I approached. So did the man with him. Very classy.

"Mr. Spenser, Inspector Downes, of the police. I asked him to join us, if that's all right with you."

I wondered what happened if it weren't all right. Did Downes back away out of the restaurant, bowing apologetically?

"Fine with me," I said. We shook hands. The waiter pulled out my chair. We sat down.

"A drink?" Flanders said.

"Draught beer," I said.

"Whiskey," Downes said.

Flanders ordered Kir.

"Inspector Downes worked on the Dixon case," Flanders said, "and is a specialist in this kind of urban guerrilla crime that we see so much of these days."

Downes smiled modestly. "I'm not sure expert is appropriate, but I've dealt with a good many, you know."

The waiter returned with the drinks. The beer was cold, at least, but much flatter than American beer. I drank some. Flanders sipped at his Kir. Downes had his whiskey straight without ice or water, in a small tumbler, and sipped it like a cordial. He was fair-skinned with a big round face and shiny pink cheekbones. His body under the black civil-servicey-looking suit was heavy and sort of slack. Not fat, just quite relaxed. There was a sense of slow power about him.

"Oh, before I forget," Flanders said. He took an envelope from inside his coat and handed it to me. On the outside in red pen was written, "Spenser, 1400." "The exchange rate is very good these days," Flanders said. "Your gain and our loss, isn't it."

I nodded and stuck the envelope in my jacket pocket. "Thank you," I said. "What have you got to tell me?"

"Let's order first," Flanders said. He had salmon, Downes had roast beef and I ordered mutton. Always try the native cuisine. The waiter looked like Barry Fitzgerald. He seemed delighted with our choices.

"Faith and begorra," I murmured.

Flanders said, "I beg your pardon?"

I shook my head. "Just an old American saying. What have you got?"

Downes said, "Really not much, I'm afraid. A group called Liberty has claimed responsibility for the Dixon murders and we have no reason to doubt them."

"What are they like?"

"Young people, apparently very conservative, recruited from all over western Europe. Headquarters might be in Amsterdam."

"How many?"

"Oh, ten, twelve. The figure changes every day. Some join, others leave. It doesn't seem a very well organized affair. More like a random group of juveniles larking about."

"Goals?"

"Excuse me?"

"What are the goals of their organization? Do they wish to save the great whales? Free Ireland? Smash apartheid? Restore Palestine? Discourage abortion?"

"I think they are anticommunist."

"That doesn't explain blowing Dixon up. Dixon industries aren't practicing state socialism, are they?"

Downes smiled and shook his head. "Hardly. The bombing was random violence. Urban guerrilla tactics. Disruption, terror, that sort of thing. It unravels the fabric of government, creates confusion, and allows the establishment of a new power structure. Or some such."

"How are they progressing?"

"The government seems to be holding its own."

"They do much of this sort of thing?"

"Hard to say," Downes sipped at his Scotch some more and rolled it around over his tongue. "Damned fine. It's hard to say because we get so bloody much of this sort of thing from so many corners. Gets difficult to know who is blowing up whom and why."

Flanders said, "But, as I understand it, Phil, this is not a major group. It doesn't threaten the stability of the country."

Downes shook his head, "No, surely not. Western civilization is in no immediate danger. But they do hurt people. We all have reason to know that," Flanders said. "Does any of this help?"

"Not so far," I said. "If anything it hurts. As Downes knows, the more amateurish and unorganized and sappy a group like this is, the harder it is to get a handle on them. The big well organized ones I'll bet you people have infiltrated already."

Downes shrugged and sipped at his Scotch. "You're certainly right about the first part anyway, Spenser. The random childishness of it makes them much more difficult to deal with. The same random childishness limits their effectiveness in terms of revolution or whatever in hell they want. But it makes them damned hard to catch."

"Have you anything?"

"If you were from the papers," Downes said, "I'd reply that we were developing several promising possibilities. Since you're not from the papers I can be more brief. No. We haven't anything."

"No names? No faces?"

"Only the sketches we took from Mr. Dixon. We've circulated them. No one has surfaced."

"Informants?"

"No one knows anything about it."

"How hard have you been looking?"

"As hard as we can," Downes said. "You've not been over here long, but as you may know, we are pressed. The

Irish business occupies most of our counterinsurgency machinery."

"You haven't looked hard."

Downes looked at Flanders. "Not true. We have given it as much attention as we can."

"I'm not accusing you of anything. I understand your kind of problems. I used to be a cop. I'm just saying it so Flanders will understand that you have not been able to conduct an exhaustive search. You've sifted the physical evidence. You've put out flyers, you've checked the urban guerilla files and the case is still active. But you don't have a lot of bodies out beating the bushes on Egdon Heath or whatever."

Downes shrugged and finished his Scotch. "True," he said.

Barry Fitzgerald came back with food. He brought with him a man in a white apron who pushed a large copper-hooded steam table. At tableside he opened the hood, and carved to my specifications a large joint of mutton. When he was finished he stood back with a smile. I looked at Flanders. Flanders tipped him.

While the carver was carving, Barry put out the rest of the food. I ordered another beer. He seemed delighted to get it for me.

CHAPTER SIX

I REJECTED FLANDERS's offer of a cab and strolled back up the Strand toward the Mayfair in the slowly gathering evening. It was a little after eight o'clock. I had nowhere to be till morning and I walked randomly. Where the Strand runs into Trafalgar Square I turned down Whitehall. I stopped halfway down and looked at the two mounted sentries in the sentry box outside the Horse Guards building. They had leather hip boots and metal breastplates and old-time British Empire helmets, like statues, except for the young and ordinary faces that stared out under the helmets and the eyes that moved. The faces were kind of a shock. At the end of Whitehall was Parliament and Westminster Bridge, and across Parliament Square, Westminster Abbey. I'd walked through it some years back with Brenda Loring and a stampede of tourists. I'd like to walk through it when it was empty sometime.

I looked at my watch: 8:50. Subtract six hours, it was ten of three at home. I wondered if Susan was in her counseling class. It probably didn't meet every day. But maybe in the summer. I walked a little way out into Westminster Bridge and looked down at the river. The Thames. Jesus Christ. It had flowed through this city when only Wampanoags were on the Charles. Below me to the left was a landing platform where excursion boats loaded and unloaded. Susan and I had gone the year before to Amsterdam and had a wine and cheese cruise by candlelight along the canals and looked at the high seventeenth-century fronts of the canal houses. Shakespeare must have crossed this river. I had some vague recollection that the Globe Theatre was on the other side. Or had been. I also had the vague feeling that it no longer existed.

I looked at the river for a long time and then turned and leaned on the bridge railing with my arms folded and watched the people for a while. I was striking, I thought, in blue blazer, gray slacks, white oxford button-down and blue and red rep striped tie. I'd opened the tie and let it hang down casually against the white shirt, a touch of informality, and it was only a matter of time until a swinging London bird in a leather miniskirt saw that I was lonely and stopped to perk me up.

Miniskirts didn't seem prevalent. I saw a lot of harem pants and a lot of the cigarette look with Levis tucked into the top of high boots. I would have accepted either substitute, but no one made a move on me. Probably had found out I was foreign. Xenophobic bastards. No one even noticed the brass touch on the tassels on my loafers. Suze noticed them the first time I had them on.

I gave it up after a while. I hadn't smoked in ten or twelve years, but I wished then I'd had a cigarette that I could have taken a final drag on and flipped still burning into the river as I turned and walked away. Not smoking gains in the area of lung cancer, but it loses badly in the realm of dramatic gestures. At the edge of St. James's Park there was something called Birdcage Walk and I took it. Probably my Irish romanticism. It led me along the south side of St. James's Park to Buckingham Palace.

I stood outside awhile and stared in at the wide bare hard-paved courtyard. "How you doing, Queen," I murmured. There was a way to tell if they were there or not but I'd forgotten what it was. Didn't matter much. They probably wouldn't make a move on me either.

From the memorial statue in the circle in front of the palace a path led across Green Park toward Piccadilly and my hotel. I took it. I felt strange walking through a dark place of grass and trees an ocean away from home, alone. I thought about myself as a small boy and the circumstantial chain that connected that small boy with the middle-aging man who found himself alone in the night in a park in London. The little boy didn't seem to be me very much. And neither did the middle-aging man. I was incomplete. I missed Susan and I'd never missed anyone before.

I came out on Piccadilly again, turned right and then left onto Berkeley. I walked past the Mayfair and looked at Berkeley Square, long and narrow and very neat-looking. I didn't hear a nightingale singing. Someday maybe I'd come back here with Susan, and I would. I went back to the hotel and had room service bring me four beers.

"How many glasses, sir?"

"None," I said in a mean voice.

When it came I overtipped the bellhop to make up for the mean voice, drank the four beers from the bottle and went to bed.

In the morning I went out early and placed an ad in

the *Times*. The ad said: "REWARD. One thousand pounds offered for information about organization called Liberty and death of three people in bombing of Steinlee's Restaurant last August 21. Call Spenser, Hotel Mayfair, London."

Downes had promised the previous evening to have the file on Dixon sent over to my hotel and by the time I got back it was there, in a brown manila envelope, folded in half the long way and crammed in the mail box back of the front desk. I took it up to my room and read it. There were Xerox copies of the first officer's report, statements taken from witnesses, Dixon's statement from his hospital bed, copies of the Identikit sketches that had been made and regular reports of no progress submitted by various cops. There was also a Xerox of a note from Liberty claiming credit for the bombing and claiming victory over the "communist goons." And there was a copy of a brief history of Liberty, presumably culled from the newspaper files.

I lay on the bed in my hotel room with the airshaft window open and read it over three times, alert for clues the English cops had missed. There weren't any. If they had overlooked anything, I had too. It was almost as if I weren't any smarter than they were. I looked at my watch: 11:15. Almost time for lunch. If I went out and walked in leisurely fashion to a restaurant and ate slowly then I would have only four or five hours to kill till dinner. I looked at the material again. There was nothing in it. If my ad didn't produce any action, I didn't have any idea what to do next. I could drink a lot of beer and tour the country but Dixon might get restless about that after I'd gone through a couple of five grand advances.

I went out, went to a pub in Shepherd's Market near Curzon Street, had lunch, drank some beer, then walked up to Trafalgar Square and went into the National Gallery. I spent the afternoon there looking at the paintings, staring most of the time at the portraits of people from another time and feeling the impact of their reality. The fifteenth-century woman in profile whose nose seemed to have been broken. Rembrandt's portrait of himself. I found myself straining after them. It was after five when I left and walked in a kind of head-buzzing sense of separateness out into Trafalgar Square and the current reality of the pigeons. The ad would run in the morning, they had told me. I had nothing to do tonight. I didn't feel like sitting alone in a restaurant and eating dinner, so I went back to my room, had a plateful of sandwiches sent up with some beer and ate in my room while I read my book.

The next morning the ad was there, as promised. As far as I could tell I was the only one who'd seen it. No one called that day, nor the next. The ad kept running. I hung around the hotel waiting until I got crazy, and then I went out and hoped they'd leave a message. During the next five days I visited the British Museum and looked at the Elgin Marbles, and visited the Tower of London and looked at the initials scratched in the walls of tower cells. I observed the changing of the guard, and jogged regularly through Hyde Park along the Serpentine.

I came in six days after the ad was placed, my shirt wet with sweat, my blue sweat pants worn stylishly with the ankle zippers open, my Adidas Cross-Countries still new-looking. I asked as always were there any messages, and the clerk said "Yes" and took a white envelope out of the box and gave it to me. It was sealed and said on it only "Spenser."

"This was delivered?" I said.

"Yes, sir."

"Not phoned in? This isn't your envelope?"

"No, sir, that was delivered by a young gentleman, I believe, sir. Perhaps half an hour ago."

"Is he still here?" I said.

"No, sir, I don't believe I see him about. You might try the coffee shop."

"Thanks."

Why hadn't they phoned it in? Because they wanted to see who I was, maybe, and they could do that by dropping off an envelope and posting someone to watch who opened it. Then they'd know who I was and I wouldn't know who they were. I walked toward one of the armchairs in the lobby where every afternoon tea was served. There was glass panel-ing on the far wall and I sat in a chair facing it so I could look in the mirror. I had on my sunglasses and I peeked out from behind them at the mirror while I opened the envelope. It was thin and unsuspicious. I doubted a letter bomb. For all I knew it might be a note from Flanders inviting me to join him for high tea at the Connaught. But it wasn't. It was what I wanted.

The note said, "Be at the cafeteria end of the east tunnel near the north gate entrance to the London Zoo in Regent's Park tomorrow at ten in the morning."

I pretended to read it again and surveyed the lobby from behind my shades as far as the mirror would let me. I didn't see anything suspicious, but I didn't expect to. I was trying to memorize all the faces in the place so if I saw one again I'd remember it. I put the letter back in the envelope and turned thoughtfully in my chair, tapping my teeth with a corner of the envelope. Pensive, deep in thought, looking hard as a bastard around the hotel lobby. No one was carrying a Sten gun. I went out the front door and strolled up toward Green Park.

It is not easy to follow someone without being spotted, if the someone is trying to catch you doing it. I caught her crossing Piccadilly. She'd been in the hotel lobby buying postcards, and now she was crossing Piccadilly toward Green Park half a block down the street. I was still in my sweat pants and I didn't have a gun. They might want to burn me right now right quick once they had me spotted.

In Green Park I stopped, did a few deep knee bends and stretching exercises for show and then started an easy jog down toward the Mall. If she wanted me she'd have to run to keep up. If she started running to keep up, I'd know she didn't care about being spotted, which would mean she was probably going to shoot me, or point me out to someone else who would shoot me. In which case I would hang a U-turn and run like hell for Piccadilly and a cop.

She didn't run. She let me go, and by the time I reached the Mall she was gone. I walked back up to Piccadilly along Queen's Walk, crossed the street and walked down to the Mayfair. I didn't see her and she wasn't in the lobby. I went up to my room and took a shower with my gun lying on the top of the toilet tank. I felt good. After a week of watching the sun set on the British Empire I was working again. And I was one up on somebody who thought they were one up on me. If she was from Liberty then they thought they had me spotted and I didn't know them. If they weren't, if they wanted just to see if they could screw me out of the thousand pounds and were taking a look at how hard I looked, I was still even. I knew them and they thought I didn't, and moreover they thought that's where they were. There were drawbacks. They knew all of me and I only knew one of them. On the other hand, I was a professional and they were amateurs. Of course, if one of them laid a bomb on me, the bomb might not know the difference between amateurs and professionals.

I put on jeans, a white Levi shirt, and white Adidas Roms with blue stripes. I didn't want the goddamned limeys to think an American sleuth didn't know color coordination. I got a black woven-leather shoulder rig out of the suitcase and slipped into it. They aren't as comfortable as hip holsters, but I wanted to wear a short Levi jacket and the hip holster would show. I put my gun in the holster and put on the Levi jacket, and left it unbuttoned. It was dark blue corduroy. I looked at myself in the mirror over the bureau. I turned up the collar. Elegant. Clean-shaven, fresh-showered, with a recent haircut. I was the image of the international adventurer. I tried a couple of fast draws to make sure the shoulder holster worked right, did one perfect Bogart imitation at myself in the mirror, "All right, Louis, drop the gun," and I was ready for action.

The room had been made up already so there was no need for a maid to come in again. I took a can of talcum powder, and, standing in the hall, I sprinkled it carefully and evenly over the rug in front of the door inside my room. Anyone who came in would leave a footprint inside and tracks outside when he left. If they were observant they might notice and wipe out the tracks. But unless they were carrying a can of talc they would have trouble covering the footprints inside.

I shut the door carefully over the smooth layer of talcum and took the can with me. There was a wastebasket by

33

the elevators and I dropped the empty talc can in. I'd get another on my way back tonight.

I walked down to Piccadilly Circus and took a subway to Regent's Park. I had my map of London folded and creased in my hip pocket and I got it out and sneaked a look at it, trying not to look just like a tourist. I figured out the best walk through the park, nodded knowingly in case anyone was watching, as if I was just confirming what I knew already, and headed on up to the north gate. I wanted a look at the territory before I showed up there tomorrow.

I went past the cranes, geese, and owls at north gate entrance and across the bridge over Regent's Canal. A water bus chugged by underneath. By the insect house a tunnel led under a zoo office building and emerged beside the zoo restaurant. To the left was a cafeteria. To the right a restaurant and bar. Past the cafeteria were some flamingos in a little grass park. Flamingos on the grass, alas. If they wanted to burn me, the tunnel was their best bet. It wasn't much of a tunnel, but it was straight and without alcoves. No place to hide. If someone came at me from each end they could cut me in two without much trouble. Stay out of the tunnel.

At the photo shop in the cafeteria I bought a guide to the zoo that had a map inside the back cover. The south gate, down by Wolf Wood, looked like a good spot to come in tomorrow. I walked down to take a look. Past the parrot house and across from something labeled *Budgerigars,* there were kids taking camel rides and shrieking with laughter at the camel's rolling asymmetrical gait.

The south gate was just past the birds of prey aviary, which seemed ominous, past the wild dogs and foxes, and next to the Wolf Wood. That wasn't too encouraging either. I went back up and looked at the cafeteria setup. There was a pavilion and tables. The food was served from an open-faced arcadelike building. If I sat on the pavilion at an open-air table I was a good target from almost any point. There was little cover. I ordered a steak and kidney pudding from the cafeteria and took it to a table. It was cold and tasted like a Nerf ball. While I gagged it down, I looked at my situation. If they were going to shoot me, there was little to prevent them. Maybe they weren't going to shoot me, but I couldn't plan much on that.

"You can't plan on the enemy's intentions," I said. "You have to plan on what he can do, not what he might."

A boy cleaning the tables looked at me oddly. "Beg pardon, sir?"

"Just remarking on military strategy. Ever do that? Sit around and talk to yourself about military strategy?"

"No, sir."

"You're probably wise not to. Here, take this with you."

I dropped most of my steak and kidney pie into his trash bucket. He moved on. I wanted two things, maybe three, depending on how you counted. I wanted not to get killed. I wanted to decommission some of the enemy. I wanted at least one of them to get away with me following. Decommission. Nice word. Sounds better than kill. But I am thinking about killing a couple of people here. Calling it decommission isn't going to make it better. It's their choice though. I won't shoot if I'm not taking fire. They try to kill me, I'll fight. I'm not setting them up. They are setting me up . . . Except I'm setting them up to set me up so I can set them up. Messy. But you're going to do it anyway, kid, whether it's messy or not, so there's not too much point to analyzing its ethical implications. Yeah, I guess I am. I guess I'll just see if it feels good afterward.

They were experienced with explosives. And they didn't worry about who got hurt. We knew that. If I were they I might wait till I got inside the tunnel, then roll in some explosives and turn me into a cave painting. Or they could do me in on the bridge over the canal.

I knew who they were. I knew the girl and I had the pictures that Dixon had given me. Only the girl knew who I was. She'd have to be there to spot me. Maybe I could spot them first. How many would they send? If they were going to trap me in the tunnel, at least two plus the spotter. They'd at least want one at each end. But when they blew up the Dixons there were nine of them that Dixon spotted. They didn't need nine. It must have been their sense of community. The group that blasts together lasts together.

My bet was they'd show up in force. And they'd be careful. They'd be looking for a police setup. Anyone would. They wouldn't be that stupid. So they'd be watching too. I stood up. There was nothing to do but blunder into it. I'd stay out of the tunnel, and I'd keep away from open areas as best I could, and I'd look very carefully at everything. I knew them and they didn't know it. Only one of them knew me. That was as much edge as I was going to get. The shoulder holster under my coat felt awkward. I wished I had more fire power.

The steak and kidney pie felt like a bowling ball in my stomach as I headed out onto Prince Albert Road and caught a red double-decker bus back to Mayfair.

CHAPTER SEVEN

ON THE WAY back to my hotel I got off the bus on Piccadilly and went into a men's specialty store. I bought a blond wig, a blond mustache, and some make-up cement to attach it. Spenser, man of a thousand faces. Outside my door there was a white talcum powder footprint. I kept on going past my room and on down the corridor. When it intersected with a cross corridor I turned right and leaned against the wall. There was no sign of anyone lurking. A standard approach to this kind of business would be one on the inside and one on the outside, but that didn't seem the case.

Of course it could have been a hotel employee on innocent business. But it might be someone who wanted to shoot me dead. I put the bag with my disguise in it on the floor and slid my gun out of the shoulder holster. I held it in my right hand and folded my arms across my chest so the gun was concealed under my arm. There was no one in the corridor. I peeked around the corner. There was no one in that corridor either.

I went down the corridor softly to my room. Took the key out of my pocket with my left hand; my right had the gun in it, chest-high now, and visible. The dim sounds of the hotel's muffled machinery whirred on around me. The elevators going and stopping. The sound of air-conditioning apparatus, faintly a television playing somewhere. The hotel door was dark oak, the room numbers in brass.

I stood outside my room and listened. There was no sound. Standing to the right of the door and reaching with my left hand, I put the key as gently as I could into the lock and turned it. Nothing happened. I opened the door a fraction to free the catch. Then I wiggled the key out, and slipped it back in my pocket. I took a deep breath. It was hard to swallow. I shoved the door open with my left hand and rolled back out of sight against the wall to the right of the door. I had the hammer back on my gun. Nothing happened. No one made a sound.

The lights were off, but the afternoon sun was shining and the room shed some light into the corridor. I edged a few steps down the corridor so that I could get a better angle on the door, and crossed. If someone came out shooting they'd expect me to be where I had been, to the right of the door, on the same wall. I folded my arms again to hide the gun, and leaned against the wall and looked at the open door and waited.

The elevator stopped to my right and a man in a tattersall vest got off with a lady in a pink pantsuit. He was bald, her hair was bluish gray. They looked past me, rigorously not being curious as they walked by. They were equally careful not to look into the open door of the room. I watched them as they went on. They didn't look like bombers but who can tell a bomber by his appearance. You have to be a little suspicious of anyone who wears a tattersall vest anyway. They went into a room about ten doors down. Nothing else moved.

I would feel like a terrible numb-nuts if the room

turned out to be empty and I was poised out here like agent X-15 for hours. But I would be a terrible numb-nuts if I just walked in there and found it flourishing with assassins, and bought the farm right here in Merry England because I wasn't patient. I would wait.

He would wait, too, apparently. But I was betting the tension would get him. The open door would get wider and wider open as he looked at it. If there were two of them it would take longer. One guy gets scareder than two guys. But I had nowhere to go till ten next morning. I was betting I could wait longer.

An Indian woman in a white uniform rolled a laundry cart past me, looked curiously into the open room but paid me no attention. I was finding that more and more women were paying me no attention these days. Perhaps tastes were drifting away from the matinee idol type.

The light from my room waned. I kept my eyes on it because I knew there'd be a shadow when the assassin made his move. Or maybe he knew that too and was waiting till dark.

Two African men came off the elevator and walked down past me. They both wore gray business suits with very narrow lapels. They both wore dark narrow ties and white broadcloth shirts with collars that turned up slightly at the ends. The one nearest me had tribal marks scarred into his cheeks. His companion had round gold-framed glasses on. They were speaking in British-accented English as they went by me, and paid no attention to me or the door. I watched them peripherally as I watched the door too. Anyone could be an accomplice.

The phone was near the door, and in the reeking silence I was pretty sure that the assassin couldn't call without me hearing him. But there might have been a signal of some sort from the window, or there might be a prearranged time when if he didn't call the back-up came looking.

It was hard watching both the door and the corridor traffic. I was getting tired of holding the gun. My hand was stiff, and with the thing cocked I had to hold it carefully. I thought about shifting it to my left hand. I wasn't as good with my left hand, and I might need to be very good all of a sudden. I wouldn't be too good if my gun hand had gone to sleep, however. I shifted the thing to my left hand and exercised my right. The gun felt clumsy in my left. I ought to practice left-handed more. I hadn't anticipated a gun hand going to sleep. *How'd you get shot, Spenser? Well, it's this way, Saint Pete. I was staked out in a hotel corridor but my hand went to sleep. Then after a while my entire body nodded off. Did Bogie's hand ever go to sleep, Spenser? Did Kerry Drake's? No, sir, I don't think we can admit you here to Private-Eye Heaven, Spenser.*

I was getting soft standing out there in the corridor. My right hand felt better and I shifted the gun back. No more light came out of the open door of my room. A family of four, complete with Instamatics and shoulder bags, came out of the elevator and walked past me down the corridor. The kids looked into the open door. The father said, "Keep walking." He had an American accent and his voice was tired. The mom had an admirable backside. They turned right at the cross corridor and disappeared. It was getting late. I was working overtime here. Sudden-death overtime. Ah, Spenser, what a way you have with words. Sudden-death overtime. Dynamite.

My feet hurt. I was beginning to experience lower back pain from standing so long. Why do you get more tired standing than walking? An imponderable. Waiting for someone to jump out of a dark doorway and shoot at you is tiring too. Pay attention. Don't let the mind wander. You tended to lose sight for a minute when the mom with the backside walked past. If that had been fight time you'd have cashed it in right there, kid.

I looked hard at the door. The assassin would have to appear from the right. The open door was flush against the left-hand wall. He'd roll around the right wall looking for me down the corridor. Or maybe not, maybe he'd come on his belly, close to the floor. That's what I would do. Or would I? Maybe I'd dive out of the door and get an angle on me from across the corridor, try to be too quick for the guy who's been standing there getting hypnotized by staring at the door.

Or maybe I wouldn't even be there. Maybe I would be an empty room and some nervous dimwit would stand outside and stare at the emptiness for a number of hours. I could call hotel security and tell them I'd found my door open. But if there was someone in there the first person through the door was going to get blasted. The assassin had been in there too long to make fine distinctions. And if he was a Liberty type he didn't care much who got killed anyway. I couldn't ask someone else to walk in there for me. I'd wait. I could wait. It was one of the things I was good at. I could hang on.

Up the corridor past me a room service waiter, dark-skinned in a white coat, wheeled a table full of covered dishes off the service elevator and around the corner to the right. A faint baked potato smell drifted back down the corridor to me. After my steak and kidney pie I had thought about extensive fasting, but the baked potatoe smell made me reconsider.

The assassin came out in a scrabbling crouch, and fired one shot down the corridor toward the elevator on the wall opposite to where I was, before he realized I wasn't there. He was quick, and half turned to shoot toward me when I shot him in the chest, my arm straight, my body half turned, not breathing while I squeezed off the shot. At close range my bullet spun him half around. I shot him again as he fell on his side with his knees up. The gun skittered out of his hand as he fell. Small caliber. Long barrel. Target gun. I jumped over and dove through the open door of my room, landed on my shoulder and rolled past the bed. There was a second man, and his first bullet took a piece out of the door frame behind me. His second one caught me with a sharp tug in the back of my left thigh. Half sitting, I shot three times into the middle of his dark form, in faint silhouette against the window. He went backward over a straight chair and lay on his back with one foot draped on the chair seat.

I raised to a full sit-up against the wall. That's why they could wait so long. There were two. My breath was coming very heavy and I could feel my heart pumping in the middle of my chest. I'm not gonna get shot, I'm gonna have cardiac arrest some day.

I took in deep breaths of air. In the right-hand breast pocket of my blue corduroy Levi jacket were twelve extra shells. I opened the cylinder of my gun and popped out the spent cartridges. There was one live round left. I felt down at the back of my left leg. It didn't hurt yet, but it was warm and I knew I was bleeding. The gun shots in the enclosed corridor had been very loud. That should bring some cops pretty quick.

I edged over to the dark shape with his foot on the chair. I felt for pulse and found none. I got to my feet and walked a little unsteadily to the door. The first man I shot lay as he had fallen. The long-barreled target pistol a foot from his inert hand. His knees drawn up. There was blood on the hall carpet. I put my gun back in its holster and walked over to him. He was dead too. I went back into my room. The back of my leg was beginning to hurt. I sat down on the bed and picked up the phone when I heard the footsteps in the hall. Some of them stopped a little way from my room and some came on to the door. I put the phone back down.

"All right in there, come out with your hands up. This is the police."

"It's okay," I said. "There's a guy dead in here and I'm wounded. Come on in. I'm on your side."

A young man in a light raincoat stepped quickly into the room and pointed a revolver at me. Behind him came an older man with graying hair and he pointed a revolver at me too.

"Stand up, please," the younger man said, "and put your hands on top of your head, fingers clasped."

"There's a gun in the shoulder holster under my left arm," I said. Several uniformed bobbies and two more guys in civilian clothes crowded into the room. One of them went directly to the phone and began to talk. The guy with the graying hair patted me down, took my gun, took the seven remaining bullets from my jacket pocket and stepped back.

The young one said to the man on the phone, "He's

bleeding. He'll need medical attention." The guy on the phone nodded.

The young cop said to me, "All right, tell us about it, please."

"I'm a good guy," I said. "I'm an American investigator. I'm over here working on a case. If you'll get hold of Inspector Downes in your department he'll vouch for me."

"And these gentlemen," he nodded at the body on the floor and included, with a sweep of his chin, the guy I had dumped in the corridor.

"I don't know. I'd guess they were going to put me away because I was on this case. I came back to the room and they were waiting for me."

The gray cop said, "You killed them both?"

"Yeah."

"This is the gun?"

"Yeah."

"Some identification, please?"

I handed it over, including the British gun permit.

The gray cop said to the one on the phone, "Tell them to get hold of Phil Downes. We've got an American investigator here named Spenser that claims to know him."

The cop on the phone nodded. As he talked he stuck a cigarette in his mouth and lit it.

A man came in with a small black doctor bag. He had on a dark silk suit and a lavender shirt with the collar spread out over the suit lapels. Around his neck were small turquoise beads on a choker necklace.

"Name's Kensy," he said. "Hotel physician."

"You staid British doctors are all the same," I said.

"No doubt. Please drop your pants and lie across the bed, face down."

I did what I was told. The leg was hurting a lot now, and I knew the back of my pants leg was soaked with blood. Dignity is not easy, I thought. But it is always possible. The doctor went into the bathroom to wash.

The cop in the light raincoat said, "You know either of these people, Mr. Spenser?"

"I haven't even gotten a look at them yet."

The doctor came back. I couldn't see him but I could hear him fumbling around. "This may sting a bit." I smelled alcohol and felt it sting as the doctor swabbed off the area.

"The bullet still in there?" I asked.

"No, went right through. Clean wound. Some blood loss, but nothing, I think, to be concerned over."

"Good, I'd just as soon not be carrying a slug around in the upper thigh," I said.

"You may choose to call it that if you wish," the doctor said, "but in point of fact, my man, you've been shot in the arse."

"There's marksmanship," I said. "And in the dark too."

CHAPTER EIGHT

THE DOCTOR put a pressure bandage on my, ah, thigh, and gave me some pills for the pain. "You'll walk funny for a few days," he said. "After that you should be fine. Though you'll have an extra dimple in your cheeks now."

"I'm glad there's socialized medicine," I said. "If only there was a vow of silence that went with it."

Downes showed up as the doctor was leaving. And he and I explained my situation to the gray cop and the young one. Two guys came with body bags and before they took away the bodies we looked at them. I got out my Identikit pictures and both of them were in the pictures. Neither one was out of his twenties. Or ever would be.

Downes looked at the Identikit picture and the fallen kid, and nodded. "How much you get for him?"

"Twenty-five hundred dollars."

"What will that buy in your country?"

43

"Half a car."

"Luxury car?"

"No."

Downes looked at the kid again. He had long blond hair and his fingernails were very recently clipped and clean. His still hands looked very vulnerable.

"Half an inexpensive car," Downes said.

"He ambushed me," I said. "I didn't lay in wait for either of them."

"You say."

"Oh come on, Downes. Is this the way I'd do it?"

Downes shrugged. He was looking at the traces of talcum powder still in front of the door. White partial footprints were now all over the room.

"You powdered the room before you left," he said.

"Yeah."

"If one of them hadn't?"

"I'd have opened the door very slowly and carefully and checked the floor inside before I went in," I said.

"And you waited them out. Shoved the door open and stood in the corridor until they made their move."

"Yeah."

"Well now, you're intrepid enough, aren't you."

"The very word for it," I said.

"The problem is," Downes said, "we can't have you running around London shooting down suspected anarchists at random and collecting the bounty."

"That's not my plan, Downes. I don't shoot people I don't have to shoot. I'm here doing a job that needs to be done, that you people are too busy to do. These two clowns tried to kill me, remember. I didn't shoot them because they were suspected anarchists. I shot them to keep them from shooting me."

"Why did you powder the floor when you left?"

"Can't be too careful in a foreign land," I said.

"And the ad you placed in the *Times?*"

I shrugged. "I had to get their attention."

"Apparently you succeeded."

A uniformed cop came in with my bag of disguises and handed it to Downes. "Found this down the corridor, sir, around the corner."

"That's mine," I said. "I left it there when I discovered the assassins."

"Assassins, is it," Downes said. He reached in the bag and took out my wig and mustache and make-up cement. His broad placid face brightened. He smiled a large smile that pushed his cheeks up and made his eyes almost close. He held the mustache under his nose. "How do I look, Grimes?" he said to the bobby.

"Like a ruddy guardsman, sir."

"My ass is hurting," I said. "And I don't think it's the wound."

"Why a disguise, Spenser? Did they know who you were?"

"I think one of them spotted me yesterday."

"And you arranged a meeting?"

I didn't want Downes at the meeting. I was afraid he'd scare off my quarry and I needed to make another contact.

"No, they just left a letter in my mailbox and when they saw me take it and read it they knew who I was. There's no meeting yet. The letter said they'd be in touch. I think it was a setup. So I thought I'd change my appearance a bit."

Downes looked at me silently for maybe a minute.

"Well," he said, "certainly there will be little grieving over these two. I do hope you'll keep in touch with us as things develop. And I do hope that you do not plan to bring all of these people to justice this way."

"Not if I have a choice," I said.

The technicians zipped up the second body bag and trundled it out on a dolly.

"Half an inexpensive car," Downes said.

"What kind of gun did the guy in here have? The one that shot me?"

The cop in the light raincoat said, "Same as the one in the hall, Colt twenty-two target pistol. They probably stole a

45

crate of them somewhere. You're lucky they didn't steal a forty-five caliber, or a Magnum."

"Might have taken a good deal more of your butt than it did," Downes said.

"Thigh," I said. "Upper thigh wound."

Downes shrugged. "I'd lock my door if I were you, and be quite alert, all right?"

I nodded. Downes and the other two were all that were left in the room now.

"Keep in touch, won't you?" Downes said.

I nodded again. Downes gestured at the door with his head and the three of them got up and left. I closed the door behind them and slid the bolt. The doctor had given me some pills for the pain if it got bad. I didn't want to take them yet. I needed to think. I sat on the bed and changed my mind quickly. Lying was a better idea. Lying on my stomach was the best idea of all. Shot in the ass. Susan would doubtless find that funny. Only hurts when I laugh.

This was not a dumb group. They had me thinking about tomorrow and while I was thinking about tomorrow they would ace me tonight. Not bad. But now what. Would they show up tomorrow? Yes. They would be there looking to see if I were there looking to see if they were there. I couldn't know that tonight's trouble was them. They didn't know I had Identikit drawings. Even if I did, I wouldn't know—hell, I didn't know—that the people who wanted to see me were the same ones who tried to blow me away tonight. Maybe there really was an informant. Maybe tonight's people were trying to stop me from getting to the informant. I'd have to go tomorrow.

I left a wake-up call for seven-thirty, took two painkillers, and in a little while I went to sleep on my stomach. It was a pill and pain sleep, fitful, and full of brief awakenings. Killing two kids didn't help any. I was up before the wake-up call, relieved at the dawn, feeling like I'd backed into a stove. I had slept in my clothes and my pants were stiff with dried blood when I took them off. I showered and did my best to keep the bandage dry. I brushed my teeth and shaved and put on clean

46

clothes. Gray slacks, blue-and-white-striped shirt with a button-down collar, blue knit tie, black-tasseled loafers, shoulder holster with gun. Continuity in the midst of change. I pasted on my fake mustache, adjusted my wig, put on a pair of pink-tinted aviator glasses and slid into my blue blazer with the brass buttons and the full tattersall lining. You *can* trust a guy with a tattersall lining. I checked the mirror. The roll in my collar wasn't quite right. I loosened the tie and redid it not quite as tight.

I stepped back for a look in the full-length mirror. I looked like the bouncer in a gay bar. But it might do. I looked a lot different than I had yesterday in sweat pants and track shoes in the lobby. I put six more bullets in my inside coat pocket and I was ready. I powdered the floor again, and went to the hotel coffee shop. I hadn't eaten since the steak and kidney pudding and it was past time. I ate three eggs sunny side up and ham and coffee and toast. It was eight-ten when I got through. In front of the hotel I got a cab and rode up to the zoo in comfort. Leaning a little to the right as I sat.

CHAPTER NINE

THEY WERE THERE. The girl I'd spotted before was looking at the flamingos as I walked up from the south gate past the hawks and eagles in the birds of prey displays. I stoped with my back to her and looked at the parrots in the parrot house. She didn't know I had spotted her before so she made no attempt to hide. She just looked casual as she strolled over to the crows' cage. She didn't take any note of me. Spenser, master illusionist.

For the next two hours we did something difficult and complex like the ritual mating dance of ring-necked pheasants. She looked for me without appearing to and I watched her without appearing to. There had to be some others around. People with guns. They didn't know what I looked like, though they probably had a description. I didn't really know what they looked like unless the Identikit drawings were very accurate and they were the same people who had wasted the Dixons.

She strolled to the chimps' lawn. I strolled to the cockatoos. She walked to the parrots, I moved to the north end of the gibbons' cage. She looked at the budgies while keeping an eye out for me. I had a cup of coffee at the garden kiosk while making sure I didn't lose her. She was wondering if there were undercover cops around. I was looking for members of her group. We were both trying to look like ordinary zoo patrons who chose to stay around the east tunnel area of the zoo. My part was complicated by the fact that I felt like a horse's ass with my wig and my mustache. I was having a little trouble with the coffee because of the mustache. If it fell off that might give the bad guys a hint that something was up.

The strain of it was physical. By eleven o'clock I was sweating and the back of my neck hurt. My wound was hurting all the time. And not limping was a matter of concentration all the time. It must have been hard for her too, though she hadn't been shot in the back of the lap. As far as I knew.

She was a pretty good-looking person. Not as young as the people I'd met last night. Thirty maybe, with straight hair, very blond that reached her shoulders. Her eyes were very round and noticeable, and as close as I'd gotten they looked black. Her breasts were a little too large but her thighs were first quality. She had on black sandals and white slacks and a white open-necked blouse with a black scarf knotted at the neck. She had a big black leather shoulder bag, and I was betting a gun in it. Handgun probably. The bag wasn't quite big enough for an antitank gun.

At eleven-forty-five by the clock tower she gave up. I was nearly two hours late. She shook her head twice, vigorously, at someone I couldn't see and headed for the tunnel. I went after her. The tunnel was something I wanted to avoid, but I didn't see how I could. I didn't want to lose her. I'd gone to a lot of trouble for this contact and I wanted to get something out of it. But if they caught me in the tunnel I was dead. I had no choice. Disguise, do your duty. I went into the tunnel after her.

There was no one in it. I walked through slowly, whistling and unconcerned, with the trapezius muscles across my back in a state of tension. As I came out of the tunnel I ditched the pink-shaded glasses in a trash basket and put on my normal sunglasses. I took my tie off and stuck it in my pocket and opened the collar of my shirt three buttons. I read in a Dick Tracy Crime Stopper that a small change in appearance can be helpful when following someone surreptitiously.

She wasn't hard to follow. She wasn't looking for me. And she was walking. She walked east on Prince Albert Road and turned down Albany Street. We went south on Albany across Marylebone onto Great Portland Street.

To the left the Post Office Tower stuck up above the city. She turned left ahead of me and started up Carburton Street. The area was getting more neighborhood and small grocery store. More middle class and student. I had a dim memory that east of the Post Office Tower was Bloomsbury and the University of London and the British Museum. She turned right onto Cleveland Street. She had a hell of a walk. I liked to watch it and I had been now for ten or fifteen minutes. It was a free, long-striding, hip-swing walk with a lot of spring to it. It was fast pace for walking wounded, and I felt the gunshot wound with every step. At the corner of Tottenham Street, diagonally across from a hospital, she turned into one of the brick-faced buildings, up three steps and in the front door.

I found a doorway with some sun and stood in it, and leaned against the wall where I could see the door she'd gone in, and waited. She didn't come out until almost two-thirty in the afternoon. Then it was just to walk half a block to a grocery store and back with a bag of groceries. I never had to leave my doorway.

Okay, I thought, this is where she lives. So what? One

of the things about my employment was the frequency with which I didn't know what I was doing or what to do next. Always a fresh surprise. I have tracked the beast to its lair, I thought. Now what do I do with her? Beast wasn't the right word, but it didn't sound right to say I've tracked the beauty to her lair.

As so often in dilemmas of this kind, I came upon the perfect thing to do. Nothing. I decided I'd better wait and watch and see what happened. If at first you don't succeed put it off till tomorrow. I looked at my watch. After four. I had been watching the girl and her doorway since before nine this morning. Every natural appetite and need pressed upon me. I was hungry and thirsty and nearly incontinent and the pain in my backside was both real and symbolic. If I was going to do this for very long I was going to need help. By six I had to pitch it in.

It was less than two blocks from the Post Office Tower. They had most of what I needed and I headed for it. On the way I took off my wig and mustache and stuffed them in my pocket. The dining room opened at six twenty and the second thing I did after I reached it was to get a table by the window and order a beer. The restaurant was on top of the tower and rotated slowly so that in the course of a meal you saw the whole 360-degree panorama of London from much the highest building. I knew that rotating restaurants like this atop a garish skyscraper were supposed to be touristy and cheap and I tried to be scornful of it. But the view of London below me was spectacular, and I finally gave up and loved it. Furthermore, the restaurant carried Amstel, which I could no longer get at home, and to celebrate I had several bottles. It was midweek and early and the restaurant wasn't yet crowded. No one hurried me.

The menu was large and elaborate and seemed devoid of steak and kidney pudding. That in itself was worth another drink. As the restaurant inched around I could look south at the Thames and to the east at St. Paul's with its massive dome, squat and Churchillian, so different from the upward soar of the great continental cathedrals. Its feet were planted firmly in the English bedrock. I was beginning to feel the four Dutch beers on an empty stomach. Here's looking at you, St. Paul's, I said to myself.

The waiter took my order and brought me another beer. I sipped it. Regent's Park edged into view from the north. There was a lot of green in this huge city. This sceptered isle, this England. I drank some more beer. Here's looking at you, Billy boy. The waiter brought my veal piccata and I ate it without biting his hand, but just barely. For dessert I had an English trifle and two cups of coffee, and it was after eight before I was out on the street heading for home.

There had been enough beer to make my wound feel okay and I wanted to walk off the indulgence, so I brought out my London street map and plotted a pleasant stroll back to Mayfair. It took me down Cleveland to Oxford Street, west on Oxford and then south on New Bond Street. It was after nine and the beer had worn off when I turned up Bruton Street to Berkeley Square. The walk had settled the food and drink, but my wound was hurting again and I was thinking about a hot shower and clean sheets. Ahead of me up Berkeley Street was the side door of the Mayfair. I went in past the hotel theater, up two stairs into the lobby. I saw no one in the lobby with a lethal engine. The elevator was crowded and unthreatening. I went up two floors above mine and got off and walked down toward the far end of the corner and took the service elevator, marked EMPLOYEES ONLY, to my floor.

No sense walking like a fly into the parlor. The service elevator opened into a little foyer where linen was stored. Four doors down toward my room from the service elevator the cross corridor intersected. Leaning near the corner and occasionally peering out around the corner down toward my door was a fat man with kinky blond hair and rosy cheeks. He was wearing a gray gabardine raincoat and he kept his right hand in the pocket. He didn't have to be waiting to ambush me but I couldn't think what else he'd be doing there. Where was the other one? They'd send two, or more, but not one.

He should be at the other end of my corridor so they could get me in a crossfire. They would know who I was when

I stopped and put the key in my door. I stood very quietly inside the linen foyer and watched. At the far end of the corridor the elevator doors slid back and three people got out, two young women and a fortyish man in a three-piece corduroy suit. As they came down the corridor toward me a man appeared beyond the elevator and watched them. All three passed my door and the guy down the corridor disappeared. The one closer to me turned and looked down the cross corridor as if he were waiting for his wife.

Okay, so they were trying again. Industrious bastards. Hostile, too. All I did was put an ad in the paper. I got back in the service elevator and went up three floors. I got out, went down an identical corridor to the public elevators and looked in behind them. The stairway was there. I descended around the elevator shaft and it was in the stairway that the other shooter was hiding three floors below. I'd take him from above. He wouldn't be looking for me to come down. He'd be waiting for me to come up.

I took off my coat, rolled my sleeves back over the elbows and took off my shoes and socks. It was psychological on the sleeves, I admit, but they bothered me and made me feel encumbered, and so what if I humor a fetish. The fifty-dollar black-tasseled loafers were lovely to look at, delightful to own, but awful to fight in, and they made noise when you snuck up on assassins. Stocking feet tend to be slippery. With my shoes off, my cuffs dragged and I had to roll them up. I looked like I was going wading. Huck Finn.

I went down the stairs in my bare feet without a sound. The stairshaft was neat and empty. To my right the workings of the elevator purred and halted, purred and halted. At the bend before my floor I stopped and listened. I heard someone sniff, and the sound of fabric scraping against the wall. He was on my side of the fire door. He listened for the elevator stop, and if it was this floor he'd step out after the doors closed and take a look. That made it easier. He was leaning against the wall. That was the fabric scrape I heard. He'd be facing the fire doors, leaning against the wall. He'd want the gun hand free. Unless he was left-handed that meant he'd be on the left-hand wall. Most people weren't left-handed.

I stepped around the corner and there he was, four steps down, leaning against the left-hand wall with his back to me. I jumped the four steps and landed behind him just as he caught a reflected movement in the wired-glass fire doors. He half turned, pulling the long-barreled gun out of his waistband, and I hit him with my forearm across the right side of the face, high. He bounced back against the wall, and fell over on the floor, and was quiet. You break your hand hitting a man in the head hard enough to put him out. I picked up the gun. Part of the same shipment. Long barreled .22 target gun. Not a lot of pizzazz, but if they shot the right part of you they would do. I felt him over for another weapon, but the .22 was it.

I ran back up the two flights, put my shoes and jacket back on, rolled down my pants legs, stuffed the pistol in my belt at the small of my back and ran back downstairs. My man was not moving. He lay on his back with his mouth open. I noticed he had those whiskers like one of the Smith Brothers that starts at the corner of the mouth and runs back to the ears. Ugly.

I opened the fire door and stepped into the hall. The man in the other corridor wasn't visible. I walked straight down the hall past my door. I could sense a slight movement at the corner of the corridor. I turned the corridor corner and he was standing a little uncertainly, trying to look unconcerned but half suspicious. I must look like his description, but why hadn't I gone into my room. His hand was still in his raincoat pocket. The raincoat was open.

I walked past him three steps, turned around and yanked the open raincoat down over his arms. He struggled to get his arm out of his pocket. Without letting go of his coat I took the gun out from under my arm with my right hand and pressed it into the hollow behind his ear. "England swings," I said, "like a pendulum do."

CHAPTER TEN

"TAKE YOUR RIGHT hand about one inch out of your pocket," I said, "and stop."

He did. There was no gun in it. "Okay, now put both hands behind your back and clasp them." I let go of his coat with my left hand and reached around and took the pistol out of his pocket. Target gun number four. I stuck it in my left-hand jacket pocket where it sagged very unfashionably. I patted him down quickly with my left hand. He didn't have another piece.

"Very good. Now put both hands back in your pockets."

He did.

"What's your name?"

"Suck my ass," he said.

"Okay, Suck," I said. "We're going down the corridor and pick up your buddy. If you have an itch, don't scratch it. If you hiccup or sneeze or yawn or bat your eyes I am going to shoot a hole through your head." I held the back of his collar with my left hand and kept the muzzle of my gun pressed in behind his right ear and we walked down the corridor. Past the elevator, behind the fire doors there was nobody. I hadn't hit him hard enough and whiskers was up and away. He didn't have a weapon and I didn't think he'd try me without one. I had already killed two of his buddies armed.

"Suck, my boy," I said, "I think you've been forsaken. But I won't turn my back on you. We'll go to my place and rap."

"Don't call me Suck, you bloody bastard." His English sounded upper class but not quite native.

I took out my room key and gave it to him. The gun still at his neck. "Open the door, Scum Bag, and step in."

54

He did. No bomb went off. I went in after him and kicked the door shut.

"Sit there," I said and shoved him toward the armchair near the airshaft.

He sat. I put the gun back in my shoulder holster. Put the two target pistols on the top shelf of the closet, took my wig and mustache and tie out of my pockets, took off my blue blazer and hung it up.

"What's your name?" I said.

He stared at me without speaking.

"You English?"

He was silent.

"Do you know that I get twenty-five hundred dollars for you alive or dead, and dead is easier?"

He crossed one pudgy leg over the other one and locked his hands over his knees. I went to the bureau and took out a pair of brown leather work gloves and slipped them on, slowly, like I'd seen Jack Palance do in *Shane,* wiggling my fingers down into them till they were snug.

"What is your name?" I said.

He gathered some saliva in his mouth and spit on the rug in my direction.

I took two steps toward him, grabbed hold of his chin with my left hand and yanked his face up at mine. He took a gravity knife out of his sock and made a pass at my throat. I leaned back and the point just nicked me under the chin. I caught the knife hand at the wrist as it went by with my right, stepped around behind him, put my left hand into his armpit and dislocated his elbow. The knife fell to the carpet. He made a harsh, half-stifled yell.

I kicked the knife across the room and let go of his arm. It hung at an odd angle. I stepped away from him and went to look at my chin in the mirror over the bureau. There was already blood all over my chin and dripping on my shirt. I took a clean handkerchief from the drawer and blotted up enough of the blood to see that the cut was minor, little more than a razor nick, maybe an inch long. I folded the handkerchief over and held it against the cut.

"Sloppy frisk," I said. "My own fault, Suck."

He sat still in the chair, his face tight and pale with pain.

"When you tell me what I want to know I'll get a doctor. What's your name?"

"Up your bleeding ass."

"I could do the other arm the same."

He was silent.

"Or the same one again."

"I am not going to say nothing," he said, his voice strained and shallow as he held against the pain. "No matter what you do. No bloody red sucking Yankee thug is going to make me say anything I don't want."

I took my Identikit sketches out and looked at them. He could have been one of them. I couldn't be sure. Dixon would have to ID him. I put the sketches away, took out the card that Downes had given me, went over to the phone and called him.

"I guess I got another one, Inspector. Fat little guy with blond hair and a Colt .22 target pistol."

"Are you at your hotel?"

"Yes, sir."

"I'll come over there, then."

"Yes, sir, and he needs a doctor. I had to bend his arm some."

"I'll call the hotel and have their man sent up."

The doctor arrived about five minutes before Downes did. It was Kensy, same doctor who'd been in to treat me. Today he had on a three-piece gray worsted suit with the waist nipped in and a lot of shoulder padding and a black silk shirt with long collar rolled out over the lapels.

"Well, sir," he said as he came in, "how's your arse?" And put his head back and laughed.

"What do you wear in surgery," I said, "a hot pink surgical mask?"

"My dear man, I don't do surgery. I'd better have a look at that chin though."

"Nope, just look at this guy's arm," I said.

He knelt beside the chair and looked at the kid's arm.

"Dislocated," he said. "Have to go to a hospital to have it set." He looked at me. "You do this?"

I nodded. "You're quite the lethal chap, aren't you?" he said.

"My entire body is a dangerous weapon," I said.

"Mm, I would think so," he said. "I'll put a kind of splint on that, my man," he said to the kid, "and give you something for the pain. And then we'd best bundle you off to the hospital and have an orthopedic man deal with it. I gather you have to wait on the authorities, however."

The kid didn't speak. "Yeah, he has to do that," I said.

Kensy took an inflatable splint from his bag and very gently put it onto the kid's damaged arm. Then he blew it up. He filled a hypodermic needle and gave him a shot. "You should feel better," he said, "in just a minute."

Kensy was putting the needle back in the bag when Downes came in. He looked at the kid with his arm in the temporary cast that looked like a transparent balloon. "Another half a car, Spenser?"

"Maybe. I think so, but it's hard to be sure."

There was a uniformed cop and a young woman in civilian clothes with Downes. "Tell me about this one," Downes said. The young woman sat down and took out a notebook. The uniformed bobby stood by the door. Kensy had his bag closed and headed for the door.

"That's only a temporary cast," he said to Downes. "Best get him prompt orthopedic attention."

"We'll get him to the hospital straight away," Downes said. "Fifteen minutes, no more."

"Good," Kensy said. "Try to avoid hurting anyone for a day or two, would you, Spenser. I'm going on holiday tonight, and I won't be back until Monday."

"Have a nice time," I said.

He left.

"Can you hold him for Dixon to look at?" I said.

"I imagine we can. What charges are you suggesting?"

"Oh, what, possession of a stolen weapon, possession of an unlicensed weapon, assault."

"You assaulted me, you red sucking son of a bitch," he said.

"Using profanity in front of a police officer," I said.

"We'll find an appropriate charge," Downes said. "Right now I'd like to hear the story."

I told him. The young lady wrote down everything we said.

"And the other one ran off on you," Downes said. "Unfortunate. You'd have had the start, perhaps, on another car."

"I could have killed him," I said.

"I am aware of that, Spenser. It's one reason I am not pressing you harder about all this." He looked at the bobby. "Gates," he said. "Take this gentleman down to the car. Be careful of his arm. I'll be right along and we'll take him to the hospital. Murray," he said to the young lady, "you go along with them."

The three of them left. The kid never looked at me. I was still holding the handkerchief to my chin. "You ought to clean that up and get a bandage on it," Downes said.

"I will in a minute," I said.

"Yes, well, I have two things I wish to say, Spenser. One, I would get some help, were I you. They've tried twice in two days. There's no reason to think that they will not try again. I don't think this is a one-man job."

"I was thinking the same thing. I'll put in a call to the States tonight."

"That's the second thing I wish to say. I am ambivalent about this entire adventure. So far you have probably done the British government and the city of London a favor by taking three terrorists out of circulation. I appreciate that. But I am not comfortable about an armed counterinsurgency movement developing in my city, conducted by Americans who operate without very much concern for British law or indeed for British custom. If you must import help, I will not allow an army of hired thugs to run loose in my city shooting terrorists on sight, and, in passing, making my department look rather bad."

"No sweat, Downes. If I get help it will be just one guy, and we'll stay out of the papers."

"You hope to stay out of the papers. But it will not be easy. The *Evening Standard* and the *Evening News* have been very insistent on getting the story of last night's shooting. I've put them off but inevitably someone will give them your name."

"I don't want ink," I said. "I'll shoot them away."

"I hope so," Downes said. "I hope too that you'll not be staying with us a great many more days, hmm?"

"We'll see," I said.

"Yes," Downes said. "Of course we will."

CHAPTER ELEVEN

I SAT ON THE BED and read the dialing instructions on the phone. I was exhausted. It was hard even to read the instructions. I had to run through them twice before I figured out that by dialing a combination of area codes I could call Susan Silverman direct. I tried it. The first time nothing happened. The second time I got a recorded message that I had screwed up. The third time it worked. The wires hummed a little bit, relays clicked in beneath the hum, a sound of distance and electricity hovered in the background, and then the phone rang and Susan answered, sounding just as she did. Mr. Watson, come here, I need you.

"It's your darling," I said.

"Which one," she said.

"Don't be a smartass," I said.

"Where are you?" she said.

"Still in London. I just dialed a few numbers and here we are."

"Oh, I had hoped you were at the airport wanting a ride home."

"Not yet, lovey," I said. "I called for two reasons. One to say that I love your ass. And second, to ask you to do me a service."

"Over the phone?"

"Not that kind of service," I said. "I want you to make a phone call for me. Got a pencil?"

"Just a minute . . . okay."

"Call Henry Cimoli,"—I spelled it—"at the Harbor Health Club in Boston. It's in the book. Tell him to get hold of Hawk and tell Hawk I've got work for him over here. You got that so far?"

"Yes."

"Tell him to get the first plane he can to London and call me at the Mayfair Hotel when he gets to Heathrow."

"Mm hmm."

"Tell him money is no problem. He can name his price. But I want him now. Or sooner."

"It's bad," Susan said.

"What's bad?"

"Whatever you're doing. I know Hawk, I know what he's good at. If you need him it means that it's bad."

"No, not too bad. I need him to see that it doesn't get bad. I'm okay, but tell Henry to make sure that Hawk gets here. I don't want Hawk to come to the hotel. I want him to call me from Heathrow, and I'll get to him. Okay?"

"Okay. Who is Henry Cimoli?"

"He's like the pro at the Harbor Health Club. Little guy, used to fight. Pound for pound he's probably the strongest man I know. Before it got fancy, the Harbor Health Club used to be a gym. Hawk and I both trained there when we were fighting. Henry sort of trained us. He'll know where Hawk is."

"I gather you don't have Hawk's address. I would be willing to talk with him direct."

"I know you would. But Hawk doesn't have an address. He lives mostly with women, and between women he lives in hotels."

"What if he won't come?"

"He'll come."

"How can you be sure?"

"He'll come," I said. "How's Techniques of Counseling doing?"

"Fine, I got an A– on the midterm."

"Minus," I said. "That sonovabitch. When I come home I want his address."

"First thing?"

"No."

There was a small pause.

"It's hard on the phone," I said.

"I know. It's hard at long distance in any event. And . . . it's like having someone in the war. I don't like you sending for Hawk."

"It's just to help me do surveillance. Even Lord Peter Wimsey has to whiz occasionally."

Susan's laugh across the ocean, only slightly distorted by distance, made me want to cry. "I believe," she said. "that Lord Peter's butler does it for him."

"When this is over maybe you and I can come," I said. "It should be very fine for you and me to go around and look at the sights and maybe up to Stratford or down to Stonehenge. London gives me that feeling, you know. That excited feeling, like New York."

"If a man tires of London, he is tired of life," Susan said.

"Would you come over?"

"When?"

"Whenever I'm through. I'll send you some of my profits and meet you here. Would you come?"

"Yes," she said.

There was another small pause.

"We'd better hang up," she said. "This must be costing a great deal of money."

"Yeah, okay. It's Dixon's money, but there's not much else to say. I'll call tomorrow at this same time to see if Henry got Hawk. Okay?"

"Yes, I'll be home."

"Okay. I love you, Suze."

"Love."

"Goodbye."

"Goodbye." She hung up and I listened to the transoceanic buzz for a minute. Then I put the phone down, leaned back on the bed, and fell asleep fully dressed with the lights on and my folded handkerchief still pressed against my chin.

When I woke up in the morning the dried blood made the handkerchief, now unfurled, stick to my chin, and the first thing I had to do when I got up was to soak it off in cold water in the sink in the bathroom.

Getting the handkerchief off started the cut bleeding again, and I got a butterfly bandage out of my bag and put it on. I showered even more carefully than yesterday, keeping the water off both bandages. Not easy. If they kept after me in a while I'd have to start going dirty. I shaved around the new cut and toweled off. I changed the dressing on my bullet wound, turning half around and watching in the mirror to do it. There didn't seem to be any infection. I bundled last night's clothes into a laundry bag and left it for the hotel laundry. My shirt was a mess. I didn't have much hope for it. If I stayed here long enough they'd probably hire a blood removal specialist.

I had juice, oatmeal and coffee for breakfast, and went back out to watch my suspect. It was raining and I put on my light beige trench coat. I didn't have a hat but there was a shop on Berkeley Street and I bought one of those Irish walking hats. Me and Pat Moynihan. When I got home I could wear it to the Harvard Club. They'd think I was faculty. With the hat turned down over my eyes and my trench coat collar up I wasn't terribly recognizable. But I was terribly silly-looking. The broken nose and the scar tissue around the eyes somehow didn't go with the Eton and Harrow look.

It was a pleasant rain and I didn't mind walking in it.

In fact I liked it. Come on with the rain, there's a smile on my face. I varied my route, going east on Piccadilly and Shaftesbury and up Charing Cross and Tottenham Court Road. All the way I kept an eye out for a tail, doubling back on my route a couple of times. I came in Tottenham Street to her apartment building staying close to the wall. The only way she could see me was if she stuck her head out the window and looked straight down. If anyone was following me they were very goddamned good.

I turned into her apartment house doorway and looked in the foyer. There were three apartments. Two were Mr. and Mrs. One was simply K. CALDWELL. I was betting on K. Caldwell.

I rang the bell. Over the intercom a voice, distorted by the cheap equipment but recognizably female, said, "Yes?"

"Mr. Western?" I said, reading the name above Caldwell's.

"Who?"

"Mr. Western."

"You've pushed the wrong button, mate. He lives upstairs." The intercom went dead. I went out of the foyer and across the street and by the hospital, underneath an overhang, and waited concealed by some shrubbery. Shortly before noon she came out and headed up Cleveland Street. She turned right on Howland and was out of sight. I waited five minutes. She didn't reappear. I walked across to the foyer again and rang the bell under K. CALDWELL. No answer. I rang it again and kept my thumb on it. No one.

The front door to the building wasn't even locked. I went in and up to the second floor. Her door was locked. I knocked. No answer. I got out my small lock picker and went to work. I'd made the lock picker myself. It looked a little like a buttonhook made of thin stiff wire, and it had a small L on the tip. The idea was to slip it into the keyhole and then one by one turn the tumbler, working by feel. Some locks if you got it in one of the tumbler slots all the tumblers would turn at once. Sometimes, in better locks, you had to turn several. K. Caldwell did not have a good lock. It took about thirty-five seconds to get her apartment door open. I stepped in. It was empty. There's a feel to a place almost as soon as you step in that says if it's empty or not. I was rarely wrong about that. Still, I took my gun out and walked through the place.

It looked as if it were ready for inspection.

Everything was immaculate. The living room was furnished in angular plastic and stainless steel. On one wall was a bookcase with books in several languages. The books were perfectly organized. Not by language or topic, but by size, highest books in the center, smallest at each end, so that the shelves were symmetrical. Most of the books I'd never heard of, but I recognized Hobbes, and *Mein Kampf.* There were four magazines stacked on the near right-hand corner of the coffee table. The one on top was in a Scandinavian language. The title was spelled with one of those little o's with a slash through it. Like in Søren Kierkegaard. On the far left-hand corner was crystal sculpture that looked sort of like a water jet, frozen. In the center, exactly between the magazines and the crystal, was a round stainless steel ashtray with no trace of ash in it.

I moved to the bedroom. It too was furnished in early Bauhaus. The bedspread was white and drawn so tight across the bed that a quarter probably would have bounced on it. There were three Mondrian prints in stainless steel frames on the white walls. One on each. The fourth wall was broken by the window. Everything in the room was white except the Mondrians and a steel-gray rug on the floor.

I opened the closet. There were skirts and blouses and dresses and slacks precisely folded and creased and hung in careful groupings on hangers. The clothes were all gray or white or black. On the shelf were six pairs of shoes in order. There was nothing else in the closet. The bathroom was entirely white except the shower curtain, which was black with silver squares on it. The toothpaste tube on the sink was neatly rolled up from the bottom. The water glass was clean. In the medicine cabinet was underarm deodorant, a safety razor, a comb, a brush, a container of dental floss, a bottle of castor oil, and a can of feminine deodorant spray. No sign of make-up.

I went back in the bedroom and began to go through the bureau. The top two drawers contained sweaters and blouses, gray, black, white and one beige. The bottom drawer was locked. I picked the lock and opened it. It contained underwear. Perhaps twelve pairs of French string bikini underpants in lavender, cerise, emerald, peach and flowered patterns. There were bras in 36C that matched the underpants. Most of them trimmed with lace, and diaphanous. There was a black lace garter belt and three pairs of black fishnet stockings. I thought pantyhose had put the garter belt people out of business. There was also a collection of perfume and a negligee.

The drawer was heavy. I measured the inside roughly with my hand span. Then I did the outside. The outside was about a hand span deeper. I felt the inside bottom of the drawer all around the edge. At one spot it gave, and when I pressed it the bottom tilted. I lifted it out and there were four guns, .22 caliber target pistols, and ten boxes of ammunition. There were six hand grenades of a type I hadn't seen. There was also a notebook with lists of names I'd never heard of, and addresses next to them. There were four passports. All with the girl's picture on them. One Canadian, one Danish, one British, one Dutch. Each one had a different name. I copied them into my notebook. The British one had the name Katherine Caldwell. There were a couple of letters in the Scandinavian language full of o's, and one bayonet that said U.S. on it. The letters were postmarked in Amsterdam. I took down the address. I looked at the list of names. It was too long to copy. The addresses were street addresses without cities attached, but obviously some were not English, and, as far as I could tell, none was American. My name wasn't on the list.

Neither was Dixon's. It could be a list of victims, or a list of safe houses, or a list of Liberty recruits, or a list of people who'd sent her Christmas cards last winter. I put the false bottom back in the drawer and slid it back and locked it.

The rest of the house didn't tell me much else. I found

out that Katherine was into bran cereal and fruit juices. That she dusted under the bed and behind the sofa, and that she owned neither television nor radio. Probably spent her free time reading *Leviathan* and breaking bricks with the edge of her hand.

CHAPTER TWELVE

I WAS BACK out in the street by the hospital behind my shrub in the rain when Katherine returned. Her real name was probably none of the four, but Katherine was the easiest one so I called her that. Having a name made her easier to think about.

She was wearing a white belted raincoat and carrying a transparent plastic umbrella that had a deep bow so that she was able to protect her whole head and shoulders. There were black slacks and black boots showing under the raincoat. I speculated on the undies. Hot pink perhaps? She went in her apartment and didn't come out again. No one else went in. I stood in the rain for three more hours. My feet were very wet and very tired of being stood on. I walked back to the Mayfair.

That night I made a sixty-three-dollar phone call to Susan. The first dollar's worth told me that Henry had got in touch with Hawk and Hawk would be over right away. The next sixty-two dollars were about who missed who and what we'd do and see when she came over. There was some brief talk about whether anyone was going to do me in. I maintained that no one was, and Susan said she hoped I was right. I thought I wouldn't mention my wounds right then.

I hung up feeling worse than I had for a while. Talking on the phone from 5000 miles away was like the myth of Tantalus. It was better not to. The telephone company has lied to us for years, I thought. Always tell you that long distance is the next best thing to being there. All those people call up and feel swell afterward. I didn't. I felt like beating up a nun.

I had room service bring up some beer and sandwiches and I sat in my chair by the airshaft and read *Regeneration Through Violence* and ate sandwiches and drank beer for nearly four hours. Then I went to bed and slept.

Hawk didn't make it the next day, and I didn't either. Katherine stayed in her apartment all day, modeling her lingerie and spraying herself with deodorant or whatever she did. I stayed outside in the rain modeling my walking hat and trench coat and listening to my shoes squish. No urban guerrillas appeared. No one went in or out of the apartment building that looked even vaguely like he might carry a knuckle knife. The rain was hard and steady and persistent. No one wanted to be out in it. There was little movement on Katherine's street, almost none in or out of her building. From where I stood I could see the call buttons in the foyer. No one pushed hers. I spent my time figuring out the time sequence for Hawk's likely arrival. To expect him today was cutting it too close. Tomorrow he'd come. I kept adding and subtracting six hours to all my calculations until my head began to hurt and I thought about other things.

Interesting girl, old Katherine. Everything black and white and stainless steel. Spotless and deodorized and exactly symmetrical and a drawer full of peepshow underwear. Times Square sexy. Repression. Maybe I should pick up a copy of Krafft-Ebing on my way back to the Mayfair. Then I could call up Susan and have her explain it to me. While I stood, I ate a Hershey bar with almonds, and a green apple. Lunch. I don't remember James Bond doing this, I thought. He was always having stone crab and pink champagne. I called it quits at dinner time and went back to the Mayfair, did a repeat of the previous evening. High adventure in swinging London. I was in bed before ten.

In the morning I followed Katherine to the Reading Room in the British Museum. She got a desk and began to read. I stood around outside in the entry foyer and looked into the enormous high-domed room. There was a grand and august quality about it all. It looked like one thought it would. Lots of places don't. Times Square, for instance. Or Piccadilly, for that matter. But when I'd first seen Stonehenge it was everything it should have been, and so was the British Museum. I could imagine Karl Marx writing the *Communist Manifesto* there, hunched over one of the desks in the whispering semi-silence beneath the enormous dome. At noon she came out of the Reading Room and went to have lunch in the small cafeteria downstairs beyond the Mausoleum Room. When she was seated, I left her and went back to call the hotel.

"Yes, sir, there is a message for you," the clerk said. "A Mr. Stepinfetchit is waiting for you near the Pan American ticket counter at Heathrow Airport." There was nothing incorrect in the clerk's voice, and if the name struck him as odd he didn't let on.

"Thank you," I said. Time to leave Katherine and go get Hawk. I got a cab on Great Russell Street and rode out to the airport. Hawk was easy to spot if you knew what you were looking for. I saw him leaning back in a chair with his feet on a suitcase and a white straw hat with a lavender band and a broad brim tipped forward over his face. He had on a dark blue three-piece suit, with a fine pinstripe of light gray, a white shirt with a collar pin underneath the small tight four-in-hand knot of a lavender silk tie. The points of a lavender handkerchief showed in his breast pocket. His black over-the-ankle boots gleamed with wax. The suitcase on which they rested must have cost half a grand. Hawk was stylish.

I said, "Excuse me, Mr. Fetchit, I've seen all your movies and was wondering if you'd care to join me for a bite of watermelon."

Hawk didn't move. His voice came from under the hat, "Y'all can call me Stepin, bawse."

The seat next to him was empty. I sat down beside him. "I'm sorry," I said, "things must be going bad for you, Hawk, having to wear that rag over here and all."

"Boy, I brought this last time I was here. Bond Street. The man fitted it right to my body." He took his hat off and held it in his lap while he looked at me. He was completely bald and his black skin glistened in the airport fluorescence. Everything fitted Hawk well. His skin was smooth and tight over his face and skull. The cheekbones were high and prominent.

"You got a gun," I said.

He shook his head. "I didn't want no hassle at the customs. You know I got no license."

"Yeah, okay. I can supply one. How you feel about a Colt .22 target pistol?"

Hawk looked at me. "What you doing with that trash? You showing off how good you are?"

"Nope, I took it off somebody."

Hawk shrugged. "It's better than nothing, till I can accumulate something better. What you into?"

I told him I was bounty-hunting.

"Twenty-five hundred a head," he said. "How much of that is mine?"

"None, you're overhead. I'll pay a hundred fifty a day and expenses, and bill it to Dixon."

Hawk shrugged. "Okay."

I gave him 500 pounds. "Get a room at the Mayfair. Pretend you don't know me. They are trying to tail me and if they see us together they'll know you too." I gave him my room number. "You can call me after you've checked in and we'll get together."

"How you know they didn't tail you out here and spot us together, old buddy?"

I scowled at him. "Are you kidding," I said.

"O yeah, tha's you, babe, Mr. Humble."

"Nobody tailed me. These people are dangerous but they are amateurs," I said.

"And you and me ain't," Hawk said. "We surely ain't."

An hour later, I was back at my room at the Mayfair waiting for Hawk to call. When he did, I got one of the .22 target pistols I'd taken from the assassins and went down to see him. He was four floors below me but I went up and down and on and off the elevator a few times to make sure I didn't have a tail.

Hawk was in his underwear, hanging up his clothes very carefully and sipping champagne from a tall tulip-shaped glass. His shorts were lavender-colored silk. I took the .22 out of the waist band of my pants and put it on the table.

"I see you've already found the room service number," I said.

"I surely have. There's some beer in the bathroom sink." Hawk rehung a pair of pearl gray slacks on a hanger so that the creases in each pant leg were exactly even. I went into the bathroom. Hawk had filled the sink with ice and put six bottles of Amstel beer and another bottle of Taittinger champagne in to chill. I opened a beer on the bottle opener by the bathroom door and stepped back into the bedroom. Hawk had the clip out of the .22 I had brought and was checking the action. Shaking his head.

"The bad guys use these over here?"

"Not all the time," I said. "It's just what they could get."

Hawk shrugged and slipped the clip back in the butt. "Better than screaming for help," he said. I drank some beer. Amstel. No one imported it at home anymore. Fools.

Hawk said, "While I'm hanging up the vines, man, you might want to talk some more about why I'm here."

I did. I gave him everything, from the first time I'd met Hugh Dixon on the terrace in Weston, until this morning when I'd left Katherine sorting her French bikini undies and musing passionately about the teachings of Savonarola.

"Shit," Hawk said. "French bikinis. What she look like?"

"She's up to your standards, Hawk, but we've come to follow Katherine, not to screw her."

"Doing one don't mean you can't do the other."

"We'll threaten her with that when we want information," I said.

Hawk drank some more champagne. "You hungry?"

I nodded. I couldn't ever really remember when I hadn't been.

"I'll have them send up something," Hawk said. "How about a mess of shrimp cocktail?" He didn't bother to look at the room service menu on the bureau.

I nodded again. Hawk ordered. The first bottle of champagne was gone and he popped the cork on the second. He showed no sign that he'd drunk anything. In fact in the time I'd known Hawk I'd never seen him show a sign of anything. He laughed easily and he was never off balance. But whatever went on inside stayed inside. Or maybe nothing went on inside. Hawk was as impassive and hard as an obsidian carving. Maybe that was what went on inside. He sipped some champagne.

"And you want me to keep your ass covered while you chase these crazies."

"Yes."

"What do we do with them when you catch them?"

"That's sort of up to them."

"You mean if they give us trouble we whack them out?"

"If we have to."

"Why not go the easy route and whack 'em out right off?"

I shook my head.

Hawk laughed. "Same old Spenser. You still go the hard way."

I shrugged and got another Amstel from the sink. The room service waiter arrived with the shrimp cocktail and I stayed in the bathroom out of sight until he was gone. When the door closed, Hawk said, "Okay, Spenser. I paid for it, you can come out."

"You can't tell who they have in their employ," I said. On the room service cart were ten shrimp cocktails, each in its individual ice dish, and two forks. Hawk ate a shrimp.

"Not bad," he said. "Okay. I can dig it. You paying the ace and a half a day, you say how we do it."

I nodded again.

"What we going to do first?"

"We'll eat this shrimp and drink this beer and wine and go to sleep. Tomorrow morning I'm going to watch Katherine some more. I'll call you before I leave and you can cover me."

"Okay. Then what?"

"Then we'll see what happens."

"What happens if I pick up somebody tagging after you?"

"Just watch them. Don't let them shoot me."

"Do mah best." Hawk grinned, his teeth flawless and white in the glistening ebony face. "Long as I don't get too distracted by the lady with the French bikinis."

"You can probably bribe her with a pair of yours," I said.

CHAPTER THIRTEEN

WE FOLLOWED my plan for nearly a week. No one killed me. No one tried. Hawk drifted around behind me in $5000 worth of clothes earning his $150 a day. We saw nothing interesting. We spotted no one on my list of crazies. We stood around and watched Kathie's apartment and followed her to the British Museum and the grocery store.

"You scared them," Hawk said while we ate dinner in his room. "They sent their best people after you twice and you ate them alive. They scared. They laying low now."

"Yeah. They're not even watching me. Unless they are so good neither one of us has spotted them."

Hawk said, "Haw."

"Yeah. We'd have spotted them. You think Kathie has spotted me?"

Hawk shook his head.

"So they don't know if I'm still after them or not."

"Maybe check the hotel once in a while, see if you still registered."

"Yeah. They could do that," I said. "And they will just keep it cool till I leave."

"Or maybe they got nothing to keep cool," Hawk said.

"Yeah, it may not be all that organized anyway and there's nothing in the works whether I'm here or not."

"Maybe."

"Could be. I'm getting sick of waiting around. Let's put some pressure on old Kath."

"I can dig that."

"Not that kind of pressure, Hawk. I'll let her spot me. If she gets scared maybe she'll run. If she runs maybe we can follow her and find some people."

"And when she runs I'll be behind her," Hawk said. "She'll think she lost you."

"Yeah. Keep in mind that these people aren't necessarily English. If she bolts she may head for another country and you better be ready."

"I am always ready, my man. Whatever I'm wearing is home."

"That's another thing," I said. "Try not to wear your shellpink jumpsuit when you tail her. Sometimes people notice things like that. I know that's your idea of inconspicuous, but . . ."

"You ever hear of me losing somebody or getting spotted by someone I didn't want to spot me?"

"Just a suggestion. I am, after all, your employer."

"Yowsah boss, y'all awful kind to hep ol Hawk lak yew do."

"Why don't you can that Aunt Jemima crap," I said. "You're about as down-home darkie as Truman Capote."

Hawk sipped some champagne, and put the glass down. He sliced a small portion of Scottish smoked salmon and ate it. He drank some more champagne.

"Just a poor old colored person," he said. "Trying to get along with the white folks."

"Well, I'll give you credit, you were one of the first to integrate leg-breaking on an interracial basis in Boston."

"A man is poor indeed if he don't do something for his people."

"Who the hell are your people, Hawk?"

"Those good folks regardless of race, creed or color, who have the coin to pay me."

"You ever think about being black, Hawk?"

He looked at me for maybe ten seconds. "We a lot alike, Spenser. You got more scruples maybe, but we alike. Except one thing. You never been black. That's something I know that you won't ever know."

"So you do think about it. How is it?"

"I used to think about it, when I had to. I don't have to no more. Now I ain't nigger any more than you honkie. Now I drink the wine and screw the broads and take the money and nobody shoves me. Now I just play all the time. And the games I play nobody can play as good." He drank some more champagne, his movements clean and sure and delicate. He was eating with no shirt on and the overhead light made the planes of muscle cast fluid and intricate highlights on the black skin. He put the champagne glass back on the table, cut another slice of salmon and stopped with the portion halfway to his mouth. He looked at me again and his face opened into a brilliant, oddly mirthless grin. "'Cept maybe you, babe," he said.

"Yeah," I said, "but the game's not the same."

Hawk shrugged. "Same game, different rules."

"Maybe," I said. "I never been sure you had any rules."

"You know better. I just got fewer than you. And I ain't softhearted. But you know, I say I gonna do something I do it. It gets done. I hire on for something, I stay hired. I do what I take the bread for."

"I remember a time you didn't stay hired for King Powers."

"That's different," Hawk said. "King Powers is a douche bag. He got no rules, he don't count. I mean you, or

Henry Cimoli. I tell you something, you can put it in the bank."

"Yeah. That's so," I said. "Who else?" Hawk had drunk a lot of Taittinger and I had drunk a lot of Amstel.

"Who else what?"

"Who else can trust you?"

"Quirk," Hawk said.

"Martin Quirk," I said. "Detective Lieutenant Martin Quirk?"

"Yeah."

"Quirk wants to put you in the joint."

"Sure he does," Hawk said. "But he knows how a man acts. He knows how to treat a man."

"Yeah, you're right. Anyone else?"

"That's enough. You, Henry, Quirk. That's more than a lot of people ever know."

"I don't guess Henry will give you trouble," I said. "But Quirk or I may shoot you someday."

Hawk finished his salmon and turned the big bright grin at me again. "If you can, man. If you can."

Hawk pushed the plate away, and stood up. "Got something to show you," he said.

I sipped at my beer while he went to the closet and brought out something that looked like a cross between a shoulder holster and a backpack. He slipped his arms through the loops and stepped back from the closet. "What do you think?"

The rig was a shoulder holster for a sawed-off shotgun. The straps went around each shoulder and the gun hung, butt down along his spine.

"Watch this," he said. He slipped his coat on over his naked skin. The coat covered the gun entirely. Unless you were looking you didn't even see a bulge. With his right hand he reached behind him under the skirt of his suit jacket, gave a brief twisting movement and brought the shotgun out.

"Can you dig it?"

"Lemme see," I said. And Hawk put the shotgun in my hand. It was an Ithaca double-barreled 12 gauge. The stock had been cut off and both barrels were cut back. The whole thing was no more than eighteen inches long. "Do a lot more damage than a target pistol," I said.

"And it's no problem. Just go buy a shotgun and cut it down. If we have to go to another country I ditch this and buy a new one where we going. Take me an hour maybe to modify the mother."

"Got a hack saw?"

Hawk nodded. "And a couple of C clamps. That's all I need."

"Not bad," I said. "What you going to do next, modify an Atlas missile and walk around with it tucked in your sock?"

"No harm," Hawk said, "to fire power."

The next morning I got up early and went up and burgled Kathie's apartment while she was at the laundromat. I was neat about it, but sloppy enough to let her know someone had been there. I wasn't looking for anything, I just wanted her to know someone had been there. I was in and out in about five minutes. When she came back I was leaning in the doorway of the next apartment house wearing sunglasses. As she passed I turned away so she wouldn't see my face. I wanted her to spot me but I didn't want to overact.

I used to know a guy named Shelley Walden when I was with the cops who would get spotted tailing a guy through a rock concert. I never knew why he was so bad at it. He had a small, innocuous look about him and he wasn't clumsy, but he couldn't keep out of sight. I tried to run this stakeout like Shelley would have.

If she spotted me when she went by she didn't let on. I knew Hawk was somewhere behind her but I didn't see him. When she went into her apartment I walked casually across the street and leaned on a lamppost and took out a newspaper and started to read it. That would have been Shelley's style. The old Bogart movies where he pulls back the curtain and there's a guy under a lamppost reading a newspaper. I figured she'd see that someone had been rummaging in her apartment and that would get her nervous. It did.

About two minutes after she went in, I saw her looking out her window. I was looking surreptitiously over my newspaper and for a moment our eyes met. I looked back down at the newspaper. She knew I was there. She should recognize me. It was sunny and I wasn't wearing my Irish walking hat. No mistaking me for Rex Harrison.

She had reason to be nervous about being spotted. She had phony passports and stolen guns in her bedroom. That would be enough to bust her. But I wanted them all. She was the string and they were the balloon. If I cut her off I lost the balloon. She was all the handle I had.

What she should have done was sit tight, but she didn't know that. She would either call out the shooters again, or she'd run. She sat in her apartment and looked at me looking at her for nearly four hours, and then she ran. Hawk had been right. The shooters must be getting wary of me. Or maybe I'd cleaned them out. Maybe all the shooters the organization had had been used up, except the one guy that got away. I wasn't dealing here with the KGB. Liberty's resources were probably limited.

She came out of her apartment at about two in the afternoon. She was wearing a tan safari jacket and matching pants and carrying a very large shoulder bag. The same one she'd had at the zoo. She was careful not to pay me any attention as she went past me on Cleveland and headed up Goodge Street toward Bloomsbury. For a half hour it was hare and hounds with Kathie dekeing and diving the side streets of Bloomsbury with me behind her and Hawk behind me. At every turn I kept before me the clear image of Shelley Walden. When in doubt I asked myself, "What would Shelley do?" Everywhere she went, she saw me behind her. Only once in all of this did I catch sight of Hawk. He was in Levis and a corduroy sport coat, surprisingly innocuous, on the opposite side of the street going the other way.

I let her lose me in the Russell Square Underground. She got on and I got on. At the last minute she got off and I let her go. As the train pulled out she was heading back out of the station and, behind her, Hawk, with his hands in his hip pockets and the faint bulge of the shotgun along his spine. He was smiling as the train went into the tunnel.

CHAPTER FOURTEEN

I WENT BACK and staked out Kathie's apartment, but she never came back. Good. She was probably headed for a new place. Any pattern break was better than none at this point. After dinner that night I finished up *Regeneration Through Violence* and was thumbing through the *International Herald Tribune* when Hawk called.

"Where are you?" I said.

"Copenhagen, babe, the Paris of the North."

"Where is she?"

"She here too. She checked into an apartment here. You coming over?"

"Yeah. Be there tomorrow. Anyone with her?"

"Not yet. She just flew over, came to the apartment and went in. She ain't come out."

"The revolutionaries do lead an exciting life, don't they?"

"Like you and me, babe, international adventurers. I'm at the Sheraton Copenhagen watching Danish television. What you doing, man?"

"I was glancing through the *Herald Tribune* when you called. Very interesting. An enriching experience."

Hawk said, "Yeah. Me too."

"I'll come over tomorrow," I said.

"Room five-two-three," Hawk said. "Have them pack up my stuff and ship it to Henry. Hate to have some limey walking around in my threads."

"Ah Hawk," I said, "you sentimental bastard."

"You gonna like it here, babe," Hawk said.

"Why is that?"

"The broads are all blond and they sell beer in the Coke machine."

"Maybe I'll come over tonight," I said. But I didn't. I slept another night in England. In the morning I arranged for Hawk's stuff to be shipped to the States. I called Flanders and told him where I was going. Then I packed my gun as before, in my luggage, and flew to Denmark. Have gun, will travel. Did Paladin do vengeance? Probably.

The airport at Copenhagen was modern and glassy, with a lot of level escalators to move people around the airport. I took a bus in from the airport to the SAS terminal in the Royal Hotel. On the way I spotted the Sheraton. A short walk from the terminal. I made the walk carrying my flight bag, my suitcase and my garment bag, feeling the odd excited buzz I always felt in a place I'd never been.

The Sheraton looked like Sheratons I'd seen in New York, Boston and Chicago. Newer maybe than New York and Chicago. More like Boston. It looked as Danish as Bond bread. I checked in. The desk clerk spoke English with no accent. Embarrassing. I didn't even know how to say Søren Kierkegaard. The hell with him. How many one-armed push-ups can he do?

I unpacked and dialed room 523. No answer. The air conditioner was purring under the window but wasn't cooling the room. The temperature was about 96. I opened the windows and looked out. There was a broad park across the street with a lake in it. The park extended several blocks down to the right. Across the park I could see another hotel. The open window's help was largely psychological, but I didn't feel quite as bad. I reassembled my gun, loaded it, put it in its shoulder holster and hung the rig on a chair back. My shirt was wet. I took it off. The rest of me was wet too. I took off my clothes, brought the gun and holster with me into the bathroom, hung it on the door knob and took a shower. Then I toweled off, put on clean clothes and looked out the window some more.

About two in the afternoon there was a knock on the door. I took my gun out, stood to one side of the door and said, "Yeah."

"Hawk."

I opened the door and he came in. He was wearing white Nikes with a red slash, and white duck pants and an off-white safari jacket with short sleeves. He was carrying two open bottles of Carlsberg beer.

"Fresh from the machine," he said, and gave me one.

I drank most of it. "I thought Scandinavia was cool and northern," I said.

"Heat wave," Hawk said. "Never had one like this before, they keep saying. That's why the air conditioners don't do shit. They never really use them."

I finished the beer. "Right in the Coke machine, you say?"

"Yeah, man, right on your floor here, around the corner from the elevator. You got any kroner?"

I nodded. "I exchanged some at the desk when I checked in."

"Come on, we'll get us a couple more. Helps with the heat."

We went out and got two more beers and came back in.

"Okay, where is she?" I said. The beer was very cool in my throat.

"About a block down that way," Hawk said. "You lean far enough out your window, you probably see her place."

"Why aren't you poised outside watching her every move?"

"She went in about eleven, nothing happened since. I was thirsty and I figured I'd come see if you got in."

"Anything shaking since I talked with you before?"

"Naw. She hasn't done a thing. Somebody else staking her out though."

"Ah hah," I said.

"What you say?"

"I said, Ah hah."

"That what I thought you say. You honkies do talk strange."

"They spot you?" I said.

"Course they didn't spot me. Would they spot you?"

"No. I withdraw the question."

"Damn right."

"What can you tell me about him?"

"Dark fella. Not a brother. Maybe a Syrian, something, some kind of Arab."

"Tough?"

"Oh yeah. He got a look. I think he had a piece. Saw him sort of shrug like the shoulder holster straps was aggravating him."

"How big?"

"Tall, taller than me. Not too heavy, sort of stoop-shouldered. Big beaky nose. Thirty, maybe thirty-five years old, crew-cut."

I had out my descriptions and my Identikit drawings.

"Yeah," I said. "He's one."

"Why is he watching her?" Hawk said.

"Maybe he's not watching her, maybe he's looking for me," I said.

"Yeah," Hawk said. "That's why she don't do much. Since I tailed her over she just take a couple walks, and come back. Each time the dude with the big honker he follow her, very loose. He stay back of her. He looking for you, see if she was followed."

I nodded. "Okay," I said. "She's got some people here. We'll play their match. I'll watch her. I'll let Big Nose watch me, and you can watch him. Then we'll see what happens."

"Maybe Big Nose burn you the first time he see you."

"You're not supposed to let him do that."

"Yeah."

The beer was gone. I looked at the empty bottle with sadness.

"Let's get to it," I said. "Sooner we get them all, the sooner I get home."

"You don't like foreigners?"

"I miss Susan."

"Can't blame you for that, man, she got one of the finest ass . . ."

I looked up.

Hawk said, "Cancel that, man. I sorry. That ain't your kind of talk about Susan. It ain't mine either. I forgot myself."

I nodded.

CHAPTER FIFTEEN

I WENT OUT of the Sheraton and turned left on Vester Søgade. Most of the buildings along the street were low apartment buildings, relatively new, and middle-class or better. Number 36 was hers. Brick, with a small open porch on the front. Before I got there I crossed the street and lingered inconspicuously near some bushes in the park. A lot of people must walk their dogs, I noticed, along a narrow path that skirted the lake. A light blue Simca cruised by with one man at the wheel. I stayed where I was. I didn't see Hawk. In a few minutes the Simca was back. A little one, square and boxy. It went past me going the other way and parked a half block up toward the hotel. I stood. It sat.

After another ten minutes a black Saab station wagon pulled up in front of Kathie's apartment. Three men got out and two of them began to walk toward me, the third went into Kathie's. I looked in the other direction toward the Simca. A tall, dark, stoop-shouldered man with a big nose and a gray crew-cut was getting out. Behind me was the lake. One of us was sort of cornered. The two men from the Saab fanned out a little as they came so that if I had wanted to I couldn't run straight ahead and split the defense and get away. I didn't want to. I stood still with my feet about a foot apart, my hands clasped loosely in front of me, slightly below my belt buckle. The three men reached me and spread out in a little circle around me. The tall guy with the nose stood behind me.

The two men from the Saab looked like brothers. Young and ruddy-cheeked. One of them had a scar that ran from the corner of his mouth halfway across his cheek. The other had very small eyes and very light eyebrows. Both were wearing loud sport shirts hanging outside their pants. I guessed why. The one with the scar took a .38 automatic out of his waistband and pointed it at me. He said something in German.

"I speak English," I said.

"Put your hands on top of your head," he said.

"Wow," I said, "you hardly have an accent."

He gestured with the gun barrel. I rested my hands loosely on my head. "That seems dumb to me," I said. "Should ein cop come by he might notice that I was standing here with my hands on my head. He might pause to ask why, nein?"

"Put your hands down at your sides."

I put them down. "Which of you is Hans?"

The guy with the gun ignored me. He said something in German to the big-nosed guy behind me.

"I'll bet you're Hans," I said to Scarface. "And you're Fritz."

Big Nose patted me down, found my gun, and took it. He slipped it into his belt under his shirt. "That's the Captain behind me."

They didn't seem to be fans of the Katzenjammer Kids. They didn't seem to be fans of me either. The guy with the small eyes said, "Come." And we walked across the street from the park and into the apartment building. I was careful not to look for Hawk.

Kathie's apartment was first floor right, looking out on the park. She was there when we went in, sitting on the couch, half turned so she could look out the window. She was wearing a white corduroy jumpsuit with a black chain for a belt. The man in the room with her was small and wiry with a wide, strong nose and a harsh mouth. He had a big gray mustache that extended beyond his lips, and he wore wire-rimmed glasses. He was nearly bald, probably, but he had let what little hair he had grow very long on the left side and then combed it up and across. Thus his part started just above his left ear. To keep it in place he seemed to have lacquered it with hair spray. He was wearing work shoes and tight-legged corduroy jeans. His white shirt was frayed at the collar. The sleeves were rolled up and his forearms looked strong. He was dark, like Big Nose, and middle-aged. He didn't look like a German, or a crazy. He looked like a mean grownup.

He spoke in German to Scarface.

Scarface said, "English."

"Why are you following this young woman?" the guy said to me. He had an accent, but I couldn't say what kind.

"Why do you want to know?" I said.

He took two steps across the room and punched me in the jaw with his right hand. He was a strong little man and the punch hurt. Hans and Fritz both had their guns out. Fritz's was a Luger. Big Nose stayed behind me.

"At least you gave me a straight answer," I said.

"Why are you following this young woman?"

"She and a number of her associates blew up the family of a rich and vengeful American," I said. "He hired me to get even."

"Then why did you simply not kill her when you found her?"

"One, I'm too nice a guy. Two, she was the only one I had contact with. I wanted her for a Judas goat. I wanted her to lead me to the others."

"And you think she has?"

"Some. You're new, but the guy with the big bazoo here and Hans and Fritz, they look about right."

"How many people are involved?"

"Nine."

"You have killed or captured three. You have located four more, and it has not taken you very long. You are good at your work."

I tried to look modest.

"Someone that good at his work should not have been so easy to catch standing there in the park like a statue."

I tried to look embarrassed.

"You were armed and you look dangerous. In the past you have killed two men lying in ambush for you." He looked out the window. "Have we followed her down the slaughter chute as well?"

Big Nose said something in a language I didn't know. The little guy answered him. Big Nose went out the front door, moving with a kind of shambling lope.

"We shall see," the little guy said.

"What's your part in all of this?" I said.

"I have the misfortune to have this collection of thugs and terrorists in my organization. I do not admire them. They are childish amateurs. I have business a good deal more serious to conduct than blowing up tourists in London. But I also have need of bodies and I cannot always choose the best."

"It's hard to get good help," I said.

"It is that," he said. "You would be good help, I think. I have knocked men down with punches no harder than I gave you."

"You might try it sometime when your thugs and terrorists were not around to support you."

"I am not big, but I am quick and I know many tricks," he said. "But we're going to kill you so you and I will never know."

"You are when your friend Nose-o comes back and says there's no one waiting outside with an antitank gun."

The little guy smiled. "You are not an amateur either," he said. "We'll kill you whether there is someone there or not. But it is best to know. Perhaps you would serve as a hostage. We shall see."

"What's this important work you're doing?" I said.

"It is freedom's work. Africa does not belong to the Nigras or the Communists."

"Who does it belong to?"

"It belongs to us."

"Us?"

"You and me, the white race. The race that brought it out of the cesspool of tribalism and savagery in the nineteenth century. The race that can make Africa a civilization."

"You aren't Cecil Rhodes, are you?"

"My name is Paul."

"All your people share this goal?"

"We are prowhite and anticommunist," Paul said. "That is common ground enough."

"Let me ask you a question, Kathie," I said. "You speak English, I assume."

"I speak five languages," she said. She was on the couch in the same spot she'd been in when I came in. She was very still. When she spoke only her mouth moved.

"How do you wear white pants like that without the French bikinis showing through?"

Kathie's face turned a slow red. "You are filthy," she said.

Paul hit me again, with his left hand this time, evening up the bruises.

"Do not speak so to her," he said.

Kathie got up and left the room. Paul went after her. Hans and Fritz pointed their guns at me. A key turned in the door behind me and Big Nose stepped in.

"No one," he said. Hawk stepped in right behind him with two shotgun shells in his teeth and, firing past his ear with a cutdown shotgun, blew most of Fritz's head off. I dove behind a lounge chair. Hans fired at Hawk and hit Big Nose in the middle of the forehead. Hawk fired the second barrel at Hans as Big Nose was going down. It folded him over and he was dead by the time he fell. Hawk broke open the shotgun. The spent shells popped in the air. Hawk took the fresh shells from his mouth and slid them into the breech and snapped the shotgun closed by the time the spent shells hit the floor.

I was on my feet. "Through there," I said, and pointed toward the door where Kathie and Paul had left the room. Hawk reached it while I dug my gun out of Big Nose's belt.

"Door's locked," Hawk said.

I kicked it open and Hawk went through in a low

crouch, the shotgun held in his right hand, and I went behind him. It was a bedroom and bath with sliding doors that opened onto a courtyard. The doors were open. Paul and Kathie were gone.

"Goddamn," Hawk said.

"Let's get the hell out of here," I said. We did.

CHAPTER SIXTEEN

THE NEXT MORNING we looked in the Danish papers. There was a front-page picture of Kathie's apartment and a shot of bodies being wheeled out on stretchers on page two. But neither Hawk nor I could read Danish so there wasn't much to learn. I clipped the story anyway, in case I found a translator. Hans and Fritz looked pretty much like two of the people on my list. Hawk and I looked at the Identikit sketches and agreed that they were.

"You doing pretty good," Hawk said. "That's six."

"You didn't waste a lot of time when you came through the door."

"Like halt or I'll shoot, that jive?"

"What did you do," I said, "follow Big Nose?"

"Sort of. I spotted him when he come out looking around and I figured he was checking if this was a setup. So I slipped in the hallway there and hid in the shadows back under the stairwell. You know how hard we is to spot in the dark."

"Unless you smile," I said.

"And if we keeps our eyes closed."

We were having breakfast in the hotel. Pastry and cold cuts and butter and cheese buffet style.

"Anyway," Hawk said, "he come slipping back in and

when he open the door I come right in back of him." Hawk drank some coffee.

"Who the one we lost with Kathie?" he said.

"Name's Paul, little guy, very tough. He's a lot heavier article than we been dealing with before. He's a real revolutionary, I think. Of one sort or another."

"Palestinian?"

"I don't think so," I said. "Right wing. Wants to save Africa from the Communists and the Nigras."

"South African? Rhodesian?"

"I don't think so. I mean he may be in that now, but he spoke a language more like Spanish. Maybe Portuguese."

"Angola," Hawk said.

I shrugged. "I don't know. Just said he was anticommunist and prowhite. You probably didn't do much to change his attitude."

Hawk grinned. "He got a big job. I hear there's quite some number of Nigras in Africa. He going to have to do a powerful heap of saving."

"Yeah. He may be dippy, but he's no pancake. He's trouble."

Hawk's face was bright and hard. He grinned again.

"So are we, babe," he said.

"True," I said.

"What's the program now?" Hawk said.

"I don't know. I gotta think."

"Okay, while you thinking, why don't we stroll down to Tivoli and walk around. I heard about Tivoli all my life. I want to see it."

"Yeah," I said. "Me too."

I paid the bill and we went out.

Tivoli was nice. Lots of greenery and not too much plastic. We ate lunch on the terrace of one of the restaurants. There wasn't a great deal for adults to do but watch the kids, and quite frequently the kids' moms, as they went here and there on the pleasant walks among the attractive buildings. It was fun to be there, but it was more a matter of presence, of space allotted to pleasure and thoughtfully done, that made it a pleasure. The lunch was ordinary.

"Ain't Coney Island," Hawk said.

"Ain't the Four Seasons either," I said. I was trying to chew a piece of tough veal and it made me grumpy.

"You thought enough yet?" Hawk said.

I nodded, still working on the veal.

"Should of had fish," Hawk said.

"Hate fish," I said. "Right now we are up a fjord without an oar, as we Danes say. Kathie sure as hell isn't going to go back to her apartment. We've lost her and we've lost Paul." I took out my pocket notebook.

"What I have got is an address in Amsterdam and one in Montreal that I took off her passports. I also have an address in Amsterdam that was the return address on a letter she got, and kept. The addresses are the same."

"Sounds like Amsterdam," Hawk said. He sipped some champagne and watched a young blond woman with very tight shorts and a halter top stroll by. "Too bad, Copenhagen looks good."

"Amsterdam's better," I said. "You'll like it." Hawk shrugged. I dug out some English pounds and gave them to Hawk. "You better get some new clothes. While you do that I'll set us up to Amsterdam. You can probably change the money to kroner at the railroad station. It's right across the street."

"I change it at the hotel, babe. Thought I might leave the shotgun home while I trying on clothes. Three folks got done in with a shotgun yesterday. I just as leave not explain to the Danish fuzz about what we doing."

Hawk left. I paid the bill and headed out the front exit of Tivoli Gardens. Across the street was the huge red brick Copenhagen railroad station. I went across the street and went in. I had nothing to do there but it was everything a European railroad station ought to be and I wanted to walk around in it. It was high ceilinged and arcane with an enormous barrel-arched central waiting room full of restaurants and shops, baggage rooms, backpacker kids and a babble of foreign tongues. Trains were leaving on various tracks for

Paris and Rome, for Munich and Belgrade. And the station was alive with excitement, with coming and going. I loved it. I walked around for nearly an hour by myself, soaking it up. Thinking about Europe in the nineteenth century when it had peaked. The station was thick with life.

Ah Suze, I thought, *you should have been here, you should have seen this.* Then I went back to the hotel and had the hall porter book us a flight to Amsterdam in the morning.

CHAPTER SEVENTEEN

THE KLM 727 came sweeping in low over Holland at about nine-thirty-five in the morning. I'd been there before and I liked it. It felt familiar and easy as I looked down at the flat green land patterned with canals. We were drinking awful coffee handed out by a KLM stewardess with hairy armpits.

"Don't care for the armpit," Hawk murmured.

"Can't say I do myself," I said.

"You know what it reminds me of?"

"Yes."

Hawk laughed. "Thought you would, babe. You think old Kathie gonna be in Amsterdam?"

"Hell, I don't know. It was the best I could do. Better bet than Montreal. It's closer and I got the same address from two different sources. Or she could have stayed in Denmark or gone to Pakistan. All we can do is look."

"You the boss. You keep paying me, I keep looking. Where we staying?"

"The Marriott, it's up near the Rijksmuseum. If it's slow I'll take you over and show you the Rembrandts."

"Hot dawg," Hawk said.

The seat belt sign went on, the plane settled another

notch down and ten minutes later we were on the ground. Schiphol Airport was shiny and glassy and new like the airport in Copenhagen. We got a bus into the Amsterdam railroad station, which wasn't bad but didn't match up to Copenhagen, and a cab from the station to the Marriott Hotel.

The Marriott was part of the American chain, a big new hotel, modern and color-coordinated and filled with the continental charm of a Mobil Station.

Hawk and I shared a room on the eighth floor. No point to concealing our relationship. If we found Kathie or Paul, they'd seen Hawk and would be looking over their shoulder for him again.

After we unpacked we strolled out to find the address on Kathie's passport.

Much of Amsterdam was built in the seventeenth century, and the houses along the canals looked like a Vermeer painting. The streets that separated the houses from the canals were cobbled and there were trees. We followed Leidsestraat toward the Dam Square, crossing the concentric canals as we went: Prinsengracht, Keisersgracht, Heerengracht. The water was dirty green, but it didn't seem to matter much. What cars there were were small and unobtrusive. There were bicycles and a lot of walkers. Boats, often glass-topped tour boats, cruised by on the canals. A lot of the walkers were kids with long hair and jeans and backpacks who gave no hint of nationality and very little of gender. Back when people used to speak that way, Amsterdam was said to be the hippie capital of Europe.

Hawk was watching everything. Walking soundlessly, apparently self-absorbed, as if listening to some inward music. I noticed people gave way to him as he walked, instinctively, without thought.

The Leidsestraat was the shopping district. The shops were good-looking and the clothes contemporary. There was Delftware and imitation Delftware in some quantity. There were cheese shops, and bookstores and restaurants, and a couple of wonderful-looking delicatessens with whole hams and roast geese and baskets of currants in the windows. On the square near the Mint Tower there was a herring stand.

"Try that, Hawk," I said. "You're into fish."

"Raw?"

"Yeah. Last time I was here people raved about them."

"Why don't you try one then?"

"I hate fish."

Hawk bought a raw herring from the stand. The woman at the stand cut it up, sprinkled it with raw onions and handed it to him. Hawk tried a bite.

He smiled. "Not bad," he said. "Ain't chitlins, but it ain't bad."

"Hawk," I said, "I bet you don't know what a god-damned chitlin is."

"Ah spec dat's right, bawse. I was raised on moon pies and Kool-Aid, mostly. It's called ghetto soul."

Hawk ate the rest of the herring. We bore left past the herring stand and turned down the Kalverstraat. It was a pedestrian street, no cars, devoted to shops.

"It's like Harvard Square," Hawk said.

"Yeah, a lot of stores that sell Levi's and Frye boots and peasant blouses. What the hell you doing in Harvard Square?"

"Used to shack up with a Harvard lady," Hawk said. "Very smart."

"Student?"

"No, man, I'm no chicken tapper. She was a professor. Told me I had a elemental power that turned her on. Haw."

"How'd you get along with her seeing-eye dog?"

"Shit, man. She could see. She thought I was gorgeous. Called me her savage, man. Said Adam musta looked like me."

"Jesus, Hawk, I'm going to puke on your shoe in a minute."

"Yeah, I know. It was awful. We didn't last long. She too weird for me. Surely could screw though. Strong pelvis, you know, man, strong."

"Yeah," I said, "me too. I think this is the place."

We were at an open-front bookstore. There were books and periodicals in racks and on tables out front and rows of them inside. Many of the books were in English. A sign on the wall said THREE HOT SEX SHOWS EVERY HOUR, and an arrow pointed toward the back of the store. In back was another sign that said the same thing with an arrow pointing downstairs.

"What kind of books they sell here?" Hawk said.

There were all kinds, books by Faulkner and Thomas Mann, books in English and books in French, books in Dutch. There was Shakespeare and Gore Vidal and a collection of bondage magazines with nude women on the cover so encumbered in chains, ropes, gags and leather restraints that it was hard to see them. You could buy *Hustler, Time, Paris Match, Punch,* and *Gay Love.* It was one of the things about Amsterdam that I never got over. At home you found a place that sold bondage porn sequestered in the Combat Zone and specializing. Here the bookstore with the THREE HOT SEX SHOWS EVERY HOUR was between a jewelry store and a bake shop. And it also sold the work of Saul Bellow and Jorge Luis Borges.

Hawk said, "You figure Kathie lives here, we could look on a shelf under K."

"Maybe upstairs," I said. "This is the address."

"Yeah," Hawk said. "There's a door."

It was just to the right of the bookstore, half obscured by the awning.

"Think she in there?"

"I know how we find out."

Hawk grinned. "Yeah. We watch. You want to take the first shift while I make sure she not down there among the hot sex films?"

"I didn't figure you for a looker, Hawk. I figured you for a doer."

"Maybe pick up a trick or two. Man's never too old to learn a little. Nobody's perfect."

"Yeah."

"We gonna go round the clock on this, babe?"

"No. Just daytime."

"That's good. Twelve on, twelve off ain't no fish fry."

"This time out it'll be harder. If she's in there she knows us both, and she's going to be very edgy."

"Also," Hawk said, "we camp out here long enough a Dutch cop going to come along and ask us what we doing."

"If they're any good."

"Yeah."

"We'll circulate," I said. "I'll stay up there by the dress shop for a half hour, then I'll stroll down to the place that sells broodjes and you stroll up to the dress shop. And we'll rotate that way every half hour or so."

"Yeah, okay," Hawk said, "let's make the circulation irregular. Each time we switch we'll decide how long before we switch again. Break up the rhythm."

"Yes. We'll do that. Unless there's a back way she'll have to pass one of us if she leaves."

"Why don't you anchor here for a while, babe, and I'll go around and see if I find any back way. I'll check in the store and I'll go around the block and see what I can find."

I nodded. "If she comes out and I go after her I'll meet you back at the hotel."

Hawk said, "Yowzah" and went into the bookstore. He went to the back and down the stairs. Five minutes later he was back up the stairs and out of the bookstore, his face glistening with humor.

"Get any pointers?" I said.

"Oh yeah, soon's I make a move on a pony, I gonna know just what to do."

"These Europeans are so sophisticated."

CHAPTER EIGHTEEN

HAWK FOUND no back entrance. We walked up and down a short stretch of the Kalverstraat all the rest of the day, staying close to the wall under Kathie's windows, if they were Kathie's windows, so she wouldn't spot us, if she were looking out, if she were up there.

The dress shop was featuring that season a fatigue green number that looked like a shelter half, long and formless, belted at the waist. It didn't even look good on the window dummy. The broodje shop was featuring roast beef on a soft roll, topped with a fried egg. Broodje seemed to mean sandwich. There were about thirty-five different kinds of broodjes listed behind the counter, but the roast beef with the fried egg was the hot seller.

The street was crowded all afternoon. There seemed to be a lot of tourists, Japanese and Germans with cameras, in groups. There was a fair number of Dutch sailors. More people seemed to smoke in Holland than they did at home. And there were far fewer big men. Sandals and clogs seemed more prevalent, especially for men, and occasionally a Dutch cop would stroll by in his gray-blue uniform with white trim. Nobody bothered me and nobody bothered Hawk.

At eight o'clock I said to Hawk, "It is time to go eat before I break into tears."

"I can dig that," Hawk said.

"There's a place just off to the side here called The Little Nun. I ate there last time I was here."

"What you doing here before, man?"

"Pleasure trip. Came with a lady."

"Suze?"

"Yeah."

The Little Nun was everything I remembered. Polished stone floor, whitewashed walls, low-beamed ceiling, some stained glass in the windows, flowers and very fine food. For dessert they brought out a great crock of red currants, cherries, strawberries, raspberries and blackberries that had been marinated in cassis. Everyone spoke English. In fact everyone in Holland spoke English as far as I could tell, and spoke it with very little accent.

We went to bed in the Marriott feeling good about supper but bad about tomorrow. I had the feeling that a lot of aimless walking was in store for us tomorrow.

It was. We walked up and down the Kalverstraat all day. I looked in every store window along the way until I knew the price of all the merchandise. I ate five broodjes during the day, three out of hunger and two out of boredom. The high point of the day was two trips to the public urinal near the Dutch Tourist Bureau on Rokin.

At night we had an Indonesian rijsttafel at the Bali Restaurant on Leidsestraat. There were about twenty-five different courses of meat, vegetables and rice. We drank Amstel beer with the meal. Hawk too. Champagne didn't go with a rijsttafel. Hawk drank some Amstel and said to me, "Spenser, how long we gonna walk up and down past the hot sex shows?"

"I don't know," I said. "We only been at it two days."

"Yeah, man, but we don't even know she's in there. I mean we may be walking up and down in front of some old Dutch granny."

"But no one has come out of that place or gone in it in two days. Isn't that a little strange?"

"Maybe nobody lives there."

I ate some beef with peanuts. "We'll give it another day, then we'll go in and see, okay?"

Hawk nodded. "I like going in and seeing," he said, "a lot better than hanging around and watching."

"I knew you were a doer," I said.

"I am that," he said. "And I want to do something pretty quick."

We walked back to the Marriott through night life and music along the Leidsestraat. The lobby was nearly empty. There were two kids from a South American soccer team half asleep in chairs. A bellhop leaned on the counter talking to the desk clerk. Faint music from the in-house night spot drifted down toward the elevators. We rode to the eighth floor in silence. At our room the DO NOT DISTURB sign was on the door. I looked at Hawk, he shook his head. The sign had not been there this morning. I put my ear hard against the door. I could hear the bedsprings creak, and what sounded like heavy breathing. I motioned Hawk to the door. He listened.

We had a room near the corner, and I gestured Hawk around the corner.

"Sound like one of them hot sex shows," Hawk said. "You think somebody shacking up in our room?"

"That's crazy," I said.

"Maybe a maid or something, see we're out all day, figures she'll slip in with her old man and make it while we out."

"If you can think of it somebody will do it," I said. "But I don't believe it."

"We could stand around out here awhile and see if they come out. If there's somebody in there putting the boots to his old lady, they can't stay all night."

"I been standing around in hotel corridors and on street corners since I been in Europe. I'm getting sick of it."

"Let's do it," Hawk said. He pulled the shotgun out from under his coat.

I took out the room key and we went around the corner. There was no one in the hall.

Hawk sprawled on the floor in front of the door. I slipped the key in the door. Hawk leveled the shotgun on his propped elbows and nodded. I turned the key from one side of the door out of the line of fire and swung the door open. I had my gun out.

Hawk said, "Jesus Christ," and gestured with his head.

I slid around the door, staying flat against the wall.

There were two dead men on the floor and Kathie on the bed. She wasn't dead. She was tied. I kicked open the door to the bathroom. No one there. Hawk was in behind me. He closed the room door with his left hand. The right kept the shotgun half erect in front of him. I came out of the bathroom.

"Nothing," I said, and slid my gun back in its holster.

Hawk squatted beside the two men on the floor. "They dead," he said.

I nodded. Kathie lay on the bed, her hands tied behind her, her feet bound. Her mouth was taped, and a rope around her waist fastened her to the bed.

Hawk looked down at her and said, "That what we heard. Nobody screwing, old Kathie here trying to get loose."

Kathie made a thick muffled sound of outrage and twisted against the ropes.

"What killed the stiffs on the floor?" I said.

"Somebody shot each of them behind the left ear with a small bullet."

"Twenty-two?"

"Could be. Been a while, they pretty cold."

There was an envelope stuck to Kathie's right thigh with some of the same adhesive tape that closed her mouth. I picked it up.

"Maybe we won her in a raffle," I said.

"I bet that ain't it," Hawk said. He was still holding the shotgun, but now negligently, hanging loosely at his side.

I opened the note. Kathie squirmed on the bed and made her muffled noise some more. Hawk read over my shoulder.

The note said:

We have much to do and you are in the way. Had we the time we would kill you. But you are obviously hard to kill, as is the *Schwartze*. Thus we have delivered to you what you seek. The two dead men are the last of those you sought. I shall probably be sorry that I let the woman live, but I am more sentimental than I should be. We have cared for each other and I cannot kill her.

You have no reason now to bother us further. If you persist despite that we shall turn our full attention to your deaths.

Paul.

"Sonovabitch," I said.

"*Schwartze?*" Hawk said.

"That's German for spade, I think."

"I know what it mean," Hawk said. "These two look like your sketches?"

"We'll look," I said. I got the Identikit drawings out of the top bureau drawer. With his foot Hawk turned both bodies over on their backs. I looked at the pictures and at the phony-looking dead faces staring up at me. "I'd say so." I handed the drawings to Hawk.

He nodded. "Look about right," he said.

I pointed my chin at Kathie. "And that makes number nine."

"What you going to do?"

"We could untie her."

"You think we safe?"

"There's two of us," I said.

"She awful mean and mad-looking," Hawk said.

He was right. Kathie's eyes were wide and angry. Since we had entered the room she had not stopped twisting against the ropes, squirming to get free. She grunted furiously at us.

"Actually, you know, we better pat her down. It could be a very elaborate fake. We untie her and she jumps up and shoots us."

Hawk laughed. "You are a suspicious mamma." He put the shotgun down on the night table. "But I'll check her."

I looked out the window at the street eight floors below. Nothing looked different than it should. Across the street in the light of street lamps the canal flowed past. A tour boat taking a candlelight cruise glimmered by. They served wine and cheese on the candlelight cruises. If I were with Suze we could drift through the ancient graceful city and drink the wine and eat the cheese and have a nice time. But Suze wasn't here. Hawk would probably go with me, but I didn't think he'd care for the hand-holding.

I looked back at Hawk. He was methodically patting Kathie for a hidden weapon. As he did so she began to twist and squirm, and a high locust sort of noise forced out around the tape. As he touched her thighs she arched her back and, straining against the ropes, thrust her pelvis forward. Her face was very red and her breath came in snorts through her nose.

Hawk looked at me. "She ain't armed," he said.

I reached down and carefully peeled the tape from her mouth. She breathed in gasps through her open mouth, reddened from the friction of the tape.

"Shall you," she gasped, "shall you rape me? Shall he?" She looked at Hawk. The locust hum in her voice had softened to a kind of hiss. A little saliva bubbled at the left corner of her mouth. Her body continued to arch against the ropes.

"I'm not sure it would be rape," I said.

"Shall you both take me, gag me again. Take me while I'm helpless, voiceless, bound and writhing on the bed?"

Her mouth was open now and her tongue ran and fretted over her lower lip.

"I can't move," she gasped. "I'm bound and helpless, shall you tear my clothing, use me, degrade me, drive me mad?"

Hawk said, "Naw."

I said, "Maybe later."

Hawk pulled a jackknife from his right hip pocket and cut her free. He had to roll her over to cut the rope on her hands, and when he did he gave her a slap on the backside, light and friendly, like one ballplayer to another. She sat up abruptly.

"Nigger," she said. "Never touch me, nigger."

Hawk looked at me, his face bright. "Nigger?" he said.

"That's English for spade, I think."

"I know what it mean," Hawk said.

"What happened to take me, ravage me?" I said.

"I'll kill you both," she said, "as soon as I can."

"That gonna be awhile, hon," Hawk said. "Beside you gonna have to get in line."

She was sitting up now on the edge of the bed. Her white linen dress was badly wrinkled from her struggle against the ropes. "I want to go to the bathroom," she said.

"Go ahead," I said. "Take your time."

She walked stiffly to the bathroom and closed the door. We heard the bolt slide and then the water begin to run in the sink. Hawk walked over to one of the red vinyl armchairs, stepped carefully over the two dead men on the floor.

"What we going to do with the corpus delicti here?" Hawk said.

"Oh," I said. "You don't know either?"

CHAPTER NINETEEN

WHILE KATHIE was still in the bathroom, Hawk and I took one body each and slipped them under the twin beds.

In the bathroom, the faucet still ran in the sink, masking any other sound. "What you suppose she doing?" Hawk said.

"Nothing probably. She's probably trying to think what to do when she comes out."

"Maybe she perfuming up in case we want to rape her."

"Still waters run deep," I said. "Her idea of a good time is probably to be beaten by Benito Mussolini with a copy of *Mein Kampf.*"

"Or to be raped by you and me," Hawk said.

"Especially you, big fella. I know what they say about you black folk."

"And quick," Hawk said, "we very quick and rhythmi-cal."

"That's what I heard," I said.

I got a can of Spot-lifter off the top closet shelf and sprayed the blood stains on the rug.

"That stuff work?"

"Works on my suits," I said. "When it dries I just brush it away."

"You make a fine wife someday, babe. You cook good too."

"Yeah, but I've always wanted a career of my own."

Kathie shut off the running water and came out of the bathroom. She'd combed her hair and smoothed out her dress as much as possible.

I was on my hands and knees working on the blood stains. "Sit down," I said. "You want something to eat? Drink? Both?"

"I am hungry," she said.

"Hawk, get her something from room service."

"They got a late night special here," Hawk said. "House pâté, cheese, bread and a carafe of wine. Want that?"

Kathie nodded. "That sounds pretty good," I said to Hawk. "Why don't we all have some."

"That how it is eating that Indonesian food," Hawk said. "An hour later you hungry again."

Kathie sat in one of the straight chairs near the window, her hands in her lap, her knees together. Her head lowered looking at the crossed thumbs of her clasped hands. Hawk called and ordered. I brushed away the dried Spot-lifter and applied some cold water to what was left of the blood stain.

The room service waiter appeared with the late night special and Hawk took the table from him at the door. Hawk set the circular table into the room with the pâté and cheese, French bread and red wine.

"Go ahead, kid," Hawk said to Kathie. "Sit down, we gonna eat."

Kathie came to the table and sat down without a word.

Hawk poured her some wine. She drank a little and her hand shook enough so that some spilled on her chin. She wiped it with a napkin. Hawk cut a wedge of pâté and broke a piece of bread and said to me, "What we gonna do with Kathie?"

"Don't know," I said. I drank some wine. It had a rich mouth-filling taste. Maybe the people who didn't chill it knew what they were about.

"How about what we doing here. I mean, we gonna do what the note said? We done what you was hired for?"

"Don't know," I said. "This pâté is terrific."

"Yeah," Hawk said. "These little nuts pistachios?"

"Yeah," I said. "You want to go home?"

"Me, man? I got nothing to go home to. It's you getting moony about Susan and all."

"Yeah."

"Besides," Hawk said, "I don't like that Paul."

"Yeah."

"I don't like how he was gonna kill us, and I don't like him saying he will if we keep after him, and I don't like much how he dump his girlfriend on us when we get close."

"No. I don't like that much either. I don't like walking away from him."

"Besides," Hawk's face widened into a brilliant humorless smile, "he call me *Schwartze.*"

"Racist bastard," I said.

"Whyn't we tell him we ain't taking the deal."

Kathie ate and drank in silence.

"You know where he is, Kathie?"

She shook her head. There seemed no more venom in her.

Hawk said, "Sure you do. You must have some place where you people make contact if you get in trouble."

She shook her head. Tears had begun to run down her cheeks.

Hawk took a sip of wine, put down the glass and slapped her across the face. Her head rocked back and then she seemed to collapse in on herself, shrinking down into the chair. The tears came in sobs then, shaking her body as she bent over. She put both hands over her ears and squeezed her face between her forearms and cried. Hawk sipped some more wine and looked at her with mild interest.

"She do take on," he said.

"She's scared," I said. "Everybody gets scared. She's alone with two guys she's tried to kill and the man she loves has ditched her. She's alone. That's hard."

"It gonna get a lot harder if she don't tell us what I want her to," Hawk said.

"Beating up on a lady isn't your style, Hawk."

"Women's lib, babe. She got the same rights to have me bust her up that a man have."

"I don't like it."

"Take a walk then. When you come back, we'll know what we want to know."

I stood up. I knew we were playing good-cop bad-cop, but did Hawk?

"Oh my God," Kathie said. "Don't."

Hawk stood up too. He took off the jacket, slipped out of the shotgun shoulder rig and peeled off his shirt. Hawk had always had a lot of muscle tone. His upper body was taut and graceful. The muscles in his chest and arms swelled slightly as he made a slight loosening gesture with his shoulders. I started for the door.

"Oh God, don't leave me with him." Kathie slid out of the chair onto the floor and crawled after me. "Don't let him. Don't let him debase me. Please don't."

Hawk stepped between her and me. She grasped one of his legs. "Don't, don't, don't." The saliva was bubbling again at the corner of her mouth. She was gasping for breath. Her nose ran.

I said to Hawk, "I don't want to know this bad."

"Your biggest problem, man, you a candy ass."

I shrugged. "I still don't want to know this bad." I reached down and took Kathie's arm. "Get up," I said. "And sit in the chair. We aren't going to do anything bad to you." I put her in the chair. Then I went in the bathroom and got a facecloth and soaked it in cold water and wrung it out and brought it in and washed her face with it.

Hawk looked like he was going to puke. I gave her a glass of wine. "Drink some," I said. "And get it back together. Take your time. We got lots of time. When you're ready, we'll talk a little. Okay?"

Kathie nodded.

Hawk said, "You remember she blew up some guy's wife and kids? You remember she trying to set you up in the London Zoo? You remember she gonna stand around while her boyfriend wasted you in Copenhagen? You remember what she is?"

"I'm not worrying about what she is," I said. "I'm worrying about what I am."

"Gonna get you killed someday, babe."

"We'll do it my way, Hawk."

"You paying the money, babe, you can pick the music." He put his shirt back on.

We ate the rest of the late night special in silence.

"Okay, Kathie. Is that your name?"

"It is one of them."

"Well, I'm used to thinking of you as Kathie so I'll stick with it."

She nodded. Her eyes were red but dry. She slumped as she sat.

"Tell me about you and your group, Kathie."

"I should tell you nothing."

"Why? Who do you owe? Who is there to be loyal to?"

She looked at her lap.

"Tell me about you and your group."

"It is Paul's group."

"What is it for?"

"It is for keeping Africa white."

Hawk snorted.

"Keeping," I said.

"Keeping the control in white hands. Keeping the blacks from destroying what white civilization had made of Africa." She wouldn't look at Hawk.

"And how was blowing up some people in a London restaurant going to do that?"

"The British were wrong on Rhodesia and wrong on South Africa. It was punishment."

Hawk had stood and gone to the window. He was whistling "Saint James Infirmary Blues" through his teeth as he stood looking down into the street.

"What were you doing in England?"

"Organizing the English unit. Paul sent me."

"Any connection with IRA?"

"No."

"Try?"

"Yes."

"They're only concerned with their own hatreds," I said. "Are there many more left in England of your unit?"

"No. You . . . you overcame us all."

"Gonna overcome all the rest of you too," Hawk said from the window.

Kathie looked blank.

"What's shaking in Copenhagen?"

"I don't understand."

"Why did you go to Denmark when you left London?"

"Paul was there."

"What was he doing there?"

"He lives there sometimes. He lives many places and that's one of them."

"The apartment on Vester Søgade?"

"Yes."

"And when Hawk busted that up you and he came here."

"Yes."

"The address on the Kalverstraat?"

"Yes."

"And you spotted us watching?"

"Paul did. He is very careful."

I looked at Hawk. Hawk said, "He pretty good too. I never saw him."

"And?"

"And he called me on the telephone and made me stay inside. Then he watched you while you watched me. When you left for the night he came in."

"When?"

"Last night."

"And you moved out of that place?"

"Yes, to Paul's apartment."

"And today while we were staking out the empty place on the Kalverstraat, Paul brought you and the two stiffs here."

"Yes, Milo and Antone. They thought we were coming to ambush you. I did too."

"And when you got in here Paul burned Milo and Antone?"

"Excuse me?"

"Paul killed the two men."

"Paul and a man named Zachary. Paul said it was time for a sacrifice. Then he bound me and gagged me and left me for you. He said he was sorry."

"Where's the apartment?"

"It doesn't matter. They won't be there."

"Tell me anyway."

"It's on the Prinsengracht." She told us the number. I looked at Hawk.

He nodded, slipped into the shotgun rig, put on his jacket and went out. Hawk needed a shotgun less than most.

"What are Paul's plans now?"

"I don't know."

"You must know something. Until last night you were his darling."

Her eyes filled.

"And now you aren't. You should start getting used to that."

She nodded.

"So being as you were his darling up till today, didn't he tell you anything about his plans?"

"He told no one. When he was ready we were told what to do, but not before."

"So you didn't know what was coming down tomorrow?"

"I don't understand."

"You didn't even know what was going to be done tomorrow."

"That is right."

"And you don't think he's at the place on Prinsengracht?"

"No. No one will be there when the black man gets there."

"His name is Hawk," I said.

She nodded.

"If the police penetrated your organization, or if they raided the apartment on Prinsengracht, where would the survivors meet?"

"We have a calling system. Each person has two people to call."

"Who were you supposed to call?"

"Milo and Antone."

"Balls."

"I cannot help you."

"Maybe you can't," I said. And maybe she couldn't. Maybe I'd used her up.

CHAPTER TWENTY

HAWK WAS BACK in less than an hour. When he came in he shook his head.

"Gone?" I said.

"Uh huh."

"Clues?"

Hawk said, "Clues?"

"You know," I said, "like an airplane schedule with a flight to Beirut underlined. A hotel confirmation slip from the Paris Hilton. Some tourist brochures from Orange County, California. A tinkling piano in the next apartment. Clues."

"No clues, man."

"Anyone see them leave?"

"Nope."

"So the only thing we know for sure is he isn't in his place on Prinsengracht, and he isn't here in this room."

"He wasn't when I looked. She tell you anything?"

"Everything she knows."

"Maybe you believe that, babe. I don't."

"We've been trying. You want some more wine? I ordered some while you were gone."

"Yeah."

I poured some for Hawk and some for Kathie. "Okay, kid," I said to Kathie. "He's gone and all we've got is you. Where might he be?"

"He could be anywhere," she said. Her face was a little flushed. She'd had a lot of wine. "He can go anywhere in the world."

"Phony passport?"

"Yes. I don't know how many. Many."

Hawk had taken off his coat and hung the shotgun rig from the corner of a chair. He was leaning far back with his Frye boots crossed on the bureau and the glass of red wine balanced on his chest. His eyes almost closed.

"Where would the places be that he wouldn't go?"

"I don't understand."

"I going too fast for you, sugar? Watch my lips close. Where would he not go?"

Kathie drank some wine. She looked at Hawk the way sparrows are supposed to look at tree snakes. It was a look of fearful fascination.

"I don't know."

"She don't know," Hawk said to me. "You do take up with some winners, babe."

"What the hell are you going to do, Hawk, keep eliminating the places he wouldn't go until there's only one left?"

"You got a better idea, babe?"

"No. Where would he be least likely to go, Kathie?"

"I cannot say."

"Think a little. Would he go to Russia?"

"Oh no."

"Red China?"

"No, no. No Communist country."

Hawk made a gesture of triumph with his open palms turned up. "See, babe, eliminate half the world just like that."

"Swell," I said. "This sounds like an old Abbott and Costello routine."

Hawk said, "You know a better game?"

Kathie said, "Have they had the Olympics yet?"

Hawk and I looked at her. "The Olympic games?"

"Yes."

"They're on now."

"Last year he sent away for tickets to the Olympic games. Where are they being held?"

Hawk and I said, "In Montreal," at the same time.

Kathie drank some wine and made a small giggle and said, "Well, that's probably where he went, then."

I said, "Why in hell didn't you tell us?"

"I didn't think of it. I don't know about sports. I didn't even know when they were being held or where. I just know Paul had tickets for them."

Hawk said, "It's pretty much on the way home anyway, man."

"There's a restaurant in Montreal called Bacco's that you're going to like," I said.

"What we do with fancy pants here?" Hawk said.

"Please don't be dirty."

The white linen dress was very simple, square-necked and straight-lined. She had a thick silver chain around her neck and white sling high-heeled shoes with no stockings. Her wrists and ankles were red and marked from the ropes. Her mouth was red and her eyes were puffy and red. Her hair was matted and tangled from her long struggle on the bed. "I don't know," I said, "she's all we have."

"I'll go with you," she said. Her voice was small when she said it. Quite different from the one she'd used when she said she'd kill us when she could. Didn't mean she'd changed her mind. But it didn't mean she hadn't. I figured between us we could keep her from killing us.

"She change sides awful fast," Hawk said.

"They got changed on her," I said. "We'll take her. She may be helpful."

"She may stick something in us when we ain't looking too."

"One of us will always look," I said. "She knows this Zachary. We don't. If he's in on this he might be there. Maybe others. She's the only thing connected to Paul we have. We'll keep her."

Hawk shrugged and drank some wine.

"In the morning we'll check out and get the first flight we can to Montreal."

"What about the two stiffs?"

"We'll ditch them in the morning."

"Hope they don't start to stink before then."

"We can't ditch them before that. The cops will be all over the place. We'll never get out of here. What time is it?"

"It's three-thirty."

"About nine-thirty in Boston. Too late to call Jason Carroll. I only got his office number anyway."

"Who Jason Carroll?"

"Dixon's lawyer. He's sort of in charge of this thing. I'll feel better when I've talked with Dixon about our plans."

"Maybe your wallet feel better too."

"No, I think this one will be on me. But Dixon's got a right to know what's going on."

"And I got a right to sleep. Who she sleep with?"

"I'll put a mattress off the floor and she can sleep on the box spring."

"She look disappointed. I think she had another plan."

Kathie said, "May I take a bath?"

I said, "Sure."

I dragged the mattress off the bed closest to the door, and stretched it out across the doorway. Kathie went into the bathroom and closed the door. The lock snicked into place. I could hear the water running in the tub.

Hawk stripped to his shorts and got into bed. He took the shotgun under the covers with him. I lay down on the mattress with my pants still on. I put my gun under the pillow. It made a lump, but not as big a lump as it would make in my body if Kathie got it in the night. The lights were out and just a thin line of light came under the bathroom door. As I lay in the dark I began to smell, only vaguely so far, a smell I'd smelled before. It was the smell of bodies that had been dead too long. It would have been a lot worse without air conditioning. It wouldn't get better before morning.

Tired as I was, I didn't sleep until Kathie came out of the bathroom and stepped across me and went to bed on the box spring of the near bed.

CHAPTER TWENTY-ONE

IN THE MORNING after we checked out, Hawk stole a laundry hamper from a utility closet whose lock I picked. We put the two bodies in the hamper, covered them with dirty linen, put the hamper in an empty elevator and sent the elevator to the top floor. We did all this while keeping a close eye on Kathie, who didn't show any sign of wanting to bolt. Or kill us. She seemed to want to stay with us as badly as we wanted her. Or I wanted her. I think Hawk would have dropped her in a canal if he'd been on his own.

We got a bus from the KLM terminal in Museumplein and caught a KLM flight from Schiphol to London at nine-fifty-five, connecting with an Air Canada flight to Montreal at noon. At one-fifteen London time I was sitting on the outside seat with Kathie next to me and Hawk on the window, drinking a Labatt 50 ale and waiting for the meal to be served. Six hours later, early afternoon Montreal time, we set down in Canada, changed money, collected luggage, and by three o'clock we were standing in line at the Olympic housing office in Place Ville Marie waiting to get lodging. By four-fifteen we had gotten to the man at the desk, and by quarter of six we were in a rented Ford heading out Boulevard St. Laurent for an address near Boulevard Henri Bourassa. I felt like I had gone fifteen rounds with Dino the Boxing Rhinoceros. Even Hawk looked a little tired, and Kathie seemed to be asleep in the back seat of the car.

The address was one half of a duplex on a side street a block from Henri Bourassa Boulevard. The name was Boucher. The husband spoke English, the wife and daughter only French. They were going to their summer home on a lake and were picking up two weeks' worth of rent leasing their home to Olympic visitors. I gave them the voucher from the Olympic housing office. They smiled and showed us where things were. The wife spoke to Kathie in French, showing her the laundry and where the cookware was kept. Kathie looked blank. Hawk answered her in very polite French.

When they had gone and left us the key I said to Hawk, "Where'd you come up with the French?"

"I done some time in the Foreign Legion, babe, when things was sorta mean in Boston. You dig?"

"Hawk, you amaze me. Vietnam?"

"Yeah, and Algeria, all of that."

"Beau Geste," I said.

"The lady she think Kathie your wife," Hawk said. He smiled very wide. "I told her she your daughter and she don't know much about cooking and things."

"I told the man we brought you along to stand outside in a jockey suit and hold horses."

"Ah'm powerful good at sittin' on a bale of cotton and singin' 'Old Black Joe' too, bawse."

Kathie sat at the counter in the small kitchen and watched us without understanding.

The house was small and lovingly done. The kitchen was pine-paneled and the cabinets were new. The adjoining dining room had an antique table and on the wall a pair of antlers, obviously home-shot. The living room had little furniture and a worn rug. Everything was clean and careful. In one corner was an old television with the screen outlined in white, giving the illusion of greater screen size. There were three small bedrooms upstairs, and a bath. One of the bedrooms was obviously a room for boys, with twin beds, two bureaus and a host of wildlife pictures and stuffed animals. The bathroom was pink.

It was a house that its owners loved. It made me ill at ease to be here with Hawk and Kathie. We had no business in a house like this.

Hawk went out and bought some beer and wine and cheese and French bread, and we ate and drank in near silence. After supper Kathie went up to one of the small bedrooms, filled with dolls and dust ruffles, and went to bed, with her clothes on. She still wore the white linen dress. It was getting pretty wrinkled but there wasn't a change of clothes. Hawk and I watched some of the Olympic action on CBC. We were on the wrong side of the mountain to get U.S. stations and thus most of the coverage focused on Canadians, not many of whom were in medal contention.

We finished up the beer and wine and went to bed before eleven o'clock, exhausted from traveling and silent and out of place in the quiet suburb among artifacts of family.

I slept in the boys' room, Hawk in the master bedroom. There were early bird sounds but the room was still dark when I woke up and saw Kathie standing at the foot of the bed. The door was closed behind her. She turned the light on. Her breath in the silence was short and heavy. She wore no clothes. She was the kind of woman who should take her clothes off when she can. She looked best without them; the proportions were better than they looked dressed. She did not seem to be carrying a concealed weapon. I was naked and on top of the covers in the warm summer. It embarrassed me. I slid under the sheet until I was covered from the waist down and rolled on to my back.

I said, "Hard to sleep these hot nights, isn't it?"

She walked across the room and dropped to her knees beside the bed and settled back with her buttocks resting on her heels.

"Maybe a little warm milk," I said.

She took my left hand where it was resting on my chest and pulled it over to her and held it between her breasts.

"Sometimes counting sheep helps," I said. My voice was getting a little hoarse.

Her breath was very short, as if she'd been sprinting, and the place between her breasts was damp with sweat. She said, "Do with me what you will."

"Wasn't that the title of a book?" I said.

"I'll do anything," she said. "You may have me. I'll be your slave. Anything." She bent over, keeping my hand between her breasts and began to kiss me on the chest. Her hair smelled strongly of shampoo and her body of soap. She must have bathed before she came in.

"I'm not into slaves, Kath," I said.

Her kisses were moving down over my stomach. I felt like a pubescent billy goat.

"Kathie," I said. "I barely know you. I mean I thought we were just friends."

She kept kissing. I sat up in bed and pulled my hand away from her sternum. She slid onto the bed as I made room, her whole body insinuated against me, her left hand running along my back. "Strong," she gasped. "Strong, so strong. Press me down, force me."

I took hold of both her hands at the wrists and held them down in front of her. She twisted over and flopped on her back, her legs apart. Her mouth half open, making small creature sounds in her throat. The bedroom door opened and

Hawk stood in it in his shorts, crouched slightly, bent for trouble. His face relaxed and broadened into pleasure as he watched.

"Goddamn," he said.

"It's okay, Hawk," I said. "No trouble." My voice was very hoarse.

"I guess not," he said. He closed the door and I could hear his thick velvet laugh in the hall. He said through the closed door, "Hey, Spenser. You want me to stay out here and hum 'Boots and Saddles' sort of soft while you're, ah, subduing the suspect?"

I let that pass. Kathie seemed uninterrupted.

"Him too," she gasped. "Both at once if you wish." She was almost boneless, sprawled on the bed, arms and legs flung out, her body wet with sweat.

"Kathie, you gotta find some other way to relate with people. Killing and screwing have their place but there are other alternatives." I was croaking now. I cleared my throat loudly. My body felt like there was too much blood in it. I was nearly ready to paw the ground and whinny.

"Please," she said, her voice now barely audible, "please."

"No offense, honey, but no."

"Please," she was hissing now. Her body writhed on the bed. She arched her pelvis up, as she had when Hawk searched her in Amsterdam. "Please." I still held her hands.

The more I held her and denied her the more she seemed to respond. It was a form of abuse and it excited her. Embarrassing or not, I had to get up. I slid out from under the sheet and slipped off the bed, rolling over her legs as I did. She used the space I'd left to spread out wider in a position of enlarged vulnerability. One of the animal behaviorists would say she was in extreme submission. I was in extreme randiness. I took my Levis off the chair and put them on. I was careful zipping them up. With them on I felt better.

Kathie was alone now, I think she wasn't even aware of me. Her breath came in thin hisses as it squeezed out between her teeth. She writhed and arched on the bed, the

116

sheets a wet tangle beneath her. I didn't know what to do. I felt like sucking my thumb but Hawk might come in and catch me. I wished Susan were here. I wished I weren't. I sat on the other bed in the room, both feet on the floor, ready to jump if she came for me, and watched her.

The window got gray and then pink. The bird sounds increased, some trucks drove by somewhere outside, not many, and not often. The sun was up. In the other half of the duplex, water ran. Kathie stopped wrenching herself around. I heard Hawk get up next door and the shower start. Kathie's breathing was quiet. I got up and went to my suitcase and took out one of my shirts and handed it to her. "Here," I said. "I don't have a robe, but this might do. Later we'll buy you some clothes."

"Why," she said. Her voice was normal now but flat, and very soft.

"Because you need some. You've been wearing that dress for a couple of days now."

"I mean why didn't you take me?"

"I'm sort of spoken for," I said.

"You don't want me."

"Part of me does, I was jumping out of my skin. But it's not my style. It has to do with love. And, ah, your, your approach wasn't quite right."

"You think I'm corrupt."

"I think you're neurotic."

"You fucking pig."

"That approach doesn't do it either," I said. "Though lots of people have used it on me."

She was quiet, but a pink flush smudged across each cheekbone.

The shower stopped and I heard Hawk walk back to the bedroom.

"I guess I'll shower now," I said. "You ought to be out of here and wearing something when I'm through. Then we'll all have a nice breakfast and plan our day."

CHAPTER TWENTY-TWO

MY SHIRT REACHED nearly to Kathie's knees and she ate break-fast in it, silently, perched on a stool at the counter with her knees together. Hawk sat across the counter, splendid in a bell-sleeved white shirt. He was wearing a gold earring in his right ear, and a thin gold chain tight around his neck. The Bouchers had left some eggs and some white bread. I steam-fried the eggs with a small splash of white wine, and served the toast with apple butter.

Hawk ate with pleasure, his movements exact and sure, like a surgeon, or at least as I hoped a surgeon's would be. Kathie ate without appetite but neatly, leaving most of the eggs and half the toast on her plate.

I said, "There's some kind of clothing store down Bou-levard St. Laurent. I saw it when we came up last night. Hawk, why don't you take Kathie down there and get her some clothes?"

"Maybe she rather go with you, babe."

Kathie said in a flat voice, softly, "I'd rather go with you, Hawk." It was the first time I could remember her using his name.

"You ain't gonna make a move on me in the car, are you?"

She dropped her head.

"Go ahead," I said. "I'll clean up here and then I'll think a little."

Hawk said, "Don't hurt yourself."

I said, "Kathie, put on some clothes."

She didn't move and she didn't look at me.

118

Hawk said, "Come on, girl, shake your ass. You heard the man."

Kathie got up and went upstairs.

Hawk and I looked at each other. Hawk said, "You think she might be about to break the color barrier?"

"It's just that myth about your equipment," I said.

"Ain't no myth, man."

I took $100 Canadian out of my wallet and gave it to Hawk. "Here, buy her a hundred worth of clothes. Whatever she wants. Don't let her blow it on fancy lingerie though."

"From what I seen last night she ain't planning to wear none."

"Maybe tonight is your turn," I said.

"Didn't satisfy her, huh?"

"I didn't come across," I said. "I never do on the first date."

"Admire a man with standards, babe, I surely do. Suze be proud of you."

"Yeah."

"That why she so grouchy about you this morning. That why I looking better to her."

"She's a sicko, Hawk."

"Ah ain't planning to screw her psyche, babe."

I shrugged. Kathie came down the stairs in the wrinkled white linen. She went with Hawk without looking at me. When they were gone I washed the dishes, put everything away, and then I called Dixon's man, Jason Carroll, collect.

"I'm in Montreal," I said. "I have accounted for all the people on Dixon's list, and I suppose I should come home."

"Yes," Carroll said. "Flanders has been sending us reports and clippings. Mr. Dixon is quite satisfied with the first five. If you can verify the last four . . ."

"We'll get to that when I'm back in town. What I want to do now is talk to Dixon."

"About what?"

"I want to keep on for a while. I have the end of something and I want to pull it all the way out of its hole before I quit."

"You have been paid a good deal of money already, Spenser."

"That's why I want to talk with Dixon. You can't authorize it."

"Well, I don't . . ."

"Call him and tell him I want to talk. Then call me back. Don't act executive with me. We both know you are a glorified go-for."

"That's hardly true, Spenser, but we need not argue about that. I'll be in touch with Mr. Dixon, and I'll call you back. What is your number?"

I read him the number off the phone and hung up. Then I sat down in the sparse living room and thought.

If Paul and Zachary were here, and maybe they were, they had tickets for the Olympics. Kathie had no idea which events. But it was pretty likely that they'd show up at the stadium. It was possible they were sport fans, but it was more likely that, sport fans or not, they had a plan to do in something or someone at the Olympics. A lot of African teams were boycotting, but not all. And on their track record they were pretty loose on who they damaged on behalf of the cause. There wasn't much to be gained by going to the Canadian cops. They were already screwing the security down as tight as they could after the horror show in Munich. If we got to them, all they could do was tell us to stay out of the way. And we didn't want to stay out of the way. So we'd do this without the cops.

If Paul wanted to make a gesture, the Olympic stadium was the place. It was the center of media attention. It was the place to look for him. To do that we needed tickets. I was figuring that Dixon could do that.

The phone rang. It was Carroll. "Mr. Dixon will see you," he said.

"Why not a phone call."

"Mr. Dixon doesn't do business on the phone. He'll see you at his home as soon as you can come."

"Okay. It's an hour flight. I'll be there this afternoon sometime. I'll have to check the flight schedule."

"Mr. Dixon will be there. Any time. He never goes out and he rarely sleeps."

"I'll be there sometime today."

I hung up, called the airport, booked a flight for after lunch. Called Susan Silverman and got no answer. Hawk came back with Kathie. They had four or five bags. Hawk had a long package done in brown paper.

"Picked up a new shotgun at a sporting goods store," he said. "After lunch I'll modify it."

Kathie went upstairs with the bags.

I said to Hawk, "I'm flying to Boston this afternoon, be back tomorrow morning."

"Remember me to Suze," he said.

"If I see her."

"What do you mean if. What you going for?"

"I gotta talk to Dixon. He doesn't talk on the phone."

"You got his bread," Hawk said. "I guess you don't have to do what you don't want."

"You and Kathie can lurk around down at the stadium. If you can find a scalper you might buy tickets and go in. I figure that's where Paul's likely to show."

"What I want with Kathie?"

"Maybe Zachary will show instead of Paul. Maybe somebody else she might know. Besides, I don't like leaving her alone."

"That ain't what you said this morning."

"You know what I mean."

Hawk grinned. "What you want with Dixon?"

"I need his clout. I need tickets to the stadium. I need his weight if we run what you might call afoul of the law. And I owe him to say what I'm doing. This matters to him. He's got nothing else that matters."

"You and Ann Landers, babe. Everybody's trouble."

"My strength is as the strength of ten," I said, "because my heart is pure."

"What you want me to do with Paul or Zachary or whatever, case I should encounter their ass?"

"You should make a citizen's arrest."

"And if they resist, seeing as I ain't hardly a citizen of this country?"

"You'll do what you do best, Hawk."

"A man like to be recognized for his work, bawse. Thank you kindly."

"You keep the car," I said. "I'll get a cab to the airport."

I left my gun in the house. I wasn't taking any luggage and I didn't want to thrash around at customs. It was just after two in the afternoon when we swung in over Winthrop and headed in to the runway at Logan Airport, home.

I took a cab straight from the airport to Weston and at three-twenty I was ringing on Hugh Dixon's doorbell again the same way I had a month before. The same Oriental man answered the door and said, "Mr. Spenser, this way." Not bad, he'd seen me only once, a month before. Of course I suppose he was expecting me.

Dixon was on his patio, looking at the hills. The cat was there, asleep. It was like when you come back from the war and the front lawn looks just as it did and people are cooking supper and you realize they've been doing it all along, while you've been gone.

Dixon looked at me and said nothing.

"I've got your people, Mr. Dixon," I said.

"I know. Five for sure, I assume your word is good on the others. Carroll is looking into it. You want money for the first five. Carroll will pay you."

"We'll settle up later," I said. "I want to stay on this a little longer."

"At my expense?"

"No."

"Then why are you here?"

"I need some help."

"Carroll tells me you've employed some help. A black man."

"I need different help than that."

"What do you want to do? Why do you want to stay on? What help do you need?"

"I got your people for you, but while I was getting them

I found out that they were only the leaves of the crabgrass. I know who the root is. I want to dig him up."

"Did he have a part in the killing?"

"Not yours, no, sir."

"Then why should I care about him?"

"Because he has had a part in a lot of other killings and because he'll probably kill somebody else's family and somebody else's after that."

"What do you want?"

"I want you to get me tickets to the Olympic games. The track and field events at the stadium. And if I get into a bind I want to be able to say I work for you."

"Tell me what's going on. Leave nothing out."

"Okay, there's a man named Paul, I don't know his last name, and possibly a man named Zachary. They run a terrorist organization called Liberty. I think they are in Montreal. I think they are going to do something rash at the Olympic games."

"Start at the beginning."

I did. Dixon looked at me steadily, without movement, without interruption, as I told him everything I had done in London and Copenhagen and Amsterdam and Montreal.

When I was through, Dixon pushed a button in the arm of his wheelchair and in a minute the Oriental man appeared.

Dixon said, "Lin, bring me five thousand dollars."

The Oriental man nodded and went out.

Dixon said to me, "I'll pay for this."

"There's no need for that," I said. "I'll pick up this one."

"No," Dixon shook his head. "I have a great deal of money and no other purpose. I'll pay for this. If the police present problems I'll do what I can to remove them. I'll have no trouble with Olympic tickets, I assume. Give your Montreal address to Lin before you leave. I'll have the tickets delivered there."

"I'll need three for every day."

"Yes."

Lin returned with fifty one-hundred-dollar bills.

"Give them to Spenser," Dixon said.

Lin handed them to me. I put them in my wallet.

Dixon said, "When this is through, come back here and tell me about it in person. If you die, have the black man do it."

"I will, sir."

"I hope you don't die," Dixon said.

"Me too," I said. "Goodbye."

Lin showed me out. I asked if he could call me a cab. He said he could. He did. I sat on a bench in the stone-paved foyer while I waited for it to come. When it came, Lin let me out. I got in the cab and said to the driver, "Take me to Smithfield."

"That's a pretty good ride, man," the cabby said. "It's gonna cost some jack."

"I got some jack."

"Okay."

We wheeled down the winding drive and out onto the road and headed toward Route 128. Smithfield was about a half-hour drive. The dashboard clock in the cab worked. It was quarter to five. She should be coming home from summer school soon, if she was still in summer school. *Oh, Susanna, oh don't you cry for me, I come from Montreal with* . . .

The cabbie said, "What'd you say, man?"

"I was singing softly to myself," I said.

"Oh, I thought you was talking to me. You want to sing to yourself, go ahead."

CHAPTER TWENTY-THREE

IT WAS OUT of the way but I had the cabbie take me to Route 1. I stopped at Karl's Sausage Kitchen for some German delicatessen and then at Donovan's Package Store for four bottles of Dom Perignon. It almost took care of Dixon's expense money.

The cabbie drove me down from Route 1 to the center of town, through the hot green tunnel of July trees. Lawns were being watered, dogs were being called, bikes were being ridden, cookouts were being done, pools were being splashed, drinks were being had, tennis was being played. Suburbia writ large. There was some kind of barbecue underway on the common around the meeting house. The smoke from the barbecue wagons hung over the folding tables in a light good-smelling haze. There were dogs there and children and a balloon man. I did not hear him whistle far and wee. If he had, it wouldn't have been for me.

There were white lilacs in Susan's front yard, and the shingles on the little Cape were weathered into a nice silvery gray. I paid the cabbie and gave him a large tip. And he left me standing with my champagne and my homemade cold cuts on Susan's green lawn in the slow evening. Her little blue Nova was not in the driveway. The guy next door was hosing his grass, letting the water stream out of the pistol spray nozzle in a long easy loop, coiling languidly back and forth across the lawn. A sprinkler would have been much more efficient but nowhere near as much fun. I liked a man who fought off technology. He nodded at me as I went up to Susan's door. She never locked the house. I went in the front door. The house was quiet and empty. I put the champagne and the stuff from Karl's in the refrigerator. I went to the bedroom and turned on the air conditioner. It was ten past six by the clock on the kitchen stove.

I found some Utica Club cream ale in the refrigerator and opened a can while I unpacked my delicatessen in the kitchen. There was veal loaf and pepper loaf and beer wurst, and Karl's liverwurst, which you could slice or spread and which made my blood flow a little faster when I thought of it.

I had bought two cartons of German potato salad and some pickles and a loaf of Westphalian rye and a jar of Dusseldorf mustard. I got out Susan's kitchen china and set the table in the kitchen. She had blue-figured kitchen china and it always made me feel like folks to eat off it. I sliced the liverwurst and put the assorted cold cuts on a platter in alternating patterns. I put the rye bread in a bread basket and the pickles in a cut-glass dish and the potato salad in a large blue-patterned bowl that was probably intended for soup. Then I went in the dining room where she kept the company china and stuff and got two champagne glasses I had bought her for her birthday, and put them in the freezer to chill. They had cost $24.50 each. The store had felt that monogramming *His* and *Hers* on them would be "kitsch," I think they said. So they were plain. But they were our glasses and they were for drinking champagne out of on special occasions. Or at least I thought they were. I was always afraid I'd come in some day and find her sprouting an avocado pit in one.

Moving about in her familiar kitchen, in her house where it seemed I could smell her perfume faintly, I felt even more strongly the sense of change and strangeness. The cookouts, the watered lawns, the weekday suburban evening coming on had that effect, and the house where she lived and read and did the dishes, where she bathed and slept and watched the *Today* show, were so real that what I'd been doing seemed unreal. I'd killed two men in a hotel in London earlier this summer. It was hard to remember. The bullet wound had healed. The men were in the ground. And here, this endured, and the man next door, watering his lawn in translucent graceful curves, didn't know anything at all about it.

I opened another can of beer and went into the bathroom and took a shower. I had to move two pairs of her panty hose that were drying on the rod that held the shower curtain. She used Ivory soap. She had some kind of fancy shampoo that came in a jar like cold cream and had a flower smell to it. I used it. Ferdinand the Bull.

There were some Puma jogging shoes, blue nylon with a white stripe, that I used sometimes when I was there for a weekend, and a pair of my white duck pants that Suze had washed and ironed and hung in a part of one of her bedroom closets that we'd come to call mine. The part, not the closet. I wore the Pumas without socks, you can do that if your ankles are good, and slipped into the ducks. I was combing my hair in her bedroom mirror when I heard the crunch of tires in her driveway. I peeked out the window. It was her. She'd come in the back door. I hopped on the bed and lay on my left side, facing the door, head propped on my left elbow, one knee drawn seductively up. My left leg fully extended, toes pointing. The bedroom door was ajar. My heart was thumping. *Christ, is that corny,* I thought. *Heart pounding, mouth dry, breath a little short. I took one look at you, that's all I meant to do.* I heard the back door open. The silence. Then the door closed. I felt the apprehension in my solar plexus. I heard her walk through the kitchen to the living room. Then straight to the bedroom door. The air conditioning hummed. Then she was there. In tennis dress, still carrying a racket, her black hair off her face with a wide white band. Her lipstick very bright and her legs tan. The hum of the air conditioner seemed a little louder. Her face was a little flushed from tennis and a faint small gloss of sweat was on her forehead. It was the longest we had been apart since we'd met.

I said, "Home from the hills is the hunter."

"From the kitchen setup," she said, "it would appear that you'd bagged a German delicatessen." Then she put her tennis racket on the bedside table and jumped on top of me. She put both arms around my neck and kissed me on the

127

mouth and held it. When she stopped I said, "Nice girls don't kiss with their mouths open."

She said, "Did you have an operation in Denmark? You're wearing perfume."

I said, "No. I used your shampoo."

She said, "Oh, thank heavens," and pressed her mouth on me again.

I slid my hand down her back and under the tennis dress. I'd had small experience with tennis dresses and wasn't doing well with this one.

She lifted her face from mine. "I'm all sweaty," she said.

"Even if you weren't," I said, "you would be soon."

"No," she said, "I've got to take a bath first."

"Jesus Christ," I said.

"I can't help it," she said. "I have to." Her voice was a little hoarse.

"Well, for crissake why not a shower. A bath, for God sake. I may commit a public disgrace on your stereo by the time you run a bath."

"A shower will ruin my hair."

"Do you know the ruination I face?"

"I'll be quick," she said. "I haven't seen you in a long time either."

She got up from the bed and ran the water in the bathtub off the bedroom. Then she came back in and pulled the shades and undressed. I watched her. The tennis dress had pants underneath.

"Ah ha," I said. "That's why my progress was slower than I'm used to."

"Poor thing," she said, "you've seduced a low-class clientele. With a better upbringing you'd have learned years ago how to cope with a tennis dress." She was wearing a white bra and white bikini underpants. She looked at me with that look she had, nine parts innocence and one part evil, and said, "All the guys at the club know."

"If they only knew what to do after they'd gotten the dress off," I said. "How come you wear pants under pants?"

128

"Only a cheap hussy would play tennis without underwear." She took off the bra.

"Or kiss with her mouth open," I said.

"Oh no," she said as she wiggled out of the underpants, "everyone at the club does that."

I'd seen her naked now enough times to stop counting. But I never lost interest. She wasn't fragile. She was strong-looking. Her stomach was flat and her breasts didn't sag. She was beautiful and she always looked a little uncomfortable naked, as if someone might burst in and say, "Ah hah!"

"Take your bath, Suze," I said. "Tomorrow I may go beat up the club."

She went into the bathroom and I could hear her splashing around in the water.

"If you're playing with a rubber ducky in there I'm going to drown you."

"Patience," she yelled. "I'm soaking in an herbal bubble bath that will drive you wild."

"I'm wild enough," I said. I took off my white ducks and my Pumas.

She came out of the bathroom with a towel tucked under her chin. It hung to her knees. With her right hand she removed it, the way you open a curtain, and said, "Tada."

"Not bad," I said. "I like a person who stays in shape."

She dropped the towel and got on the bed with me. I opened my arms and she got inside. I hugged her.

"I'm glad you're back in one piece," she said, her mouth very close to mine.

"Me too," I said, "and speaking of one piece . . ."

"Now," she said, "I'm not sweaty."

I kissed her. She pressed harder against me and I could hear her breath go in deep once through her nose and come out slowly in a long sigh. She ran her hand over my hip and down along my backside. It stopped when she felt the scar of the bullet wound.

With her lips lightly against mine she said, "What's this?"

"Bullet wound."

"I gather you weren't attacking," she said.

"I am now," I said.

And then we didn't talk.

CHAPTER TWENTY-FOUR

"In the ass?" Susan said.

"I like to think of it as a hamstring wound," I said.

"I'll bet you do," she said. "Was it bad?"

"Undignified but not serious," I said.

We were eating deli and drinking champagne in her kitchen. I had my white ducks back on and my Pumas. She had on a bathrobe. Outside it was dark now. Nonurban night sounds drifted in through the open back door. Night insects pinged against the screen.

"Tell me. All of it. From the beginning."

I put two slices of veal loaf on some rye bread, added a small application of Dusseldorf mustard, put another slice of bread on top and bit. I chewed and swallowed.

"Two shots in the ass and I was off on the greatest adventure of my career," I said. I took a bite of half sour pickle. It clashed a little with the champagne, but life is flawed.

"Be serious," Susan said. "I want to hear about it. Have you had a bad time? You look tired."

"I am tired," I said. "I've just been screwing my brains out."

"Oh really?"

"Oh really," I said. "How come you were doing all that sighing and moaning?"

130

"Boredom," she said. "Those weren't sighs and moans. Those were yawns."

"Nice talk to a wounded man."

"Well," she said, "I am glad the bullet didn't go all the way through."

I poured some champagne in her glass and mine. I put the bottle down, raised the glass and said, "Here's looking at you, kid."

She smiled. The smile made me want to say *Oh boy,* but I'm too worldly to say it out loud.

"Begin at the beginning," she said. "You got on the plane after you left me and . . . ?"

"And I landed in London about eight hours later. I didn't like leaving you."

"I know," she said.

"And a guy named Flanders that works for Hugh Dixon met me at the airport . . ." and I told her all, the people that tried to kill me, the people I killed, all of it.

"No wonder you look tired," she said when I finished. We were on the last bottle of champagne and most of the food was gone. She was easy to tell things to. She understood quickly, she supplied missing pieces without asking questions, and she was interested. She wanted to hear.

"What do you think about Kathie?" I said.

"She needs a master. She needs structure. When you destroyed her structure, and her master turned her out, she latched on to you. When she wanted to solidify the relationship by complete submission, which for her must be sexual, you turned her out. I would guess she'll be Hawk's as long as he'll have her. How's that for instant psychoanalysis. Just add a bottle of champagne and serve off the top of the head."

"I'd say you were right, though."

"If you report accurately, and it's something you're good at," Susan said, "certainly she's a rigid and repressed personality. The way her room was, the colorless clothing and the flashy underwear, the tight-lipped commitment to a kind of Nazi absolutism."

"Yeah, she's all of that. She's some kind of masochist.

Maybe that's not quite the right term. But when she was tied up and gagged on the bed she liked it. Or at least it aroused her to be tied like that and have us there. She went crazy when Hawk searched her while she was tied."

"I'm not sure masochist is the right word. But obviously she finds some connection between sex and helplessness and helplessness and humiliation and humiliation and pleasure. Most of us have conflicting tendencies toward aggression and passivity. If we have healthy childhoods and get through adolescence okay we tend to work them out. If we don't, then we confuse them and tend to be like Kathie, who hasn't worked out her passivity impulses." Susan smiled. "Or you, who are quite aggressive."

"But gallant," I said.

"How do you think Hawk will deal with her?" Susan said.

"Hawk has no feelings," I said. "But he has rules. If she fits one of his rules, he'll treat her very well. If she doesn't, he'll treat her any way the mood strikes him."

"Do you really think he has no feelings?"

"I have never seen any. He's as good as anyone I ever saw at what he does. But he never seems happy or sad or frightened or elated. He never, in the twenty-some years I've known him, here and there, has shown any sign of love or compassion. He's never been nervous. He's never been mad."

"Is he as good as you?" Susan was resting her chin on her folded hands and looking at me.

"He might be," I said. "He might be better."

"He didn't kill you last year on Cape Cod when he was supposed to. He must have felt something then."

"I think he likes me, the way he likes wine, the way he doesn't like gin. He preferred me to the guy he was working for. He sees me as a version of himself. And, somewhere in there, killing me on the say-so of a guy like Powers was in violation of one of the rules. I don't know. I wouldn't have killed him either."

"Are you a version of him?"

"I got feelings," I said. "I love."

"Yes, you do," Susan said. "And quite well too. Let us take this last bottle of champagne to the bedroom and lie down and drink it and continue the conversation and perhaps once more you would care to, as the kids at the high school say, do it."

"Suze," I said, "I'm a middle-aged man."

"I know," Susan said. "I see it as a challenge."

We went into the bedroom and lay close in the bed, sipping the champagne and watching the late movie in the air-conditioned darkness. Life may be flawed but sometimes things are just right. The late movie was *The Magnificent Seven*. When Steve McQueen looked at Eli Wallach and said, "We deal in lead, friend," I said it along with him.

"How many times have you seen this movie?" Susan asked.

"Oh, I don't know. Six, seven times, I guess. It's on a lot of late shows in hotel rooms in a lot of cities."

"How can you stand to watch it again?"

"It's like watching a dance, or listening to music. It's not plot, it's pattern."

She laughed in the darkness. "Of course it is," she said. "That's the story of your life. *What* doesn't matter. It's how you look when you do it."

"Not just how you look," I said.

"I know," she said. "My champagne is gone. Do you think you are, if you'll pardon the phrase, up for another transport of ecstasy?"

I finished the last of my champagne. "With a little help," I said, "from my friends."

She ran her hand lightly across my stomach. "I'm all the friend you've got, big fella."

"All I need," I said.

CHAPTER TWENTY-FIVE

NEXT DAY Susan drove me to the airport. We stopped on the way in the hot bright summer morning at a Dunkin' Donut shop, and had coffee and two plain donuts apiece.

"A night of ecstasy followed by a morning of delight," I said, and bit into a donut.

"Did William Powell take Myrna Loy to a Dunkin' Donut shop?"

"He didn't know enough," I said. I raised my coffee cup toward her.

She said, "Here's looking at you, kid."

I said, "How'd you know what I was going to say?"

"Lucky guess," she said.

We were quiet on the ride to the airport. Susan was a terrible driver and I spent a lot of time stomping my right foot on the floorboards.

When she stopped at the terminal she said, "I'm getting sick of doing this. How long this time?"

"Not long," I said. "Maybe a week, no longer than the Olympic games."

"You promised me London," she said. "If you don't make it back to pay off I'll be really angry with you."

I kissed her on the mouth. She kissed me back. I said, "I love you, Suze."

She said, "I love you too," and I got out and went into the terminal.

Two hours and twenty minutes later I was back in Montreal at the house near Henri Bourassa Boulevard. It was empty. There was O'Keefe's ale in the refrigerator along with several bottles of champagne. Hawk had been shopping. I opened a bottle of O'Keefe's and sat in the living room and watched some of the games on television. At about two-thirty a man knocked at the front door. I stuck my gun in my hip pocket, just in case, and answered.

"Mr. Spenser?" The man was wearing a seersucker suit and a small-brimmed straw hat with a big blue band. He sounded American, although so did half the people in Canada. At the curb with the motor running was a Dodge Monaco with Quebec plates.

"Yeah," I said, very snappy.

"I'm from Dixon Industries. I have an envelope for you, but first could I see some ID?"

I showed him my PI license with my picture on it. I looked like one of the friends of Eddie Coyle.

"Yeah," he said, "that's you."

"It disappoints me too," I said.

He smiled automatically, gave me back my license and took a thick envelope out of his side coat pocket. It had my name on it, and the Dixon Industries logo up in the left-hand corner.

I took the envelope. The man in the seersucker suit said, "Goodbye, have a nice day," went back to his waiting Monaco, and drove off.

I went in the house and opened the envelope. It was three sets of tickets for all the events at the Olympic stadium for the duration of the games. There was nothing else. Not even a preprinted card that said HAVE A NICE DAY. The world becomes impersonal.

Hawk and Kathie returned while I was on my fourth O'Keefe's.

Hawk opened some champagne and poured a glass for Kathie and one for him. "How old Suze doing?" he asked. He sat on the couch, Kathie sat beside him. She didn't say anything.

"Fine. She said hello."

"Dixon go along?"

"Yeah. I think it gave him another purpose. Something else to think about."

"Better than watching daytime TV," Hawk said.

"You turn up anything yesterday or today?"

He shook his head. "Me and Kathie been looking, but we haven't seen anyone she know. Stadium's big. We haven't looked at it all yet."

"You scalp some tickets?"

Hawk smiled. "Yeah. Hated to. But it's your bread. Been my bread I might have taken them away. Hate scalpers."

"Yeah. How's the security?"

Hawk shrugged. "Tight, but you know. How you gonna be airtight with seventy, eighty thousand people walking in and out two, three times a day. There's a lot of buttons around, but if I wanted to do somebody in there, I could. No sweat."

"And get out?"

"Sure, with a little luck. It's a big place, man. Lot of people."

"Well, tomorrow I'll see. I got us all tickets so we don't have to deal with the scalpers."

"All *right*," Hawk said.

"Hate corruption in all its aspects, don't you, Hawk."

"Been fighting it all my life, bawse." Hawk drank some more champagne. Kathie filled his glass as soon as he put it down. She sat so that her thigh touched his and watched him all the time.

I drank some ale. "Been enjoying the games, Kath?"

She nodded without looking at me.

Hawk grinned at me. "She don't like you," he said. "She say you ain't much of a man. Say you weak, you soft, say her and me we should shake you. I getting the feeling she don't care for you. She think you a degenerate."

"I got a real way with the broads," I said.

Kathie reddened but was silent, still looking at Hawk.

"I told her she was a little hasty in her judgment."

"She believe you?"

"No. You buy anything besides booze, like for supper?"

"Naw, man, you was telling me about a place called Bacco's. Figured you'd like to take me and Kath out and show her you ain't no degenerate. Treat her to a fine meal. Me too."

"Yeah," I said. "Okay. Let me take a shower."

"See that, Kath," Hawk said. "He very clean."

Bacco's was on the second floor in the old section of Montreal not far from Victoria Square. The cuisine was French Canadian and they had one of the better country pâtés that I'd eaten. It also had good French bread and Labatt 50 ale. Hawk and I had a very nice time. I was thinking that Kathie probably did not have nice times. Ever. But she was passive and polite while we ate. She'd bought a kind of dungaree suit with a vest and long coat that she was wearing, and her hair was neat and she looked good.

Old Montreal was jumping during the Olympics. There was outdoor entertainment in a square nearby, and throngs of young people drinking beer and wine and smoking and listening to the rock music.

We got in our rented car and drove back to our rented house. Hawk and Kathie went upstairs to what had become their room. I sat for a while and finished the O'Keefe's and watched the evening events, wrestling and some of the weightlifting, alone in the rented living room, on the funny old TV set with the illuminated border.

At nine o'clock I went to bed. Alone. I hadn't had much sleep the night before and I was tired. I felt middle-aged. I was lonely. It kept me awake till nine-fifteen.

CHAPTER TWENTY-SIX

WE TOOK the subway to the Olympic Stadium. Subway is probably the wrong term. If what I ride occasionally in Boston is a subway, then what we rode in Montreal was not. The stations were immaculate, the trains silent, the service on time. Hawk and I forced a small space for Kathie between us, in the jam of bodies. We changed at Berri Montigny and got off at Viau.

Being a supercool sophisticated worldly-wise full-grown hipster, I was unimpressed with the enormous complex around the Olympic Stadium. Just as I was unimpressed with going to the actual, real, live Olympic games. The excited circus feeling in my stomach was merely the manhunter's natural sensation as he closes in on his quarry. Straight ahead were food pavilions and concessions of one kind or another. Beyond was the Maisonneuve Sports Center, to my right the Maurice Richard Arena, to my left the Velodrome and, beyond it, looming like the Colosseum, the gray, not quite finished, monumental stadium. Cheering surged up from it. We started up the long winding ramp toward the stadium. As we went I sucked in my stomach.

Hawk said, "Kathie say this Zachary a bone-breaker."

"How big is he?"

Hawk said, "Kath?"

"Very big," she said.

"Bigger than me," I said, "or Hawk?"

"Oh yes. I mean really big."

"I weigh about two hundred pounds," I said. "How much would you say he weighs?"

"He weighs three hundred five pounds. I know. I heard him tell Paul one day."

I looked at Hawk. "Three hundred five?"

"But he only six feet seven," Hawk said.

"Is he fat, Kathie?" I was hopeful.

"No, not really. He used to be a weightlifter."

"Well, so, Hawk and I do a lot on the irons."

"No, I mean like those Russians. You know, a real weightlifter, he was the champion of somewhere."

"And he looks like a Russian weightlifter?"

"Yes, like that. Paul and he used to watch them on television. He has that fat look that you know is strong."

"Well, anyway, he won't be hard to spot."

"Harder here than most places," Hawk said.

"Yeah. Let's be careful and not try to put the arm on Alexeev or somebody."

Hawk said, "This dude trying to save Africa too?"

"Yes. He . . . he hates blacks worse than anyone I've seen."

"That helps," I said. "You can reason with him, Hawk."

"I got something under my coat for reasoning."

"If we run into him we're going to have trouble shooting. There's too many people."

"You think we should wrestle him, maybe?" Hawk said. "You and me good, babe, but we ain't used to no giants. And we got that other mean little sucker we got to think of."

We were at the gate. We handed in our tickets and then we were inside. There were several tiers. Our tickets were for tier one. I could hear the crowd roaring inside now. I was dying to see.

I said, "Hawk, you and Kathie start circling that way, and I'll go this way. We'll start at the first level and work up. Be careful. Don't let Paul spot you first."

"Or old Zach," Hawk said. "I be especially careful about Zach."

"Yeah. We'll keep working up to the top tier, then start back down again. If you spot them, stay with them. We'll eventually intersect again as long as we stay in the stadium."

Hawk and Kathie started off. "If you see Zachary," Hawk said over his shoulder, "and you want to do him in, it okay. You don't have to wait for me. You free to take him right there."

"Thanks," I said. "I think you ought to have a shot at the racist bastard."

Hawk went off with Kathie. He seemed to glide. I wasn't so sure he couldn't handle Zachary. I went off the other way, trying to glide. I seemed to be doing pretty well. Maybe I could manage Zachary too. I was as ready as I was going to be. Pale blue Levis, white polo shirt, blue suede Adidas with three white stripes, a blue blazer and a plaid cap for disguise. The blazer didn't go but it provided cover for the gun on my hip. I was tempted to limp a little so people would think I was a competitor, temporarily out of action. Decathlon maybe. No one seemed to be paying me any attention so I didn't bother. I went up the ramp to the first-level seating. It was better than I had imagined. The stadium seats were colorful, yellow and blue and such, and when I came out of the passageway there was a bright blaze of color. Below the stadium floor was bright green grass, ringed with red running track. Directly below me and near the side of the stadium, girls were doing the long jump. They had on white tops mostly, with large numbers affixed, and very high-cut tight shorts. The electronic scorekeeper was to my left near the pit where the jump finished. Judges in yellow blazers were at the start point, the take-off line, and the pit. A girl from West Germany started down the track in that peculiar long-gaited stride that long jumpers have, nearly straight-legged. She fouled at the take-off line.

In the middle of the stadium, men were throwing the discus. They all looked like Zachary. An African discus thrower had just launched one. It didn't look very good, and it looked even worse a minute later when a Pole threw one far beyond it.

Around the stadium there were athletes in colorful sweat clothes, jogging and stretching, loosening up and staying warm and doing what jocks always do waiting for an event. They moved and massaged muscles and bounced and shrugged.

At either end of the stadium, at the top, were score-boards, one at each end, with instant replay mechanism. I watched the Pole's huge discus toss again.

"The goddamned Olympics," I said to myself. "Jesus Christ."

I hadn't thought much about going to the games until I got off the subway. I'd been busy with the business at hand. But now that I was here looking down on the actual event, a sense of such strangeness and excitement came over me that I forgot about Zachary and Paul and the deaths at Munich and stared down at the Olympics, thinking of Melbourne and Rome and Tokyo and Mexico City and Munich, of Wilma Rudolph, and Jesse Owens, Bob Mathias, Rafer Johnson, Mark Spitz, Bill Toomey, the names flooded back at me. Cassius Clay, Emil Zatopek, the clenched fists at Mexico City, Alexeev, Cathy Rigby, Tenley Albright. Wow.

An usher said, "You seated, sir?"

"That's okay," I said. "It's over there, I just wanted to stop here a minute before I went on."

"Of course, sir," he said.

I started looking for Paul. I was wearing sunglasses, and I tipped the hat down over my forehead. Paul wouldn't expect to see me, if he were here, and Zachary didn't know me. I looked section by section, starting at the first row and moving up and down the rows slowly, one row at a time, up to the end of the section. Then I moved on. It was hard to concentrate and not begin to skim over the faces. But I concentrated and tried to pay no attention to the games right there below me. It was an outdoor sports crowd, well-dressed and able to afford the Olympic tickets. Lots of kids and cameras and binoculars. Across the stadium a group of male sprinters gathered for a 100-meter heat. I picked out the American colors. I discovered that I wanted the American to win. Son of a bitch. A patriot. A nationalist. The PA system made a little chiming sound and then an announcer said, first in French, then in English, that the qualifying heat was about to begin.

I kept drifting through the stands looking up and down the rows. A lot of Americans. The starting gun cracked across

141

the stadium and the runners broke out of the blocks. I stopped and watched. The American won. He jogged on around the track, a tall black kid with that runner's bounce, with USA on his shirt. I looked some more. It was like at a ball game, but the crowd was more affluent, more dignified, and the events below were of a different order. A vendor moved by me selling Coke.

On the field below, a platoon of Olympic officials in Olympic blazers marched out onto the near side track and picked up the long jump paraphernalia. And took it away. An American threw the discus. Farther than the African. Not as far as the Pole. I circled the whole stadium, getting tired of looking, stopping now and then to watch the games. I saw Hawk and Kathie two sections over, she was holding his arm, he was doing what I was doing. I started around again and I stopped at the second level for beer and a hot dog.

I put mustard and relish on the hot dog, took a sip of beer, a bite of hot dog (it was so-so, not Olympian) and looked out through the runway to the stands. Paul came down the runway. I turned back toward the counter and ate some more of my hot dog. A tribute to careful search and survey techniques and a masterpiece of concentration, looking over the stands aisle by aisle, and he almost walks into me while I'm eating a hot dog. Super sleuth.

Paul moved on past me without looking and headed up the ramp toward level three. I finished the hot dog and drank the beer and drifted along behind him. I didn't see anyone who looked like Zachary. I didn't mind.

At the third deck Paul went to a spot in the runway and looked down at the stadium floor. I went in the next ramp and watched him across the seats. The athletes looked smaller up here. But just as poised and just as agile. The squad of officials was breaking out low hurdles as we looked down at them. The discus throwers were leaving and the officials for that event formed into a small phalanx and marched out. Paul looked around, glanced up at the top of the stadium and back into the runway behind him. I stayed half inside my runway, a section away, and watched him sideways behind my sunglasses underneath my plaid cap.

Paul came back up the runway and turned down along the ramp that ran beneath the stands. I followed. There was a large kiosk where the washroom was located, and between it and the wall beneath the stands there was a narrow space. Paul stood looking at the space. I leaned on the wall and read a program, across the width of the ramp by a support pillar. Paul walked through the space beyond the washroom and into another ramp, then he came back up the ramp and stood in the space beyond the washroom staring down toward the ramp.

There wasn't much activity under the stands, and I stayed back of the post with just a slot between it and the edge of the washroom kiosk to see. I was okay as long as Hawk didn't show up with Kathie and run into Paul. If he did we'd take him right there, but I wanted to see what he'd do. He glanced over his shoulder back toward the washroom. No one came out. He leaned against the wall at the corner and took out what looked like a spyglass. He aimed the spyglass down the ramp, leaning it against the corner of the kiosk. He adjusted the focus, raised and lowered a little, then took a large Magic Marker and drew a small black stripe under the spyglass, holding the spyglass like a straight edge against the building. He put the Magic Marker away, sighted the spyglass again by holding it against the line on the wall, and then collapsed it and slipped it away in his pocket. Without looking around he went in the men's room.

Maybe three minutes later he came out. It was noon. The morning games were ending and the crowd began to pour out. From almost empty, the corridors under the stands became jammed. I forced my way after Paul and stayed with him to the subway. But as the train for Berri Montigny pulled out of Viau I was standing three rows back on the boarding platform calling the man in front of me an asshole.

CHAPTER
TWENTY-SEVEN

BY THE TIME I got back to the stadium it had cleared. Ticket holders for the afternoon games would not be admitted for an hour. I hung around the entrance marked for our ticket section and Hawk showed up in five minutes. Kathie wasn't holding his arm. She was walking a little behind him. When he saw me he shook his head.

I said, "I saw him."

"He alone?"

"Yeah. I lost him, though, in the subway."

"Shit."

"He'll be back. He was marking out a position up on the second deck. This afternoon we'll go take a look at it."

Kathie said to Hawk, "Can we eat?"

"Want to try the Brasserie down there?" Hawk said to me.

"Yeah."

We moved down toward the open area before the station stairs near the Sports Center. There were small hot-dog and hamburg stands, souvenir stands, a place to buy coins and stamps, a washroom, and a big festive-looking tent complex with the sides open and banners flying from the tent-pole peaks. Inside were big wooden tables and benches. Waiters and waitresses circulated, taking orders and bringing food and drink.

We ate, beer and sausage, and watched the excited people eating at the other tables. A lot of Americans. More than anything else, maybe more than Canadians. Kathie went to stand in the line at the ladies' room. Hawk and I had a second beer.

144

"What you figure?" Hawk said.

"I don't know. I'd guess he's got a shooting stand marked. He was looking through a telescope and marked a spot on the wall at shoulder level. I'd like to get a look at what you can see from that spot."

Kathie came back. We walked back up toward the stadium. The afternoon crowd was beginning to go in. We went in with them and went right to the second level. On the wall by the corner of the washroom near the entry ramp was Paul's mark. Before we went to it we circled around the area. No sign of Paul.

We looked at the mark. If you sighted along it, pressing your cheek against the wall, you would look straight down into the stadium at the far side of the infield, this side of the running track. There was nothing there now but grass. Hawk took a look.

"Why here?" he said.

"Maybe the only semi-concealed place with a shot at the action."

"Then why the mark? He can remember where it is."

"Must be something here. In that spot. If you were going to burn somebody for effect at the Olympic games, what would you choose?"

"The medals."

"Yeah. Me too. I wonder if the awards ceremonies take place down there?"

"Haven't seen one. There ain't many at the beginning of the games."

"We'll watch."

And we did. I watched the mark and Hawk circulated through the stadium with Kathie. Paul didn't reappear. No medals were awarded. But the next day they were, and looking down along Paul's mark on the washroom wall I could see the three white boxes and the gold medalist in the discus standing on the middle one.

"Okay," I said to Hawk. "We know what he's going to do. Now we have to hang around and catch him when."

"How you know he ain't got half a dozen marks like this all over the stadium?"

"I don't but I figured you'd keep looking for them and if you didn't see any we could count on this one."

"Yeah. You stay on this one, Kathie and me we keep circulating. Program say there's no more finals today. So I guess he ain't gonna do it today."

And he didn't. And he didn't the next day, but the next day he showed and he brought Zachary with him.

Zachary was nowhere near as big as an elephant. In fact he wasn't much bigger than a Belgian draught horse. He had a blond crew cut and a low forehead. He wore a blue-and-white striped sleeveless tank top jersey and knee-length plaid Bermuda shorts. I was staked out by the shooting mark when they arrived and Hawk was circulating with Kathie.

Paul, carrying a blue equipment bag with OLYMPIQUE MONTREAL, 1976 stenciled on the side, checked his watch, put the equipment bag down, took out a small telescope and sighted along his mark. Zachary folded his incredible arms across his monumental chest and leaned against the side of the washroom wall, shielding Paul. Behind Zachary, Paul knelt and opened his bag. Down the curve of the stadium ramp I could see Hawk and Kathie appear. I didn't want them spotted. Paul wasn't looking and Zachary didn't know me. I stepped out from my alcove behind the pillar and strolled on down toward Hawk. When he saw me coming he stopped and moved against the wall. When I reached them he said, "They here?"

"Yeah, up by the mark. Zachary too."

"How you know it's Zachary for sure?"

"It's either Zachary or there's a whale loose in the stands."

"Big as she said, huh?"

"At least that big," I said. "You're going to love him."

From inside the stadium came a sound of chimes and then the PA speaker's voice in French.

"Awards ceremony," Hawk said.

"Okay," I said. "We gotta do it now." We moved, Kathie behind us.

Around the corner, behind Zachary, Paul had assembled a rifle, with a scope. I brought my gun out of my hip holster and said, "Hold it right there." Clever. Hawk had the cutdown shotgun out and level.

He looked at Zachary and said, "Shit," stretching the word into two syllables.

Zachary had a small automatic pistol in his hand, hidden against his thigh. He raised it as I spoke. Paul whirled with the sniper rifle level and all four of us froze there. Three women and two children came out of the washroom and stopped. One of the women said, "Oh my god."

Kathie came around the other corner of the washroom kiosk and began to hit Paul in the face with both hands. He slapped her away with the rifle barrel. The three women and their daughters were screaming now and trying to get out of the way, and some other people appeared. I said to Hawk, "Don't shoot."

He nodded, reversed his hands on the shotgun and swung it like a baseball bat. He hit Paul across the base of the skull with the stock of the shotgun, and Paul went down without a sound. Zachary fired at me and missed, and I chopped at his gun hand with the barrel of my gun. I missed, but it caused him to jerk his arm and he missed again at close range. I tried to get my gun up against him so I could shoot without hitting anyone else, and he twisted it away from me with his left hand and it clattered on the floor. I grabbed onto his right with both hands and pushed the gun away from me.

Hawk hit him with the shotgun but Zachary hunched his shoulders and Hawk hit him too low, catching the massed-up trapezius muscles. While I hung onto his right arm Zachary half spun and caught Hawk with the left arm, like the boom coming across on a sailboat, and sent him and the shotgun in different directions. While he was distracted I was able to get his grip loosened on the pistol. It was the strength of both my hands against his fingers and I almost lost. I twisted

147

his forefinger back as hard as I could and the automatic hit the cement floor.

Zachary grunted and folded me in against him with his right arm. He brought the left one around too, but before he could close it around me Hawk was back up and got hold of it. I butted Zachary under the nose and then twisted down and away. He flung Hawk from him again, and as he did I rolled away from him and back up on my feet.

There were a lot of people around now and I heard someone yelling about police and there was a kind of murmurous babble of fright in different languages. Zachary had backed a couple of steps away from us, against the wall, Hawk was to his right and I was to his left in a ring of people milling about. Zachary's breath was heavy and there was sweat on his face. To my right I could see Hawk moving into the boxer's shuffle that I'd seen him use before. There was a bruise swelling along the cheekbone under his right eye. His face was shiny and bright and he was smiling. His breath was quiet, and his hands moved slightly in front of him, chest-high. He was whistling almost inaudibly through his teeth, "Do Nothing Till You Hear from Me."

Zachary looked at Hawk, then at me. I realized I was in almost the same stance Hawk was in. Zachary looked back at Hawk. At me. At Hawk. Time was with us. If we held him there, in a little while there would be cops and guns and he knew it. He looked at me again. Then took a breath.

"Hawk," I said. And Zachary charged. Hawk and I both grabbed at him and bounced off, Hawk from his right shoulder, me off his left thigh. I had tried to get low but he was quicker than he should have been and I didn't get down low enough fast enough. The milling crowd scattered like pigeons, swooping aside and settling back as Zachary burst through them, heading for the ramp. I tasted blood in my mouth as I got up, and Hawk's nose seemed to be bleeding.

We went after Zachary. He was pounding down the ramp ahead of us. Hawk said to me, "We can catch him okay, but what we gonna do with him?"

"No more Mr. Nice Guy," I said. My lip was puffing and

148

it was hard to speak clearly. We were out of the stadium now, past two startled ushers and running along the outside terrace that led down to the eating and concession areas.

Zachary went down the stairs two at a time at the end of the terrace. He was agile and very fast for a guy the size of a drive-in movie. He cut left at the bottom of the stairs toward the swimming and diving building. I put a hand on the railing and vaulted over the retaining wall and landed on him eight feet below. My weight hitting him made him stumble forward, and we both sprawled on the concrete. I had one hand locked around his neck as we hit, but he rolled over on top of me and tore loose. Hawk came around the corner of the stairs and kicked Zachary in the side of the head as he started to get up. It didn't stop him. He was on his feet and running. Hawk hit him with a right hook in the throat and Zachary grunted and ran over Hawk and kept going. Hawk and I looked at each other on the ground. I said, "You may have to turn in your big red S."

"He can run," Hawk said, "but he can't hide," and we went after him. Past the swimming arena Zachary turned right up a long steady hill toward the park that spread out around that end of the stadium complex.

"The hill's gonna kill him," I said to Hawk.

"Ain't doing me that goddamned much good either," Hawk said. But his breathing was still easy and he still moved like a series of springs.

"Three hundred pounds moving uphill is going to hurt. He'll be tired when we catch him."

Ahead of us Zachary churned on. Even at fifty yards we could see the sweat soaked through his striped shirt. Mine was wet too. I glanced down as I ran. It was wet with blood that must be running from my cut lip. I looked at Hawk. The lower half of his face was covered with blood and his shirt was spattered too. One eye had started to close.

We began to close. All the years of jogging, three, four, five miles a day, was staying with me. The legs felt good, my breath was coming easy and as the sweat began to come it seemed to make everything go smoother. There weren't many people here. And the ones we saw didn't register. The running got hypnotic as we pressed after Zachary. A steady rhythm of our feet, the swing of our arms, Hawk's feet were almost soundless as they hit the ground going up the long hill. Near the top we were right behind Zachary and at the top he stopped, his chest heaving, his breath rasping in his damaged throat, the sweat running on his face. Slightly ahead of us, slightly above, with the sun behind him, he stood and waited, high and huge, as if he had risen on his hind legs. We had bayed him.

CHAPTER TWENTY-EIGHT

HAWK AND I slowed and stopped about five feet away. Two athletes, a man and a woman, were jogging and they stopped a short distance away and stared.

Hawk moved to Zachary's right. Zachary turned slightly toward him, I moved a little more to his left. He turned back. Hawk moved closer. He turned slightly toward Hawk and I edged in. Zachary made a grunting sound. Maybe he was trying to speak. But it came out a kind of snarling grunt. He took a step toward me and Hawk stepped in and hit him again in the throat.

Zachary croaked and swung at Hawk. Hawk had moved out of reach and I was inside of Zachary's arm hitting him in the body, left, right, left, right. It was like working on the heavy bag. He croaked again and squeezed his arms around me. When he did, Hawk was behind him, hitting him in the kidneys, left hook, right hook, the punches thudded home without any seeming effect. He squeezed harder. He was going to do me in, then turn at Hawk. I chopped both hands in along the edge of his jawline, where his head joined his neck. He squeezed harder. I was beginning to see spots. I put both hands under his chin and pressed my back against his grasp, pushing his head back very slowly. Hawk stepped around and, one finger at a time, began to pry his hands loose from each other. The grip broke, and I pushed free.

Hawk hit him with a combination left jab, right hook right on the chin. It snapped Zachary's head back but that's all. Hawk stepped out away from Zachary, shaking his right hand. As he did, Zachary caught him with the back of his right hand and Hawk went down.

I kicked Zachary in the groin. He half turned and I half missed, but he grunted with the pain. Hawk scrambled away and got to his feet. He was covered with blood and so was Zachary. We were all bleeding now and smeared with each other's blood. Zachary was breathing hard. He seemed to be having trouble, as if his throat were closing where Hawk had caught him earlier. In the distance was a siren but no one was where we were.

Hawk circled in at Zachary, bobbing a little. "Nigger," Zachary rasped. He spit at Hawk. I circled the other way. We kept narrowing the circle. Finally we were too close. Zachary got hold of Hawk. I jumped on Zachary's back and tried to set a full nelson. He was too big and too strong. He broke it on me before I could set it, but Hawk got loose and pounded two more punches into Zachary's throat. Zachary grunted in pain.

I was still on his back. We were both slippery with sweat now, and blood, and rancid with body odor and exhaustion. I got one arm partly under his chin but I couldn't raise it. He reached behind him with his right arm and grabbed me by the shirt. Hawk hit him again, twice in the throat, and the pain was real. I could feel the tremor in his body, and the croak was more anguished. We were making progress.

He hauled me up over his shoulder with one arm, got his hand inside my thigh and threw me into Hawk. We both went down and Zachary came at us kicking. He got me in the ribs and I saw the spots again. Then I was up and Hawk was up and we were moving in our slow circle. Zachary's chest heaved as he dragged air in. In front of my eyes, exhaustion miasma danced. Hawk spit out a tooth. The siren was louder.

Hawk said, "We don't do him in soon, cops will be here."

"I know," I said, and moved in on Zachary again. He swung at me massively, but slow. He was tired. And was having trouble breathing. I ducked under the arm and hit him in the stomach. He chopped down on me with his fist but missed again, and Hawk hit him again in the kidneys. Hard expert punches. Zachary groaned. He turned at Hawk, but slowly, ponderously, like the last lurch of a broken machine.

I hit him in the neck behind the ear, not boxing now, throwing my fist like a sling from as far back as I could pull it, letting my whole two hundred pounds go into the punch. We had him now and I wanted to end it. He staggered, he half turned back. Hawk hit him as I had, haymaker right-hand punches, and he staggered again. I stepped in close and hit him again in the solar plexus, right, left, right, and Hawk caught him from behind with first his left elbow, then his right forearm, delivered in swinging sequence against the back of Zachary's neck. He turned again, and swinging his arm like a tree limb he knocked Hawk sprawling.

Then he lurched at me. I put two left jabs on his nose but he got hold of me with his left hand. He held me by the shirtfront and began to club me with his right fist. I covered up, pulling my head down inside my shoulders as far as I could, keeping my arms beside my head, elbows covering my body. It didn't help much. I felt something break in my left forearm. I didn't hurt much, just a snap. And I knew a bone had broken.

I drove the side of my right fist into his windpipe as hard as I could and brought my forearm around and hit Zachary along the jawline. He gasped. Then Hawk was behind Zachary and kicked him with the side of his foot in the small of his back. He bent back, half turned, and Hawk hit him a rolling, lunging right hand on the jaw, and Zachary loosened his grip on me and his knees buckled and he fell forward on his face on the ground. I stepped out of the way as he fell.

Hawk was swaying slightly as he stood on the other side of Zachary's fallen body. His face and chest and arms were covered with blood and sweat, his upper lip was swollen so badly that the pink inside showed. His right eye was closed. His sunglasses were gone and much of his shirt was shredded. One sleeve was gone entirely. A part of his lower lip moved and I think he was trying to smile. He looked down at Zachary and tried to spit. A little bloody saliva trickled on his chin. He said, "Honkie."

My left arm was bent a funny way above the wrist: It still didn't hurt much but my hand twitched and jumped involuntarily and I knew it was going to hurt. The front of my shirt was gone. My chest was covered with blood. My nose felt like it was broken too. That would make six times. I stepped toward Hawk and staggered. I realized I was weaving like he was.

A Montreal police car, with the light flashing and siren whooping, came up the road toward us. Several people were pointing up in our direction, running toward the car. The car came to a skidding halt and two cops rolled out of it, guns in hand.

Hawk said to me, "Didn't need no fucking cops, babe."

I put my right hand out, palm up. It was shaking. Hawk slapped his down limply on it. We were too tired to shake. We simply clutched hands, swaying back and forth with Zachary motionless on the ground in front of us.

"Didn't need no jive-fucking cops, babe," Hawk said again, and a noise came hoarsely out of his throat. I realized he was laughing. I started to laugh too. The two Montreal cops stood looking at us with the guns half raised and the doors of the cruiser swung open. Down the hill another cop car was coming.

One of them said, "Qu'est-ce que c'est?"

"Je parle anglais," I said with the blood running off me. Laughing and gasping for breath. "Je suis Americain, mon gendarme."

Hawk was nearly hysterical with laughter. Now his body was rocking back and forth, hanging on to my good hand.

"What the hell are you doing?" the cop said.

Trying to control his laughter, Hawk said, "We just copped the gold medal in outdoor scuffling." It was the funniest thing I'd ever heard, or so it seemed at the time, and the two of us were still giggling when they loaded us into the car and hauled us off to a hospital.

CHAPTER TWENTY-NINE

THEY SET MY arm and packed my nose and cleaned me up, and put me in the hospital overnight with Hawk in the next bed. They didn't arrest us, but there was a cop at the door all night. My arm was hurting now and they gave me a shot. I went to sleep for the rest of the day and night. When I woke up, a man in plain clothes was there from the RCMP. Hawk was sitting up in bed reading the *Montreal Star* and sipping some juice from a big styrofoam cup through a straw from one corner of his mouth. The swelling was down a bit in his eye. He could see out of it, but the lip was still very puffy and I could see the black thread from the stitches.

"My name's Morgan," the man from RCMP said. He showed me his shield. "We'd like to hear about what happened."

Hawk said, with difficulty, "Paul dead. Kathie shot him with the rifle while he trying to escape."

"Escape?" I said.

Hawk said, "Yeah." There was no expression on his face.

154

"Where is she now?"

Morgan said, "We're holding her for the moment."

I said, "How's Zachary?"

Morgan said, "He'll live. We have looked into him a bit. He's in our files, in fact."

"I'll bet he is," I said. I shifted a little in bed. It hurt. I was sore all over. My left arm was in a cast from knuckles to elbow. The cast felt warm. There was tape over my nose and the nostrils were packed.

"Naturally with the games established in Montreal we kept a file of known terrorists. Zachary was quite well known. Several countries want him. What business were you doing with him?"

"We were preventing him from shooting a gold medalist. Him and Paul."

Morgan was a strong-looking middle-sized man with thick blondish hair and a thick mustache. His jaw stuck out and his mouth receded. The mustache helped. He wore rimless glasses. I hadn't seen those for years. The principal of my elementary school had worn rimless glasses.

"We rather figured that out from the witnesses and what Kathie told us. That doesn't appear, incidentally, to be her real name."

"I know. I don't know what it is."

Morgan looked at Hawk, "You?"

Hawk said, "I don't know."

Morgan looked back at me, "Anyway the rifle with the scope, the mark on the wall, that sort of thing. We were able to figure out pretty well what the plan had been. What we're interested in is a bit of information on how you happened to be there at the proper time and place. There were quite a number of weapons at the scene. None of you seemed able to hang on. There was a thirty-eight caliber Smith and Wesson revolver for which you have a permit, Mr. Spenser. And there was a modified shotgun, which is illegal in Canada, for which there is no permit, but for which your companion seems to have had a shoulder rig."

155

Hawk looked at the ceiling and shrugged. I didn't say anything.

"The other guns," Morgan went on, "doubtless belonged to this Paul, and to Zachary."

I said, "Yeah."

Morgan said, "Let us not bullshit around anymore. You are not tourists, either of you. Spenser, I have already checked you out. Your investigator's license was in your wallet. We called Boston and have talked about you. This gentleman," he nodded at Hawk, "admits only to being called Hawk. He carries no identification. The Boston Police, however, suggested that a man of that description who used that name was sometimes known to associate with you. They described him, I believe, as a leg-breaker. It was not a pair of tourists who took Mr. Zachary, either. Tell me. I want to hear."

I said, "I want to make a phone call."

Morgan said, "Spenser, this is not a James Cagney movie."

I said, "I want to call my employer. He has a right to some anonymity and the right to be consulted before I violate it. If I violate it."

Morgan nodded his head at the phone on the bedside table. I called Jason Carroll. He was in. I had the feeling he was always in. Always at the alert for a call from Dixon.

I said, "This is Spenser. Don't mention the name of my client and yours, but I have finished what we agreed I'd do and the cops are involved and they are asking questions."

Carroll said, "I think our client will not approve of that. Are you at your Montreal address?"

"No. I'm in the hospital." The number was on the phone and I read it off to him.

"Are you badly hurt?"

"No. I'll be out today."

"I will call our client. Then I will be in touch."

I hung up. "I have no desire to be a pain in the ass," I said to Morgan. "Just give me a few hours till I talk with my client. Go out, have lunch, come back. We cleaned up something for you. We prevented a very bad scene for you."

Morgan nodded. "I know that. We are treating you very nicely," he said. "You've had experience with the police. We don't have to be this nice."

From the next bed Hawk said, "Haw."

I said, "True. Give me a few hours till I hear from my client."

Morgan nodded again. "Yes. Certainly. I'll be back before dinner." He smiled. "There will be an officer outside your door if you need anything."

"He got on a bright red coat?" Hawk said.

"Just for formal occasions," Morgan said. "For the Queen, yes. Not for you."

He left. I said to Hawk, "You really think she shot him trying to escape?"

Hawk said, "Hell no. The minute we took off after Zachary she picked up the rifle and shot him. You know goddamned well that's what she did."

"Yeah, that's my guess."

"I don't think they know different, though. Morgan don't look dumb but he got nobody to swear it wasn't like she telling it, I think. I bet everybody looking at you and me and old lovable Zach, when she done it."

"Yeah," I said. "I think that too."

Three hours and fifteen minutes later, the door opened and Hugh Dixon came in in a motor-driven wheel chair and stopped beside my bed.

I said, "I did not expect to see you here."

He said, "I did not expect to see *you here.*"

"It's not bad, I've had worse." I gestured at the next bed. "This is Hawk," I said. "This is Hugh Dixon."

Hawk said, "How do you do."

Dixon nodded his head once, without speaking. Behind him in the doorway was the Oriental man who had opened doors for me the last two times. A couple of nurses looked in through the half open door. Dixon looked at me some more.

"In a way it's too bad," he said. "Now I have nothing."

"I know," I said.

"But that's not your fault. You did what you said you'd do. My people have verified everyone. I understand they have the last one in jail here."

I shook my head. "Nope. She's not in it. I missed the last one."

Hawk looked over at me without saying anything. Dixon looked at me a long time.

I said, "How'd you get here so fast?"

"Private plane," Dixon said, "Lear jet. She's not the one?"

"No, sir," I said. "I missed the girl."

He looked at me some more. "All right. I'll pay you the full sum anyway." He took an envelope from his inside pocket and handed it to me. I didn't open it. "I've sent Carroll to the police," Dixon said. "There should be no difficulty for you. I have some influence in Canada."

"Get the girl out too," I said.

Again he looked at me. I could almost feel the weight of his look. Then he nodded. Once. "I will," he said. We were silent then, except for a faint whirr from his wheel chair.

"Carroll will take care of your medical bills," Dixon said.

"Thank you," I said.

"Thank you," Dixon said. "You did everything I wanted done. I am proud to have known you." He put out his hand. We shook hands. He rolled the chair over to Hawk and shook hands with him. He said to us both, "You are good men. If you need help from me at any time I will give it to you." Then he turned the chair and went out. The Oriental man closed the door behind him and Hawk and I were alone in the room. I opened the envelope. The check was for fifty thousand dollars.

I said to Hawk, "He doubled the fee. I'll give you half."

Hawk said, "Nope. I'll take what I signed up for."

We were quiet. Hawk said, "You gonna let that little psycho loose?"

"Yeah."

"Sentimental, dumb. You don't owe her nothing."

"She was a Judas goat but she was my Judas goat," I said. "I don't want to send her into the slaughter house too. Maybe she can stay with you."

Hawk looked at me and said again, "Haw."

"Okay, it was just a thought."

"She belong in the joint," Hawk said. "Or in the funny farm."

"Yeah, probably. But I'm not going to put her there."

"Somebody will."

"Yeah."

"And she might do somebody in 'fore they do."

"Yeah."

"You crazy, Spenser. You know that. You crazy."

"Yeah."

CHAPTER THIRTY

THE THAMES was glistening and firm below us as Susan and I stood on Westminster Bridge. My left arm was still in a cast and I was wearing my classic blue blazer with four brass buttons on the cuff, draped over my shoulders like David Niven. I could get the cast through my shirt sleeve but not through the coat. Susan had on a white dress with dark blue polka dots all over it. She had a wide white belt around her waist and white sling high-heeled shoes. Her bare arms were tan and her black hair glistened in the English twilight. We were leaning on the railing looking down at the water. I wasn't wearing a gun. I could smell her perfume.

"Ah," I said, "this sceptered isle, this England."

Susan turned her face toward me, her eyes invisible behind her enormous opaque sunglasses. There were faint parenthetical smile lines at her mouth and they deepened as she looked at me.

"We have been here for about three hours," she said. "You have sung 'A Foggy Day in London Town,' 'A Nightingale Sang in Berkeley Square,' 'England Swings Like a Pendulum Do,' 'There'll Be Blue Birds Over the White Cliffs of Dover.' You have quoted Samuel Johnson, Chaucer, Dickens and Shakespeare."

"True," I said. "I also assaulted you in the shower at the hotel."

"Yes."

"Where would you like to eat dinner?"

"You say," she said.

"Post Office Tower."

"Isn't that kind of touristy?"

"What are we, residents?"

"You're right. The tower it is."

"Want to walk?"

"Is it far?"

"Yes."

"Not in these shoes, then."

"Okay, we'll take a cab. I got a lot of bread. Stick with me, babe, and you'll be wearing ermine."

I gestured to a cab. He stopped. We climbed in and I gave him the address.

"Hawk wouldn't take half the money?" Susan said. In the cab she rested her hand lightly on my leg. Would the driver notice if I assaulted her in the cab? Probably.

I said, "Nope. He gave me a bill for his expenses and the fee for his time. It's his way of staying free. As I said, he has rules."

"And Kathie?"

I shrugged, and my jacket slipped off my shoulders. Susan helped me slip it back on. "Dixon got her released and we never saw her. She never went back to the rented house. I haven't seen her since."

"I think you were wrong to let her go. She's not someone who should be walking around loose."

160

"You're probably right," I said. "But she got to be one of us. I couldn't be the one to put her away. When you come down to it, Hawk shouldn't be running loose either."

"I suppose not. So how do you decide?"

I started to shrug again, remembered my jacket, and stopped. "Sometimes I guess, sometimes I trust my instincts, sometimes I don't care. I do what I can."

She smiled. "Yes, you do," she said. "I noticed that at the hotel while I was trying to shower. Even with one arm."

"I'm very powerful," I said.

"A lot of people died this trip out," she said.

"Yes."

"That bothers you some."

"Yes."

"This time worse than many."

"There was a lot of blood. Too much," I said. "People die. Some people probably ought to. But this time there was a lot. I needed to get rid of it. I needed to get clean."

"The fight with Zachary," she said.

"Goddamn," I said. "You don't miss anything, do you?"

"I don't miss very much about you," she said. "I love you. I have come to know you very well."

"Yeah, the fight with Zachary. That was a kind of—what—sweating out the poison, maybe. I don't know. For Hawk too, I think. Or maybe for Hawk it was just competition. He doesn't like to lose. He's not used to it."

"I understand that," she said. "I begin to wonder about myself sometimes. But I understand what you mean."

"Do you understand that there's more?"

"What?"

"You," I said. "The shower assault. It's like I need to love you to come back whole from where I sometimes go."

She rubbed the back of her left hand on my right cheek. "Yes," she said, "I know that too."

The cab pulled up at the Post Office Tower. I paid and overtipped. We held hands going up in the elevator. It was early evening on a week night. We were seated promptly.

"Touristy," Susan murmured to me. "Very touristy."

"Yes," I said, "but you can have Mateus Rosé and I can have Amstel beer and we can watch the evening settle onto London. We can eat duckling with cherries and I can quote Yeats."

"And later," she said, "there's always another shower."

"Unless I drink too much Amstel," I said, "and eat too much duck with cherries."

"In which likelihood," Susan said, "we can shower in the morning."

LOOKING FOR RACHEL WALLACE

For Joan, David and Daniel—
my good fortune.

CHAPTER ONE

LOCKE-OBER'S RESTAURANT is on Winter Place, which is an alley off Winter Street just down from the Common. It is Old Boston the way the Custom House tower is Old Boston. The decor is plain. The waiters wear tuxedos. There are private dining rooms. Downstairs is a room which used to be the Men's Bar until it was liberated one lunchtime by a group of humorless women who got into a shouting match with a priest. Now anybody can go in there and do what they want. They take Master Charge.

I didn't need Master Charge. I wasn't paying, John Ticknor was paying. And he didn't need Master Charge, because he was paying with the company's money. I ordered lobster Savannah. The company was Hamilton Black Publishing, and they had ten million dollars. Ticknor ordered scrod.

"And two more drinks, please."

"Very good." The waiter took our menus and hurried off. He had a hearing aid in each ear.

Ticknor finished his Negroni. "You drink only beer, Mr. Spenser?"

The waiter returned with a draft Heineken for me and another Negroni for Ticknor.

"No. I'll drink wine sometimes."

"But no hard liquor?"

"Not often. I don't like it. I like beer."

"And you always do what you like."

"Almost always. Sometimes I can't."

He sipped some more Negroni. Sipping didn't look easy for him.

"What might prevent you?" he said.

"I might have to do something I don't like in order to get to do something I like a lot."

Ticknor smiled a little. "Metaphysical," he said.

I waited. I knew he was trying to size me up. That was okay, I was used to that. People didn't know anything about hiring someone like me, and they almost always vamped around for a while.

"I like milk, too," I said. "Sometimes I drink that."

Ticknor nodded. "Do you carry a gun?" he said.

"Yes."

The waiter brought our salad.

"How tall are you?"

"Six one and something."

"How much do you weigh?"

"Two-oh-one and a half, this morning, after running."

"How far do you run?"

The salad was made with Boston lettuce and was quite fresh.

"I do about five miles a day," I said. "Every once in a while I'll do ten to sort of stretch out."

"How did your nose get broken?"

"I fought Joe Walcott once when he was past his prime."

"And he broke your nose?"

"If he'd been in his prime, he'd have killed me," I said.

"You were a fighter then."

I nodded. Ticknor was washing down a bite of salad with the rest of his Negroni.

"And you've been on the police?"

I nodded.

"And you were dismissed?"

"Yeah."

"Why?"

"They said I was intractable."

"Were they right?"

"Yeah."

The waiter brought our entrée.

"I am told that you are quite tough."

"You betcha," I said. "I was debating here today whether to have lobster Savannah or just eat one of the chairs."

Ticknor smiled again, but not like he wanted me to marry his sister.

"I was also told that you were—I believe the phrase was, and I'm quoting—'a smart-mouthed bastard'—though it was not said without affection."

I said, "Whew."

Ticknor ate a couple of green peas from the side dish. He was maybe fifty and athletic-looking. Squash probably, tennis. Maybe he rode. He wore rimless glasses, which you don't see all that often anymore, and had a square-jawed Harvardy face, and an unkempt gray crew cut like Archibald Cox. Not a patsy even with the Bryn Mawr accent. Not soft.

"Were you thinking of commissioning a biography of me, or do you want to hire me to break someone's arm?"

"I know some book reviewers," he said, "but . . . no, neither of those." He ate five more peas. "Do you know very much about Rachel Wallace?"

"Sisterhood," I said.

"Really?"

"Yeah. I have an intellectual friend. Sometimes she reads to me."

"What did you think of it?"

"I thought Simone de Beauvoir already said most of it."

"Have you read *The Second Sex?*"

"Don't tell the guys down the gym," I said. "They'll think I'm a fairy."

"We published *Sisterhood.*"

"Oh, yeah?"

"Nobody ever notices the publisher. But yes, we did. And we're publishing her new book."

"What is that called?"

"*Tyranny.*"

"Catchy title."

"It is an unusual book," Ticknor said. "The tyrants are people in high places who discriminate against gay women."

"Catchy idea," I said.

Ticknor frowned for a moment. "The people in high places are named. Ms. Wallace has already had threats against her if the book is published."

"Ah-hah," I said.

"I beg your pardon?"

"My role in this is beginning to take on definition."

"Oh, yes, the threats. Well, yes. That's it essentially. We want you to protect her."

"Two hundred dollars a day," I said. "And expenses."

"Expenses?"

"Yeah, you know. Sometimes I run out of ammunition and have to buy more. Expenses."

"There are people I can get for half that."

"Yeah."

The waiter cleared the lunch dishes and poured coffee.

"I'm not authorized to go that high."

I sipped my coffee.

"I can offer one hundred thirty-five dollars a day."

I shook my head.

Ticknor laughed. "Have you ever been a literary agent?" he said.

"I told you, I don't do things I don't like to do if I can avoid it."

"And you don't like to work for a hundred and thirty-five a day."

I nodded.

"Can you protect her?"

"Sure. But you know as well as I do that it depends on what I protect her from. I can't prevent a psychopath from sacrificing himself to kill her. I can't prevent a horde of hate-crazed sexists from descending on her. I can make her harder to hurt, I can up the cost to the hurter. But if she wishes to live anything like a normal life, I can't make her completely safe."

"I understand that," Ticknor said. He didn't look happy about it, though.

"What about the cops?" I said.

"Ms. Wallace doesn't trust them. She sees them as, quote, 'agents of repression.'"

"Oh."

"She has also said she refuses to have, and once again I quote, 'a rabble of armed thugs following me about day and night.' She has agreed to a single bodyguard. At first she insisted on a woman."

"But?"

"But if there were to be but one, we felt a man might be better. I mean if you had to wrestle with an assassin, or what-ever. A man would be stronger, we felt."

"And she agreed?"

"Without enthusiasm."

"She gay?" I said.

"Yes," Ticknor said.

"And out of the closet?"

"Aggressively out of the closet," Ticknor said. "Does that bother you?"

"Gay, no. Aggressive, yes. We're going to spend a lot of time together. I don't want to fight with her all day."

"I can't say it will be pleasant, Spenser. She's not an easy person. She has a splendid mind, and she has forced the world to listen to her. It has been difficult. She's tough and cynical and sensitive to every slight."

"Well, I'll soften her up," I said. "I'll bring some candy and flowers, sweet-talk her a little . . . ."

Ticknor looked like he'd swallowed a bottle cap.

"My God, man, don't joke with her. She'll simply ex-plode."

Ticknor poured some more coffee for me and for him-self from the small silver pot. There was only one other table occupied now. It made no difference to our waiter. He sprang forward when Ticknor put the coffeepot down, took it away, and returned almost at once with a fresh pot.

"The only reservation I have," Ticknor said when the waiter had retreated, "is the potential for a personality clash."

I leaned back in my chair and folded my arms.

"You look good in most ways," Ticknor said. "You've got the build for it. People who should know say you are as tough as you look. And they say you're honest. But you work awfully hard sometimes at being a wise guy. And you look like everything Rachel hates."

"It's not hard work," I said.

"What isn't?"

"Being a wise guy. It's a gift."

"Perhaps," Ticknor said. "But it is not a gift that will endear you to Rachel Wallace. Neither will the muscles and the machismo."

"I know a guy would lend me a lavender suit," I said.

"Don't you want this work?" Ticknor said.

I shook my head. "What you want, Mr. Ticknor, is someone feisty enough to get in the line of someone else's fire, and tough enough to get away with it. And you want him to look like Winnie-the-Pooh and act like Rebecca of Sunnybrook Farm. I'm not sure Rebecca's even got a gun permit."

He was silent for a moment. The other table cleared, and now we were alone in the upstairs dining room, except for several waiters and the maître d'.

"God damn it," Ticknor said. "You are right. If you'll take the job, it's yours. Two hundred dollars a day and expenses. And God help me, I hope I'm right."

"Okay," I said. "When do I meet Ms. Wallace?"

172

CHAPTER TWO

I MET RACHEL WALLACE on a bright October day when Ticknor and I walked down from his office across the Common and the Public Garden through the early turn-of-fall foliage and visited her in her room at the Ritz.

She didn't look like Carry Nation. She looked like a pleasant woman about my age with a Diane Von Furstenberg dress on and some lipstick, and her hair long and black and clean.

Ticknor introduced us. She shook hands firmly and looked at me carefully. If I'd had tires, she'd have kicked them. "Well, you're better than I expected," she said.

"What did you expect?" I said.

"A wide-assed ex-policeman with bad breath wearing an Anderson Little suit."

"Everybody makes mistakes," I said.

"Let's have as few as possible between us," she said. "To insure that, I think we need to talk. But not here. I hate hotel rooms. We'll go down to the bar."

I said okay. Ticknor nodded. And the three of us went down to the bar. The Ritz is all a bar should be—dark and quiet and leathery, with a huge window that looks out onto Arlington Street and across it to the Public Garden. The window is tinted so that the bar remains dim. I always like to drink in the Ritz Bar. Ticknor and Rachel Wallace had martinis on the rocks. I had beer.

"That figures," Rachel Wallace said, when I ordered the beer.

"Everybody laughs at me when I order a Pink Lady," I said.

"John has warned me that you are a jokester. Well, I

am not. If we are to have any kind of successful association, you'd best understand right now that I do not enjoy humor. Whether or not successful."

"Okay if now and then I enjoy a wry, inward smile if struck by one of life's vagaries?"

She turned to Ticknor, and said, "John, he won't do. Get rid of him."

Ticknor took a big drink of his martini. "Rachel, damn it. He's the best around at what we need. You did needle him about the beer. Be reasonable, Rachel."

I sipped some beer. There were peanuts in a small bowl in the center of the table. I ate some.

"He's read your book," Ticknor said. "He'd read it even before I approached him."

She took the olive on a toothpick out of her drink and bit half of it off and held the other half against her bottom lip and looked at me. "What did you think of *Sisterhood?*"

"I think you are rehashing Simone de Beauvoir."

Her skin was quite pale and the lipstick mouth was very bright against it. It made her smile more noticeable. "Maybe you'll do," she said. "I prefer to think that I'm reapplying Simone de Beauvoir to contemporary issues. But I'll accept 'rehashing.' It's direct. You speak your mind."

I ate some more peanuts.

"Why did you read Simone de Beauvoir?"

"My friend gave it to me for my birthday. She recommended it."

"What did you feel was her most persuasive insight?"

"Her suggestion that women occupied the position of *other.* Are we having a quiz later?"

"I wish to get some insight into your attitude toward women and women's issues."

"That's dumb," I said. "You ought to be getting insight into how well I can shoot and how hard I can hit and how quick I can dodge. That's what somebody is giving me two hundred a day for. My attitude toward women is irrelevant. So are my insights into *The Second Sex.*"

She looked at me some more. She leaned back against

the black leather cushions of the corner banquette where we sat. She rubbed her hands very softly together.

"All right," she said. "We shall try. But there are ground rules. You are a big attractive man. You have probably been successful in your dealings with some women. I am not like those women. I am a lesbian. I have no sexual interest in you or any other man. Therefore there is no need for flirtatious behavior. And no need to take it personally. Does the idea of a gay woman offend you or titillate you?"

"Neither of the above," I said. "Is there a third choice?"

"I hope so," she said. She motioned to the waiter and ordered another round. "I have work to do," she went on. "I have books to write and publicize. I have speeches to give and causes to promote and a life to live. I will not stay in some safe house and hide while my life goes by. I will not change what I am, whatever the bigots say and do. If you want to do this, you'll have to understand that."

"I understand that," I said.

"I also have an active sex life. Not only active but often diverse. You'll have to be prepared for that, and you'll have to conceal whatever hostility you may feel toward me or the women I sleep with."

"Do I get fired if I blush?"

"I told you before, I have no sense of humor. Do you agree or disagree?"

"Agree."

"Finally, except when you feel my life is in danger, I want you to stay out of my way. I realize you will have to be around and watchful. I don't know how serious the threats are, but you have to assume they are serious. I understand that. But short of a mortal situation I do not want to hear from you. I want a shadow."

I said, "Agree," and drank the rest of my beer. The waiter came by and removed the empty peanut bowl and replaced it. Rachel Wallace noticed my beer was gone and gestured that the waiter should bring another. Ticknor looked at his glass and at Rachel Wallace's. His was empty, hers wasn't. He didn't order.

"Your appearance is good," she said. "That's a nice suit, and it's well tailored. Are you dressed up for the occasion or do you always look good?"

"I'm dressed up for the occasion. Normally I wear a light-blue body stocking with a big red **S** on the front." It was dim in the bar, but her lipstick was bright, and I thought for a moment she smiled, or nearly smiled, or one corner of her mouth itched.

"I want you presentable," she said.

"I'll be presentable, but if you want me appropriate, you'll have to let me know your plans ahead of time."

She said, "Certainly."

I said thank you. I tried to think of things other than the peanuts. One bowl was enough.

"I've had my say, now it is your turn. You must have some rules or questions, or whatever. Speak your mind."

I drank beer. "As I said to Mr. Ticknor when he and I first talked, I cannot guarantee your safety. What I can do is increase the odds against an assassin. But someone dedicated or crazy can get you."

"I understand that," she said.

"I don't care about your sex life. I don't care if you elope with Anita Bryant. But I do need to be around when it happens. If you make it with strangers, you might be inviting your murderer to bed."

"Are you suggesting I'm promiscuous?"

"You suggested it a little while ago. If you're not, it's not a problem. I don't assume your friends will kill you."

"I think we'll not discuss my sex life further. John, for God's sake order another drink. You look so uncomfortable, I'm afraid you'll discorporate."

He smiled and signaled the waiter.

"Do you have any other statements to make?" she said to me.

"Maybe one more," I said. "I hired on to guard your body, that's what I'll do. I will work at it. Part of working at it will include telling you things you can do and things you can't do. I know my way around this kind of work a lot better than

176

you do. Keep that in mind before you tell me to stick it. I'll stay out of your way when I can, but I can't always."

She put her hand out across the table, and I took it. "We'll try it, Spenser," she said. "Maybe it won't work, but it could. We'll try."

CHAPTER THREE

"OKAY," I SAID, "tell me about the death threats."

"I've always gotten hate mail. But recently I have gotten some phone calls."

"How recently?"

"As soon as the bound galleys went out."

"What are bound galleys? And who do they go out to?"

Ticknor spoke. "Once a manuscript is set in type, a few copies are run off to be proofread by both author and copy editor. These are called galley proofs."

"I know that part," I said. "What about the bound ones going out?"

"Galleys normally come in long sheets, three pages or so to the sheet. For reviewers and people from whom we might wish to get a favorable quote for promotional purposes, we cut the galleys and bind them in cheap cardboard covers and send them out." Ticknor seemed more at ease now, with the third martini half inside him. I was still fighting off the peanuts.

"You have a list of people to whom you send these?"

Ticknor nodded. "I can get it to you tomorrow."

"Okay. Now, after the galleys went out, came the phonecalls. Tell me about them."

She was eating her martini olive. Her teeth were small and even and looked well cared-for. "A man's voice," she said.

177

"He called me a dyke, 'a fucking dyke,' as I recall. And told me if that book was published, I'd be dead the day it hit the streets."

"Books don't hit the streets," I said. "Newspapers do. The idiot can't get his clichés straight."

"There has been a call like that every day for the last week."

"Always say the same thing?"

"Not word for word, but approximately. The substance is always that I'll die if the book is published."

"Same voice all the time?"

"No."

"That's too bad."

Ticknor said, "Why?"

"Makes it seem less like a single cuckoo getting his rocks off on the phone," I said. "I assume you've rejected the idea of withdrawing the book."

Rachel Wallace said, "Absolutely."

Ticknor said, "We suggested that. We said we'd not hold her to the contract."

"You also mentioned returning the advance," Rachel Wallace said.

"We run a business, Rachel."

"So do I," she said. "My business is with women's rights and with gay liberation and with writing." She looked at me. "I cannot let them frigthen me. I cannot let them stifle me. Do you understand that?"

I said yes.

"That's your job," she said. "To see that I'm allowed to speak."

"What is there in the new book," I said, "that would cause people to kill you?"

"It began as a book about sexual prejudice. Discrimination in the job market against women, gay people, and specifically gay women. But it has expanded. Sexual prejudice goes hand in hand with other forms of corruption. Violation of the equal employment laws is often accompanied by violation of other laws. Bribery, kickbacks, racket tie-ins. I have named names as I found them. A lot of people will be hurt by my book. All of them deserve it."

"Corporations," Ticknor said, "local government agencies, politicians, city hall, the Roman Catholic Church. She has taken on a lot of the local power structure."

"Is it all Greater Boston?"

"Yes," she said. "I use it as a microcosm. Rather than trying to generalize about the nation, I study one large city very closely. Synecdoche, the rhetoricians would call it."

"Yeah," I said, "I bet they would."

"So," Ticknor said, "you see there are plenty of potential villains."

"May I have a copy of the book to read?"

"I brought one along," Ticknor said. He took his briefcase off the floor, opened it, and took out a book with a green dust jacket. The title, in salmon letters, took up most of the front. Rachel Wallace's picture took up most of the back. "Just out," Ticknor said.

"I'll read it tonight," I said. "When do I report for work?"

"Right now," Rachel Wallace said. "You are here. You are armed. And quite frankly I have been frightened. I won't be deflected. But I am frightened."

"What are your plans for today?" I said.

"We shall have perhaps three more drinks here, then you and I shall go to dinner. After dinner I shall go to my room and work until midnight. At midnight I shall go to bed. Once I am in my room with the door locked, I should think you could leave. The security here is quite good, I'm sure. At the slightest rustle outside my door I will call the hotel security number without a qualm."

"And tomorrow?"

"Tomorrow you should meet me at my room at eight o'clock. I have a speech in the morning and an autographing in the afternoon."

"I have a date for dinner tonight," I said. "May I ask her to join us?"

"You're not married," she said.

"That's true," I said.

"Is this a casual date or is this your person?"

"It's my person," I said.

Ticknor said, "We can't cover her expenses, you know."

"Oh, damn," I said.

"Yes, of course, bring her along. I hope that you don't plan to cart her everywhere, however. Business and pleasure, you know."

"She isn't someone you cart," I said. "If she joins us, it will be your good fortune."

"I don't care for your tone, buster," Rachel Wallace said. "I have a perfectly legitimate concern that you will not be distracted by your lady friend from doing what we pay you to do. If there's danger, would you look after her first or me."

"Her," I said.

"Then certainly I can suggest that she not always be with us."

"She won't be," I said. "I doubt that she could stand it."

"Perhaps I shall change my mind about this evening," Rachel Wallace said.

"Perhaps I shall change mine, too," I said.

Ticknor said, "Wait. Now just wait. I'm sure Rachel meant no harm. Her point is valid. Surely, Spenser, you understand that."

I didn't say anything.

"Dinner this evening, of course, is perfectly understandable," Ticknor said. "You had a date. You had no way to know that Rachel would require you today. I'm sure Rachel will be happy to have dinner with you both."

Rachel Wallace didn't say anything.

"Perhaps you could call the lady and ask her to meet you."

Rachel Wallace didn't like Ticknor saying "lady," but she held back and settled for giving him a disgusted look. Which he missed, or ignored—I couldn't tell which.

"Where are we eating?" I said to Rachel.

"I'd like the best restaurant in town," she said. "Do you have a suggestion?"

"The best restaurant in town is not *in* town. It's in Marblehead, place called Rosalie's."

"What's the cuisine?"

"Northern Italian Eclectic. A lot of it is just Rosalie's."

"No meatball subs? No pizza?"

"No."

"Do you know this restaurant, John?"

"I've not been out there. I've heard that it is excellent."

"Very well, we'll go. Tell your friend that we shall meet her there at seven. I'll call for reservations."

"My friend is named Susan. Susan Silverman."

"Fine," Rachel Wallace said.

CHAPTER FOUR

ROSALIE'S IS IN a renovated commercial building in one of the worst sections of Marblehead. But the worst section of Marblehead is upper middle class. The commercial building had probably once manufactured money clips.

The restaurant is up a flight and inside the door is a small stand-up bar. Susan was at the bar drinking a glass of Chablis and talking to a young man in a corduroy jacket and a plaid shirt. He had a guardsman's mustache twirled upward at the ends. I thought about strangling him with it.

We paused inside the door for a moment. Susan didn't see us, and Wallace was looking for the maître d'. Susan had on a double-breasted camel's-hair jacket and matching skirt. Under the jacket was a forest-green shirt open at the throat. She had on high boots that disappeared under the skirt. I always had the sense that when I came upon her suddenly in a slightly unusual setting, a pride of trumpets ought to play alarms and flourishes. I stepped up to the bar next to her and

181

said, "I beg your pardon, but the very sight of you makes my heart sing like an April day on the wings of spring."

She turned toward me and smiled and said, "Everyone tells me that."

She gestured toward the young man with the guardsman's mustache. "This is Tom," she said. And then with the laughing touch of evil in her eyes she said, "Tom was nice enough to buy me a glass of Chablis."

I said to Tom, "That's *one.*"

He said, "Excuse me?"

I said, "It's the tag line to an old joke. Nice to meet you."

"Yeah," Tom said, "same here."

The maître d', in a dark velvet three-piece suit, was standing with Rachel Wallace. I said, "Bring your wine and come along."

She smiled at Tom and we stepped over to Wallace. "Rachel Wallace," I said, "Susan Silverman."

Susan put out her hand. "Hi, Rachel," she said. "I think your books are wonderful."

Wallace smiled, took her hand, and said, "Thank you. Nice to meet you."

The maître d' led us to our table, put the menus in front of us, and said, "I'll have someone right over to take your cocktail order."

I sat across from Susan, with Rachel Wallace on my left. She was a pleasant-looking woman, but next to Susan she looked as if she'd been washed in too much bleach. She was a tough, intelligent national figure, but next to Susan I felt sorry for her. On the other hand I felt sorry for all women next to Susan.

Rachel said, "Tell me about Spenser. Have you known him long?"

"I met him in 1973," Susan said, "but I've known him forever."

"It only seems like forever," I said, "when I'm talking."

Rachel ignored me. "And what is he like?"

182

"He's like he seems," Susan said. The waitress came and took our cocktail order.

"No, I mean in detail, what is he like? I am perhaps dependent on him to protect my life. I need to know about him."

"I don't like to say this in front of him, but for that you could have no one better."

"Or as good," I said.

"You've got to overcome this compulsion to understate your virtues," Susan said. "You're too self-effacing."

"Can he suspend his distaste for radical feminism enough to protect me properly?"

Susan looked at me and widened her eyes. "Hadn't you better answer that, snookie?" she said.

"You're begging the question, I think. We haven't established my distaste for radical feminism. We haven't even in fact established that you are a radical feminist."

"I have learned," Rachel Wallace said, "to assume a distaste for radical feminism. I rarely err in that."

"Probably right," I said.

"He's quite a pain in the ass, sometimes," Susan said. "He knows you want him to reassure you and he won't. But I will. He doesn't much care about radical feminism one way or the other. But if he says he'll protect you, he will."

"I'm not being a pain in the ass," I said. "Saying I have no distaste for her won't reassure her. Or it shouldn't. There's no way to prove anything to her until something happens. Words don't do it."

"Words can," Susan said. "And tone of voice. You're just so goddamned autonomous that you won't explain yourself to anybody."

The waitress came back with wine for Susan and Beck's beer for me, and another martini for Rachel Wallace. The five she'd had this afternoon seemed to have had no effect on her.

"Maybe I shouldn't cart her around everyplace," I said to Rachel.

"Machismo," Rachel said. "The machismo code. He's locked into it, and he can't explain himself, or apologize, or cry probably, or show emotion."

"I throw up good, though. And I will in a minute."

Wallace's head snapped around at me. Her face was harsh and tight. Susan patted her arm. "Give him time," she said. "He grows on you. He's hard to classify. But he'll look out for you. And he'll care what happens to you. And he'll keep you out of harm's way." Susan sipped her wine. "He really will," she said to Rachel Wallace.

"And you," Rachel said, "does he look out for you?"

"We look out for each other," Susan said. "I'm doing it now."

Rachel Wallace smiled, her face loosened. "Yes," she said. "You are, aren't you?"

The waitress came again, and we ordered dinner.

I was having a nice time eating Rosalie's cream of carrot soup when Rachel Wallace said, "John tells me you used to be a prizefighter."

I nodded. I had a sense where the discussion would lead.

"And you were in combat in Korea?"

I nodded again.

"And you were a policeman?"

Another nod.

"And now you do this."

It was a statement. No nod required.

"Why did you stop fighting?"

"I had plateaued," I said.

"Were you not a good fighter?"

"I was good. I was not great. Being a good fighter is no life. Only great ones lead a life worth too much. It's not that clean a business, either."

"Did you tire of the violence?"

"Not in the ring," I said.

"You didn't mind beating someone bloody."

"He volunteered. The gloves are padded. It's not

pacifism, but if it's violence, it is controlled and regulated and patterned. I never hurt anyone badly. I never got badly hurt."

"Your nose has obviously been broken."

"Many times," I said. "But that's sort of minor. It hurts, but it's not serious."

"And you've killed people."

"Yes."

"Not just in the army."

"No."

"What kind of a person does that?" she said.

Susan was looking very closely at some of the decor in Rosalie's. "That is a magnificent old icechest," she said. "Look at the brass hinges."

"Don't change the subject for him," Rachel Wallace said. "Let him answer."

She spoke a little sharply for my taste. But if there was anything sure on this earth, it was that Susan could take care of herself. She was hard to overpower.

"Actually," she said, "I was changing the subject for me. You'd be surprised at how many times I've heard this conversation."

"You mean we are boring you."

Susan smiled at her. "A tweak," she said.

"I bore a lot of people," Rachel said. "I don't mind. I'm willing to be boring to find out what I wish to know."

The waitress brought me veal Giorgio. I ate a bite.

"What is it you want to know?"

"Why you engage in things that are violent and dangerous."

I sipped half a glass of beer. I took another bite of veal. "Well," I said, "the violence is a kind of side-effect, I think. I have always wanted to live life on my own terms. And I have always tried to do what I can do. I am good at certain kinds of things; I have tried to go in that direction."

"The answer doesn't satisfy me," Rachel said.

"It doesn't have to. It satisfies me."

"What he won't say," Susan said, "and what he may not even admit to himself is that he'd like to be Sir Gawain.

185

He was born five hundred years too late. If you understand that, you understand most of what you are asking."

"Six hundred years," I said.

CHAPTER FIVE

WE GOT THROUGH the rest of dinner. Susan asked Rachel about her books and her work, and that got her off me and onto something she liked much better. Susan is good at that. After dinner I had to drive Rachel back to the Ritz. I said goodbye to Susan in the bank parking lot behind Rosalie's where we'd parked.

"Don't be mean to her," Susan said softly. "She's scared to death, and she's badly ill at ease with you and with her fear."

"I don't blame her for being scared," I said. "But it's not my fault."

From the front seat of my car Rachel said, "Spenser, I have work to do."

"Jesus Christ," I said to Susan.

"She's scared," Susan said. "It makes her bitchy. Think how you'd feel if she were your only protection."

I gave Susan a pat on the fanny, decided a kiss would be hokey, and opened the door for her before she climbed into her MG. I was delighted. She'd gotten rid of the Nova. She was not Chevy. She was sports car.

Through the open window Susan said, "You held the door just to spite her."

"Yeah, baby, but I'm going home with her."

Susan slid into gear and wheeled the sports car out of the lot. I got in beside Rachel and started up my car.

"For heaven's sake, what year is this car?" Rachel said.

"1968," I said. "I'd buy a new one, but they don't make convertibles anymore." Maybe I should get a sports car. Was I old Chevy?

"Susan is a very attractive person," Rachel said.

"That's true," I said.

"It makes me think better of you that she likes you."

"That gets me by in a lot of places," I said.

"Your affection for each other shows."

I nodded.

"It is not my kind of love, but I can respond to it in others. You are lucky to have a relationship as vital as that."

"That's true, too," I said.

"You don't like me."

I shrugged.

"You don't," she said.

"It's irrelevant," I said.

"You don't like me, and you don't like what I stand for."

"What is it you stand for?" I said.

"The right of every woman to be what she will be. To shape her life in conformity to her own impulse, not to bend her will to the whims of men."

I said, "Wow."

"Do you realize I bear my father's name?"

"I didn't know that," I said.

"I had no choice," she said. "It was assigned me."

"That's true of me, too," I said.

She looked at me.

"It was assigned me. Spenser. I had no choice. I couldn't say I'd rather be named Spade. Samuel Spade. That would have been a terrific name, but no. I had to get a name like an English poet. You know what Spenser wrote?"

"The Faerie Queen?"

"Yeah. So what are you bitching about?"

We were out of Marblehead now and driving on Route 1A through Swampscott.

"It's not the same," she said.

"Why isn't it?"

"Because I'm a woman and was given a man's name."

"Whatever name would have been without your consent. Your mother's, your father's, and if you'd taken your mother's name, wouldn't that merely have been your grandfather's?"

There was a blue Buick Electra in front of me. It began to slow down as we passed the drive-in theater on the Lynnway. Behind me a Dodge swung out into the left lane and pulled up beside me.

"Get on the floor," I said.

She said, "What—" and I put my right hand behind her neck and pushed her down toward the floor. With my left hand I yanked the steering wheel hard over and went inside the Buick. My right wheels went up on the curb. The Buick pulled right to crowd me, and I floored the Chevy and dragged my bumper along his entire righthand side and spun off the curb in front of him with a strong smell of skun rubber behind me. I went up over the General Edwards Bridge with the accelerator to the floor and my elbow on the horn, and with the Buick and the Dodge behind me. I had my elbow on the horn because I had my gun in my hand.

The Lynnway was too bright and too busy, and it was too early in the evening. The Buick swung off into Point of Pines, and the Dodge went with it. I swerved into the passing lane to avoid a car and swerved back to the right to avoid another and began to slow down.

Rachel Wallace crouched, half fetal, toward the floor on the passenger's side. I put the gun down on the seat beside me. "One of the advantages of driving a 1968 Chevy," I said, "is you don't care all that much about an occasional dent."

"May I sit up?" she said. Her voice was strong.

"Yeah."

She squirmed back up onto the seat.

"Was that necessary?"

"Yeah."

"Was there someone really chasing us?"

"Yeah."

"If there was, you handled it well. My reactions would not have been as quick."

I said, "Thank you."

"I'm not complimenting you. I'm merely observing a fact. Did you get their license numbers?"

"Yes, 469AAG, and D60240, both Mass. But it won't do us any good unless they are bad amateurs, and the way they boxed me in on the road before I noticed, they aren't amateurs."

"You think you should have noticed them sooner?"

"Yeah. I was too busy arguing patristic nomenclature with you. I should never have had to hit the curb like that."

"Then partly it is my fault for distracting you."

"It's not your line of work. It is mine. You don't know better. I do."

"Well," she said, "no harm done. We got away."

"If the guy in front of us in the Buick was just a mohair better, we wouldn't have."

"He would have cut you off?"

I nodded. "And the Dodge would have blasted us."

"Actually would he not have blasted you? I was on the floor, and you were much closer anyway."

I shrugged. "It wouldn't have mattered. If you survived the crash they'd have waited and blasted you."

"You seem, so, so at ease with all of this."

"I'm not. It scares me."

"Perhaps. It scares me, too. But you seem to expect it. There's no moral outrage. You're not appalled. Or offended. Or . . . aghast. I don't know. You make this seem so commonplace."

"*Aghast* is irrelevant, too. It's useless. Or expressing it is useless. On the other hand I'm not one of the guys in the other car."

We went past the dog track and around Bell Circle. There was no one noticeable in the rearview mirror.

"Then you do what you do in part from moral outrage."

I looked at her and shook my head. "I do what I do because I'm comfortable doing it."

"My God," she said, "you're a stubborn man."

"Some consider it a virtue in my work," I said.

She looked at the gun lying on the seat.

"Oughtn't you to put that away?"

"I think I'll leave it there till we get to the Ritz."

"I've never touched a gun in my life."

"They're a well-made apparatus," I said. "If they're good. Very precise."

"Is this good?"

"Yes. It's a very nice gun."

"No gun is nice," she said.

"If those gentlemen from the Lynnway return," I said, "you may come to like it better."

She shook her head. "It's come to that. Sometimes I feel sick thinking about it."

"What?"

"In this country—the land of the free and all that shit—I need a man with a gun to protect me simply because I am what I am."

"That's fairly sickening," I said.

CHAPTER SIX

I PICKED RACHEL WALLACE up at her door at eight thirty the next morning, and we went down to breakfast in the Ritz Café. I was wearing my bodyguard outfit—jeans, T-shirt, corduroy Levi jacket, and a daring new pair of Pumas: royal-blue suede with a bold gold stripe. Smith and Wesson .38 Police Special in a shoulder holster.

Rachel Wallace said, "Well, we are somewhat less formal this morning, aren't we? If you're dressed that way tonight, they won't let you in the dining room."

"Work clothes," I said. "I can move well in them."

She nodded and ate an egg. She wore a quiet gray

dress with a paisley scarf at her throat. "You expect to have to move?"

"Probably not," I said. "But like they say at the Pentagon, you have to plan for the enemy's capacity, not his intentions."

She signed the check. "Come along," she said. She picked up her briefcase from under the table, and we walked out through the lobby. She got her coat from the check room, a pale tan trenchcoat. It had cost money. I made no effort to hold it for her. She ignored me while she put it on. I looked at the lobby. There were people, but they looked like they belonged there. No one had a Gatling gun. At least no one had one visible. In fact I'd have been the only one I would have been suspicious of if I hadn't known me so well, and so fondly.

A young woman in a green tweed suit and a brown beret came toward us from the Arlington Street entrance.

"Ms. Wallace. Hi. I've got a car waiting."

"Do you know her?" I said.

"Yes," Rachel said. "Linda Smith."

"I mean by sight," I said. "Not just by hearing of her or getting mail from her."

"Yes, we've met several times before."

"Okay."

We went out onto Arlington Street. I went first. The street was normal 9:00 AM busy. There was a tan Volvo sedan parked at the yellow curb with the motor running and the doorman standing with his hand on the passenger door. When he saw Linda Smith, he opened the passenger door. I looked inside the car and then stepped aside. Rachel Wallace got in; the doorman closed the door. I got in the back, and Linda Smith got in the driver's seat.

As we pulled into traffic Rachel said, "Have you met Mr. Spenser, Linda?"

"No, I haven't. Nice to meet you, Mr. Spenser."

"Nice to meet you, Ms. Smith," I said. Rachel would like the *Ms.*

"Spenser is looking after me on the tour," Rachel said.

"Yes, I know. John told me." She glanced at me in the

rearview mirror. "I don't think I've ever met a bodyguard before."

"We're just regular folks," I said. "If you cut us, do we not bleed?"

"Literary, too," Linda Smith said.

"When are we supposed to be in Belmont?"

"Ten o'clock," Linda said. "Belmont Public Library."

"What for?" I said.

"Ms. Wallace is speaking there. They have a Friends of the Library series."

"Nice liberal town you picked."

"Never mind, Spenser," Rachel Wallace said. Her voice was brusque. "I told them I'd speak wherever I could and to whom I could. I have a message to deliver, and I'm not interested in persuading those who already agree with me."

I nodded.

"If there's trouble, all right. That's what you're being paid for."

I nodded.

We got to the Belmont Library at a quarter to ten. There were ten men and women walking up and down in front of the library with placards on poles made of strapping.

A Belmont Police cruiser was parked across the street, two cops sitting in it quietly.

"Park behind the cops," I said.

Linda swung in behind the cruiser, and I got out. "Stay in the car a second," I said.

"I will not cower in here in front of a few pickets."

"Then look menacing while you sit there. This is what I'm paid for. I just want to talk to the cops."

I walked over to the cruiser. The cop at the wheel had a young wise-guy face. He looked like he'd tell you to stick it, at the first chance he got. And laugh. He was chewing a toothpick, the kind they put through a club sandwich. It still had the little cellophane frill on the end he wasn't chewing.

I bent down and said through the open window, "I'm escorting this morning's library speaker. Am I likely to have any trouble from the pickets?"

He looked at me for ten or twelve seconds, worrying the toothpick with his tongue.

"You do, and we'll take care of it," he said. "You think we're down here waiting to pick up a copy of *Gone with the Wind?*"

"I figured you more for picture books," I said.

He laughed. "How about that, Benny?" he said to his partner. "A hot shit. Haven't had one today." His partner was slouched in the seat with his hat tipped over his eyes. He didn't say anything or move. "Who's the speaker you're escorting?"

"Rachel Wallace," I said.

"Never heard of her."

"I'll try to keep that from her," I said. "I'm going to take her in now."

"Good show," he said. "Shouldn't be any trouble for a hot shit like you."

I went back to the car and opened the door for Rachel Wallace.

"What did you do?" she said as she got out.

"Annoyed another cop," I said. "That's three hundred sixty-one this year, and October's not over yet."

"Did they say who the pickets were?"

I shook my head. We started across the street, Linda Smith on one side of Rachel and me on the other. Linda Smith's face looked tight and colorless; Rachel's was expressionless.

Someone among the pickets said, "There she is." They all turned and closed together more tightly as we walked toward them. Linda looked at me, then back at the cops. We kept walking.

"We don't want you here!" a woman shouted at us.

Someone else yelled, "Dyke!"

I said, "Is he talking to me?"

Rachel Wallace said, "No."

A heavy-featured woman with shoulder-length gray hair was carrying a placard that said, A Gay America is a Communist Goal. A stylish woman in a tailored suit carried a sign that read, Gay's Can't Reproduce. They Have to Convert.

I said, "I bet she wanted to say proselytize; but no one knew how to spell it."

No one laughed; I was getting used to that. As we approached the group they joined arms in front of us, blocking the entrance. In the center of the line was a large man with a square jaw and thick brown hair. Looked like he'd been a tight end perhaps, at Harvard. He wore a dark suit and a pale gray silk tie. His cheeks were rosy, and his eye was clear. Probably still active in his alumni association. A splendid figure of a man, the rock upon which the picket line was anchored. Surely a foe of atheism, Communism, and faggotry. Almost certainly a perfect asshole.

Rachel Wallace walked directly up to him and said, "Excuse me, please."

There was no shouting now. It was quiet. Square Jaw shook his head, slowly, dramatically.

Rachel said, "You are interfering with my right of free speech and free assembly, a right granted me by the Constitution."

Nobody budged. I looked back at the cops. The wiseguy kid was out of the squad car now, leaning against the door on the passenger side, his arms crossed, his black leather belt sagging with ammunition, Mace, handcuffs, nightstick, gun, come-along, and a collection of keys on a ring. He probably wanted to walk over and let us through, but his gunbelt was too heavy.

I said to Rachel, "Would you like me to create an egress for you?"

"How do you propose to do it," she said.

"I thought I would knock this matinee idol on his kiester, and we could walk in over him."

"It might be a mistake to try, fellow," he said. His voice was full of money, like Daisy Buchanan.

"No," I said. "It would not be a mistake."

Rachel said, "Spenser." Her voice was sharp. "I don't stand for that," she said. "I won't resort to it."

I shrugged and looked over at the young cop. His partner appeared not to have moved. He was still sitting in the squad car with his hat over his eyes. Maybe it was an econ- omy move; maybe the partner was really an inflatable dummy. The young cop grinned at me.

"Our civil rights are in the process of violation over here!" I yelled at him. "You have any plans for dealing with that?"

He pushed himself away from the car and swaggered over. His half-chewed toothpick bobbed in his mouth as he worked it back and forth with his tongue. The handle of his service revolver thumped against his leg. On his uniform blouse were several military service ribbons. Vietnam, I fig- ured. There was a Purple Heart ribbon and a service ribbon with battle stars and another ribbon that might have been the Silver Star.

"You could look at it that way," he said when he reached us. "Or you could look at it that you people are caus- ing a disturbance."

"Will you escort us inside, officer?" Rachel Wallace said. "I would say that is your duty, and I think you ought to do it."

"We are here to prevent the spreading of an immoral and pernicious doctrine, officer," Square Jaw said. "That is *our* duty. I do not think you should *aid* people who wish to destroy the American family."

The cop looked at Rachel.

"I will not be caught up in false issues," Rachel said. "We have a perfect right to go into that library and speak. I have been invited, and I will speak. There is no question of right here. I have a right and they are trying to violate it. Do your job."

Other people were gathering, passing cars slowed down and began to back up traffic while the drivers tried to see what was happening. On the fringes of the crowd post- high-school kids gathered and smirked.

Square Jaw said, "It might help you to keep in mind, officer, that I am a close personal friend of Chief Garner, and I'm sure he'll want to hear from me exactly what has hap- pened and how his men have behaved."

The young cop looked at me. "A friend of the chief," he said.

"That's frightening," I said. "You better walk softly around him."

The young cop grinned at me broadly. "Yeah," he said. He turned back to Square Jaw. "Move it, Jack," he said. The smile was gone.

Square Jaw rocked back a little as if someone had jabbed at him.

"I beg your pardon?" he said.

"I said, Move your ass. This broad may be a creep, but she didn't try to scare me. I don't like people to try and scare me. These people are going in—you can tell the chief that when you see him. You can tell him they went in past you or over you. You decide which you'll tell him."

The young cop's face was half an inch away from Square Jaw's, and since he was three inches shorter, it was tilted up. The partner had appeared from the car. He was older and heavier, with a pot belly and large hands with big knuckles. He had his night stick in his right hand, and he slapped it gently against his thigh.

The people on either side of Square Jaw unlinked their arms and moved away. Square Jaw looked at Rachel, and when he spoke he almost hissed. "You foul, contemptible woman," he said. "You bulldyke. We'll never let you win. You queer . . ."

I pointed down the street to the left and said to the two cops, "There's trouble."

They both turned to look, and when they did I gave Square Jaw a six-inch jab in the solar plexus with my right fist. He gasped and doubled up. The cops spun back and looked at him and then at me. I was staring down the street where I'd pointed. "Guess I was mistaken," I said.

Square Jaw was bent over, his arms wrapped across his midsection, rocking back and forth. A good shot in the solar plexus will half-paralyze you for a minute or two.

The young cop looked at me without expression. "Yeah, I guess you were," he said. "Well, let's get to the library."

As we walked past Square Jaw the older cop said to him, "It's a violation of health ordinances, Jack, to puke in the street."

CHAPTER SEVEN

INSIDE THE LIBRARY, and downstairs in the small lecture room, there was no evidence that a disturbance had ever happened. The collection of elderly people, mostly women, all gray-haired, mostly overweight, was sitting placidly on folding chairs, staring patiently at the small platform and the empty lectern.

The two cops left us at the door. "We'll sit around out-side," the young one said, "until you're through." Rachel Wallace was being introduced to the Friends of the Library president, who would introduce her to the audience. The young cop looked at her. "What did you say her name was?"

"Rachel Wallace," I said.

"She some kind of queer or something?"

"She's a writer," I said. "She's a feminist. She's gay. She's not easy to scare."

The cop shook his head, "A goddamned lezzy," he said to his partner. "We'll be outside," he said to me. They started up the stairs. Three steps up the young cop stopped and turned back to me. "You got a good punch," he said. "You don't see a lot of guys can hit that hard on a short jab." Then he turned and went on up after his partner. Inside the room Rachel Wallace was sitting on a folding chair beside the lectern, her hands folded in her lap, her ankles crossed. The president was introducing her. On a table to the right of the lectern were maybe two dozen of Rachel Wallace's books. I leaned against the wall to the right of the door in the back and

197

looked at the audience. No one looked furtive. Not all of them looked awake. Linda Smith was standing next to me.

"Nice booking," I said to her.

She shrugged. "It all helps," she said. "Did you hit that man outside?"

"Just once," I said.

"I wonder what she'll say about that," Linda Smith said.

I shrugged.

The president finished introducing Rachel and she stepped to the lectern. The audience clapped politely.

"I am here," Rachel said, "for the same reason I write. Because I have a truth to tell, and I will tell it."

I whispered to Linda Smith, "You think many of these people have read her books?"

Linda shook her head. "Most of them just like to come out and look at a real live author."

"The word *woman* is derived from the Old English *wifmann* meaning 'wife-person.' The very noun by which our language designates us does so only in terms of men."

The audience looked on loyally and strained to understand. Looking at them, you'd have to guess that the majority of them couldn't find any area where they could agree with her. At least a plurality probably couldn't find an area where they understood what she was talking about. They were library friends, people who had liked to read all their lives, and liked it in the library and had a lot of free time on their hands. Under other circumstances they would have shot a lesbian on sight.

"I am not here," Rachel Wallace was saying, "to change your sexual preference. I am here only to say that sexual preference is not a legitimate basis for discriminatory practices, for maltreatment in the marketplace. I am here to say that a woman can be fulfilled without a husband and children, that a woman is not a breeding machine, that she need not be a slave to her family, a whore for her husband."

An elderly man in a gray sharkskin suit leaned over to his wife and whispered something. Her shoulders shook with silent laughter. A boy about four years old got up from his seat beside his grandmother and walked down the center aisle to sit on the floor in front and stare up at Rachel. In the very last row a fat woman in a purple dress read a copy of *Mademoiselle.*

"How many books does this sell?" I whispered to Linda Smith.

She shrugged. "There's no way to know, really," she whispered. "The theory is that exposure helps. The more the better. Big scenes like the *Today Show,* small ones like this. You try to blanket a given area."

"Are there any questions?" Rachel said. The audience stared at her. A man wearing white socks and bedroom slippers was asleep in the front row, right corner. In the silence the pages turning in *Mademoiselle* were loud. The woman didn't seem to notice.

"If not, then thank you very much."

Rachel stepped off the low platform past the small boy and walked down the center aisle toward Linda and me. Outside the hall there were multicolored small cookies on a table and a large coffee maker with a thumbprint near the spigot. Linda said to Rachel, "That was wonderful."

Rachel said, "Thank you."

The president of the Friends said, "Would you like some coffee and refreshments?"

Rachel said, "No, thank you." She jerked her head at me, and the three of us headed for the door.

"You sure you don't want any refreshment?" I said, as we went out the side door of the library.

"I want two maybe three martinis and lunch," Rachel said. "What have I this afternoon, Linda?"

"An autographing in Cambridge."

Rachel shivered. "God," she said.

There was no one outside now except the two cops in the squad car. The pickets were gone, and the lawn was empty and innocent in front of the library. I shot at the young cop with my forefinger and thumb as we got into Linda Smith's car. He nodded. We drove away.

"You and the young officer seem to have developed some sort of relationship. Have you met him before?"

"Not him specifically, but we know some of the same things. When I was his age, I was sort of like him."

"No doubt," she said, without any visible pleasure. "What sort of things do you both know? And how do you know you know them?"

I shrugged. "You wouldn't get it, I don't think. I don't even know how we know, but we do."

"Try," Rachel said. "I am not a dullard. Try to explain."

"We know what hurts," I said, "and what doesn't. We know about being scared and being brave. We know applied theory."

"You can tell that, just by looking?"

"Well, partly. He had some combat decorations on his blouse."

"Military medals?"

"Yeah, cops sometimes wear them. He does. He's proud of them."

"And that's the basis of your judgment?"

"No, not just that. It's the way he walks. How his mouth looks, the way he holds his head. The way he reacted to the protest leader."

"I thought him a parody of machismo."

"No, not a parody," I said. "The real thing."

"The real thing is a parody," she said.

"I didn't think you'd get it," I said.

"Don't you patronize me," she said. "Don't use that oh-women-don't-understand-tone with me."

"I said you didn't understand. I didn't say other women don't. I didn't say it was because you're a woman."

"And," she snapped, "I assume you think you were some kind of Sir Galahad protecting my good name when you punched that poor sexist fool at the library. Well, you were not. You were a stupid thug. I will not have you acting on my behalf in a manner I deplore. If you strike another person except to save my life, I will fire you at that moment."

200

"How about if I stick my tongue out at them and go *bleaaah*."

"I'm serious," she said.

"I'll say."

We were perfectly quiet then. Linda Smith drove back through Watertown toward Cambridge.

"I really thought the talk went very well, Rachel," she said. "That was a tough audience, and I thought you really got to them."

Rachel Wallace didn't answer.

"I thought we could go into Cambridge and have lunch at the Harvest," Linda said. "Then we could stroll up to the bookstore."

"Good," Rachel said. "I'm hungry, and I need a drink."

CHAPTER EIGHT

IN MY MOUTH there was still the faint taste of batter-fried shrimp with mustard fruits as I hung around the front door of the Crimson Book Store on Mass. Ave. and watched Rachel Wallace sign books. Across the street Harvard Yard glistened in the fall rain that had started while we were eating lunch.

Rachel was at a card table near the check-out counter in the front of the store. On the card table were about twenty copies of her new book and three blue felt-tipped pens. In the front window a large sign announced that she'd be there from one until three that day. It was now two ten, and they had sold three books. Another half dozen people had come in and looked at her and gone out.

Linda Smith hung around the table and drank coffee and steered an occasional customer over. I looked at everyone who came in and learned nothing at all. At two fifteen a teenage girl came in wearing Levi's jeans and a purple warmup jacket that said Brass Kaydettes on it.

"You really an author?" she said to Rachel.

Rachel said, "Yes, I am."

"You write this book?"

"Yes."

Linda Smith said, "Would you like to buy one? Ms. Wallace will autograph a copy."

The girl ignored her. "This book any good?" she said.

Rachel Wallace smiled. "I think so," she said.

"What's it about?"

"It's about being a woman and about the way people discriminate against women, and about the way that corruption leads to other corruption."

"Oh, yeah? Is it exciting?"

"Well, I wouldn't, ah, I wouldn't say it was exciting, exactly. It is maybe better described as powerful."

"I was thinking of being a writer," the kid said.

Rachel's smile was quite thin. "Oh, really?"

"Where do you get your ideas?"

"I think them up," Rachel said. The smile was so thin it was hard to see.

"Oh, yeah?" The girl picked up a copy of Rachel's book and looked at it, and turned it over and looked at the back. She read the jacket flap for a minute, then put the book down.

"This a novel?" the girl said.

"No," Rachel said.

"It's long as a novel."

"Yes," Rachel said.

"So why ain't it a novel?"

"It's nonfiction."

"Oh."

The girl's hair was leaf-brown and tied in two pigtails that lapped over her ears. She had braces on her teeth. She picked the book up again and flipped idly through the pages. There was silence.

Rachel Wallace said, "Are you thinking of buying a copy?"

The girl shook her head, "Naw," she said, "I got no money anyway."

"Then put the book down and go somewhere else," Rachel said.

"Hey, I ain't doing any harm," the girl said.

Rachel looked at her.

"Oh, I'm through anyway," the girl said and left the store.

"You got some smooth way with the reading public," I said.

"Little twerp," Rachel said. "Where do I get my ideas? Jesus Christ, where does she think I get them? Everyone asks me that. The question is inane."

"She probably doesn't know any better," I said.

Rachel Wallace looked at me and said nothing. I didn't have a sense that she thought me insightful.

Two young men came in. One was small and thin with a crew cut and gold-rimmed glasses. He had on a short yellow slicker with a hood up and blue serge pants with cuffs that stopped perhaps two inches above the tops of his wingtipped cordovan shoes. He had rubbers on over the shoes. The other one was much bigger. He had the look of a fat weightlifter. He couldn't have been more than twenty-five, but he was starting to get bald. He wore a red-and-black plaid flannel shirt, a black down vest, and chino pants rolled up over laced work boots. The sleeves of his shirt were turned up.

The small one carried a white cardboard pastry box. I edged a little closer to Rachel when they came in. They didn't look bookstorish. As they stopped in front of Rachel's table I put my hand inside my jacket on the butt of my gun. As the small one opened the pastry box I moved. He came out with a chocolate cream pie and had it halfway into throwing position when I hit him with my shoulder. He got it off, side-armed and weakly, and it hit Rachel in the chest. I had the gun out now, and when the fat one grabbed at me I hit him on the wrist with the barrel. The small one bowled over backwards and fell on the floor.

I said, "Everybody freeze," and pointed my gun at them. Always a snappy line.

The fat one was clutching his wrist against his stomach. "It was only a freaking pie, man," he said.

The small one had scrunched up against the wall by the door. The wind was knocked out of him, and he was working on getting it back. I looked at Rachel. The pie had hit her on the left breast and slid down her dress to her lap, leaving a wide trail of chocolate and whipped cream.

I said to the men, "Roll over on the floor, face down. Clasp your hands back of your head."

The little one did what I said. His breath was back. The fat one said, "Hey, man, I think you broke my freaking wrist."

"On the floor," I said.

He went down. I knelt behind them and searched them quickly with my left hand, keeping the gun clear in my right. They had no weapons.

The bookstore manager and Linda Smith were busy with paper towels trying to wipe the chocolate cream off Rachel; customers gathered in a kind of hushed circle—not frightened, embarrassed rather. I stood up.

Rachel's face was flushed, and her eyes were bright. "Sweets for the sweet, my dear," I said.

"Call the police," she said.

"You want to prefer charges?" I said.

"Absolutely," she said. "I want these two boars charged with assault."

From the floor the fat one said, "Aw, lady, it was only a freaking pie."

"Shut up," she said. "Shut your foul, stupid mouth now. You grunting ass. I will do everything I can to put you in jail for this."

I said, "Linda, could you call the buttons for us?"

She nodded and went over to the telephone behind the counter.

Rachel turned and looked at the five customers and two clerks in a small semicircle looking uncomfortable.

"What are you people looking at?" she said. "Go about your business. Go on. Move."

They began to drift away. All five customers went out. The two clerks went back to arranging books on a display table downstairs.

"I think this autographing is over," Rachel said.

"Yeah," I said, "but the cops are coming. You gotta wait for them. They get grouchy as hell when you call them and screw."

Linda Smith hung up the phone. "They'll be right along," she said.

And they were—a prowl car with two cops in uniform. They wanted to see my license and my gun permit, and they shook down both the assault suspects routinely and thoroughly. I didn't bother to tell them I'd already done it; they'd have done it again anyway.

"You want to prefer assault charges against these two, lady?" one of the prowlies said.

"My name is Rachel Wallace. And I certainly do."

"Okay, Rachel," the cop said. There was a fine network of red veins in each cheek. "We'll take them in. Sergeant's gonna like this one, Jerry. Assault with a pie."

They herded the two young men toward the door. The fat one said, "Geez, lady, it was just a freaking pie."

Rachel leaned toward him a little and said to him very carefully, "Eat a shit sandwich."

CHAPTER NINE

WE DROVE BACK to the Ritz in silence. The traffic wasn't heavy yet, and Linda Smith didn't have to concentrate on driving as much as she did. As we went over the Mass. Ave. Bridge I looked at the way the rain dimpled the surface of the river. The sweep of the Charles from the bridge down toward the basin was very fine from the Mass. Ave. Bridge—much better when you walked across it, but okay from a car. The red-brick city on Beacon Hill, the original one, was prominent from here, capped by the gold dome of the Bulfinch State House. The high-rises of the modern city were all around it, but from here they didn't dominate. It was like looking back through the rain to the way it was, and maybe should have been.

Linda Smith turned off Mass. Ave. and onto Commonwealth. "You don't think I should have preferred charges," Rachel said to me.

"Not my business to think about that," I said.

"But you disapprove."

I shrugged. "Tends to clog up the court system."

"Was I to let them walk away after insulting and degrading me?"

"I could have kicked each one in the fanny," I said.

"That's your solution to everything," she said, and looked out the window.

"No, but it's a solution to some things. You want them punished. What do you think will happen to them. A night in jail and a fifty dollar fine, maybe. To get that done will involve two prowl-car cops, a desk sergeant, a judge, a prosecutor, a public defender, and probably more. It will cost the state about two thousand dollars, and you'll probably have to spend the morning in court and so will the two arresting officers. I could have made them sorry a lot sooner for free."

She continued to stare out the window.

"And," I said, "it was only a freaking pie, lady."

She looked at me and almost smiled. "You were very quick," she said.

"I didn't know it was going to be a pie."

"Would you have shot him?" she said. She wasn't looking out the window now; she stared straight at me.

"If I had to. I almost did before I saw it was a pie."

"What kind of a man would do that?"

"Throw a pie at someone?"

206

"No," she said. "Shoot someone."

"You asked me that before," I said. "I don't have a better answer this time except to say, Isn't it good you've got one? At the rate we're going, you'll be attacked by a horde of chauvinist cameldrivers before the week is out."

"You sound as if it were my fault. It is not. I do not cause trouble—I am beset by it because of my views."

Linda Smith pulled the car onto Arlington Street and into the open space in front of the Ritz. I said, "Stay in the car till I tell you."

I got out and looked both ways and into the lobby. The doorman hustled forward to open the door for Rachel. She looked at me. I nodded. She stepped out of the car and walked into the hotel.

"We'll have a drink in the bar," she said.

I nodded and followed her in. There were a couple of business types having Scotch on the rocks at a table by the window, and a college-age boy and girl sitting at another table, very dressed up and a little ill at ease. He had beer. She had a champagne cocktail. Or at least it looked like a champagne cocktail. I hoped it was.

Rachel slid onto a bar stool, and I sat next to her and turned my back to the bar and surveyed the room. No one but us and the business types and the college kids. Rachel's coat had a hood. She slid the hood off but kept the coat on to cover up the pie smear down the front of her dress.

"Beer, Spenser?"

"Yes, please."

She ordered. Beer for me and a martini for her. For the Ritz Bar I was spectacularly underdressed. I thought the bartender paled a little when I came in, but he said nothing and tended the bar just as if I were not offensive to his sight.

A young woman came into the bar alone. She had on a long cream-colored wool skirt and heavy black boots, the kind that seem to have extra leather. Her blouse was white. There was a black silk scarf at her neck, and she carried a gray leather coat over her arm. Very stylish. The skirt fit well, I noticed, especially around the hips. She looked around the room and spotted us at the bar and came directly to us. The kid can still attract them, I thought. Still got the old whammo.

The young woman reached us and said, "Rachel," and put her hand out.

Rachel Wallace turned and looked at her and then smiled. She took the outstretched hand in both of hers. "Julie," she said. "Julie Wells." She leaned forward and Julie Wells put her face down and Rachel kissed her. "How lovely to see you," she said. "Sit down."

Julie slid onto the bar stool on the other side of Rachel.

"I heard you were in town again," she said, "and I knew you'd be staying here, so I got through work early and came over. I called your room, and when there was no answer, I thought, well, knowing Rachel, chances are she's in the bar."

"Well, you do know me," Rachel said. "Can you stay? Can you have dinner with me?"

"Sure," Julie said, "I was hoping you'd ask."

The bartender came over and looked questioningly at Julie. "I'll have a Scotch sour on the rocks," she said.

Rachel said, "I'll have another martini. Spenser, another beer?"

I nodded. The bartender moved away. Julie looked at me. I smiled at her. "We're on tour," I said. "Rachel plays the hand organ, and I go around with a little cup and collect money."

Julie said, "Oh, really," and looked at Rachel.

"His name is Spenser," Rachel said. "There have been some threats about my new book. The publisher thought I should have a bodyguard. He thinks he's funny."

"Nice to meet you," Julie said.

"Nice to meet you, too," I said. "Are you an old friend of Rachel's?"

She and Rachel smiled at each other. "Sort of, I guess," Julie said. "Would you say so, Rachel?"

"Yes," Rachel said, "I would say that. I met Julie when I was up here doing the research for *Tyranny,* last year."

"You a writer, Julie?"

She smiled at me, very warm. *Zing* went the strings of my heart. "No," she said, "I wish I were. I'm a model."

"What agency?"

"Carol Cobb. Do you know the modeling business?"

"No, I'm just a curious person."

Rachel shook her head. "No, he's not," she said. "He's screening you. And I don't like it." She looked at me. "I appreciate that you have to do your job, and that today may have made you unduly suspicious. But Julie Wells is a close personal friend of mine. We have nothing to fear from her. I'll appreciate it if in the future you trust my judgment."

"Your judgment's not as good as mine," I said. "I have no involvement. How close a personal friend can someone be that you met only last year?"

"Spenser, that's enough," Rachel said. There was force in her voice and her face.

Julie said, "Rachel, I don't mind. Of course he has to be careful. I pray that he is. What are these threats? How serious are they?"

Rachel turned toward her. I sipped a little beer. "I've had phone calls threatening me if *Tyranny* is published."

"But if you're on the promotion tour, it means it's been published already."

"In fact, yes, though technically publication date isn't until October fifteenth. The book is already in a lot of bookstores."

"Has anything happened?"

"There was an incident last night, and there have been protests. But I don't think they're related."

"The incident last night was the real goods," I said. "The other stuff was probably what it seemed."

"What happened last night?" Julie said.

"Spenser contends that someone tried to run us off the road last night in Lynn."

"Contends?" Julie said.

"Well, I was on the floor, and he swerved around a lot and then the car behind us was gone. I can't speak for sure myself. And if I were convinced no one were after me, Spenser would be out of work."

"Aw, you'd want me around anyway. All you chicks like a guy to look after you."

She threw her drink at me. She threw like a girl; most of it landed on my shirt front.

"Now we're both messy," I said. "A his-and-hers outfit."

The bartender slid down toward us. Julie put her hand on Rachel's arm. The bartender said, "Is there something wrong, ma'am?"

Rachel was silent. Her breath blew in and out through her nose.

I said to the bartender, "No, it's fine. She was kidding with me, and the drink slipped."

The bartender looked at me as if I were serious, smiled as if he believed me, and moved off down the bar. In maybe thirty seconds he was back with a new martini for Rachel. "This is on the house, ma'am," he said.

Julie said to me, "Why do you feel last night was serious?"

"It was professional," I said. "They knew what they were doing. We were lucky to get out of it."

"Rachel is hard sometimes," Julie said. She was patting the back of Rachel's left hand. "She doesn't mean everything she says and does always. Sometimes she regrets them, even."

"Me, too," I said. I wonder if I should pat the other hand. My T-shirt was wet against my chest, but I didn't touch it. It's like getting hit with a pitch. You're not supposed to rub.

Rachel said, "Julie and I will dine in our room tonight. I won't need you until tomorrow at eight."

"I better wait until Julie leaves," I said.

They both looked at me. Then Rachel said, "That's when she is going to leave."

I said, "Oh." Always the smooth comeback, even when I've been dumb. Of course they were very good friends.

"I'll walk up with you and hang around in the hall till the waiter has come and gone."

"That won't be necessary," Rachel said. She wouldn't look at me.

"Yeah, it will," I said. "I work at what I do, Rachel. I'm not going to let someone buzz you in the lobby just because you're mad at me."

She looked up at me. "I'm not mad at you," she said. "I'm ashamed of the way I behaved a moment ago."

Behind her Julie beamed at me. *See?* her smile said, *See? She's really very nice.*

"Either way," I said. "I'll stick around and wait till you've locked up for the night. I won't bother you—I'll lurk in the hall."

She nodded. "Perhaps that would be best," she said.

We finished our drinks, Rachel signed the bar tab, and we headed for the elevators. I went first; they followed. When we got in the elevator, Julie and Rachel were holding hands. The skirt still fit Julie's hips wonderfully. Was I a sexist? Was it ugly to think, *What a waste?* On Rachel's floor I got out first. The corridor was empty. At her room I took the key from Rachel and opened the door. The room was dark and silent. I went in and turned on the lights. There was no one there and no one in the bathroom. Rachel and Julie came in.

I said, "Okay, I'll say good night. I'll be in the hall. When room service comes, open the door on the chain first, and don't let him in unless I'm there, too. I'll come in with him."

Rachel nodded. Julie said, "Nice to have met you, Spenser."

I smiled at her and closed the door.

CHAPTER TEN

THE CORRIDOR WAS silent and Ritz-y, with gold-patterned wallpaper. I wondered if they'd make love before they ordered dinner. I would. I hoped they wouldn't. It had been a while since lunch and would be a long wait for dinner if it worked out wrong.

I leaned against the wall opposite their door. If they were making love, I didn't want to hear. The concept of love between two women didn't have much affect on me in the abstract. But if I imagined them at it, and speculated on exactly how they went about it, it seemed sort of too bad, demeaning. Actually maybe Susan and I weren't all that slick in the actual doing ourselves. When you thought about it, maybe none of us were doing Swan Lake. "What's right is what feels good afterwards," I said out loud in the empty corridor. Hemingway said that. Smart man, Hemingway. Spent very little time hanging around hotel corridors with no supper.

Down the corridor to my left a tall thin man with a black mustache and a double-breasted gray pinstripe suit came out of his room and past me, heading for the elevator. There was a silver pin in his collar under the modest knot of his tie. His black shoes glistened with polish. Class. Even more class than a wet Adidas T-shirt. The hell with him. He probably did not have a Smith and Wesson .38 caliber revolver with a four-inch barrel. And I did. *How's that for class?* I mumbled at his back as he went into the elevator.

About fifteen minutes later a housekeeper went bustling past me down the corridor and knocked on a door. No one answered, and the housekeeper let herself in with a key on a long chain. She was in for maybe a minute and came back past me and into the service elevator. She probably didn't have a .38 either.

I amused myself by trying to see how many lyrics I could sing to songs written by Johnny Mercer. I was halfway through "Memphis in June" when a pleasant-looking gray-haired man with a large red nose got out of the elevator and walked down the corridor toward me. He had on gray slacks and a blue blazer. On the blazer pocket was a small name plate that said Asst. Mgr.

His blazer also hung funny over his right hip, the way it does when you are carrying a gun in a hip holster. He smiled as he approached me. I noticed that the blazer was unbuttoned and his left hand was in a half fist. He sort of tapped it against his thigh, knuckles toward me.

"Are you locked out of your room, sir?" he said with a big smile. He was a big guy and had a big stomach, but he didn't look slow and he didn't look soft. His teeth had been capped.

I said, "House man, right?"

"Callahan," he said. "I'm the assistant night manager."

"Spenser," I said. "I'm going to take out my wallet and show you some ID."

"You're not registered here, Mr. Spenser."

"No, I'm working. I'm looking out for Rachel Wallace, who is registered here."

I handed him my license. He looked at it and looked at me. "Nice picture," he said.

"Well, that's my bad side," I said.

"It's full face," he said.

"Yeah," I said.

"Do I detect a weapon of some sort under your left arm, Mr. Spenser?"

"Yes. It makes us even—you got one on your right hip."

He smiled again. His half-clenched left fist tapped against his thigh.

"I'm in kind of a puzzle, Mr. Spenser. If you really are guarding Miss Wallace, I can't very well ask you to leave. On the other hand you could be lying. I guess we better ask her."

"Not right now," I said. "I think she's busy."

213

"'Fraid we'll have to anyway."

"How do I know you're really the house dick?"

"Assistant manager," he said. "Says so right on my coat."

"Anyone can get a coat. How do I know this isn't a ploy to get her to open the door?"

He rolled his lower lip out. "Got a point there," he said. "What we do is go down the end of the hall by the elevators and call on the house phone. You can see the whole corridor and I can see you that way."

I nodded. We walked down to the phone side by side, watching each other and being careful. I was paying most attention to the half-closed fist. For a man his size it was a small fist. At the phones he tucked the phone between his cheek and shoulder and dialed with his right hand. He knew the number without looking. She took a long while to answer.

"Sorry to bother you, Miss Wallace. . . . Ms. Wallace. . . . Yeah. . . . Well, this is Callahan, the assistant manager. Do you have a man named Spenser providing personal security for you? . . . Unh-huh. . . . Describe him to me, if you would. . . . No, we just spotted him outside your room and thought we'd better check. . . . Yes, ma'am. Yes, that'll be fine. Thank you." He hung up.

"Okay," he said with a big friendly smile. "She validated you." He put his left hand into the side pocket of his blazer and took it out.

"What did you have in your hand?" I said. "Roll of quarters?"

"Dimes," he said. "Got a small hand."

"Who whistled on me—the housekeeper."

He nodded.

I said, "Are you looking out for Ms. Wallace special?"

"We're a little special on her," he said. "Got a call from a homicide dick said there'd been threats on her life."

"Who called you—Quirk?"

"Yeah, know him?"

I nodded.

"Friend of his?"

"I wouldn't go that far," I said.

We walked back down the corridor toward Rachel's room. "Good cop," Callahan said.

I nodded. "Very tough," I said.

"So I hear. I hear he's as tough as there is in this town."

"Top three," I said.

"Who else?"

"Guy named Hawk," I said. "He ever shows up in your hotel, don't try to take him with a roll of dimes."

"Who's the third?"

I smiled at him and ducked my head. "Aw, hell," I said.

He did his big friendly smile again. "Well, good we don't have to find that out," he said. His voice was steady. He seemed able to repress his terror. "Not tonight anyway." He nodded at me. "Have a good day," he said, and moved off placidly down the corridor. I must have frightened him to death.

I went back to my Johnny Mercer lyrics. I was on the third verse of "Midnight Sun" when a room service waiter came off the elevator pushing a table. He stopped at Rachel's door and knocked. He smiled at me as he waited. The door opened on the chain and a small vertical plane of Rachel Wallace's face appeared.

I said, "It's okay, Rachel. I'm here." The waiter smiled at me again, as if I'd said something clever. The door closed and in a moment re-opened. The waiter went in, and I came in behind him. Rachel was in a dark-brown full-length robe with white piping. She wore no makeup. Julie Wells wasn't in the room. The bathroom door was closed, and I could hear the shower going. Both beds were a little rumpled but still made.

The waiter opened up the table and began to lay out the supper. I leaned against the wall by the window and watched him. When he was through, Rachel Wallace signed the bill, added in a tip, and gave it back to him. He smiled—smiled at me—and went out.

Rachel looked at the table. There were flowers in the center.

"You can go for tonight, Spenser," she said. "We'll eat and go to bed. Be here at eight tomorrow."

"Yes, ma'am," I said. "Where we going first?"

"We're going out to Channel Four and do a talk show."

Julie Wells came out of the bathroom. She had a small towel wrapped around her head and a large one wrapped around her body. It covered her but not by much. She said, "Hi, Spenser," and smiled at me. Everyone smiled at me. Lovable. A real pussycat.

"Hello." I didn't belong there. There was something powerfully non-male in the room, and I felt its pressure. "Okay, Rachel. I'll say good night. Don't open the door. Don't even open it to push that cart into the hall. I'll be here at eight."

They both smiled. Neither of them said anything. I went to the door at a normal pace. I did not run. "Don't forget the chain," I said. "And the deadbolt from inside."

They both smiled at me and nodded. Julie Wells's towel seemed to be shrinking. My mouth felt a little dry. "I'll stay outside until I hear the bolt turn."

Smile. Nod.

"Good night," I said, and went out and closed the door. I heard the bolt slide and the chain go in. I went down in the elevator and out onto Arlington Street with my mouth still dry, feeling a bit unlovely.

CHAPTER ELEVEN

I LEANED AGAINST the cinder-block wall of studio two at Channel Four and watch Rachel Wallace prepare to promote her book and her cause. Off camera a half-dozen technician types in jeans and beards and sneakers hustled about doing technical things.

Rachel sat in a director's chair at a low table. The interviewer was on the other side and on the table between them was a copy of *Tyranny,* standing upright and visible on a small display stand. Rachel sat calmly looking at the camera. The interviewer, a Styrofoam blonde with huge false eyelashes, was smoking a kingsized filter-tipped mentholated Salem cigarette as if they were about to tie her to a post and put on the blindfold. A technician pinned a small microphone to the lapel of Rachel's gray flannel jacket and stepped out of the way. Another technician with a clipboard crouched beneath one of the cameras a foot and a half from the interviewer. He wore earphones.

"Ten seconds, Shirley," he said. The interviewer nodded and snuffed her cigarette out in an ashtray on the floor behind her chair. A man next to me shifted in his folding chair and said, "Jesus Christ, I'm nervous." He was scheduled to talk about raising quail after Rachel had finished. The technician squatting under the front camera pointed at the interviewer.

She smiled. "Hi," she said to the camera. "I'm Shirley. And this is *Contact.* We have with us today feminist and lesbian activist Rachel Wallace. Rachel has written a new book, *Tyranny,* which takes the lid off of some of the ways government and business exploit women and especially gay women. We'll be back to talk with Rachel about her book and these issues after this word." A commercial for hair coloring came on the monitor overhead.

The guy with the earphones crouching beneath the camera said, "Good, Shirl." Shirl took another cigarette from a box on the table behind Rachel's book and lit up. She was able to suck in almost half of it before the guy under the camera said, "Ten seconds." She snuffed this one out, leaned forward slightly, and when the picture came on the monitor, it caught her profile looking seriously at Rachel.

"Rachel," she said, "do you think lesbians ought to be allowed to teach at a girls' school?"

"Quite the largest percentage," Rachel said, "of child molestations are committed by heterosexual men. As I pointed out in my book, the incidence of child molestation by lesbians is so small as to be statistically meaningless."

"But what kind of role model would a lesbian provide?"

"Whatever kind she was. We don't ask other teachers about their sexual habits. We don't prevent so-called frigid women from teaching children, or impotent men. Children do not, it seems to me, have much chance in public school to emulate the sexual habits of their teachers. And if the teacher's sexual preference is so persuasive to his or her students, why aren't gays made straight by exposure to heterosexual teachers?"

"But might not the gay teacher subtly persuade his or her students toward a homosexual preference?"

Rachel said, "I just answered that, Shirley."

Shirley smiled brilliantly. "In your book you allege frequent violations of civil rights in employment both by the government and the private sector. Many of the offenders are here in Massachusetts. Would you care to name some of them?"

Rachel was beginning to look annoyed. "I named all of them in my book," she said.

"But," Shirley said, "not all of our viewers have read it."

"Have you?" Rachel said.

"I haven't finished it yet," Shirley said. "I'm sorry to say." The guy crouching below the camera lens made a gesture with his hand, and Shirley said, "We'll be right back with more interesting revelations from Rachel Wallace after this message."

I whispered to Linda Smith, who stood in neat tweeds beside me, "Shirley doesn't listen to the answers."

"A lot of them don't," Linda said. "They're busy looking ahead to the next question."

"And she hasn't read the book."

Linda smiled and shook her head. "Almost none of

them ever do. You can't blame them. Sometimes you get several authors a week plus all the other stuff."

"The pressure must be fearful," I said. "To spend your working life never knowing what you're talking about."

"Lots of people do that," Linda said. "I only hope Rachel doesn't let her annoyance show. She's a good interview, but she gets mad too easy."

"That's because if *she* had been doing the interview, she'd have read the book first."

"Maybe," Linda said, "but Shirley North has a lot of fans in the metropolitan area, and she can sell us some books. The bridge club types love her."

A commercial for pantyhose concluded with a model holding out the crotch to show the ventilated panel, then Shirley came back on.

"In your book, Rachel, you characterize lesbianism as an alternative way of loving. Should everyone try it?"

"Everyone should do what she wants to do," Rachel said. "Obviously people to whom the idea is not attractive should stay straight. My argument is, and has been, that those who do find that alternative desirable should not be victimized for that preference. It does no one any harm at all."

"Is it against God's law?"

"It would be arrogant of me to tell you God's law. I'll leave that to the people who think they have God's ear. All I can say is that I've had no sign that He disapproves."

"How about the argument that it is unnatural?"

"Same answer. That really implies a law of nature that exists immutably. I'm not in a position to know about that. Sartre said that perhaps existence precedes essence, and maybe we are in the process of making the laws of nature as we live."

"Yes, certainly. Do you advocate lesbian marriage?"

"Shirley," Rachel said. "I have documented corruption on several levels of local and state government, in several of the major corporations in the country, and you've asked me only about titillating things. In essence you've asked only about sex. That seems unbalanced to me."

219

Shirley's smile glowed. Her splendiferous eyelashes fluttered. "Isn't that an interesting thought, Rachel? I wish we could spend more time, but I know you have to rush." She picked up *Tyranny*. "Get Rachel's book, *Tyranny,* published by Hamilton Black. You'll love it, as I did. Thanks a million, Rachel. Come back again."

Rachel muttered, "Thank you."

Shirley said, "Now this message."

The guy squatting under the camera stood up and said, "Okay, next segment. Thanks a lot Mrs. Wallace. Shirley, you're on the den set." A technician took off Rachel's lapel mike, and she got up and walked away. Shirley didn't say goodbye. She was getting as much mentholated smoke into her as she could before the deodorant commercial ended.

Linda Smith said, "Oh, Rachel, you were dynamite."

Rachel looked at me. I shrugged. Rachel said, "What's that mean?"

I said, "It means you did your best in a difficult situation. You can't look good being interviewed by Shirley North."

Rachel nodded. Linda said, "Oh, no, I thought you were super."

Rachel said nothing as we walked out of the studio and down the long corridor past the news set, empty now and shabby, then along the corridor where people sat in small offices and typed, and out into the lobby and reception area. On the big monitor opposite the reception desk Shirley was leaning toward the man who raised quail.

I frowned the way Shirley did and said in a high voice, "Tell me, do quails like to do it with anything but other quails?"

Rachel gave a snort. Linda smiled. Outside we parted—Rachel and I in my car, Linda in hers.

We wheeled along Soldiers' Field Road with the Charles, quite small and winding this far up, on our left. I looked at Rachel. She was crying. Tears ran in silence down her cheeks. Her hands were folded in her lap. Her shoulders were a little hunched, and her body shook slightly. I looked back at the road. I couldn't think of anything to say. She didn't cry any harder and she didn't stop. The only sound was the unsteady inhaling and exhaling as she cried. We went past Harvard Stadium.

I said, "Feel like a freak?"

She nodded.

"Don't let them do that to you," I said.

"A freak," she said. Her voice was a little thick and a little unsteady, but if you didn't see the tears, you wouldn't be sure she was crying. "Or a monster. That's how everyone seems to see us. Do you seduce little girls? Do you carry them off for strange lesbian rites? Do you use a dildo? God. God damn. Bastards." Her shoulders began to shake harder.

I put my right hand out toward her with the palm up. We passed the business school that way—me with my hand out, her with her body shaking. Then she put her left hand in my right. I held it hard.

"Don't let them do that to you," I said.

She squeezed back at me and we drove the rest of the way along the Charles like that—our hands quite rigidly clamped together, her body slowly quieting down. When I got to the Arlington Street exit, she let go of my hand and opened her purse. By the time we stopped in front of the Ritz, she had her face dry and a little makeup on and herself back in place.

The doorman looked like I'd made a mess on his foot when I got out and nodded toward the Chevy. But he took it from me and said nothing. A job is a job. We went up in the elevator and walked to her room without saying a word. She opened the door. I stepped in first; she followed.

"We have to go to First Mutual Insurance Company at one. I'm addressing a women's group there. Could you pick me up about twelve thirty?" Her voice was quite calm now.

"Sure," I said.

"I'd like to rest for a while," she said, "so please excuse me."

"Sure," I said. "I'll be here at quarter to one."

"Yes," she said. "Thank you."

"Lock the door behind me," I said.

She nodded. I went out and waited until I heard the bolt click behind me. Then I went to the elevator and down.

CHAPTER TWELVE

"I'M MEETING WITH a caucus of women employees at First Mutual Insurance," Rachel said. "This is their lunch hour and they've asked me to eat with them. I know you have to be close by, but I would like it if you didn't actually join us." We were walking along Boylston Street.

"Okay," I said. "As I recall from your book, First Mutual is one of the baddies."

"I wouldn't put it that way, but yes. They are discriminatory in their hiring and wage practices. There are almost no women in management. They have systematically refused to employ gay people and have fired any that they discovered in their employ."

"Didn't you turn up discriminatory practices in their sales policy?"

"Yes. They discourage sales to blacks."

"What's the company slogan?"

Rachel smiled. "We're in the people business."

We went into the lobby of First Mutual and took an elevator to the twentieth floor. The cafeteria was at one end of the corridor. A young woman in camel's-hair slacks and vest topped with a dark-brown blazer was waiting outside. When she saw Rachel she came forward and said, "Rachel Wallace?" She wore small gold-rimmed glasses and no makeup. Her hair was brown and sensible.

Rachel put out her hand. "Yes," she said. "Are you Dorothy Collela?"

222

"Yes, come on in. We're all at a table in the corner." She looked at me uncertainly.

"My name is Spenser," I said. "I just hang around Ms. Wallace. Don't think about me for a moment."

"Will you be joining us?" Dorothy said.

Rachel said, "No. Mr. Spenser is just going to stay by if I need anything."

Dorothy smiled a little blankly and led Rachel to a long table at one end of the cafeteria. There were eight other women gathered there. I leaned against the wall maybe twenty feet away where I could see Rachel and not hear them and not be in the flow of diners.

There was a good deal of chair-scraping and jostling at the table when Rachel sat down. There were introductions and people standing and sitting, and then all but two of the women got up and went to the food line to get lunch. The luncheon special was Scrambled Hamburg Oriental, and I decided to pass on lunch.

The cafeteria had a low ceiling with a lot of fluorescent panels in it. The walls were painted a brilliant yellow on three sides with a bank of windows looking out over Back Bay on the fourth side. The bright yellow paint was almost painful. Music filtered through the cafeteria noise. It sounded like Mantovani, but it always does.

Working with a writer, you get into the glamour scene. After we left here, we'd probably go down to Filene's basement and autograph corsets. Maybe Norman would be there, and Truman and Gore. Rachel took her tray and sat down. She had eschewed the Oriental hamburg. On her tray was a sandwich and a cup of tea.

A girl not long out of the high-school corridors came past me wearing very expensive clothes, very snugly. She had on blue harlequin glasses with small jewels on them, and she smelled like a French sunset.

She smiled at me and said, "Well, foxy, what are you looking at?"

"A size-nine body in a size-seven dress," I said.

"You should see it without the dress," she said.

"I certainly should," I said.

She smiled and joined two other kids her age at a table. They whispered together and looked at me and laughed. The best-dressed people in the world are the single kids that just started working.

Two men in business suits and one uniformed guard came into the cafeteria and walked over to Rachel's table. I slid along behind and listened in. It looked like my business. It was.

"We invited her here," Dorothy was saying.

One of the business suits said, "You're not authorized to do that." He looked like Clark Kent. Three-piece suit with a small gray herringbone in it. Glasses, square face. His hair was short, his face was clean shaved. His shoes were shined. His tie was knotted small but asserted by a simple pin. He was on the way up.

"Who are you?" Rachel said.

"Timmons," he said. "Director of employee relations." He spoke very fast. "This is Mr. Boucher, our security coordinator." Nobody introduced the uniformed guard; he wasn't on the way up. Boucher was sort of plumpish and had a thick mustache. The guard didn't have a gun, but the loop of a leather strap stuck out of his right hip pocket.

"And why are you asking me to leave?" Rachel was saying.

"Because you are in violation of company policy."

"How so?"

"No soliciting is allowed on the premises," Timmons said. I wondered if he was nervous or if he always spoke that fast. I drifted around behind Rachel's chair and folded my arms and looked at Timmons.

"And what exactly am I supposed to be soliciting?" Rachel said.

Timmons didn't like me standing there, and he didn't quite know what to do about it. He looked at me and looked away quickly and then he looked at Boucher and back at me and then at Rachel. He started to speak to Rachel and stopped and looked at me again.

"Who are you?" he said.

"I'm the tooth fairy," I said.

"The what?"

"The tooth fairy," I said. "I loosen teeth."

Timmons's mouth opened and shut. Boucher said, "We don't need any smart answers, mister."

I said, "You wouldn't understand any."

Rachel said, "Mr. Spenser is with me."

"Well," Boucher said, "you'll both have to leave or we'll have you removed."

"How many security people you got?" I said to Boucher.

"That's no concern of yours," Boucher said. Very tough.

"Yeah, but it could be a concern of yours. It will take an awful lot of people like you to remove us."

The uniformed guard looked uncomfortable. He probably knew his limitations, or maybe he just didn't like the company he was keeping.

"Spenser," Rachel said, "I don't want any of that. We will resist, but we will resist passively."

The dining room was very quiet except for the yellow walls. Timmons spoke again—probably encouraged by the mention of passive resistance.

"Will you leave quietly?" he said.

"No," Rachel said, "I will not."

"Then you leave us no choice," Boucher said. He turned to the uniformed guard. "Spag," he said, "take her out."

"You can't do that," Dorothy said.

"You should wait and discuss this with your supervisor," Timmons said, "because I certainly will."

Spag stepped forward and said softly, "Come on, miss."

Rachel didn't move.

Boucher said, "Take her, Spag."

Spag took her arm, gently. "Come on, miss, you gotta go," he said. He kept a check on me with frequent sideshifting glances. He was probably fifty and no more than 170 pounds, some of it waistline. He had receding brown hair and tattoos on both forearms. He pulled lightly at Rachel's arm. She went limp.

Boucher said, "God damn it, Spag, yank her out of that chair. She's trespassing. You have the right."

Spag let go of Rachel's arm and straightened up. "No," he said. "I guess not."

Timmons said, "Jesus Christ."

Boucher said to him, "All right, we'll do it. Brett, you take one arm." He stepped forward and took Rachel under the left arm. Timmons took her right arm, and they dragged her out of the chair. She went limp on them, and they weren't ready for it. They couldn't hold her dead weight, and she slipped to the floor, her legs spread, her skirt hitched halfway up her thighs. She pulled it down.

I said to Spag, "I am going to make a move here. Are you in or out?"

Spag looked at Rachel on the floor and at Timmons and Boucher. "Out," he said. "I used to do honest work."

Boucher was behind Rachel now and had both his arms under hers. I said to him, "Let her go."

Rachel said, "Spenser, I told you we were going to be passive."

Boucher said, "You stay out of this, or you'll be in serious trouble."

I said, "Let go of her, or I'll hit you while you're bent over."

Timmons said, "Hey," but it wasn't loud.

Boucher let Rachel go and stood up. Everyone in the dining room was standing and watching. There was a lot on the line for Boucher. I felt sorry for him. Most of the onlookers were young women. I reached my hand down to Rachel. She took it and got up.

"God damn you," she said. I turned toward her and Boucher took a jump at me. He wasn't big, but he was slow. I dropped my shoulder and caught him in the chest. He grunted. I straightened up, and he staggered backwards and bumped into Timmons.

I said, "If you annoy me, I will knock you right over that serving counter." I pointed my finger at him.

Rachel said, "You stupid bastard," and slapped me

across the face. Boucher made another jump. I hit him a stiff jab in the nose and then crossed with my right, and he went back into the serving line and knocked down maybe fifty plates off the counter and slid down to the floor. "Into is almost as good as over," I said. Timmons was stuck. He had to do something. He took a swing at me; I pulled my head back, slapped his arm on past me with my right hand. It half turned him. I got his collar in my left hand and the seat of his pants in my right and ran him three steps over to the serving counter, braced my feet, arched my back a little, and heaved him up and over it. One of his arms went in the gravy. Mashed potatoes smeared his chest, and he went over the counter rolling and landed on his side on the floor behind it.

The young girl with the tight clothes said, "All *right*, foxy," and started to clap. Most of the women in the cafeteria joined in. I went back to Rachel. "Come on," I said. "Someone must have called the cops. We'd best walk out with dignity. Don't slap me again till we're outside."

CHAPTER THIRTEEN

"YOU DUMB son of a bitch," Rachel said. We were walking along Boylston Street back to the Ritz. "Don't you realize that it would have been infinitely more productive to allow them to drag me out in full view of all those women?"

"Productive of what?"

"Of an elevated consciousness on the part of all those women who were standing there watching the management of that company dramatize its sexism."

"What kind of a bodyguard stands around and lets two B-school twerps like those drag out the body he's supposed to be guarding?"

"An intelligent one. One who understands his job. You're employed to keep me alive, not to exercise your Arthurian fantasies." We turned left on Arlington. Across the street a short gray-haired man wearing two topcoats vomited on the base of the statue of William Ellery Channing.

"Back there you embodied everything I hate," Rachel said. "Everything I have tried to prevent. Everything I have denounced—machismo, violence, that preening male arrogance that compels a man to defend any woman he's with, regardless of her wishes and regardless of her need."

"Don't beat around the bush," I said. "Come right out and say you disapprove of my conduct."

"It demeaned me. It assumed I was helpless and dependent, and needed a big strong man to look out for me. It reiterated that image to all those young women who broke into mindless applause when it was over."

We were in front of the Ritz. The doorman smiled at us—probably pleased that I didn't have my car.

"Maybe that's so," I said. "Or maybe that's a lot of theory which has little to do with practice. I don't care very much about theory or the long-range consequences to the class struggle, or whatever. I can't deal with that. I work close up. Right then I couldn't let them drag you out while I stood around."

"Of course from your viewpoint you'd be dishonored. I'm just the occasion for your behavior, not the reason. The reason is pride—you didn't do that for me, and don't try to kid yourself."

The doorman's smile was getting a little forced.

"I'd do it again," I said.

"I'm sure you would," Rachel said, "but you'll have to do it with someone else. You and I are terminated. I don't want you around me. Whatever your motives, they are not mine, and I'll not violate my life's convictions just to keep your pride intact."

She turned and walked into the Ritz. I looked at the doorman. He was looking at the Public Garden. "The hell of it is," I said to him, "I think she was probably right."

"That makes it much worse," he said.

I walked back along Arlington and back up Boylston for a block to Berkeley Street. I had several choices. I could go down to the Dockside Saloon and drink all their beer, or I could drive up to Smithfield and wait till Susan came home from school and tell her I flunked Women's Lib. Or I could do something useful. I opted for useful and turned up Berkeley.

Boston Police Headquarters was a block and a half up Berkeley Street on the right, nestled in the shadows of big insurance companies—probably made the cops feel safe. Martin Quirk's office at the end of the Homicide squadroom was just as it always was. The room was neat and spare. The only thing on the desk was a phone and a plastic cube with pictures of his family in it.

Quirk was on the phone when I appeared in his doorway. He was tilted back in his chair, his feet on the desk, the phone hunched against his ear with his shoulder. He pointed at the straight chair beside his desk, and I sat down.

"Physical evidence," Quirk said into the phone. "What have you got for physical evidence?" He listened. His tweed jacket hung on the back of his chair. His white shirt was crisp and starchy. The cuffs were turned under once over his thick wrists. He was wearing over the ankle cordovan shoes with brass buckles. The shoes shined with fresh polish. The gray slacks were sharply creased. The black knit tie was knotted and in place. His thick black hair was cut short with no sign of gray.

"Yeah, I know," he said into the phone. "But we got no choice. Get it." He hung up and looked at me. "Don't you ever wear a tie?" he said.

"Just the other day," I said. "Dinner at the Ritz."

"Well, you ought to do it more often. You look like a goddamned overage hippie."

"You're jealous of my youthful image," I said. "Just because you're a bureaucrat and have to dress up like Calvin Coolidge doesn't mean I have to. It's the difference between you and me."

"There's other differences," Quirk said. "What do you want?"

"I want to know what you know about threats on the life of Rachel Wallace."

"Why?"

"Until about a half hour ago I was her bodyguard."

"And?"

"And she fired me for being too masculine."

"Better than the other way around, I guess," Quirk said.

"But I figured since I'd been hired by the day I might as well use the rest of it to see what I could find out from you."

"There isn't much to tell. She reported the threats. We looked into it. Nothing much surfaced. I had Belson ask around on the street. Nobody knew anything."

"You have any opinion on how serious the threats are?"

Quirk shrugged. "If I had to guess, I'd guess they could be. Belson couldn't find any professional involvement. She names a lot of names and makes a lot of embarrassing charges about local businesses and government figures, but that's all they are—embarrassing. Nobody's going to go to jail or end his career, or whatever."

"Which means," I said, "if the threats are real, they are probably from some coconut, or group of coconuts, that are anti-feminist or anti-gay, or both."

"That would be my guess," Quirk said. "The busing issue in this town has solidified and organized all the redneck crazies. So any radical issue comes along, there's half a dozen little fringe outfits available to oppose it. A lot of them don't have anything to do now that busing is getting to be routine. For crissake they took the state cops out of South Boston High this year."

"Educational reform," I said. "One comes to expect such innovation in the Athens of America."

Quirk grunted and locked his hands behind his head as he leaned back further in his chair. The muscles in his upper arm swelled against the shirt sleeve.

"So who's looking after her now?" he said.

"Nobody that I know of. That's why I'm interested in the reality of the threats."

"You know how it is," Quirk said. "We got no facts. How can we? Anonymous phone calls don't lead anywhere. If I had to guess, I guess there might be some real danger."

"Yeah, me too," I said. "What bothers you?"

"Well, the threat to harm her if the book wasn't suppressed. I mean, there were already copies of the damned thing around in galleys or whatever they are. The damage had been done."

"Why doesn't that make you feel easier?" I said. "Why isn't it just a crank call, or a series of crank calls?"

"How would a crank caller even know about the book? Or her? I'm not saying it's sure. I mean it could be some numb-nuts in the publishing company, or at the printer, or anywhere that they might see the book. But it feels worse than that. It has a nice, steady hostile feel of organized opposition."

"Balls," I said.

"You don't agree," Quirk said.

"No. I do. That's what bothers me. It feels real to me, too. Like people who want that book suppressed not because it tells secrets, but because it argues something they don't want to hear."

Quirk nodded. "Right. It's not a matter of keeping a secret. If we're right, and we're both guessing, it's opposition to her opinion and her expression of it. But we are both guessing."

"Yeah, but we're good guessers," I said. "We have some experience in the field."

Quirk shrugged. "We'll see," he said.

"Also, somebody made what looked like a professional try at her a couple nights ago."

"Good how promptly you reported it to the authorities," Quirk said.

"I'm doing that now," I said. "Listen."

He listened.

I told him about the two-car incident on the Lynnway.

I told him about the pickets in Belmont and the pie-throwers in Cambridge. I told him about the recent unpleasantness in the First Mutual cafeteria.

"Don't you free-lance types have an exciting time of it?" Quirk said.

"It makes the time pass," I said.

"The business on the Lynnway is the only thing that sounds serious," Quirk said. "Gimme the license numbers."

I did.

"Course they could be merely harassing you like the others."

"They seemed to know their way around."

"Shit, everybody knows his way around. They watch *Baretta* and *Kojak*. They know all about that stuff."

"Yeah," I said. "Could be. Could even be a pattern."

"Conspiracy?" Quirk raised both eyebrows.

"Possible."

"But likely?"

I shrugged. "There are stranger things in this world than in all your philosophies, Horatio."

"The only other guy I ever met as intellectual as you," Quirk said, "was a child molester we put away in the late summer of 1967."

"Smart doesn't mean good," I said.

"I've noted that," Quirk said. "Anyway, I'm not ready to buy a conspiracy without more."

"Me either," I said. "Can you do anything about keeping an eye on her?"

"I'll call Callahan over at the Ritz again. Tell him you're off the thing, and he should be a little carefuller."

"That's it?"

"Yeah," Quirk said, "that's it. I need more people than I've got now. I can't put a guard on her. If she makes a public appearance somewhere, maybe I can arrange to beef up her security a little. But we both know the score—I can't protect her and neither can you, unless she wants us to. And even then"—he shrugged—"depends on how bad somebody wants her."

"But after someone does her in, you'll swing into action. Then you'll be able to spare a dozen men."

"Take a walk," Quirk said. The lines from his nose to the corners of his mouth were deep. "I don't need to get lectured about police work. I'm still here—I didn't quit."

I stood up. "I apologize," I said. "I feel very sour about things now. I'm blaming you."

Quirk nodded. "I get anything on those numbers, you want to know?"

"Yeah."

"Okay."

I left.

CHAPTER FOURTEEN

SUSAN AND I were at the raw bar in the middle of Quincy Market eating oysters and drinking beer, and arguing. Sort of.

"So why didn't you keep out of it?" Susan said. "Rachel had asked you to."

"And stand there and let them drag her out?"

"Yes." Susan slurped an oyster off the shell. They don't offer forks at the raw bar. They just serve oysters or clams or shrimp, with beer in paper cups. There are bowls of oyster crackers and squeeze bottles of cocktail sauce. They named the place the Walrus and the Carpenter, but I like it anyway.

"I couldn't do that," I said. Under the vaulted ceiling of the market, people swirled up and down the main aisle. A bearded man wearing a ski cap and a green turtleneck sweater eyed Susan and whispered something to the man with him. The man with him looked at Susan and nodded. They both smiled, and then they both caught me looking at

233

them and looked away and moved on. I ordered another beer. Susan sipped a little of hers.

"Why couldn't you do that?" Susan said.

"It violates something."

"What?"

I shrugged. "My pride?"

Susan nodded. "Now we're getting somewhere. And while we're at it, if somebody wants to admire my figure, why not let them? I am pleased. Would it be better if they didn't?"

"You mean those two clowns a minute ago?"

"Yes. And a man who admires my ass isn't necessarily a clown."

"I didn't do anything," I said.

"You glared at them."

"Well, they scare easy."

"Would you have liked it better if they'd told me to start wearing a girdle?"

I said, "Grrrrr."

"Exactly. So what are you glaring at them for?"

"My pride?"

"Now we're getting somewhere."

"Didn't we just have this conversation?"

She smiled and gestured at the bartender for another beer. "Yes, but we haven't finished it."

"So what should I have done when those two upwardly mobile assholes took hold of her?"

"Stood by, made sure they didn't hurt her. Been available if she called for help. Held the door as they went out."

"Jesus Christ," I said.

"Or you could have locked arms with her and gone limp when they touched you and made it that much harder."

"No," I said. "I couldn't do that. Maybe I could have stood by, or maybe if there were a next time I could. But I couldn't lie down and let them drag me out."

"No. You couldn't. But you didn't have to deprive Rachel of a chance for a triumph."

"I didn't think of it in just that way."

"Of course you didn't—just as you don't perceive it that

way when we're at a party and someone makes a pass at me and you're at his shoulder with the look."

"Depriving you of the chance to deal with it successfully yourself."

"Of course," she said. There was a small streak of cocktail sauce at one corner of her mouth. I reached over and wiped it away with my thumb. "I don't normally need you to protect me. I got along quite well without you for quite some years. I fended off the people I wanted to fend off, all by myself."

"And if they don't fend?"

"I call you. You're not far. I've not seen you ten feet from me at a party since we met."

I finished my beer. "Let's walk up toward the Faneuil Hall end," I said. It was nearly four thirty and the crowds were thin, for the market. "Maybe I'll buy you a croissant."

"I'm not bitching about me," she said. She put her arm through mine. Her head came a little above my shoulder. Her hair had a faint flowery smell. "I understand you, and I kind of like your proprietary impulses. Also I love you, and it changes one's perspective sometimes.".

"We could slip into that stairwell and make out," I said.

"Later. You promised a lot of walking and eating and drinking and looking at people."

"And after that?"

"Who knows?" Susan said. "Maybe ecstasy."

"Let's walk faster then."

Quincy Market is old and lovingly restored. It is vast and made of granite blocks. Along each side of the long center aisle there were stalls selling yogurt with fruit topping, kielbasy on a roll with sauerkraut, lobster rolls, submarine sandwiches, French bread, country pâté, Greek salad, sweet and sour chicken, baklava, cookies, bagels, oysters, cheese, fresh fruit on a stick, ice cream, cheesecake, barbecued chicken, pizza, doughnuts, cookies, galantine of duck, roast beef sandwiches with chutney on fresh-baked bread, bean sprouts, dried peaches, jumbo cashews and other nuts. There are also butchershops, cheese stores, a place that sells custom-ground coffee, fruit stands, and a place that sells Korean ginseng root. Outside on either side are arcades with more stalls and terrace cafés, and in restored brick buildings parallel were clothing stores and specialty shops and restaurants. It claims to be the number-one tourist attraction in Boston, and it should be. If you were with a girl in the market area, it would be hard not to hold hands with her. Jugglers and strolling musicians moved around the area. The market is never empty, and in prime time it is nearly unmanageable. We stopped and bought two skewers of fresh fruit and melon, and ate them as we walked.

"What you say makes sense, babe," I said, "but it doesn't feel right."

"I know," she said. "It probably never will for you. You were brought up with a fierce sense of family. But you haven't got a family, and so you transfer that great sea of protective impulse to clients, and me."

"Maybe not you, but usually clients need protection."

"Yes. That's probably why you're in business. You need people who need protection. Otherwise what would you do with the impulse?"

I threw my empty skewer in a trash barrel. "Concentrate it all on you, chickie," I said.

Susan said, "Oh, God."

"I don't think I'm going to change," I said.

"Oh, I hope you don't. I love you. And I understand you, and you should stay as sweet as you are. But you can see why Rachel Wallace might have reservations about you."

"Yeah, except I'm so goddamned cute," I said.

"You certainly are that," Susan said. "Want to split a yogurt?"

CHAPTER FIFTEEN

IT WAS THREE weeks before Christmas, and it was snowing big sporadic flakes outside my office window when I found out that they'd taken Rachel Wallace.

I was sitting with my feet up, drinking black coffee and eating a doughnut and waiting for a guy named Anthony Gonsalves to call me from Fall River when the phone rang. It wasn't Gonsalves.

A voice said, "Spenser? John Ticknor from Hamilton Black. Could you get over here right now? It appears Rachel Wallace has been kidnaped."

"Did you call the cops?" I said.

"Yes."

"Okay, I'm on my way."

I hung up, put my fleece-lined jacket on over my black turtleneck and shoulder holster, and went. My office that year was on the corner of Mass. Ave. and Boylston Street, on the second floor, in a small three-sided turret over a smokeshop. My car was parked by a sign that said No Parking Bus Stop. I got in and drove straight down Boylston. The snow was melting as it hit the street but collecting on the margins of the road and on the sidewalks and building ledges.

The Christmas tree in the Prudential Center was lit already although it was only three forty-five. I turned left at Charles and right onto Beacon and parked at the top of the hill in front of the State House in a space that said Reserved for Members of the General Court. They meant the legislature, but Massachusetts calls it the Great and General Court for the same reason they call themselves a Commonwealth. It has something to do I think with not voting for Nixon. To my right the Common sloped down to Tremont Street, its trees strung with Christmas lights, a very big Nativity scene stretching out near the Park Street end. The snow was holding on the grass part of the Common and melting on the walkways. Down near the information booth they had some reindeer in pens, and a guy with a sandwich board was standing by the pens handing leaflets to people who were trying to feed popcorn to the deer.

Ticknor's office was on the top floor looking out over the Common. It was high-ceilinged and big-windowed and cluttered with books and manuscripts. Across from the desk was a low couch, and in front of the couch was a coffee table covered with manila folders. Ticknor was sitting on the couch with his feet on the coffee table looking out at the guy on the Common who was handing out leaflets by the reindeer pens. Frank Belson, who was a detective-sergeant, sat on the couch beside him and sipped some coffee. A young guy with a face from County Mayo and a three-piece suit from Louis was standing behind Ticknor's desk talking on the phone.

Belson nodded at me as I came in. I looked at the kid with the County Mayo face and said, "DA's office?"

Belson nodded. "Cronin," he said. "Assistant prosecutor."

Ticknor said, "Spenser, I'm glad you could come. You know Sergeant Belson, I gather."

I nodded.

Ticknor said, "This is Roger Forbes, our attorney."

I shook hands with a tall gray-haired man with high cheekbones and sunken cheeks who stood—a little uncomfortably, I thought—in the corner between the couch and a book shelf.

Cronin said into the phone, "We haven't said anything to the media yet."

I said to Belson, "What have you got?"

He handed me a typewritten sheet of paper. It was neatly typed, double-spaced. No strikeovers, no x-ed out portions. Margins were good. Paragraphs were indented five spaces. It was on a plain sheet of Eaton's Corrasable Bond. It read:

Whereas Rachel Wallace has written several books offensive to God and country; whereas she has advocated lesbian love in direct contradiction of the Bible and common decency; whereas she has corrupted and continues to corrupt our nation and our children through the public media, which mindlessly exploits her for greed; and whereas our public officials, content to be the dupes of any radical conspiracy, have taken no action, therefore we have been forced to move.

We have taken her and are holding her. She has not been harmed, and unless you fail to follow our instructions, she will not be. We want no money. We have taken action in the face of a moral imperative higher than any written law, and we shall follow that imperative though it lead to the grave.

Remain alert for further communication. We will submit our demands to you for communication to the appropriate figures. Our demands are not negotiable. If they are not met, the world will be better for the death of Rachel Wallace.

R(estore) A(merican) M(orality)
RAM

I read it twice. It said the same thing both times. "Some prose style," I said to Ticknor.

"If you'd been able to get along with her," Ticknor said, "perhaps the note would never have been written." His face was a little flushed.

I said to Belson, "And you've checked it out."

"Sure," Belson said. "She's nowhere. Her hotel room is empty. Suitcases are still there, stuff still in drawers. She was supposed to be on a radio talk show this afternoon and never showed. Last time anyone saw her was last night around nine o'clock, when the room service waiter brought up some sandwiches and a bottle of gin and one of vermouth and two glasses. He says there was someone taking a shower, but he

239

doesn't know who. The bathroom door was closed, and he heard the water running."

"And you got nothing for a lead."

"Not a thing," Belson said. He was lean and thin-faced with a beard so heavy that the lower half of his face had a blue cast to it, even though he shaved at least twice a day. He smoked five-cent cigars down to the point where the live end burned his lip, and he had one going now that was only half-way there but already chewed and battered-looking.

"Quirk coming in on this?" I said.

"Yeah, he'll be along in a while. He had to be in court this afternoon, and he sent me down to get started. But now that you showed up, he probably won't need to."

Cronin hung up the phone and looked at me. "Who are you?"

Ticknor said, "Mr. Spenser was hired to protect her. We thought he might be able to shed some light on the situation."

"Sure did a hell of a job protecting," Cronin said. "You know anything?"

"Not much," I said.

"Didn't figure you would. They want you around, okay by me, but don't get in the way. You annoy me, and I'll roast your ass."

I looked at Belson. He grinned. "They're turning them out tougher and tougher up the heights," Belson said.

"This must be their supreme achievement," I said. "They'll never get one tougher than this."

"Knock off the shit," Cronin said. "Sergeant, you know this guy?"

"Oh, yes, sir, Mr. Cronin. I know him. You want me to shoot him?"

"What the hell is wrong with you, Belson? I asked you a simple question."

"He's all right," Belson said. "He'll be a help."

"He better be," Cronin said. "Spenser, I want you to give Sergeant Belson a rundown on anything you know about this case. Belson, if there's anything worth it, get a formal statement."

"Yeah, sure," Belson said. "Get right on it." He winked at me.

Cronin turned to Ticknor. "You're in the word business. You recognize anything from the way it's written, the prose style?"

"If it were a manuscript, we'd reject it," Ticknor said. "Other than that I haven't anything to say about it. I can't possibly guess who wrote it."

Cronin wasn't really listening. He turned toward Forbes, the lawyer. "Is there a room around here where we can meet with the media people, Counselor?" He addressed Forbes almost like an equal; law-school training probably gave him an edge.

"Certainly," Forbes said. "We've a nice conference room on the second floor that will do, I think." He spoke to Ticknor. "I'll take him to the Hamilton Room, John."

"Good idea," Ticknor said. Forbes led the way out. Cronin stopped at the door. "I want everything this guy knows, Sergeant. I want him empty when he leaves."

I said to Belson, "I don't want my face marked up."

"Who could tell?" he said.

Cronin went out after Forbes.

I sat on the edge of Ticknor's desk. "I hope he doesn't go armed," I said.

"Cronin?" Belson laughed. "He got out of law school in 1973, the year I first took the lieutenant's exam. He thinks if he's rough and tough, people won't notice that he doesn't know shit and just wants to get elected to public office."

"He figures wrong," Ticknor said. Belson raised his eyebrows approvingly. Ticknor was behind him and didn't see.

I said to Ticknor, "How'd you get the letter?"

"Someone delivered it to the guard at the desk downstairs," Ticknor said. He handed me the envelope. It was blank except for Ticknor's name typed on the front.

"Description?"

Belson answered. "They get a hundred things a day delivered down there. Guard paid no attention. Can't remember for sure even whether it was a man or a woman."

"It's not his fault," Ticknor said. "We get all sorts of deliveries from the printers—galleys, pages, blues—as well as manuscripts from agents, authors, and readers, artwork, and half a dozen other kinds of material at the desk every day. Walt isn't expected to pay attention to who brings it."

I nodded. "Doesn't matter. Probably someone hired a cabby to bring it in anyway, and descriptions don't help much, even if they're good ones."

Belson nodded. "I already got somebody checking the cab companies for people who had things delivered here. But they could just as easy have delivered it themselves."

"Should the press be in on this?" Ticknor said.

"I don't think it does much harm," I said. "And I don't think you could keep them out of here if Cronin has any say. This sounds like an organization that wants publicity. They said nothing about keeping it from the press, just as they said nothing about keeping the police out."

"I agree," Belson said. "Most kidnapings have something about 'don't go to the police,' but these political or social or whatever-the-hell-they-are kidnapings usually are after publicity. And anyway Cronin has already told the press so the question is—what? What word am I after?"

Ticknor said, "Academic. Hypothetical. Aimless. Too late. Merely conjectural."

"Okay, any of those," Belson said.

"So what do we do?" Ticknor said.

"Nothing much," Belson said. "We sit. We wait. Some of us ask around on the street. We check with the FBI to see if they have anything on RAM. We have the paper analyzed and the ink, and learn nothing from either. In a while somebody will get in touch and tell us what they want."

"That's all?" Ticknor was offended. He looked at me.

"I don't like it either," I said. "But that's about all. Mostly we have to wait for contact. The more contact the better. The more in touch they are, the more we have to work on, the better chance we have to find them. And her."

"But how can we be sure they'll make contact?"

Belson answered. "You can't. But you figure they will. They said they would. They did this for a reason. They want something. One of the things you can count on is that everybody wants something." The cigar had burned down far enough now so that Belson had to tilt his head slightly to keep the smoke from getting in his eyes.

"But in the meantime—what about Rachel? My God, think how she must feel. Suppose they abuse her? We can't just sit here and wait."

Belson looked at me. I said, "We haven't got anything else to do. There's no profit in thinking about alternatives when you don't have any. She's a tough woman. She'll do as well as anyone."

"But alone," Ticknor said, "with these maniacs. . . ."

"Think about something else," Belson said. "Have you any idea who this group might be?"

Ticknor shook his head briskly, as if he had a fly in his ear. "No," he said. "No. No idea at all. What do they call themselves? RAM?"

Belson nodded. "Anyone in the publishing community that you know of that has any hostility toward Ms. Wallace?"

"No, well, I mean, not like this. Rachel is abrasive and difficult, and she advocates things not everyone likes, but nothing that would cause a kidnaping."

"Let us decide that. You just give me a list of everybody you can think of that didn't like her, that argued with her, that disagreed with her."

"My God, man, that would include half the reviewers in the country."

"Take your time," Belson said. He had a notebook out and leaned back in his chair.

"But, my God, Sergeant, I can't just start listing names indiscriminately. I mean, I'll be involving these people in the investigation of a capital crime."

"Aren't you the one was worried about how poor Rachel must be feeling?" Belson said.

I knew the conversation. I'd heard variations on it too many times. I said, "I'm going to go out and look for Rachel. Let me know when you hear from them."

"I'm not authorized to employ you on this, Spenser," Ticknor said.

Belson said, "Me either." His thin face had the look of internal laughter.

"All part of the service," I said.

I went out of Ticknor's office, past two detectives questioning a secretary, into the elevator down to the street, and out to start looking.

CHAPTER SIXTEEN

THE BOSTON *Globe* is in a building on Morrissey Boulevard which looks like the offspring of a warehouse and a suburban junior high school. It used to be on Washington Street in the middle of the city and looked like a newspaper building should. But that was back when the *Post* was still with us, and the *Daily Record*. Only yesterday. When the world was young.

It was the day after they took Rachel and snowing again. I was talking to Wayne Cosgrove in the city room about right-wing politics, on which he'd done a series three years earlier.

"I never heard of RAM," he said. Cosgrove was thirty-five, with a blond beard. He had on wide-wale corduroy pants and a gray woolen shirt and a brown tweed jacket. His feet were up on the desk. On them he wore leather boots with rubber bottoms and yellow laces. A blue down parka with a hood hung on the back of his chair.

"God you look slick, Wayne," I said. "You must have been a Nieman Fellow some time."

"A year at Harvard," he said, "picks up your taste like a bastard." He'd grown up in Newport News, Virginia, and still had the sound of it when he talked.

"I can see that," I said. "Why don't you look in your files and see if you have anything on RAM?"

"Files," Cosgrove said. "I don't need to show no stinking files, gringo." He told me once that he'd seen *The Treasure of the Sierra Madre* four times at a revival house in Cambridge.

"You don't have any files?"

He shrugged. "Some, but the good stuff is up here, in the old coconut. And there ain't nothing on RAM. Doesn't matter. Groups start up and fold all the time, like sub sandwich shops. Or they change the name, or a group splinters off from another one. If I had done that series day before yesterday, I might not have heard of RAM, and they might be this week's biggie. When I did the series, most of the dippos were focused on busing. All the mackerel-snappers were afraid of the niggers' fucking their daughters, and the only thing they could think of to prevent that was to keep the niggers away from their daughters. Don't seem to speak too highly of their daughters' self-control, but anyway if you wanted to get a group started, then you went over to Southie and yelled *nigger nigger.*"

He pronounced it *niggah.*

"Isn't that a technique that was developed regionally?"

"Ahhh, yes," Cosgrove said. "Folks down home used to campaign for office on that issue, whilst you folks up north was just a tsk-tsking at us and sending in the feds. Fearful racism there was, in the South, in those days."

"Didn't I hear you were involved in freedom riding, voter registration, and Communist subversion in Mississippi some years back?"

"I had a northern granddaddy," Cosgrove said. "Musta come through on a gene."

"So where are all the people in this town who used to stand around chanting *never* and throwing rocks at children?"

Cosgrove said, "Most of them are saying, 'Well, hardly ever.' But I know what you're after. Yeah, I'd say some of them, having found out that a lot of the niggers don't want to fuck their daughters, are now sweating that the faggots will bugger their sons and are getting up a group to throw rocks at fairies."

"Any special candidates?"

Cosgrove shrugged. "Aw, shit, I don't know, buddy. You know as well as I do that the hub of any ultra-right-wing piece of business in this metropolitan area is Fix Farrell. For Christ's sake, he's probably anti-Eskimo."

"Yeah, I know about Farrell, but I figure a guy like him wouldn't involve himself in a thing like this."

"'Cause he's on the city council?" Cosgrove said. "How the hell old are you?"

"I don't argue he's honest, I just argue he doesn't need this kind of action. I figure a guy like him benefits from people like Rachel Wallace. Gives him someone to be against. Farrell wouldn't want her kidnaped and her book suppressed. He'd want her around selling it at the top of her lungs so he could denounce her and promulgate plans to thwart her."

Cosgrove tapped his teeth with the eraser end of a yellow pencil. "Not bad," he said. "You probably got a pretty good picture of Fix at that."

"You think he might have any thoughts on who I should look into?"

Cosgrove shook his head very quickly. "No soap. Farrell's never going to rat on a possible vote—and anybody opposed to a gay feminist activist can't be all bad in Fix's book."

"You think the RAM people would trust him?" I said.

"How the fuck would I know?" Cosgrove said. "Jesus, Spenser, you are a plugger, I'll say that for you."

"Hell of a bodyguard, too," I said.

246

Cosgrove shrugged. "I'll ask around; I'll talk it up in the city room. I hear anything, I'll give you a buzz."

"Thank you," I said, and left.

CHAPTER SEVENTEEN

I KNEW A guy who was in the Ku Klux Klan. His name was Manfred Roy, and I had helped bust him once, when I was on the cops, for possession of pornographic materials. It was a while ago, when possession of pornographic materials was more serious business than it is now. And Manfred had weaseled on the guy he bought it from and the friends who were with him when he bought it, and we dropped the charges against him and his name never got in the papers. He lived with his mother, and she would have been disappointed in him if she had known. After I left the cops, I kept track of Manfred. How many people do you know that actually belong to the Ku Klux Klan? You find one, you don't lose him.

Manfred was working that year cutting hair in a barbershop on the ground floor of the Park Square Building. He was a small guy, with white-blond hair in a crew cut. Under his barber coat he had on a plaid flannel shirt and chino pants and brown penny-loafers with a high shine. It wasn't a trendy shop. The only razor cut you got was if somebody nicked you while they were shaving your neck.

I sat in the waiting chair and read the *Globe*. There was an article on the city council debate over a bond issue. I read the first paragraph because Wayne Cosgrove had a byline, but even loyalty flagged by paragraph two.

There were four barbers working. One of them, a fat guy with an Elvis Presley pompadour sprayed into rigid stillness, said, "Next?"

I said, "No thanks. I'll wait for him," and pointed at Manfred.

He was cutting the hair of a white-haired man. He glanced toward me and then back at the man and then realized who I was and peeked at me in the mirror. I winked at him, and he jerked his eyes back down at the white hair in front of him.

In five minutes he finished up with Whitey and it was my turn. I stepped to the chair. Manfred said, "I'm sorry, sir, it's my lunch hour, perhaps another barber. . . ?"

I gave him a big smile and put my arm around him. "That's even better, Manfred. Actually I just wanted to have a good rap with you anyway. I'll buy you lunch."

"Well, actually, I was meeting somebody."

"Swell, I'll rap with them, too. Come on, Manfred. Long time no see."

The barber with the pompadour was looking at us. Manfred slipped off his white barber coat, and we went together out the door of the shop. I took my coat from the rack as I went by.

In the corridor outside Manfred said, "God damn you, Spenser, you want to get me fired?"

"Manfred," I said, "Manfred. How unkind. Un-Christian even. I came by to see you and buy you lunch."

"Why don't you just leave me alone?" he said.

"You still got any of those inflatable rubber nude girls you used to be dealing?"

We were walking along the arcade in the Park Square Building. The place had once been stylish and then gotten very unstylish and was now in renaissance. Manfred was looking at his feet as we walked.

"I was different then," Manfred said. "I had not found Christ yet."

"You, too?" I said.

"I wouldn't expect you to understand."

Near the St. James Avenue exit was a small stand that sold sandwiches. I stopped. "How about a sandwich and a cup of coffee, Manfred? On me, any kind. Yogurt too, and an apple if you'd like. My treat."

"I'm not hungry," he said.

"Okay by me," I said. "Hope you don't mind if I dine."

"Why don't you just go dine and stop bothering me?"

"I'll just grab a sandwich here and we'll stroll along, maybe cross the street to the bus terminal, see if any miscegenation is going on or anything."

I bought a tuna on whole wheat, a Winesap apple, and a paper cup of black coffee. I put the apple in my pocket and ate the sandwich as we walked along. At the far end of the arcade, where the Park Square Cinema used to be, we stopped. I had finished my sandwich and was sipping my coffee.

"You still with the Klan, Manfred?"

"Certainly."

"I heard you were regional manager or Grand High Imperial Alligator or whatever for Massachusetts."

He nodded.

"Dynamite," I said, "next step up is playing intermission piano at a child-abuse convention."

"You're a fool, like all the other liberals. Your race will be mongrelized; a culture that took ten thousand years and produced the greatest civilization in history will be lost. Drowned in a sea of half-breeds and savages. Only the Communists will gain."

"Any culture that produced a creep like you, Manfred," I said, "is due for improvement."

"Dupe," he said.

"But I didn't come here to argue ethnic purity with you."

"You'd lose," he said.

"Probably," I said. "You're a professional bigot. You spend your life arguing it. You are an expert. It's your profession. And it ain't mine. I don't spend two hours a month debating racial purity. But even if I lose the argument, I'll win the fight afterwards."

"And you people are always accusing us of violence,"

Manfred said. He was standing very straight with his back against the wall near the barren area where the advertisements for the Cinema used to be. There was some color on his cheeks.

"*You people?*" I said. "*Us?* I'm talking about me and you. I'm not talking about *us* and about *you people.*"

"You don't understand politics," Manfred said. "You can't change society talking about *you* and *me.*"

"Manfred, I would like to know something about a group of people as silly as you are. Calls itself RAM, which stands for Restore American Morality."

"Why ask me?"

"Because you are the kind of small dogturd who hangs around groups like this one and talks about restoring morality. It probably helps you to feel like less of a dogturd."

"I don't know anything about RAM."

"It is opposed to feminism and gay activism—probably in favor of God and racial purity. You must've heard about them?"

Manfred shook his head. He was looking at his feet again. I put my fist under his chin and raised it until he was looking at me. "I want to know about this group, Manfred," I said.

"I promise you, I don't know nothing about them," Manfred said.

"Then you should be sure to find out about them, Manfred."

He tried to twist his chin off my fist, but I increased the upward pressure a little and held him still.

"I don't do your dirty work."

"You do. You do anyone's. You're a piece of shit, and you do what you're told. Just a matter of pressure," I said.

His eyes shifted away from me. Several people coming out of the bank to my right paused and looked at us, and then moved hurriedly along.

"There are several kinds of pressure, Manfred. I can come into work every day and harass you until they fire you. I can go wherever you go and tell them about how we busted you for possession of an inflatable lover, and how you sang like the Mormon Tabernacle Choir to get off." There was more color in his cheeks now. "Or," I said, "I could punch your face into scrapple once a day until you had my information."

With his teeth clenched from the pressure of my fist, Manfred said, "You miserable prick." His whole face was red now. I increased the pressure and brought him up on his toes.

"Vilification," I said. "You people are always vilifying us." I let him go and stepped away from him. "I'll be around tomorrow to see what you can tell me," I said.

"Maybe I won't be here," he said.

"I know where you live, Manfred. I'll find you."

He was still standing very straight and stiff against the wall. His breath was hissing between his teeth. His eyes looked bright to me, feverish.

"Tomorrow, Manfred. I'll be by tomorrow."

CHAPTER EIGHTEEN

I WENT OUT to Arlington Street and turned left and walked down to Boylston eating my Winesap apple. On Boylston Street there were lots of Christmas decorations and pictures of Santa Claus and a light, pleasant snow falling. I wondered if Rachel Wallace could see the snow from where she was. 'Tis the season to be jolly. If I had stayed with her. . . . I shook my head. Hard. No point to that. It probably wasn't much more unpleasant to be kidnaped in the Christmas season than any other time. I hadn't stayed with her. And thinking I should have wouldn't help find her. Got to concentrate on the priority items, babe. Got to think about finding her. Automatically, as I went by Brentano's, I stopped and looked in the window at the books. I didn't have much hope for Manfred—

he was mean and bigoted and stupid. Cosgrove was none of those things, but he was a working reporter on a liberal newspaper. Anything he found out, he'd have to stumble over. No one was going to tell him.

I finished my apple and dropped the core in a trash basket attached to a lamp post. I looked automatically in Malben's window at the fancy food. Then I could cross and see what new Japanese food was being done at Hai Hai, then back this side and stare at the clothes in Louis, perhaps stop off at the Institute of Contemporary Art. Then I could go home and take a nap. Shit. I walked back to my office and got my car and drove to Belmont.

The snow wasn't sticking as I went along Storrow Drive, and it was early afternoon with no traffic. On my right the Charles was very black and cold-looking. Along the river people jogged in their winter running clothes. A very popular model was longjohns under shorts, with a hooded sweatshirt and blue New Balance shoes with white trim. I preferred a cutoff sweat shirt over black turtleneck sweater, with blue warm-up pants to match the New Balance 320's. Diversity. It made America great.

I crossed the Charles to the Cambridge side near Mt. Auburn Hospital and drove through a slice of Cambridge through Watertown, out Belmont Street to Belmont. The snow was beginning to collect as I pulled into a Mobil station on Trapelo Road and got directions to the Belmont Police Station on Concord Avenue.

I explained to the desk sergeant who I was, and he got so excited at one point that he glanced up at me for a moment before he went back to writing in a spiral notebook.

"I'm looking for one of your patrol car people. Young guy, twenty-five, twenty-six. Five ten, hundred eighty pounds, very cocky, wears military decorations on his uniform blouse. Probably eats raw wolverine for breakfast."

Without looking up the desk sergeant said, "That'd be Foley. Wise mouth."

"Man's gotta make his mark somehow," I said. "Where do I find him?"

252

The sergeant looked at something official under the counter. "He's cruising up near the reservoir," he said. "I'll have the dispatcher call him. You know the Friendly's up on Trapelo?"

"Yeah, I passed it coming in," I said.

"I'll have him meet you in the parking lot there."

I thanked him and went out and drove up to Friendly's ice-cream parlor. Five minutes after I got there, a Belmont cruiser pulled in and parked. I got out of my car in the steady snowfall and walked over to the cruiser and got in the back seat. Foley was driving. His partner was the same older cop with the pot belly, still slouched in the passenger seat with his hat over his eyes.

Foley shifted sideways and grinned at me over the seat. "So someone snatched your lez, huh?"

"How gracefully you put it," I said.

"And you got no idea who, and you come out grabbing straws. You want me to ID the cluck you hit in the gut, don't you?"

I said to the older cop, "How long you figure before he's chief?"

The older cop ignored me.

"Am I right or wrong?"

"Right," I said, "you know who he is?"

"Yeah, after we was all waltzing together over by the library that day, I took down his license number when he drove off, and I checked into him when I had time. Name's English—Lawrence Turnbull English, Junior. Occupation, financial consultant. Means he don't do nothing. Family's got twelve, fifteen million bucks. He consults with their trust officer on how to spend it. That's as much as he works. Spends a lot of time taking the steam, playing racquetball, and protecting democracy from the coons and the queers and the commies and the lower classes, and the libbers and like that."

The old cop shifted a little in the front seat and said, "He's got an IQ around eight, maybe ten."

"Benny's right," Foley said. "He snatched that broad, he'd forget where he hid her."

253

"Where's he live?" I said.

Foley took a notebook out of his shirt pocket, ripped out a page, and handed it to me. "Watch your ass with him though. Remember, he's a friend of the chief's," Foley said.

"Yeah," I said. "Thanks."

A plow rumbled by on Trapelo Road as I got out of the cruiser and went back to my car. The windows were opaque with snow, and I had to scrape them clean before I could drive. I went into the same Mobil station and got my tank filled and asked for directions to English's house.

It was in a fancy part of Belmont. A rambling, gabled house that looked like one of those old nineteenth century resort hotels. Probably had a hunting preserve in the snow behind it. The plow had tossed up a small drift in front of the driveway, and I had to shove my car through it. The driveway was clear and circled up behind the house to a wide apron in front of a garage with four doors. To the right of the garage there was a back door. I disdained it. I went back around to the front door. A blow for the classless society. A young woman in a maid suit answered the bell. Black dress, little white apron, little hat—just like in the movies.

I said, "Is the master at home?"

She said, "Excuse me?"

I said, "Mr. English? Is he at home?"

"Who shall I say is calling, please?"

"Spenser," I said, "representing Rachel Wallace. We met once, tell him, at the Belmont Library."

The maid said, "Wait here, please," and went off down the hall. She came back in about ninety seconds and said, "This way, please."

We went down the hall and into a small pine-paneled room with a fire on the hearth and a lot of books on built-in shelves on either side of the fireplace. English was sitting in a red-and-gold wing chair near the fire, wearing an honest-to-God smoking jacket with black velvet lapels and smoking a meerschaum pipe. He had on black-rimmed glasses and a book by Harold Robbins was closed in his right hand, the forefinger keeping the place.

He stood up as I came in but did not put out his hand—probably didn't want to lose his place. He said, "What do you want, Mr. Spenser?"

"As you may know, Rachel Wallace was kidnaped yesterday."

"I heard that on the news," he said. We still stood.

"I'm looking for her."

"Yes?"

"Can you help?"

"How on earth could I help?" English said. "What have I to do with her?"

"You picketed her speech at the library. You called her a bulldyke. As I recall, you said you'd 'never let her win' or something quite close to that."

"I deny saying any such thing," English said. "I exercised my Constitutional right of free speech by picketing. I made no threats whatsoever. You assaulted me."

So he hadn't forgotten.

"We don't have to be mad at each other, Mr. English. We can do this easy."

"I wish to do nothing with you. It is preposterous that you'd think I knew anything about a crime."

"On the other hand," I said, "we can do it the other way. We can talk this all over with the Boston cops. There's a sergeant named Belson there who'll be able to choke back the terror he feels when you mention your friend, the chief. He'd feel duty bound to drag your tail over to Berkeley Street and ask you about the reports that you'd threatened Rachel Wallace before witnesses. If you annoyed him, he might even feel it necessary to hold you overnight in the tank with the winos and fags and riffraff."

"My attorney—" English said.

"Oh, yeah," I said, "Belson just panics when an attorney shows up. Sometimes he gets so nervous, he forgets where he put the client. And the attorney has to chase all over the metropolitan area with his writ, looking into assorted pens and tanks and getting puke on his Chesterfield overcoat to see if he can find his client."

English opened his mouth and closed it and didn't say anything.

I went and sat in his red-and-gold wing chair. "How'd you know Rachel Wallace was going to be at the library?" I said.

"It was advertised in the local paper," he said.

"Who organized the protest?"

"Well, the committee had a meeting."

"What committee?"

"The vigilance committee."

"I bet I know your motto," I said.

"Eternal vigilance—" he said.

"I know," I said. "I know. Who is the head of the committee?"

"I am chairman."

"Gee, and still so humble," I said.

"Spenser, I do not find you funny," he said.

"Puts you in excellent company," I said. "Could you account for your movements since Monday night at nine o'clock if someone asked you?"

"Of course I could. I resent being asked."

"Go ahead," I said.

"Go ahead what?"

"Go ahead and account for your movements since nine o'clock Monday night."

"I certainly will not. I have no obligation to tell you anything."

"We already did this once, Lawrence. Tell me, tell Belson—I don't care."

"I have absolutely nothing to hide."

"Funny how I knew you'd say that. Too bad to waste it on me though. It'll dazzle the cops."

"Well, I don't," he said. "I don't have anything to hide. I was at a committee meeting from seven thirty Monday night until eleven fifteen. Then I came straight home to bed."

"Anybody see you come home?"

"My mother, several of the servants."

"And the next day?"

"I was at Old Colony Trust at nine fifteen, I left there at eleven, played racquetball at the club, then lunched at the club. I returned home after lunch, arrived here at three fifteen. I read until dinner. After dinner—"

"Okay, enough. I'll check on all of this, of course. Who'd you play racquetball with?"

"I simply will not involve my friends in this. I will not have you badgering and insulting them."

I let that go. He'd fight that one. He didn't want his friends at the club to know he was being investigated, and a guy like English will dig in to protect his reputation. Besides I could check it easily. The club and the committee, too.

"Badger?" I said. "Insult? Lawrence, how unkind. I am clearly not of your social class, but I am not without grace."

"Are you through?"

"I am for now," I said. "I will authenticate your—if you'll pardon the expression—alibi, and I may look further into your affairs. If the alibi checks, I'll still keep you in mind, however. You didn't have to do it, to have it done, or to know who did it."

"I shall sue you if you continue to bother me," English said.

"And if you are involved in any way in anything that happened to Rachel Wallace," I said, "I will come back and put you in the hospital."

English narrowed his eyes a little. "Are you threatening me?" he said.

"That's exactly it, Lawrence," I said. "That is exactly what I am doing. I am threatening you."

English looked at me with his eyes narrowed for a minute, and then he said, "You'd better leave."

"Okay by me," I said, "but remember what I told you. If you are holding out on me, I'll find out, and I'll come back. If you know something and don't tell me, I will find out, and I will hurt you."

He stood and opened the study door.

"A man in my position has resources, Spenser." He was still squinting at me. I realized that was his tough look.

"Not enough," I said, and walked off down the hall and out the front door. The snow had stopped. Around back, a Plymouth sedan was parked next to my car. When I walked over to it, the window rolled down and Belson looked out at me.

"Thought this was your heap," he said. "Learn anything?"

I laughed. "I just got through threatening English with you," I said, "so he'd talk to me. Now here you are, and he could just as well not have talked to me."

"Get in," Belson said. "We'll compare notes."

I got in the backseat. Belson was in the passenger seat. A cop I didn't know sat behind the wheel. Belson didn't introduce us.

"How'd you get here?" I said.

"You told Quirk about the library scene," Belson said, "and we questioned Linda Smith along with everybody else and she mentioned it to me. I had it on my list when Quirk mentioned it to me. So we called the Belmont Police and found ourselves about an hour behind you. What you get?"

"Not much," I said. "If it checks out, he's got an alibi for all the time that he needs."

"Run it past us," Belson said. "We won't mention you, and we'll see if the story stays the same."

I told Belson what English had told me. The cop I didn't know was writing a few things in a notebook. When I was through, I got out of the Plymouth and into my own car. Through the open window I said to Belson, "Anything surfaces, I'd appreciate hearing."

"Likewise," Belson said.

I rolled up the window and backed out and turned down the drive. As I pulled onto the street I saw Belson and the other cop get out and start toward the front door. The small drift of snow that had blocked the driveway when I'd arrived was gone. A man in English's position was not without resources.

CHAPTER NINETEEN

THE MAIN ENTRANCE to the Boston Public Library used to face Copley Square across Dartmouth Street. There was a broad exterior stairway and inside there was a beautiful marble staircase leading up to the main reading room with carved lions and high-domed ceilings. It was always a pleasure to go there. It felt like a library and looked like a library, and even when I was going in there to look up Duke Snider's lifetime batting average, I used to feel like a scholar.

Then they grafted an addition on and shifted the main entrance to Boylston Street. *Faithful to the spirit,* the architect had probably said. *But making a contemporary statement,* I bet he said. The addition went with the original like Tab goes with pheasant. Now, even if I went into study the literary influence of Eleanor of Aquitaine, I felt like I'd come out with a pound of hamburger and a loaf of Wonder bread.

By the big glass doors a young woman in Levi's jeans and a rabbit fur coat told me she was trying to raise money to get a bus back to Springfield. She had one tooth missing and a bruise on her right cheekbone. I didn't give her anything.

I went through the new part to the old and walked around a bit and enjoyed it, and then I went to the periodical section and started looking at the *Globe* on microfilm to see what I could find out about the Belmont Vigilance Committee. I was there all day. Next to me a fragrant old geezer in a long overcoat slept with his head resting on the microfilm viewer in front of him. The overcoat was buttoned up to his neck even though the room was hot. No one bothered him.

At noon I went out and went across the street to a Chinese restaurant and ate some Peking ravioli and some mushu pork for lunch. When I went back for the afternoon session the old man was gone, but the broad with the missing tooth was still working the entrance. At five o'clock I had seven pages of notes, and my eyes were starting to cross. If I weren't so tough, I would have thought about reading glasses. I wonder how Bogie would have looked with specs. Here's looking at you, four-eyes. I shut off the viewer, returned the last microfilm cassette, put on my coat, and went out to a package store, where I bought two bottles of Asti Spumante.

I was driving up to Smithfield to have dinner with Susan, and the traffic northbound was stationary a long way back onto Storrow Drive. I deked and dived up over the Hill and down across Cambridge Street past the Holiday Inn, behind Mass. General and got to the traffic light at Leverett Circle almost as quick as the people who just sat in line on Storrow. The radio traffic-reporter told me from his helicopter that there was a "fender-bender" on the bridge, so I turned off onto 93 and went north that way. A magician with the language—*fender-bender,* wow! It was six when I turned off of Route 128 at the Main Street-Smithfield exit. Out in the subs most of the snow was still white. There were candles in all the windows and wreaths on all the doors, and some people had Santas on their rooftops, and some people had colored lights on their shrubbery. One house had a drunken Santa clutching a bottle of Michelob under the disapproving stare of a red-nosed reindeer. Doubtless the antichrist lurks in the subs as well.

Susan's house had a spotlight on the front and a sprig of white pine hanging on the brass doorknocker. I parked in her driveway and walked to her front door, and she opened it before I got there.

"Fa-la-la-la-la," I said.

She leaned against the doorjamb and put one hand on her hip.

"Hey, Saint Nick," she said, "you in town long?"

"Trouble with you Jews," I said, "is that you mock our Christian festivals."

She gave me a kiss and took the wine, and I followed her in. There was a fire in her small living room and on the coffee table some caponata and triangles of Syrian bread. There was a good cooking smell mixed with the woodsmoke. I sniffed. "Onions," I said, "and peppers."

"Yes," she said, "and mushrooms. And rice pilaf. And when the fire burns down and the coals are right, you can grill two steaks, and we'll eat."

"And then?" I said.

"Then maybe some Wayne King albums on the stereo and waltz till dawn."

"Can we dip?"

"Certainly, but you have to wait for the music. No dipping before it starts. Want a beer?"

"I know where," I said.

"I'll say."

"White wine and soda for you?"

She nodded. I got a bottle of Beck's out of her poppy-red refrigerator and poured white wine from a big green jug into a tall glass. I put in ice, soda, and a twist of lime, and gave it to her. We went back into the living room and sat on her couch, and I put my arm around her shoulder and laid my head back against the couch and closed my eyes.

"You look like the dragon won today," she said.

"No, didn't even see one. I spent the day in the BPL looking at microfilm."

She sipped her wine and soda. "You freebooters do have an adventurous life, don't you?" With her left hand she reached up and touched my left hand as it rested on her shoulder.

"Well, some people find the search for truth exciting."

"Did you find some?" she said.

"Some," I said. Susan drew a series of small circles on the back of my hand with her forefinger. "Or at least some facts. Truth is a little harder, maybe."

I took a small triangle of Syrian bread and picked up some caponata with it and ate it and drank some beer.

"It's hard to hug and eat simultaneously," I said.

"For you that may be the definition of a dilemma," she said.

She sipped at her wine. I finished my beer. A log on the fire settled. I heaved myself off the couch and went to the kitchen for more beer. When I came back, I stood in the archway between the living room and dining room and looked at her.

She had on a white mannish-looking shirt of oxford cloth with a button-down collar, and an expensive brown skirt and brown leather boots, the kind that wrinkle at the ankles. Her feet were up on the coffee table. Around her neck two thin gold chains showed where the shirt was open. She wore them almost all the time. She had on big gold earrings; her face was thoroughly made up. There were fine lines around her eyes, and her black hair shone. She watched me looking at her. There stirred behind her face a sense of life and purpose and mirth and caring that made her seem to be in motion even as she was still. There was a kind of rhythm to her, even in motionless repose. I said, "Energy contained by grace, maybe."

She said, "I beg your pardon?"

I said, "I was just trying to find a phrase to describe the quality you have of festive tranquility."

"That's an oxymoron," she said.

"Well, it's not my fault," I said.

"You know damn well what an oxymoron is," she said. "I just wanted you to know that I know."

"You know everything you need to," I said.

"Sit down," she said, "and tell me what you found out in the library."

I sat beside her, put my feet up beside hers and my arm back around her shoulder, leaned my head back on the couch, closed my eyes, and said, "I found out that the Belmont Vigilance Committee is a somewhat larger operation than I would have thought. It was founded during the Korean war by English's father to combat the clear menace of Communist subversion in this country. Old man English managed to stave off the commies until his death in 1965, at which time the family business, which as far as I can tell is anti-Communism, passed into the hands of his only son, Lawrence

262

Turnbull English, Junior. There was a daughter, Geraldine Julia English, but she went off to Goucher College and then got married and dropped out of things. Probably got radicalized in college, mixing with all those com-symp professors. Anyway there's Lawrence Junior, Harvard '61, and his momma, who looks like Victor McLaglen, living in the old homestead, with fifteen million or so to keep them from the cold, running the committee and spreading the gospel and opening new chapters and stamping out sedition as fast as it springs up. The committee has chapters in most of the metropolitan colleges, some high schools, and most neighborhoods across the Commonwealth. Ninety-six chapters by last count, which was 1977. They sprung up like toadstools in the Boston neighborhoods when busing was hot. There's chapters in South Boston, Dorchester, Hyde Park, all over. Lawrence Junior was right there on the barricades when the buses rolled into South Boston High. He got arrested once for obstructing traffic and once for failing to obey the lawful order of a policeman. Both times his mom had someone down to post bond by the time the wagon got to the jail. Second time he filed suit alleging police brutality on the part of a big statie from Fitchburg named Thomas J. Fogarty, who apparently helped him into the wagon with the front end of his right boot. Case was dismissed."

"And that's what English does? Run the Vigilance Committee."

"I only know what I read in the papers," I said. "If they are right, that seems to be the case. A real patriot. Keeping his fifteen million safe from the reds."

"And the daughter isn't involved?"

"There's nothing about her. Last entry was about her marriage to some guy from Philadelphia in 1968. She was twenty."

"What's she do now?" Susan said. She was making her circles on the back of my hand again.

"I don't know. Why do you care?"

"I don't—I was just curious. Trying to be interested in your work, cookie."

"It's a woman's role," I said.

She said, "I spent the day talking to the parents of learning-disabled children."

"Is that educatorese for dummies?"

"Oh, you sensitive devil. No, it isn't. It's kids with dys-lexia, for instance—that sort of thing."

"How were the parents?"

"Well, the first one wanted to know if this had to go on his record. The kid is in the eleventh grade and can't really read.

"I said that I wasn't sure what she meant about the record. And she said if it were on his record that the kid was dyslexic, wouldn't that adversely affect his chances of going to a good college."

"Least she's got her priorities straight," I said.

"And the next mother—the fathers don't usually come—the next mother said it was our job to teach the kid, and she was sick of hearing excuses."

I said, "I think I might have had a better time in the library."

She said, "The coals look pretty good. Would you like to handle the steaks?"

"Where does it say that cooking steaks is man's work?" I said.

Her eyes crinkled and her face brightened. "Right above the section on what sexual activity one can look forward to after steak and mushrooms."

"I'll get right on the steaks," I said.

CHAPTER TWENTY

SUSAN WENT TO work in the bright, new-snow suburban morning just before eight. I stayed and cleaned up last night's dishes and made the bed and took a shower. There was no point banging heads with commuter traffic.

At eleven minutes after ten I walked into the arcade of the Park Square Building to talk with Manfred Roy. He wasn't there. The head man at the barber shop told me that Manfred had called in sick and was probably home in bed.

I said, "He still living down on Commonwealth Avenue?"

The barber said, "I don't know where he lives."

I said, "Probably does. I'll stop by and see how he is."

The barber shrugged and went back to trimming a neat semi-circle around some guy's ear. I went out and strolled down Berkeley Street two blocks to Commonwealth. When we had first put the arm on Manfred, he was living on the river side, near the corner of Dartmouth Street. I walked up the mall toward the address. The snow on the mall was still clean and fresh from the recent fall. The mall walkway had been cleared and people were walking their dogs along it. Three kids were playing Frisbee and drinking Miller's beer out of clear glass bottles. A woman with a bull terrier walked by. The terrier had on a plaid doggie sweater and was straining at his leash. I thought his little piggie eyes looked very embarrassed, but that was probably anthropomorphism.

At the corner of Dartmouth Street I stopped and waited for the light. Across the street in front of Manfred's apartment four men were sitting in a two-tone blue Pontiac Bonneville. One of them rolled down the window and yelled across the street, "Your name Spenser?"

"Yeah," I said, "S-p-e-n-s-e-r, like the English poet."

"We want to talk with you," he said.

"Jesus," I said, "I wish I'd thought of saying that."

They piled out of the car. The guy that talked was tall and full of sharp corners, like he'd been assembled from Lego blocks. He had on a navy watch cap and a plaid lumberman's jacket and brown pants that didn't get to the tops of his black shoes. His coat sleeves were too short and his knobby wrists stuck out. His hands were very large with angular knuckles. His jaw moved steadily on something, and as he crossed the street he spat tobacco juice.

The other three were all heavy and looked like men who'd done heavy labor for a long time. The shortest of them had slightly bowed legs, and there was scar tissue thick around his eyes. His nose was thicker than it should have been. I had some of those symptoms myself, and I knew where he got them. Either he hadn't quit as soon as I had or he'd lost more fights. His face looked like a catcher's mitt.

The four of them gathered in front of me on the mall. "What are you doing around here?" the tall one said.

"I'm taking a species count on maggots," I said. "With you four and Manfred I got five right off."

The bow-legged pug said, "He's a smart guy, George. Lemme straighten him out."

George shook his head. He said to me, "You're looking for trouble, you're going to get it. We don't want you bothering Manfred."

"You in the Klan, too?" I said.

"We ain't here to talk, pal," George said.

"You must be in the Klan," I said. "You're a smooth talker and a slick dresser. Where's Manfred—his mom won't let him come out?"

The pug put his right hand flat on my chest and shoved me about two steps backwards. "Get out of here or we'll stomp the shit out of you," he said. He was slow. I hit him two left jabs and a right hook before he even got his hands up. He sat down in the snow.

"No wonder your face got marked up so bad," I said to him. "You got no reflexes."

There was a small smear of blood at the base of the pug's nostrils. He wiped the back of his hand across, and climbed to his feet.

"You gonna get it now," he said.

George made a grab at me, and I hit him in the throat. He rocked back. The other two jumped, and the three of us went down in the snow. Someone hit me on the side of the head. I got the heel of my hand under someone's nose and rammed upward. The owner of the nose cried out in pain. George kicked me in the ribs with his steel-toed work shoes. I rolled away, stuck my fingers in someone's eyes, and rolled up onto my feet. The pug hit me a good combination as I was moving past. If I'd been moving toward him, it would have put me down. One of them jumped on my back. I reached up, got hold of his hair, doubled over, and pulled with his momentum. He went over my shoulder and landed on his back on a park bench. The pug hit me on the side of the jaw and I stumbled. He hit me again, and I rolled away from it and lunged against George. He wrapped his arms around me and tried to hold me. I brought both fists up to the level of his ears and pounded them together with his head in between. He grunted and his grip relaxed. I broke free of him and someone hit me with something larger than a fist and the inside of my head got loud and red and I went down.

When I opened my eyes there were granules of snow on the lashes; they looked like magnified salt crystals. There was no sound and no movement. Then there was a snuffing sound. I rolled my eyes to the left, and over the small rim of snow I could see a black nose with slight pink outlinings. It snuffed at me. I shifted my head slightly and said, *"Uff."* The nose pulled back. It was on one end of a dog, an apprehensive young Dalmatian that stood with its front legs stiffened and its hindquarters raised and its tail making uncertain wags.

Lifting my head was too hard. I put it back in the snow. The dog moved closer and snuffed at me again. I heard someone yell, "Digger!" The dog shuffled his feet uncertainly.

Someone yelled, "Digger!" again, and the dog moved away. I took a deep breath. It hurt my ribcage. I exhaled, inhaled again, inched my arms under me, and pushed myself up onto my hands and knees. My head swam. I felt my stomach tighten, and I threw up, which hurt the ribs some more. I stayed that way for a bit, on my hands and knees with my head hanging, like a winded horse. My eyes focused a little better. I could see the snow and the dog's footprints, beyond them the legs of a park bench. I crawled over, got hold of it, and slowly got myself upright. Everything blurred for a minute, then came back into focus again. I inhaled some more and felt a little steadier. I looked around. The mall was empty. The Dalmatian was a long way down the mall now, walking with a man and woman. The snow where I stood was trampled and churned. There was a lot of blood spattered on the snow. Across the street in front of Manfred's apartment the Pontiac was gone. I felt my mouth with my left hand. It was swollen, but no teeth were loose. My nose seemed okay, too.

I let go of the bench and took a step. My ribs were stiff and sore. My head ached. I had to wait for a moment while dizziness came and went. I touched the back of my head. It was swollen and wet with blood. I took a handful of snow from the bench seat and held it against the swollen part. Then I took another step, and another. I was under way. My apartment was three blocks away—one block to Marlborough Street, two blocks down toward the Public Garden. I figured I'd make it by sundown.

Actually I made it before sundown. It wasn't quite noon when I let myself in and locked the door behind me. I took two aspirin with a glass of milk, made some black coffee, added a large shot of Irish whiskey and a teaspoon of sugar, and sipped it while I got undressed. I examined myself in the bathroom mirror. One eye was swollen and my lower lip was puffy. There was a seeping lump on the back of my head and a developing bruise that was going to be a lulu on my right side. But the ribs didn't appear to be broken, and in fact there seemed to be nothing but surface damage. I took a long hot shower and put on clean clothes and had some more coffee and whiskey, and cooked myself two lambchops for lunch. I ate the lambchops with black bread, drank some more coffee with whiskey, and cleaned up the kitchen. I felt lousy but alive, and my fourth cup of whiskeyed coffee made me feel less lousy.

I looked into the bedroom at my bed and thought about lying down for a minute and decided not to. I took out my gun and spun the cylinder, made sure everything worked smoothly, put the gun back in my hip holster again, and went back out of my apartment.

I walked the three blocks back to Manfred's place a lot faster than I had walked from Manfred's two hours earlier. I was not sprightly, but I was moving steadily along.

CHAPTER TWENTY-ONE

WHEN I RANG the bell Manfred's mom came to the door. She was thin and small, wearing a straight striped dress and white sneakers with a hole cut in one of them to relieve pressure on a bunion. Her hair was short and looked as if it had been trimmed with a jackknife. Her face was small, and all the features were clustered in the middle of it. She wore no makeup.

I said, "Good afternoon, ma'am. Is Manfred Roy here, please?"

She looked at my face uneasily. "He's having his lunch," she said. Her voice was very deep.

I stepped partway into the apartment and said, "I'll be glad to wait, ma'am. Tell him I have some good news about Spenser."

She stood uncertainly in the doorway. I edged a little further into the apartment. She edged back a little.

269

Manfred called from another room, "Who is it, Ma?"

"Man says he has good news about Spenser," she said. I smiled at her benignly. Old Mr. Friendly.

Manfred appeared in the archway to my right. He had a napkin tucked in his belt and a small milk mustache on his upper lip. When he saw me, he stopped dead.

"The good news is that I'm not badly hurt, good buddy," I said. "Ain't that swell?"

Manfred backed up a step. "I don't know nothing about that, Spenser."

"About what?" his mother said. I edged all the way past her.

"About what, Manfred?" I said. His mom still stood with one hand on the doorknob.

"I didn't have nothing to do with you getting beat up."

"I'll not be able to say the same about you, Manfred."

Mrs. Roy said, "What do you want here? You said you had good news. You lied to get in here."

"True," I said. "I did lie. But if I hadn't lied, sort of, then you wouldn't have let me in, and I'd have had to kick in your door. I figured the lie was cheaper."

"Don't you threaten my mother," Manfred said.

"No, I won't. It's you I came to threaten, Manfred."

Mrs. Roy said, "Manfred, I'm going for the police," and started out into the hall.

"No, Ma. Don't do that," Manfred said. Mrs. Roy stopped in the hall and looked back at him. Her eyes were sick.

"Why shouldn't I go to the police, Manfred?"

"They wouldn't understand," Manfred said. "He'd lie to them. They'd believe him. I'd get in trouble."

"Are you from the niggers?" she said to me.

"I represent a woman named Rachel Wallace, Mrs. Roy. She was kidnaped. I think your son knows something about it. I spoke to him about it yesterday and said I'd come visit him today. This morning four men who knew my name and recognized me on sight were parked in a car outside your apartment. When I arrived, they beat me up."

Mrs. Roy's eyes looked sicker—a sickness that must have gone back a long way. A lifetime of hearing hints that her son wasn't right. That he didn't get along. That he was in trouble or around it. A lifetime of odd people coming to the door and Manfred hustling in and out and not saying exactly what was up. A lifetime sickness of repressing the almost-sure knowledge that your firstborn was very wrong.

"I didn't have nothing to do with that, Ma. I don't know nothing about a kidnaping. Spenser just likes to come and push me around. He knows I don't like his nigger friends. Well, some of my friends don't like him pushing me around."

"My boy had nothing to do with any of that," Mrs. Roy said. Her voice was guttural with tension.

"Then you ought to call the cops, Mrs. Roy. I'm trespassing. And I won't leave."

Mrs. Roy didn't move. She stood with one foot in the hall and one foot in the apartment.

Manfred turned suddenly and ran back through the archway. I went after him. To the left was the kitchen, to the right a short corridor with two doors off it. Manfred went through the nearest one, and when I reached him, he had a short automatic pistol halfway out of the drawer of a bedside table. With the heel of my right fist I banged the drawer shut on his hand. He cried out once. I took the back of his shirt with my left hand and yanked him back toward me and into the hall, spinning him across my body and slamming him against the wall opposite the bedroom door. Then I took the gun out of the drawer. It was a Mauser HSc, a 7.65mm pistol that German pilots used to carry in World War II.

I took the clip out, ran the action back to make sure there was nothing in the chamber, and slipped the pistol in my hip pocket.

Manfred stood against the wall sucking on the bruised fingers of his right hand. His mother had come down the hall and stood beside him, her hands at her side. "What did he take from you?" she said to Manfred.

I took the pistol out. "This, Mrs. Roy. It was in a drawer beside the bed."

"It's for protection, Ma."

"You got a license for this, Manfred?"

"Course I do."

"Lemme see it."

"I don't have to show you. You're not on the cops no more."

"You don't have a permit do you, Manfred?" I smiled a big smile. "You know what the Massachusetts handgun law says?"

"I got a license."

"The Massachusetts handgun law provides that anyone convicted of the possession of an unlicensed handgun gets a mandatory one-year jail sentence. Sentence may not be suspended nor parole granted. That's a year in the joint, Manfred."

"Manfred, do you have a license?" his mother said.

He shook his head. All four fingers of his bruised right hand were in his mouth and he sucked at them.

Mrs. Roy looked at me. "Don't tell," she said.

"Ever been in the joint, Manfred?"

With his fingers still in his mouth Manfred shook his head.

"They do a lot of bad stuff up there, Manfred. Lot of homosexuality. Lot of hatred. Small blond guys tend to be in demand."

"Don't tell," his mother said. She had moved betwen me and Manfred. Manfred's eyes were squeezed nearly shut. There were tears in the corners.

I smiled my nice big smile at his mother. Old Mr. Friendly. Here's how your kid's going to get raped in the slammer, ma'am.

"Maybe we can work something out," I said. "See, I'm looking for Rachel Wallace. If you gave me any help on that, I'd give you back your Mauser and speak no ill of you to the fuzz."

I was looking at Manfred but I was talking for his mother, too.

"I don't know nothing about it," Manfred mumbled

around his fingers. He seemed to have shrunk in on himself, as if his stomach hurt.

I shook my head sadly. "Talk to him, Mrs. Roy. I don't want to have to put him away. I'm sure you need him here to look after you."

Mrs. Roy's face was chalky, and the lines around her mouth and eyes were slightly reddened. She was beginning to breathe hard, as if she'd been running. Her mouth was open a bit, and I noticed that her front teeth were gone.

"You do what he says, Manfred. You help this man like he says." She didn't look at Manfred as she talked. She stood between him and me and looked at me.

I didn't say anything. None of us did. We stood nearly still in the small hallway. Manfred snuffed a little. Some pipes knocked.

Still looking at me, with Manfred behind her, Mrs. Roy said, "God damn you to hell, you little bastard, you do what this man says. You're in trouble. You've always been in trouble. Thirty years old and you still live with your mother and never go out of the house except to those crazy meetings. Whyn't you leave the niggers alone? Whyn't you let the government take care of them? Whyn't you get a good job or get an education or get a woman or get the hell out the house once in awhile, and not get in trouble? Now this man's going to put you in jail unless you do what he says, and you better the hell damn well goddamned do it." She was crying by the time she got halfway through, and her ugly little face looked a lot worse.

And Manfred was crying. "Ma," he said.

I smiled as hard as I could, my big friendly smile. The Yuletide spirit. 'Tis the season to be jolly.

"All my life," she said. Now she was sobbing, and she turned and put her arms around him. "All my rotten goddamn life I've been saddled with you and you've been queer and awful and I've worried all about you by myself and no man in the house."

"Ma," Manfred said, and they both cried full out.

I felt awful.

"I'm looking for Rachel Wallace," I said. "I'm going to find her. Anything that I need to do, I'll do."

"Ma," Manfred said. "Don't, Ma. I'll do what he says. Ma, don't."

I crossed my arms and leaned on the doorjamb and looked at Manfred. It was not easy to do. I wanted to cry, too.

"What do you want me to do, Spenser?"

"I want to sit down and have you tell me anything you've heard or can guess or have imagined about who might have taken Rachel Wallace."

"I'll try to help, but I don't know nothing."

"We'll work on that. Get it together, and we'll sit down and talk. Mrs. Roy, maybe you could make us some coffee."

She nodded. The three of us walked back down the hall. Me last. Mrs. Roy went to the kitchen. Manfred and I went to the living room. The furniture was brightly colored imitation velvet with a lot of antimacassars on the arms. The antimacassars were the kind you buy in Woolworth's, not the kind anyone ever made at home. There was a big new color TV set in one corner of the room.

I sat in one of the bright fuzzy chairs. It was the color of a Santa Claus suit. Manfred stood in the archway. He still had his napkin tucked into his belt.

"What you want to know?" he said.

"Who do you think took Rachel Wallace?" I said. "And where do you think she is?"

"Honest to God, Spenser, I got no idea."

"What is the most anti-feminist group you know of?"

"Anti-feminist?"

"Yeah. Who hates women's lib the most?"

"I don't know about any group like that."

"What do you know about RAM, which stands for Restore American Morality?" I said. I could hear Manfred's mom in the kitchen messing with cookware.

"I never heard of it."

"How about the Belmont Vigilance Committee?"

"Oh, sure, that's Mr. English's group. We coordinated some of the forced-busing tactics with them."

"You know English?"

"Oh, yes. Very wealthy, very important man. He worked closely with us."

"How tough is he?"

"He will not retreat in the face of moral decay and godless Communism."

"Manfred, don't make a speech at me—I'm too old to listen to horseshit. I want to know if he's got the balls to kidnap someone, or if he's crazy enough. Or if he's got the contacts to have someone do it."

"Mr. English wouldn't hesitate to do the right thing," Manfred said.

"Would he know how to arrange a kidnaping?" I said. "And don't give me all that canned tripe in the answer."

Manfred nodded.

"Who would do it for him?" I said.

Manfred shook his head. "I don't know any names, I promise I don't. I just see him with people, and, you know, they're the kind that would know about that kind of stuff."

Mrs. Roy brought in some instant coffee in white mugs that had pictures of vegetables on them. She'd put some Oreo cookies on a plate and she put the two cups and the plate down on a yellow plastic molded coffee table with a translucent plastic top that had been finished to imitate frosted glass.

I said, "Thank you, Mrs. Roy."

Manfred didn't look at her. She didn't look at him, either. She nodded her head at me to acknowledge the thanks and went back to the kitchen. She didn't want to hear what Manfred was saying.

"I heard he could get anything done and that he was a good man if you needed anything hard done, or you needed to hire anyone for special stuff."

"Like what?" I sipped at the coffee. The water had been added to the coffee before it was hot enough, and the coffee wasn't entirely dissolved. I swallowed and put the cup down.

"You know."

"No, I don't, Manfred. Like what?"

"Well, if you needed people for, like, you know, like fighting and getting things done."

"Like the baboons that pounded on me this morning?"

"I didn't hire them, Spenser. They're from the organization. They wanted to make sure I wasn't bothered."

"Because you are a Klan mucky-muck?" I said. "Second Assistant Lizard?"

"I'm an official. And they were looking out for me. We stick together."

Manfred's voice tried for dignity, but he kept staring at the floor, and dignity is hard, while you're looking at the floor.

"Ever meet his mother or his sister?"

"No."

"Know anything about them?"

"No."

"Manfred, you are not being a help."

"I'm trying, Spenser. I just don't know nothing. I never heard of Rachel Whosis."

"Wallace," I said. "Rachel Wallace."

CHAPTER TWENTY-TWO

MANFRED AND I chatted for another hour with no better results. Hardly seemed worth getting beat up for. When I left, Mrs. Roy didn't come to say goodbye, and Manfred didn't offer to shake hands. I got even—I didn't wish them Merry Christmas.

It was a little after three when I got back out onto Commonwealth. The whiskey and aspirin had worn off, and I hurt. A three-block walk and I could be in bed, but that wouldn't be looking for Rachel Wallace. That would be taking a nap. Instead I walked down to Berkeley and up three blocks to Police Headquarters to talk with Quirk.

He was there and so was Belson. Quirk had his coat off and his sleeves rolled up. He was squeezing one of those little red rubber grip strengtheners with indentations for the fingers He did ten in one hand and switched it to the other and did ten more.

"Trying to keep your weight down, Marty?" I said.

Quirk switched the grip strengthener back to his right hand. "Your face looks good," he said.

"I bumped into a door," I said.

"About fifteen times," Belson said. "You come in to make a complaint?"

I shook my head. It made my face hurt. "I came by to see how you guys are making out looking for Rachel Wallace."

"We got shit," Quirk said.

"Anything on those license-tag numbers I gave you?"

Quirk nodded. "The Buick belongs to a guy named Swisher Cody. Used to be a big basketball star at Hyde Park High in the Fifties, where he got the nickname. Dodge belongs to a broad named Mary Stevenson. Says she lets her boyfriend use it all the time. Boyfriend's name is Michael Mulready. He's a pal of Swisher's. They both tell us that they were together the night you say they tried to run you off the road and that they were playing cards with Mulready's cousin Mingo at his place in Watertown. Mingo says that's right. Cody's done time for loansharking. Mingo, too."

"So you let them go," I said.

Quirk shrugged. "Even if we didn't believe them and we believe you, what have we got them for? Careless driving? We let 'em go and we put a tail on them."

"And?"

"And nothing. They both go to work in the Sears warehouse in Dorchester. They stop on the way home for a few beers. They go to bed. Sometimes they drive out to Watertown and play cards with Cousin Mingo."

I nodded. "How about English?"

Quirk nodded at Belson.

Belson said, "Pretty much what you heard. He's chairman of the Vigilance Committee."

"Eternal vigilance is the price of liberty," Quirk said, and squeezed his grip exerciser hard so that the muscles in his forearm looked like suspension cables.

Belson said, "Spenser been lending you books again, Marty?"

Quirk shook his head. "Naw, my kid's taking U.S. History. He's almost as smart as Spenser."

"Maybe he'll straighten out," I said. "What else you got on English?"

Belson shrugged. "Nothing you don't know. He's got money—he thinks it makes him important, and he's probably right. He's got the IQ of a fieldmouse. And he's got an alibi to cover any time Rachel Wallace might have been kidnaped. Did you meet his mother?"

"No. I've seen her picture."

"Ain't she a looker?" He looked at Quirk. "We ever have to bust her, Marty, I want you to send some hard-ass kids from the tac squad. You and me'd get hurt."

"She as nice as she looks?" I said.

"Nowhere near that nice," Belson said. "She sat in while we questioned sonny and tended to answer whatever we asked him. I told her finally, why didn't she hold him on her knee and he could move his lips? She told me she'd see to it that I never worked for any police department in this state."

"You scared?" I said.

"Hell, no," Belson said. "I'm relieved. I thought she was going to kill me."

"She active in the committee?" I said.

"She didn't say," Belson said, "but I'd guess yes. I have the feeling she's active in anything sonny is active in. He doesn't get a hard-on without checking with her."

"You run any check on the family? There's a sister."

Quirk said, "What the hell do you think we do in here—make up Dick Tracy Crimestoppers? Of course we ran a check on the family. Sister's name is Geraldine."

"I know that, for crissake—Geraldine Julia English, Goucher College class of '68."

Quirk went on as if I hadn't said anything. "Geraldine Julia English. Married a guy named Walton Wells in June, 1968, divorced 1972. Works as a model in Boston."

"Wells," I said.

"Yeah, Walton Wells—slick name, huh?"

"Geraldine Julia Wells would be her married name."

Belson said, "You were wrong, Marty. Your kid couldn't be nearly as smart as Spenser."

"What model agency she with?"

Belson said, "Carol Cobb."

"She use her married name?"

"Yeah."

"And her middle name instead of her first, I bet."

Quirk said, "Nobody could be nearly as smart as Spenser."

"She bills herself as Julie Wells, doesn't she?"

Belson nodded.

"Gentlemen," I said, "what we have here is your basic clue. Julie Wells, who is Lawrence Turnbull English, Junior's, sister, was intimate with Rachel Wallace."

"Intimate intimate or just friendly intimate," Quirk said.

"Intimate intimate," I said.

"How do you know this?" Quirk said.

I told him.

"Nice you told us first thing," Quirk said. "Nice you mentioned her name at the beginning of the investigation so we could follow up every possible lead. Very nice." There was no amusement in Quirk's voice now."

"I should have told you," I said. "I was wrong."

"You bet your ass you were wrong," Quirk said. "Being wrong like that tends to put your balls in the fire, too—you know that?"

"You're not the Holy Ghost, Quirk. None of you guys are. I don't have to run in and report everything I know to you every day. I made a guess that this broad was okay, and I didn't want to smell up her rose garden by dragging her into this. Can't you see the *Herald American* headline

LESBIAN LOVER SUSPECT IN KIDNAPING."

"And maybe you guessed wrong, hot shot, and maybe your girl friend Rachel is dead and gone because you didn't tell us something."

"Or maybe it doesn't mean a goddamned thing," I said. "Maybe you're making a big goddamned event out of nothing." I was leaning back in my chair, one foot propped against the edge of Quirk's desk. He leaned over and slapped the foot away.

"And get your goddamned foot off my desk," he said.

I stood up and so did Quirk.

"Dynamite," Belson said. "You guys fight to the death, and the winner gets to look for Rachel Wallace." He scratched a wooden match on the sole of his shoe and lit a new cigar.

Still standing, Quirk said, "How much do you pay for those goddamned weeds anyway?"

Between puffs to get the cigar going Belson said, "Fifteen cents apiece."

Quirk sat down. "You get screwed," he said.

"They're cheap," Belson said, "but they smell bad."

I sat down.

Quirk said, "Okay. Julie Wells is a member of the English family." He was leaning back now in his swivel chair, his head tipped, staring up at the ceiling, his hands resting on the arms. The rubber grip squeezer lay on the nearly empty desk in front of him. "She is also an intimate of Rachel Wallace. Which means she's gay or at least bisexual." I put one foot up on Quirk's desk again. "Her brother on the other hand is out picketing Rachel Wallace and calling her a dyke and telling her she's immoral and must be stopped," Quirk said.

"We have here a family conflict," Belson said. "And at least an odd coincidence."

"It could be only that," I said.

Quirk's eyes came down from the ceiling and he let the swivel chair come forward until his feet touched the floor.

"It could be," he said. "But it don't do us a lot of good to assume that it is."

"We better get together on how we're going to handle this," I said. "We don't want to charge in and hit her with it, do we?"

"You had your chance to get together with us on this, hot shot, and you didn't take it. We'll decide how to handle it."

"You want to teach me a lesson, Quirk," I said, "or you want to find Rachel Wallace?"

"Both," he said. "Take a walk."

"How about an address for Cody and Mulready?"

"Blow," Quirk said.

I toyed with saying, "I shall return." Figured it was not appropriate and left without a word. As I left Belson blew a smoke ring at me.

CHAPTER TWENTY-THREE

I WENT HOME feeling lousy. My face hurt, so did my ribs. I'd been making people mad at me all day. I needed someone to tell me I was swell. I called Susan. She wasn't home. I had a bottle of Molson's ale, took two aspirin, made a meatloaf sandwich with lettuce, ate it, drank two more ales with it, and went to bed. I dreamed I was locked in a castle room and Susan kept walking by and smiling when I yelled for help. I woke up mad at her, at five minutes of seven in the morning.

When I got up, I forgot about being mad at Susan. I was mad at my body. I could barely walk. I clanked over to the bathroom, and got under the hot water in the shower, and stretched a little while the hot water ran over me. I was in there for maybe half an hour, and when I got out I had corn-bread and country sausage and broiled tomato for breakfast and read the *Globe.* Then I put on my gun and went looking for Mulready and Cody.

It was snowing again as I drove on the Southeast Expressway to Dorchester, and the wind was blowing hard so that the snow swirled and eddied in the air. I was going against the commuter rush, but still the traffic was slow, cautious in the snowfall. I slithered off the exit ramp at the big Sears warehouse, stopped at the guard shack, got directions to the main pick-up point, and drove to it.

Quirk had been childish not to give me the addresses. He'd already mentioned that they worked at the Sears warehouse, and he knew I'd go out and find them that way. Immature. Churlish.

I turned up the fleece collar of my jacket before I got out of the car. I put on a blue navy watch cap and a pair of sunglasses. I checked myself in the rearview mirror. Unrecognizable. One of my cleverest disguises. I was impersonating a man dressed for winter. I got out and walked to the warehouse pick-up office.

"Swisher or Michael around?" I said to the young woman behind the call desk.

"Cody and Mulready?"

I nodded.

"They're out back. I can call them on the horn here."

"Yeah, would ya? Tell them Mingo's out here."

She said into the microphone, "Swisher Cody, Michael Mulready, please report to the call desk. A Mr. Mingo is here."

There were three other people in the call office, two of them men. I stood behind the others as we waited. In less than two minutes two men came through the swinging doors behind the desk and glanced around the room. One of them was tall with a big red broken-veined nose and long sideburns. His short hair was reddish with a sprinkling of gray. The other man was much younger. He had blow-dried black hair, a thick black mustache, and a seashell necklace tight around his throat. Contemporary.

I said, "Hey, Swisher."

The tall one with the red hair turned first, then they both looked at me.

"I got a message for you guys from Mingo," I said. "Can you come around?"

Mustache started toward the hinged end of the counter and Red Hair stopped him. He said something I couldn't hear, then they both looked at me again. Then Mustache said something I couldn't hear, then they both bolted through the swinging doors back into the warehouse. So much for my disguise wizardry.

I said, "Excuse me," to the woman waiting for her pickup and vaulted the counter.

The young lady behind the counter said, "Sir, you can't . . ."

I was through the swinging doors and into the warehouse. There were vast aisles of merchandise and down the center aisle Cody and Mulready were hot-footing it to the rear. The one with the mustache, Mulready, was a step or two behind Cody. I only needed one. I caught them as they were fumbling with a door that said Emergency Only. Cody had it open when I took Mulready from behind. Cody went on out into the snow. I dragged Mulready back.

He turned and tried to knee me in the groin. I turned my hip into his body and blocked him. I got a good grip of shirt front with both hands and pressed him up and backwards until his feet were off the ground and his back was against the wall beside the door. The door had a pneumatic closer and swung slowly shut. I put my face close up to Mulready's and said, "You really got a cousin named Mingo Mulready?"

"What the fuck's wrong with you?" he said. "Lemme the fuck down. What are you, crazy?"

"You know what I'm doing, Michael baby," I said. "You know 'cause you ran when you recognized me."

"I don't know you. Lemme the fuck down."

I banged him once, hard, against the wall.

"You tried to run me and Rachel Wallace off the road a while ago in Lynn. I'm looking for Rachel Wallace, and I'm going to find her, and I don't mind if I have to break things to do it."

Behind me I could hear footsteps coming at a trot. Someone yelled, "Hey, you!"

I pulled Mulready away from the wall and banged him against the safety bar on the emergency door. It opened, and I shoved him through, sprawling into the snow. I followed him outside. The door swung shut behind me. Mulready tried to scramble to his feet. I kicked him in the stomach. I was wearing my Herman survivor boots, double-insulated with a heavy sole. He gasped. The kick rolled him over onto his back in the snow. He tried to keep rolling. I landed on his chest with both knees. He made a croaking noise.

I said, "I will beat you into whipped cream, Michael, if you don't do just what I say." Then I stood up, yanked him to his feet, got a hold on the back of his collar, and ran him toward my car. He was doubled over with pain, and the wind was knocked out of him and he was easy to move. I shoved him into the front seat, driver's side, put my foot on his backside, and shoved him across to the passenger's side, got in after him, and skidded into reverse. In the rearview mirror I could see three, then four men and the girl from the call counter coming out the emergency exit. I shifted into third and pulled out of the parking lot and past the gate house; the guard gestured at us. I turned right through the parking lot at the Howard Johnson's motel and out onto the Southeast Expressway.

In the rearview mirror all was serene. The snow slanted in across the road steadily. Beside me Mulready was getting his breath back.

"Where you going with me?" he said. His voice was husky with strain.

"Just riding," I said. "I'm going to ask you questions, and when you've answered them all, and I'm happy with what you've said, I'll drop you off somewhere convenient."

"I don't know anything about anything."

284

"In that case," I said, "I will pull in somewhere and maybe kill you."

"For what, man? We didn't do you no harm. We didn't plan to do you in. We were supposed to scare you and the broad."

"You mean Ms. Wallace, scumbag."

"Huh?"

"Call her Ms. Wallace. Don't call her 'the broad'."

"Okay, sure, Ms. Wallace. Okay by me. We weren't trying to hurt Ms. Wallace or you, man."

"Who told you to do that?"

"Whaddya mean?"

I shook my head. "You are going to get yourself in very bad trouble," I said. I reached under my coat and brought out my gun and showed it to him. "Smith and Wesson," I said, "thirty-eight caliber, four-inch barrel. Not good for long range, but perfect for shooting a guy sitting next to you."

"Jesus, man, put the piece down. I just didn't understand the question, you know? I mean, What is it you're asking, man? I'll try. You don't need the fucking piece, you know?"

I put the gun back. We were in Milton now; traffic was very thin in the snow. "I said, Who told you to scare us up on the Lynnway that night?"

"My cousin, man—Mingo. He told us about doing it. Said there was a deuce in it for us. Said we could split a deuce for doing it. Mingo, man. You know him?"

"Why did Mingo want you to scare me and Ms. Wallace?"

"I don't know, man, it was just an easy two bills. Swisher says it's a tit. Says he knows how to work it easy. He done time, Swisher. Mingo don't say why, man. He just lays the deuce on us—we ain't asking no questions. A couple hours' drive for that kind of bread, man, we don't even know who you are."

"Then how'd you pick us up?"

"Mingo gave us a picture of the bro—Ms. Wallace. We followed her when you took her out to Marblehead. We hung

285

around till you took her home, and there wasn't much traffic. You know? Then we made our move like he said—Mingo."

"What's Mingo do?"

"You mean for a living?"

"Yeah."

"He works for some rich broad in Belmont."

"Doing what?"

"I don't know. Everything. Drives her around. Carry stuff when she shops. Errands. That shit. He's got it made, man."

"What's her name?"

"The rich broad?" Mulready shrugged. His breath was back. I had put the gun away. He was talking, which was something he obviously had practiced at. He was beginning to relax a little. "I don't know," he said. "I don't think Mingo ever said."

At Furnace Brook Parkway I went off the expressway, reversed directions, and came back on heading north.

"Where we going now?" Mulready said.

"We're going to go visit Cousin Mingo," I said. "You're going to show me where he lives."

"Oh, fuck me, man. I can't do that. Mingo will fucking kill me."

"But that will be later," I said. "If you don't show me I'll kill you now."

"No, man, you don't know Mingo. He is a bad-ass son of a bitch. I'm telling you now, man, you don't want to fuck with Mingo."

"I told you, Michael. I'm looking for Rachel Wallace. I told you back in the warehouse that I'd break things if I had to. You're one of the things I'll break."

"Well, shit, man, lemme tell you, and then drop me off. Man, I don't want Mingo to know it was me. You don't know what he's fucking like, man."

"What's his real name?" I said.

"Eugene, Eugene Ignatius Mulready."

"We'll check a phonebook," I said.

In Milton I pulled off the expressway and we checked the listing in an outdoor phone booth. It didn't list Watertown.

"That's in the West Suburban book," Michael said. "They only got Boston and South Suburban here."

"Observant," I said. "We'll try Information."

"Christ, you think I'm lying? Hey, man, no way. You know? No way I'm going to bullshit you, man, with the piece you're carrying. I mean my old lady didn't raise no stupid kids, you know?"

I put in a dime and dialed Information. "In Watertown," I said. "The number for Eugene I. Mulready—what's the address, Michael?"

He told me. I told the operator.

"The number is eight-nine-nine," she said, "seven-three-seven-oh."

I said thank you and hung up. The dime came back.

"Okay, Michael, you're on your way."

"From here?"

"Yep."

"Man, I got no coat—I'll freeze my ass."

"Call a cab."

"A cab? From here? I ain't got that kind of bread, man."

I took the dime out of the return slot. "Here," I said. "Call your buddy Swiswher. Have him come get you."

"What if he ain't home?"

"You're a grown-up person, Michael. You'll figure something out. But I'll tell you one thing—you call and warn Mingo, and you won't grow up any more."

"I ain't going to call Mingo, man. I'd have to tell him I tipped you."

"That's what I figure," I said. I got in my car. Michael Mulready was standing shivering in his shirt sleeves, his hands in his pants pocket, his shoulders hunched.

"I give you one tip though, pal," he said. "You got a big surprise coming, you think you can fuck around with Mingo like you done with me. Mingo will fucking destroy you."

"Watch," I said and let the clutch out and left him on the sidewalk.

CHAPTER TWENTY-FOUR

WATERTOWN WAS NEXT to Belmont, but only in location. It was mostly working-class and the houses were shabby, often two-family, and packed close together on streets that weren't plowed well. It was slow going now, the snow coming hard and the traffic overcautious and crawling.

Mingo Mulready's house was square, two stories, with a wide front porch. The cedar shingle siding was painted blue. The asbestos shingles on the roof were multi-colored. I parked on the street and walked across.

There were two front entrance doors. The one on the left said Mulready. I rang the bell. Nothing. I waited a minute, rang it again. Then I leaned on it for about two minutes. Mingo wasn't home. I went back to my car. Mingo was probably off working at his soft job, driving the rich woman around Belmont. I turned on the radio and listened to the news at noon. Two things occurred to me. One was that nothing that ever got reported in the news seemed to have anything to do with me, and the other was that it was lunchtime. I drove about ten blocks to the Eastern Lamjun Bakery on Belmont Street and bought a package of fresh Syrian bread, a pound of feta cheese, and a pound of Calamata olives.

The bread was still warm. Then I went across the street to the package store and bought a six-pack of Beck's beer, then I drove back and parked in front of Mingo's house and had lunch, and listened to a small suburban station that played jazz and big-band music. At three I drove down the block to a gas station and filled my gas tank and used the men's room and drove back up to Mingo's and sat some more.

288

I remembered this kind of work as less boring fifteen years ago when I used to smoke. Probably not so. Probably just seemed that way. At four fifteen Mingo showed up. He was driving a tan Thunderbird with a vinyl roof. He pulled into the driveway beside the house and got out. I got out and walked across the street. We met at the front steps of his home.

I said, "Are you Mingo Mulready?"

He said, "Who wants to know?"

I said, "I say, 'I do,' then you say, 'Who are you?' then I say—"

He said, "What the fuck are you talking about, Jack?"

He was big enough to talk that way, and he must have been used to getting away with it. He was about my height, which made him just under six two, and he was probably twenty-five or thirty pounds heavier, which would have made him 230. He had one of the few honest-to-God bootcamp crew cuts I'd seen in the last eight or ten years. He also had small eyes and a button nose in a doughy face, so that he looked like a mean, palefaced gingerbread man. He was wearing a dark suit and a white shirt and black gloves. He wore no coat.

I said, "Are you Mingo Mulready?"

"I want to know who's asking," he said. "And I want to know pretty quick, or I might stomp your ass."

I was holding my right hand in my left at about belt level. While I was talking I strained the right against the left, so that when I let go with the left, the right snapped up, and the edge of my hand caught Mingo under the nose the way a cocked hammer snaps when you squeeze the trigger. I accelerated it a little on the way up, and the blood spurted from Mingo's nose, and he staggered back about two steps. It was a good shot.

"That's why I wanted to know if you were Mingo," I said. I drove a left hook into the side of his jaw. "Because I didn't want to beat the hell out of some innocent bystander." I put a straight right onto Mingo's nose. He fell down. "But you're such a pain in the ass that you need to get the hell beat out of you even if you aren't Mingo Mulready."

He was not a bunny. I'd sucker-punched him and put two more good shots in his face, and he didn't stay down. He came lunging up at me and knocked me back into the snow and scrambled on top of me. I put the heels of both hands under his chin and drove his head back and half-lifted him off me and rolled away. He came after me again, but that extra thirty pounds wasn't helping him. It was mostly fat, and he was already rasping for breath. I moved in, hit him hard twice in the gut, moved out, and hit him twice on that bloody nose. He sagged. I hit him on each side of the jaw. Left jab, right cross, left jab, right cross. He sagged more. His breath wheezed; his arms dropped. He was arm-weary in the first round.

I said, "Are you Mingo Mulready?"

He nodded.

"You sure?" I said. "I heard you were a bad ass."

He nodded again, wheezing for oxygen.

"I guess I heard wrong," I said. "You work for a rich woman in Belmont?"

He stared at me.

"If you want to keep getting your breath back, you answer what I ask. You don't answer, and you'll think what we did before was dancing."

He nodded.

"You do. What's her name?"

"English," he said.

"She tell you to hire your cousin and his pal Swisher to run me off the road in Lynn?"

He said, "You?"

"Yeah, me. Me and Rachel Wallace. Who told you to harass us?"

He looked toward the street. It was empty. The snow was thin and steady, and darkness had come on. He looked toward the house. It was dark.

He said, "I dunno what you mean."

I hit him a good left hook in the throat. He gasped and clutched at his neck.

I said, "Who told you to run Rachel Wallace off the

road? Who told you to hire your cousin and his pal? Who gave you the two bills?"

He was having trouble speaking. "English," he croacked.

"The old lady or the son?"

"The son."

"Why?"

He shook his head. I moved my left fist. He backed up. "Swear on my mother," he said. "I don't ask them questions. They pay me good. They treat me decent." He stopped and coughed and spit some blood. "I don't ask no questions. I do what they say, they're important people."

"Okay," I said. "Remember, I know where you live. I may come back and talk with you again. If I have to look for you, it will make me mad."

He didn't say anything. I turned and walked across the street to my car. It was very dark now, and in the snow I couldn't even see the car till I was halfway across the street. I opened the door. The inside light went on. Frank Belson was sitting in the front seat. I got in and closed the door.

"For crissake turn the motor on and get the heater going," he said. "I'm freezing my nuts off."

CHAPTER TWENTY-FIVE

"You want a beer?" I said. "There's four left in the backseat."

"I don't drink on duty," he said. He took two bottles of Beck's out of the carton. "For crissake, what kind of beer is this? It doesn't even have a twist-off cap."

"There's an opener in the glove compartment," I said.

Belson opened the two beers, gave one to me and took a long pull on the other bottle.

"What you get from Mingo?"

"I thought I was ostracized," I said.

"You know Marty," Belson said. "He gets mad quick, he cools down quick. What you get from Mingo?"

"Haven't you talked to him?"

"We figured you could talk with him harder than we could. We were right. But I thought he'd give you more trouble than he did."

"I suckered him," I said. "That got him off to a bad start."

"Still," Belson said, "he used to be goddamned good."

"Me, too," I said.

"I know that. What'd you get?"

"English set up the hit-and-run on the Lynnway."

"Mingo do it through his cousin?"

"Yeah."

"Cousin tell you that?"

"Yeah. Him and Cody did the work. Mingo gave them a deuce. He got the money from English. I braced Cousin Michael this morning."

"I know," Belson said.

"What the hell is this—practice teaching? You follow me around and observe?"

"I told you we had Cody and Mulready staked out," Belson said. "When you showed up, the detail called in. I told them to let you go. I figured you'd get more than we would because you don't have to sweat brutality charges. They lost you heading out of Sears, but I figured you'd end up here and I came over. Got here about one thirty and been sitting in the next block since. You get anything else?"

"No. But English is looking better and better. You look into those pie-throwers in Cambridge?"

Belson finished the beer and opened another bottle. "Yeah," he said. "There's nothing there. Just a couple of right-wing fruitcakes. They never been in jail. They don't show any

292

connection with English or Mingo Mulready or the Vigilance Committee or anybody else. They go to MIT, for crissake."

"Okay. How about Julie Wells? You talk to her yet?"

Belson held the beer between his knees while he got a half-smoked cigar out of his shirt pocket and lit it and puffed at it. Then he took the cigar out of his mouth, sipped some beer, put the cigar back in, and said around it, "Can't find her. She doesn't seem to have moved or anything, but she's not at her apartment whenever we show up. We're sort of looking for her."

"Good. You think you might sort of find her in a while?"

"If we'd known some things earlier, buddy, we'd have been more likely to have kept an eye on her."

"Know anything about Mingo? You sound like you've known him before."

"Oh, yeah, old Mingo. He's got a good-sized file. Used to work for Joe Broz once. Used to be a bouncer, did some pro wrestling, some loansharking. Been busted for assault, for armed robbery, been picked up on suspicion of murder and released when we couldn't turn a witness that would talk. English employs some sweetheart to drive the old babe around."

I said, "You people going to keep English under surveillance?"

"Surveillance? Christ, you been watching *Police Woman* again? *Surveillance*. Christ."

I said, "You gonna watch him?"

"Yeah. We'll try to keep someone on him. We ain't got all that many bodies, you know?"

"And he's got money and maybe knows a couple city councilmen and a state senator."

"Maybe. It happens. You know Marty. You know me. But you also know how it works. Pressure comes down, we gotta bend. Or get other work, you know?"

"Felt any pressure yet?"

Belson shook his head. "Nope," he said, "not yet." He finished the bottle of beer.

"Belmont cops?"

"They said they could help out a little."

"You got anybody at Julie Wells's apartment?"

"Yeah. And we check in at the agency regular. She ain't there."

I said, "You want a ride to your car?"

He nodded, and I went around the block and dropped him off on the street behind Mingo's house. "You stumble across anything, you might want to give us a buzz," Belson said as he got out.

"Yeah," I said. "I might."

He said, "Thanks for the beer," and closed my door, and I pulled away. It was almost an hour and a half in the snow and the near-motionless rush hour until I got to my aprtment. Susan was there.

"I had an Adolescent Development Workshop at B.U. this afternoon, and when I got out it was too bad to drive home, so I left my car in the lot and walked down," she said.

"You missed a golden opportunity," I said.

"For what?"

"To take off all your clothes and make a martini and surprise me at the door."

"I thought of that," Susan said, "but you don't like martinis."

"Oh," I said.

"But I made a fire," she said. "And we could have a drink in front of it."

"Or something," I said. I picked her up and hugged her.

She shook her head. "They were talking about you all day today," she said.

"At the workshop on adolescent development?"

She nodded and smiled her fallen-seraph smile at me. "You exhibit every symptom," she said.

I put her down and we went to the kitchen. "Let us see what there is to eat," I said. "Maybe pulverized rhino horn with a dash of Spanish fly."

"You whip up something, snooks," she said. "I'm going

294

to take a bath. And maybe rinse out the pantyhose in your sink."

"A man's work is never done," I said. I looked in the refrigerator. There was Molson Golden Ale on the bottom shelf. If we were snowbound, at least I had staples on hand. In the vegetable keeper there were some fresh basil leaves and a bunch of parsley I'd bought in Quincy Market. It was a little limp but still serviceable. I opened a Molson. I could hear the water running in the bathroom. I raised the bottle of ale, and said, "Here's looking at you, kid," in a loud voice.

Susan yelled back, "Why don't you make me a gimlet, blue eyes, and I'll drink it when I get out. Ten minutes."

"Okay."

In the freezer was chopped broccoli in a twenty-ounce bag. I took it out. I got out a large blue pot and boiled four quarts of water, and a smaller saucepan with a steamer rack and boiled about a cup of water. While it was coming to a boil I put two garlic cloves in my Cuisinart along with a handful of parsley and a handful of basil and some kosher salt and some oil and a handful of shelled pistachios and I blended them smooth. Susan had given me the Cuisinart for my birthday, and I used it whenever I could. I thought it was kind of a silly toy, but she'd loved giving it to me and I'd never tell. When the water boiled, I shut off both pots. I could hear Susan sloshing around in the tub. The door was ajar, and I went over and stuck my head in. She lay on her back with her hair pinned up and her naked body glistening in the water.

"Not bad," I said, "for a broad your age."

"I knew you'd peek," she said. "Voyeurism, a typical stage in adolescent development."

"Not bad, actually, for a broad of anyone's age," I said.

"Go make the gimlet now," she said. "I'm getting out."

"Gin or vodka?" I said.

"Gin."

"Animal," I said.

I went back to the kitchen and mixed five parts gin to one part Rose's lime juice in a pitcher and stirred it with ice and poured it into a glass with two icecubes. Susan came into the kitchen as I finished, wearing the half-sleeved silk shaving robe she'd given me last Christmas, which I never wore, but which she did when she came and stayed. It was maroon with black piping and a black belt. When I tried it on, I looked like Bruce Lee. She didn't.

She sat on one of my kitchen stools and sipped her gimlet. Her hair was up and she had no makeup and her face was shiny. She looked fifteen, except for the marks of age and character around her eyes and mouth. They added.

I had another Molson and brought my two pots to a boil again. In the big one I put a pound of spaghetti. In the small one with the steamer rack I put the frozen broccoli. I set the timer for nine minutes.

"Shall we dine before the fire?" I said.

"Certainly."

"Okay," I said. "Put down the booze and take one end of the dining-room table."

We moved it in front of the fire and brought two chairs and set the table while the spaghetti boiled and the broccoli steamed. The bell on the timer rang. I went to the kitchen and drained the broccoli and tried the spaghetti. It needed another minute. While it boiled I ran the Cuisinart another whirl and reblended my oil and spices. Then I tried the pasta. It was done. I drained it, put it back in the pot and tossed it with the spiced oil and broccoli. I put out the pot, the leftover loaves of Syrian bread that I bought for lunch, and a cold bottle of Soave Bolla. Then I held Susan's chair. She sat down. I put another log on the fire, poured a dash of wine in her glass. She sipped it thoughtfully, then nodded at me. I filled her glass and then mine.

"Perhaps madam would permit me to join her," I said.

"Perhaps," she said.

I sipped a little wine.

"And perhaps later on," she said, "we might screw."

I laughed halfway through a swallow of wine and choked and gasped and splattered the wine all over my shirt front.

"Or perhaps not," she said.

"Don't toy with me while I'm drinking," I said, when I was breathing again. "Later on I may take you by force."

"Woo-woo," she said.

I served her some pasta with broccoli and some to myself. Outside it was snowing steadily. There was only one light on in the room; most of the light came from the fire, which was made of applewood and smelled sweet. The glow of the embers behind the steady low flame made the room faintly rosy. We were quiet. The flame hissed softly as it forced the last traces of sap from the logs. I wasn't nearly as sore as I had been. The pasta tasted wonderful. The wine was cold. And Susan made my throat ache. If I could find Rachel Wallace, I might believe in God.

CHAPTER TWENTY-SIX

THE SUN THAT brief December day rose cheerlessly and invisibly over one hell of a lot of snow in the city of Boston. I looked at the alarm clock. Six AM. It was very still outside, the noise of a normal morning muffled by the snow. I was lying on my right side, my left arm over Susan's bare shoulder. Her hair had come unpinned in the night and was in a wide tangle on the pillow. Her face was toward me and her eyes were closed. She slept with her mouth open slightly, and the smell of wine on her breath fluttered faintly across the pillow. I pushed up on one elbow and looked out the window. The snow was still coming—steadily and at a slant so I knew the wind was driving it. Without opening her eyes, Susan pulled me back down against her and shrugged the covers back up over us. She made a snuggling motion with her body and lay still.

I said, "Would you like an early breakfast, or did you have another plan?"

297

She pressed her face into the hollow of my shoulder. "My nose is cold," she said in a muffled voice.

"I'm your man," I said. I ran my hand down the line of her body and patted her on the backside. She put her right hand in the small of my back and pressed a little harder against me.

"I had always thought," she said, her face still pressed in my shoulder, "that men of your years had problems of sexual dysfunction."

"Oh, we do," I said. "I used to be twice as randy twenty years ago."

"They must have kept you in a cage," she said. She walked her fingers up my backbone, one vertebra at a time.

"Yeah," I said, "but I could reach through the bars."

"I bet you could," she said, and with her eyes still closed she raised her head and kissed me with her mouth open.

It was nearly eight when I got up and took a shower.

Susan took hers while I made breakfast and built another fire. Then we sat in front of the fire and ate cornbread made with buttermilk, and wild-strawberry jam and drank coffee.

At nine fifteen, with the cornbread gone and the strawberry jam depleted and the *Globe* read and the *Today Show* finished, I called my answering service. Someone had left a telphone number for me to call.

I dialed it, and a woman answered on the first ring. I said, "This is Spenser. I have a message to call this number."

She said, "Spenser, this is Julie Wells."

I said, "Where are you?"

She said, "It doesn't matter. I've got to see you."

I said, "We're in an old Mark Stevens movie."

"I beg your pardon?"

"I want to see you, too," I said. "Where can I meet you?"

"There's a snow emergency, you know."

They never said that in the old Mark Stevens movies. "Name a place," I said. "I'll get there."

"The coffee shop at the Parker House."

"When?"

"Ten thirty."

"See you then."

"I don't want anyone else to know I'm there, Spenser."

"Then you say, 'Make sure you're not followed.' And I say, 'Don't worry. I'll be careful.' "

"Well, I don't. I mean it."

"Okay, kid. I'll be there."

We hung up. Susan was in the bathroom doing makeup. I stuck my head in and said, "I have to go out and work for a while." She was doing something with a long thin pencilish-looking item to the corner of her mouth. she said, "Unh-huh," and kept on doing it.

When Susan concentrates, she concentrates. I put on my white wide-wale corduroy pants, my dark-blue all-wool Pendleton shirt, and my Herman survivors. I put my gun in its hip holster on my belt; I got into my jacket, turned up the fleece collar, pulled on my watch cap, slipped on my gloves, and went forth into the storm.

Except for the snow, which still fell hard, the city was nearly motionless. There was no traffic. The streets were snow-covered, maybe two feet deep, and the snow had drifted in places high enough to bury a parked car. Arlington Street had been partially plowed, and the walking was easier. I turned right on Beacon and headed up the hill, leaning now into the wind and the snow. I pulled my watch cap down over my ears and forehead. It didn't look rakish, but one must compromise occasionally with nature. An enormous yellow bulldozer with an enclosed cab and a plow blade approximately the size of Rhode Island came churning slowly down Beacon Street. There were no people and no dogs, just me and the bulldozer and the snow. When the bulldozer passed, I had to climb over a snowbank to get out of the way of the plow spill, but after it had passed, the walking was much better. I walked up the middle of Beacon Street with the old elegant brick houses on my left and the empty Common on my right. I could see the houses okay, but ten feet past the iron fence the Common disappeared into the haze of snow and strong wind.

At the top of the hill I could see the State House but not the gold dome. Nothing was open. It was downhill from there and a little easier. By the time I got to the Parker House, where Beacon ends at Tremont, I was cold and a little strange with the empty swirling silence in the middle of the city.

There were people hanging around in the lobby of the Parker House and the coffee shop on the Tremont Street side was nearly full. I spotted Julie Wells alone at a table for two by the window looking out at the snow.

She had on a silver ski parka which she'd unzipped but not removed; the hood was thrown back, and the fur trim tangled with the edges of her hair. Underneath the parka she wore a white turtleneck sweater, and with her big gold earrings and her long eyelashes she looked like maybe 1.8 million. Susan was a two million.

I rolled my watch cap back up to rakish and then walked over and sat down across from her. The Parker House used to be Old Boston and kind of an institution. It had fallen on hard times and was now making a comeback, but the coffee shop with the window on Tremont Street was a good place. I unzipped my coat.

"Good morning," I said.

She smiled without much pleasure and said, "I am glad to see you. I really didn't know who else to call."

"I hope you didn't have to walk far," I said. "Even an Olympic walker like myself experienced some moments of discomfort."

Julie said, "There's someone after me."

I said, "I don't blame him."

She said, "There really is. I've seen him outside my apartment. He's followed me to and from work."

"You know the cops have been looking for you."

"About Rachel?"

I nodded. The waitress came, and I ordered coffee and

whole-wheat toast. There was a plate with most of an omelet still left on it in front of Julie Wells. The waitress went away.

"I know about the police," she said. "I called the agency, and they said the police had been there, too. But they wouldn't follow me around like that."

I shrugged. "Why not tell the cops about this guy that's following you. If it's one of them, they'll know. If it's not, they can look into it."

She shook her head.

"No cops?"

She shook her head again.

"Why not?"

She poked at the omelet with the tines of her fork, moving a scrap of egg around to the other side of the plate.

"You're not just hiding out from the guy that's following you?" I said.

"No."

"You don't want to talk with the cops either."

She started to cry. Her shoulders shook a little, and her lower lip trembled a little, and some tears formed in her eyes. It was discreet crying though—nothing the other customers would notice.

"I don't know what to do," she said. "I don't want to be involved in all of this. I want people to leave me alone."

"You got any thoughts on where Rachel might be?" I said.

She blew her nose in a pink Kleenex and inhaled shakily.

"What shall I do?" she said to me. "I don't know anyone else to ask."

"You know where Rachel is?"

"No, of course not. How would I? We were friends, lovers if you'd rather, but we weren't in love or anything. And if people—"

"You don't want people to know that you're a lesbian."

She made a little shiver. "God, I hate the word. It's so . . . . clinical, like classifying an odd plant."

"But you still don't want it known?"

"Well, I'm not ashamed. You put it so badly. I have made a life choice that's not like yours, or some others, and I have no reason to be ashamed. It's as natural as anyone else."

"So why not talk with the cops? Don't you want to find Rachel Wallace?"

She clasped her hands together and pressed the knuckles against her mouth. Tears formed again. "Oh, God, poor Rachel. Do you think she's alive?"

The waitress brought my toast and coffee.

When she left, I said, "I don't have any way to know. I have to assume she is, because to assume she isn't leaves me nothing to do."

"And you're looking for her?"

"I'm looking for her."

"If I knew anything that would help, I'd say so. But what good will it do Rachel to have my name smeared in the papers? To have the people at the model agency—"

"I don't know what good," I said. "I don't know what you know. I don't know why someone is following you, or was—I assume you've lost him."

She nodded. "I got away from him on the subway."

"So who would he be? Why would he follow you? It's an awful big coincidence that Rachel is taken and then someone follows you."

"I don't know, I don't know anything. What if they want to kidnap me? I don't know what to do." She stared out the window at the empty snow-covered street.

"Why not stay with your mother and brother?" I said.

She looked back at me slowly. I ate a triangle of toast.

"What do you know about my mother and brother?"

"I know their names and I know their politics and I know their attitude toward Rachel Wallace, and I can guess their attitude toward you if they knew that you and Rachel were lovers."

"Have you been . . . did you . . . you don't have the right to . . ."

302

"I haven't mentioned you to them. I did mention you to the cops, but only when I had to, quite recently."

"Why did you have to?"

"Because I'm looking for Rachel, and I'll do anything I have to to find her. When I figured out that you were Lawrence English's sister, I thought it might be a clue. It might help them find her. They're looking, too."

"You think my brother—"

"I think he's in this somewhere. His chauffeur hired two guys to run me and Rachel off the road one night in Lynn. Your brother organized a picket line when she spoke in Belmont. Your brother has said she's an ungodly corruption or some such. And he's the head of an organization of Ritz crackers that would be capable of such things."

"I didn't used to know I was gay," she said. "I just thought I was not very affectionate. I got married. I felt guilty about being cold. I even did therapy. It didn't work. I was not a loving person. We were divorced. He said I was like a wax apple. I looked wonderful, but there was nothing inside—no nourishment. I went to a support group meeting for people recently divorced, and I met a woman and cared for her, and we developed a relationship, and I found out I wasn't empty. I could love. I could feel passion. It was maybe the moment in my life. We made love and I felt. I"—she looked out the window again, and I ate another piece of toast—"I reached orgasm. It was as if, as if . . . I don't know what it was as if."

"As if a guilty verdict had been overturned."

She nodded. "Yes. Yes. I wasn't bad. I wasn't cold. I had been trying to love the wrong things."

"But Mom and brother?"

"You've met them?"

"Brother," I said. "Not yet Momma."

"They could never understand. They could never accept it. It would be just the worst thing that could be for them. I wish for them—maybe for me, too—I wish it could have been different, but it can't, and it's better to be what I am than to be failing at what I am not. But they mustn't ever know. That's why I can't go to the police. I can't let them know. I don't mind the rest of the world. It's them. They can't know. I don't know what they would do."

"Maybe they'd kidnap Rachel," I said.

CHAPTER TWENTY-SEVEN

THE WAITRESS SAID, "May I get you anything else?"

I shook my head, so did Julie. The waitress put the check down, near me, and I put a ten down on top of it.

Julie said, "They wouldn't. They couldn't do that. They wouldn't know what to do."

"They could hire a consultant. Their chauffeur has done time. Name's Mingo Mulready, believe it or not, and he would know what to do."

"But they don't know."

"Maybe they don't. Or maybe the guy that was following you around was your brother's. You haven't been living at home."

"Spenser, I'm thirty years old."

"Get along with the family?"

"No. They didn't approve of my marriage. They didn't approve of my divorce. They hated me going to Goucher. They hate me being a model. I couldn't live with them."

"They worry about you?"

She shrugged. Now that she was thinking, she wasn't crying, and her face looked more coherent. "I suppose they did," she said. "Lawrence likes to play father and man of the house, and Mother lets him. I guess they think I'm dissolute and weak and uncommitted—that kind of thing."

"Why would they have a thug like Mulready driving them around?"

Julie shrugged her shoulders. "Lawrence is all caught up in his Vigilance Committee. He gets into situations, I guess, where he feels he needs a bodyguard. I assume this Mulready is someone who would do that."

"Not as well as he used to," I said.

The waitress picked up my ten and brought back some change on a saucer.

"If they did take Rachel," I said, "where would they keep her?"

"I don't know."

"Sure you do. If you were your brother and you had kidnaped Rachel Wallace, where would you keep her?"

"Oh, for God's sake, Spenser . . ."

"Think," I said. "Think about it. Humor me."

"This is ridiculous."

"I walked a half-mile through a blizzard because you asked me to," I said. "I didn't say it was ridiculous."

She nodded. "The house," she said.

The waitress came back and said, "Can I get you anything else?"

I shook my head. "We better vacate," I said to Julie, "before she gets ugly."

Julie nodded. We left the coffee shop and found an overstuffed loveseat in the lobby.

"Where in the house?" I said.

"Have you seen it?"

"Yeah. I was out there a few days ago."

"Well, you know how big it is. There's probably twenty rooms. There's a great big cellar. There's the chauffeur's quarters over the garage and extra rooms in the attic."

"Wouldn't the servants notice?"

"They wouldn't have to. The cook never leaves the kitchen, and the maid would have no reason to go into some parts of the house. We had only the cook and the maid when I was there.

"And of course old Mingo."

"They hired him after I left. I don't know him."

"Tell you what," I said. "We'll go back to my place. It's just over on Marlborough Street, and we'll draw a map of your brother's house."

"It's my mother's," Julie said.

"Whoever," I said. "We'll make a map, and later on I'll go take a look."

"How will you do that?"

"First the map. Then the B-and-E plans. Come on."

"I don't know if I can make a map."

"Sure you can. I'll help and we'll talk. You'll remember."

"And we're going to your apartment?"

"Yes. It's quite safe. I have a woman staying with me who'll see that I don't molest you. And on the walk down we'll be too bundled up."

"I didn't mean that."

"Okay, let's go."

We pushed out into the snow again. It seemed to be lessening, but the wind was whipping it around so much, it was hard to tell. A half-block up Beacon Street Julie took my arm, and she hung on all the way up over the hill and down to Marlborough. Other than two huge yellow pieces of snow equipment that clunked and waddled through the snow, we were all that moved.

When we got to my apartment, Susan was on the couch by the fire reading a book by Robert Coles. She wore a pair of jeans she'd left there two weeks ago and one of my gray T-shirts with the size, XL, printed in red letters on the front. it hung almost to her knees.

I introduced them and took Julie's coat and hung it in the hall closet. As I went by the bathroom, I noticed Susan's lingerie hanging on the shower rod to dry. It made me speculate about what was under the jeans, but I put it from me. I was working. I got a pad of lined yellow paper, legal size, from a drawer in the kitchen next to the phone and a small translucent plastic artist's triangle and a black ballpoint pen, and Julie and I sat at the counter in my kitchen for three hours and diagrammed her mother's house—not only the rooms, but what was in them.

"I haven't been there in a year," she said at one point.

"I know, but people don't usually rearrange the big pieces. The beds and sofas and stuff are usually where they've always been."

We made an overall diagram of the house and then did each room on a separate sheet. I numbered all the rooms and keyed them to the separate sheets.

"Why do you want to know all this? Furniture and everything?"

"It's good to know what you can. I'm not sure even what I'm up to. I'm just gathering information. There's so much that I can't know, and so many things I can't predict, that I like to get everything I can in order so when the unpredictable stuff comes along I can concentrate on that."

Susan made a large plate of ham sandwiches while we finished up our maps and we had them with coffee in front of the fire.

"You make a good fire for a broad," I said to Susan.

"It's easy, " Susan said, "I rubbed two dry sexists together."

"This is a wonderful sandwich," Julie said to Susan.

"Yes. Mr Macho here gets the ham from someplace out in eastern New York State."

"Millerton," I said. "Cured with salt and molasses. Hickory-smoked, no nitrates."

Julie looked at Susan. "Ah, what about that other matter."

"The shadow?" I said.

She nodded.

"You can go home and let him spot you, and then I'll take him off your back."

"Home?"

"Sure. Once he lost you, if he's really intent on staying with you, he'll go and wait outside your home until you show up. What else can he do?"

"I guess nothing. He wouldn't be there today, I wouldn't think."

"Unless he was there yesterday, " Susan said. "The governor's been on TV. No cars allowed on the highway. No buses are running. No trains. Nothing coming into the city."

"I don't want to go home," Julie said.

"Or you can stay hiding out for a while, but I'd like to know where to get you."

She shook her head.

"Look, Julie," I said. "You got choices, but they are not limitless. You are part of whatever happened to Rachel Wallace. I don't know what part, but I'm not going to let go of you. I don't have that much else. I need to be able to find you."

She looked at me and at Susan, who was sipping her coffee from a big brown mug, holding it in both hands with her nose half-buried in the cup and her eyes on the fire. Julie nodded her head three times.

"Okay," she said. "I'm in an apartment at one sixty-four Tremont. One of the girls at the agency is in Chicago, and she let me stay while she's away. Fifth floor."

"I'll walk you over," I said.

CHAPTER TWENTY-EIGHT

THE DAY AFTER the big blizzard was beautiful, the way it always is. The sun is shining its ass off, and the snow is still white, and no traffic is out, and people and dogs are walking everywhere and being friendly during shared duress.

Susan and I walked out to Boylston and up toward Mass. Ave. She had bought a funky-looking old raccoon coat

with padded shoulders when we'd gone antiquing in New
Hampshire in November, and she was wearing it with big
furry boots and a woolen hat with a big pom-pom. She looked
like a cross between Annette Funicello and Joan Crawford.

We'd been living together for two and a half days, and
if I had known where Rachel Wallace was, I would have been
having a very nice time. But I didn't know where Rachel Wallace was, and what was worse, I had a suspicion where she
might be, and I couldn't get there. I had called Quirk and told
him what I knew. He couldn't move against a man of English's
clout without some probable cause, and we agreed I had none.
I told him I didn't know where Julie Wells was staying. He
didn't believe me, but the pressure of the snow emergency was
distracting the whole department, and no one came over with
a thumbscrew to interrogate me.

So Susan and I walked up Boylston Street to see if
there was a store open where she could buy some under-
clothes and maybe a shirt or two, and I walked with her in a
profound funk. All traffic was banned from all highways. No
trains were moving.

Susan bought some very flossy-looking lingerie at
Saks, and a pair of Levi's jeans and two blouses. We were back
out on Boylston when she said, "Want to go home and model
the undies?"

"I don't think they'd fit me," I said.

"I didn't mean you," she said.

I said, "God damn it, I'll walk out there."

"Where?"

"I'll walk out to Belmont."

"Just to avoid modeling the undies?"

I shook my head. "It's what? Twelve, fifteen miles?
Walk about three miles an hour. I'll be there in four or five
hours."

"You're sure she's there?"

"No. But she might be, and if she is, it's partly my
fault. I have to look."

"It's a lot of other people's fault much more than yours.
Especially the people who took her."

"I know, but if I'd been with her, they wouldn't have taken her."

Susan nodded.

"Why not call the Belmont Police?" she said.

"Same as with Quirk. They can't just charge in there. They have to have a warrant. And there has to be some reasonable suspicion, and I don't have anything to give them. And . . . I don't know. They might screw it up."

"Which means that you want to do it yourself."

"Maybe."

"Even if it endangers her?"

"I don't want to endanger her. I trust me more than I trust anyone else. Her life is on the line here. I want me to be the one who's in charge."

"And because you have to even up with the people that took her," Susan said, "you're willing to go after her alone and risk the whole thing, including both your lives, because your honor has been tarnished, or you think it has."

I shook my head. "I don't want some Belmont cop in charge of this whose last bust was two ninth-graders with an ounce of Acapulco gold."

"And Quirk or Frank Belson can't go because they don't have jurisdiction, and they don't have a warrant and all of the above?"

I nodded.

We turned the corner onto Arlington and walked along in the middle of the bright street, like a scene from Currier and Ives.

"Why don't you find Hawk and have him go with you?"

I shook my head.

"Why not?"

"I'm going alone."

"I thought you would. What if something happens to you?"

"Like what?"

"Like suppose you sneak in there and someone shoots you. If you're right, you are dealing with people capable of that."

"Then you tell Quirk everything you know. And tell Hawk to find Rachel Wallace for me."

"I don't even know how to get in touch with Hawk. Do I call that health club on the waterfront?"

"If something happens to me, Hawk will show up and see if you need anything."

We were on the corner of Marlborough Street. Susan stopped and looked at me. "You know that so certainly?"

"Yes."

She shook her head and kept shaking it. "You people are like members of a religion or a cult. You have little rituals and patterns you observe that nobody else understands."

"What people?"

"People like you. Hawk, Quirk, that state policeman you met when the boy was kidnaped."

"Healy."

"Yes, Healy. The little trainer at the Harbor Health Club. All of you. You're as complexly programmed as male wildebeests, and you have no common sense at all."

"Wildebeests?" I said.

"Or Siamese fighting fish."

"I prefer to think *lion, panther* maybe."

We walked to my apartment. "I suppose," Susan said, "we could settle for ox. Not as strong but nearly as smart."

Susan went to the apartment. I went to the basement and got some more firewood from the storage area and carried an armful up the back stairs. It was early afternoon. We had lunch. We watched the news. The travel ban was still with us.

"At least wait until morning," Susan said. "Get an early start."

"And until then?"

"We can read by the fire."

"When that gets boring, I was thinking we could make shadow pictures on the wall. Ever see my rooster?"

Susan said, "I've never heard it called that." I put my arm around her shoulder and squeezed her against me and we began to giggle. We spent the rest of the day before the fire on the couch. Mostly we read.

CHAPTER TWENTY-NINE

By SEVEN THIRTY the next morning I was on the road. I had a flashlight in my hip pocket, a short prying tool stuck in my belt, my packet of floor plans in my shirt pocket, and my usual jackknife and gun. Susan kissed me goodbye without getting up, and I left without hearing any more wildebeest remarks. I walked up Marlborough to the Mass. Ave. Bridge along a quiet and narrow lane, one plow-blade wide, with the snow head-high on either side of me. Below the bridge the Charles was frozen and solid white. No sign of the river. Memorial Drive had one lane cleared in either direction, and I turned west. I had learned to walk some years ago at government expense when I had walked from Pusan to the Yalu River and then back. I moved right along. After the first mile or so I had a nice rhythm and even felt just a trickle of sweat along the line of my backbone.

It was shorter than I thought. I was on Trapelo Road in Belmont by ten forty-five. By eleven I was standing two houses away from the English place, across the street. Now if I found Rachel Wallace, I wouldn't have to walk back. The cops would drive me. Maybe.

The house was three stories high. Across the front was a wide veranda. A long wing came off the back, and at the end of the wing there was a carriage house with a little pointed cupola on top. Mingo probably parked the family Caddies in the carriage house. There was a back door, which led through a back hall into the kitchen, according to Julie. Off the back hall there were back stairs. The veranda turned one corner and ran back along the short side of the house, the one without the wing. Big french doors opened out onto the library, where I'd talked with English before. The yard wasn't as big as you'd expect with a house like that. Last century when they'd built the house there was plenty of land, so no one had wanted it. Now there wasn't and they did. The neighbor's house was maybe fifty feet away on one side, a street was ten feet away on the other, and the backyard was maybe a hundred feet deep. A chainlink fence surrounded the property, except in front, where there was a stone wall, broken by the driveway. There was no sign of the driveway now and very little of the fence in the high snow. It took me nearly two and a half hours of clambering about through snowbanks and side streets to get all of the layout of the grounds and to look at the house from all sides. When I got through, I was sweaty underneath my jacket, and the shoulder rig I was wearing chafed under my left arm. I figured it was better than walking ten miles with the gun jiggling in a hip holster.

There were people out now, shoveling and walking to the store for supplies, and a lot of laughter and neighborly hellos and a kind of siege mentality that made everyone your buddy. I studied the house. The shutters on the top-floor windows were closed, all of them, on the left side and in front. I strolled around the corner and up the side street to the right of the house. The top-floor shutters were closed there, too. I went on down the road till I could see the back shutters.

I knew where I'd look first if I ever got in there. That was the only detail to work out. Julie had told me there was a burglar alarm, and that her mother had always set it before she went to bed. Going in before Mom went to bed would seem to be the answer to that. It would help if I knew who was in there. Mingo, probably. I saw what looked like his tan Thunderbird barely showing through a snowdrift back by the carriage house. There'd be a maid or two probably, and Momma and Lawrence. Whoever was in there when the storm came would be in there now. There were no tracks, no sign of shoveling, just the smooth white sea of snow out of which the old Victorian house rose like a nineteenth-century ship.

I thought about getting in. Trying the old I'm-from-

313

the-power-company trick. But the odds were bad. English knew me, Mingo knew me. At least one of the maids knew me. If I got caught and they got wise, things would be worse. They might kill Rachel. They might kill me, if they could. And that would leave Rachel with no one looking for her the way I was looking for her. Hawk would find her eventually, but he wouldn't have my motivation. Hawk's way would be prompt though. Maybe he'd find her quicker. He'd hold English out a twenty-story window till English said where Rachel was.

I thought about that. It wasn't a bad way. The question was, How many people would I have to go through to hang English out the window? There were probably at least five people in there—Mingo, English, Momma, and two maids—but the whole Vigilance Committee could be in there sharpening their pikes for all I knew.

It was two o'clock. Nothing was happening. People like English wouldn't have to come out till April. They'd have food in the pantry and booze in the cellar and fuel in the tank and nothing to make winter inconvenient. Did they have a hostage in the attic? Why hadn't there been some kind of communication? Why no more ransom notes or threats about canceling the books or anything? Had they been snowed out? I didn't know any of the answers to any of the questions, and I could only think of one way to find out.

At two fifteen I waded through the snow, sometimes waist-deep, and floundered up to the front door and rang the bell. If they knew me, they knew me. I'd deal with that if it happened. A maid answered.

I said, "Mr. English, please."

She said, "Who may I say is calling?"

I said, "Joseph E. McCarthy."

She said, "Just a moment, please," and started to close the door.

I said, "Wait a minute. It's cold, and we've had a blizzard. Couldn't I wait in the front hall?"

And she hesitated and I smiled at her disarmingly but a bit superior, and she nodded and said, "Of course, sir. I'm sorry. Come in."

I went in. She closed the door behind me and went off down the corridor and through a door and closed it behind her. I went up the front stairs as quietly as I could. There was a landing and then a short left turn, then three steps to the upstairs hall. Actually there were two upstairs halls. One ran from front to back and the other, like the cross of a capital **T**, ran the width of the house and led into the wing hall.

I had the general layout in my head. I'd spent most of my time in front of yesterday's fire looking at Julie's diagrams. The stairway to the attic was down the hall in a small back bedroom. The house was quiet. Faintly somewhere I could hear television. There was a smell of violet sachet and mothballs in the small bedroom. The door to the stairs was where it should have been. It was a green wooden door made of narrow vertical boards with a small bead along one edge. It was closed. There was a padlock on it.

Behind me I heard no hue and cry. The maid would be returning now to say that Mr. English didn't know a Joseph E. McCarthy, or that the one he knew wasn't likely to be calling here. I took my small pry bar from my belt. The padlock hasp wasn't very new, and neither was the door. The maid would look and not see me and be puzzled and would look outside and perhaps around downstairs a little before she reported to English that Mr. McCarthy had left. I wedged the blade of the pry bar under the hasp and pulled the whole thing out of the wood, screws and all. It probably wasn't much louder than the clap of Creation. It just seemed so because I was tense. The door opened in, and the stairs went up at a right angle, very steep, very narrow treads and high risers. I closed the door and went up the stairs with hand and feet touching like a hungry monkey. Upstairs the attic was pitch-black. I got out my flashlight and snapped it on and held it in my teeth to keep my hands free. I had the pry bar in my right hand.

The attic was rough and unfinished except for what appeared to be two rooms, one at each gabled end. All the windows had plywood over them. I took one quick look and noticed the plywood was screwed in, not nailed. Someone had wanted it to be hard to remove. I tried one door at the near end of the attic. It was locked. I went and tried the other. It opened, and I went in holding the pry bar like a weapon. Except for an old metal frame bed and a big steamer trunk and three cardboard boxes it was empty. The windows were covered with plywood.

If Rachel was up here, she was back in the other room at the gable end. And she was here—I could feel her. I could feel my insides clench with the certainty that she was behind the other door. I went back to it. There was a padlock, this one new, with a new hasp. I listened. No sound from the room. Downstairs I could hear footsteps. I rammed the pry bar in under the hasp and wrenched the thing loose. The adrenaline was pumping, and I popped the whole thing off and ten feet across the attic floor with one lunge. There was saliva on my chin from holding the flashlight. I took the light in my hand and shoved into the room. It stunk. I swept the flashlight around. On an ironframe bed with a gray blanket around her, half-raised, was Rachel Wallace, and she looked just awful. Her hair was a mess, and she had no makeup, and her eyes were swollen. I reversed the flashlight and shone it on my face.

"It's Spenser," I said.

"Oh, my God," she said. Her voice was hoarse.

The lights went on suddenly. There must have been a downstairs switch, and I'd missed it. The whole attic was bright. I snicked off the flashlight and put it in my pocket and took out my gun and said, "Get under the bed."

Rachel rolled onto the floor and under the bed. Her feet were bare. I heard footsteps coming up the stairs, and then they stopped. They'd spotted the ruptured door. It sounded like three sets of footsteps. I looked up. The light in this room came from a bare bulb that hung from a zinc fixture in the ceiling. I reached up with the pry bar and smashed the bulb. The room was dark except for the light from beyond the door.

Outside, a woman's voice said, "Who is in there?" It was an old voice but not quavery and not weak. I didn't say anything. Rachel made no sound.

The voice said, "You are in trespass in there. I want you out. There are two armed men out here. You have no chance."

I got down on the floor and snaked along toward the door.

In the light at the head of the stairs was Mingo with a double-barreled shotgun and English with an automatic pistol. Between them and slightly forward was a woman who looked like a man, and an ugly, mean man at that. She was maybe five eight and heavy, with a square massive face and short gray hair. Her eyebrows came straight across with almost no arch and met over the bridge of her nose. They were black.

"Give yourself up," she said. There was no uncertainty in her voice and certainly no fear. She was used to people doing what she said.

From the dark I said, "It's over, Momma. People know I'm here. They know I was looking for Rachel Wallace. And I found her. Throw down the weapons, and I'll bring her out and take her home. Then I'll call the cops. You'll have that much time to run."

"Run?" Momma said. "We want you out of there and we'll have you out now. You and that atrocious queer." Mingo had brought the shotgun to the ready and was looking into the room.

I said "Last chance," and rolled right, over once, and came up with my gun raised and steadied with my left hand. Mingo fired one barrel toward where I had been, and I shot him under the right eye. He fell backwards down the stairs. English began to shoot into the room—vaguely, I guess in the direction of my muzzle flash, but panicky and without much time to aim. He squeezed off four rounds into the dark room and I shot him, twice, carefully. One bullet caught him in the forehead and the second in the throat. He made no sound and fell forward. He was probably dead before he landed. I saw Momma start to bend, and I thought she might keel over, but then I realized she was going for the gun, and I lunged to my feet and jumped three jumps and kicked it away from her, and yanked her to her feet by the back of her collar. There was a little bubble of saliva at the corner of her mouth, and she began to gouge at my eyes with her fingers. I held her at arm's length—my arms were longer than hers—and looked down at Mingo in a tangle at the foot of the stairs. He was dead. He had the look. You see it enough, you know.

I said, "Mrs. English, they're dead. Both of them. Your son is dead."

She spat at me and dug her fingernails into my wrist and tried to bite my arm. I said, "Mrs. English, I'm going to hit you."

She bit my arm. It didn't hurt, because she was trying to bite through my coat, but it made me mad. I put my gun away, and I slapped her hard across the face. She began to scream at me. No words, just scream and claw and bite and I hit her with my right fist, hard. She fell down and began to snivel, her face buried in her son's dead back. I picked up English's gun and stuck it in my pocket and went down the stairs and got Mingo's shotgun and jacked the remaining shell out and put that in my pocket and went back up the stairs.

Rachel was standing in the doorway of the room, looking at the carnage and squinting in the light. She had the gray blanket wrapped around her and held with both hands closed at the neck.

I walked over to her and said, "Okay, Jane Eyre, I got you."

Tears began to run down her face, and I put my arms around her, and she cried. And I cried. In between crying I said, "I got you. I got you."

She didn't say anything.

CHAPTER THIRTY

THE FIRST COPS to show were cruiser people—three cars' worth despite the snow emergency—and one of them was Foley, the young cop with the ribbons and the wise-guy face. They came up the attic stairs with guns drawn, directed by the frightened maid who'd called them. He was first. He knew who Rachel was the first look he took.

"Son of a bitch," he said. "You found her."

His partner with the belly squatted down beside English and felt his neck. Then he and another prowlie half-lifted, half-helped Momma English off her son's body. While the prowlie held her, the pot-bellied cop got down on his hands and knees and listened to English's chest. He looked at the young cop and shook his head.

"Gonzo," he said. "So's the horse at the bottom." He nodded at Mingo, still sprawled at the foot of the attic stairs. They must have had to climb over him. "Two in the head," he said. He stood up and looked at me. I still had my arms around Rachel. "What the hell you crying for?" he said. "Think how these guys feel."

Foley spun around. "Shut up," he said. "I know why he's crying. You don't. Close your fucking mouth up."

The older cop shook his head and didn't say anything.

Foley said to me, "You ace these two guys?"

I nodded.

Foley said, "Chief will want to talk with you about all this. Her, too."

"Not now," I said, "now I'm taking her home."

Foley looked at me for maybe thirty seconds. "Yeah," he said. "Take her out of here."

The cop with the belly said, "For crissake, the chief

will fry our ass. This clown blasts two guys, one of them Lawrence English, and he walks while we stand around. Foley, we got two stiffs here."

I said to Foley, "I need a ride."

He nodded. "Come on."

His partner said, "Foley, are you fucking crazy?"

Foley put his face close to the older cop's face. "Benny," he said, "you're okay. You're not a bad cop. But you don't know how to act, and you're too old to learn."

"Chief will have your badge for this and mine for letting you do it."

Foley said, "Ain't your fault, Benny. You couldn't stop me."

Mom English said, "If you let that murderer escape and allow that corrupt degenerate to go with him, I'll have every one of your badges."

There were four other cops besides Foley and Benny. One of them had gone downstairs to call in. One was supporting Mrs. English. The other two stood uncertainly. One of them had his gun out, although it hung at his side and he'd probably forgotten he had it in his hand.

"They murdered my son," she said. Her voice was flat and heavy. "She has vomited filth and corruption long enough. She has to be stopped. We would have stopped her if he hadn't interfered. And you must. She is a putrefaction, a cancerous foul sore." The voice stayed flat but a trickle of saliva came from the left corner of her mouth. She breathed heavily through her nose. "She has debauched and destroyed innocent women and lured them into unspeakable acts." Her nose began to run a little.

I said, "Foley, we're going."

He nodded and pushed past Benny. We followed. Rachel still had the blanket around her.

Momma shrieked at us, "She stole my daughter."

One of the other cops said, "Jesus Christ, Fole."

Foley looked at him, and his eyes were hot. Then he went down the attic stairs, and Rachel and I went with him. In the front hall on the first floor the two maids stood, silent and fidgety. The cop on the phone was talking to someone at headquarters and as we went past he glanced up and widened his eyes.

"Where the hell you going?" he said.

Foley shook his head.

"Chief says he's on his way, Fole."

We kept going. On the porch I picked Rachel up—she was still in her bare feet—and carried her through the floundering waist-deep snow. The cruisers were there in front with the blue lights rotating.

Foley said, "First one."

We got in—Foley in front, me and Rachel in back. He hit the siren, and we pulled out.

"Where?" Foley said.

"Boston," I said. "Marlborough Street, Arlington Street end."

Foley left the siren wailing all the way, and with no traffic but cops and plows we made it in fifteen minutes. He pulled into Marlborough Street from Arlington and went up it the wrong way two doors to my apartment.

"You ain't here when we want you," Foley said, "and I'll be working next week in a carwash."

I got out with Rachel. I had been holding her all the way.

I looked at Foley and nodded once.

"Yeah," he said.

He spun the wheels pulling away, slammed the car into snowbanks on both sides of the street making a U-turn, and spun the wheels s more as he skidded out into Arlington.

I carried Rachel up to my front door and leaned on my bell till Susan said, "Who is it?" over the intercom.

I said, "Me," never at a loss for repartee.

She buzzed and I pushed and in we went. I called the elevator with my elbow and punched my floor with the same elbow and banged on my door with the toe of my boot. Susan opened it. She saw Rachel.

"Oh," she said. "Isn't that good!"

We went in and I put Rachel down on the couch.

I said, "Would you like a drink?"

She said, "Yes, very much."

"Bourbon, okay?"

"Yes, on the rocks, please."

She still had her gray blanket tightly wrapped around her. I went out in the kitchen and got a bottle of Wild Turkey and three glasses and a bucket of ice and came back out. I poured each of us a drink. Susan had kept the fire going and it went well with the Wild Turkey. Each of us drank.

"You need a doctor?" I said.

"No," she said. "I don't think so. I was not abused in that sense."

"Would you like to talk about it?" Susan said.

"Yes," Rachel said, "I think I would. I shall talk about it and probably write about it. But right now I should very much like to bathe and put on clean clothes, and then perhaps eat something." She drank some bourbon. "I've not," she said, "been eating particularly well lately." She smiled slightly.

"Sure," I said. "Spenser's the name, cooking's the game."

I started to get up. "No," she said. "Stay here a minute, both of you, while I finish this drink."

And so we sat—me and Rachel on the couch, Susan in the wing chair—and sipped the bourbon and looked at the fire. There was no traffic noise and it was quiet except for the hiss of the fire and the tick of the old steeple clock with wooden works that my father had given me years ago.

Rachel finished her drink. "I would like another," she said, "to take into the bath with me."

I mixed it for her.

She said, "Thank you."

Susan said, "If you want to give me your old clothes, I can put them through the wash for you. Lancelot here has all the latest conveniences."

Rachel shook her head. "No," she said. "I haven't any clothes. They took them. I have only the blanket."

Susan said, "Well, I've got some things you can wear."

Rachel smiled. "Thank you," she said.

Susan showed Rachel to the bathroom door. "There are clean towels," Susan said. "While he was out I was being domestic."

Rachel went in and closed the door. I heard the water begin to run in the tub. Susan walked over to me on the couch.

"How are you?" she said.

"Okay," I said.

"Was it bad?"

"Yeah," I said.

"Was it English?"

I nodded. She rubbed my head—the way you tousle a dog.

"What was that old song?" she said. " 'Joltin' Joe DiMaggio, we want you on our side.' "

"Yeah, except around here we used to sing, 'Who's better than his brother Joe? Dominic DiMaggio.' "

She rubbed my head again, "Well, anyway," she said. "I want *you* on my side, cutie."

"You're just saying that," I said, "because DiMaggio's not around."

"That's true," she said.

CHAPTER THIRTY-ONE

WHILE RACHEL WAS in the bath I made red beans and rice. Susan put out the rest of the cornbread and I chopped green peppers and scallions. When Rachel finally came to dinner, she had put on some of Susan's makeup and a pair of Susan's jeans and a sweat shirt of mine that was considerably big. The sleeves were rolled up and made a bulky ring around her arms above the elbow. Her hair had been washed and blown dry and looked very straight.

I said, "You want some more bourbon?"

She said yes.

I gave her some more, with ice, and she sat at the table in the dining area and sipped it. I served the beans and rice with the chopped vegetables and some canned chopped tomato on top and put out a dish of grated cheddar cheese. Susan and I drank beer with the meal. Rachel stayed with the bourbon. Like the martinis she'd been drinking when we met first, the bourbon seemed to have no effect.

There was very little talk for the first few minutes. Rachel ate rapidly. When she had nearly finished, she said, "Julie is that woman's daughter, did you know that?"

"Yes," I said.

"They took me because of her, you know."

"I thought they might have."

"They wanted to punish me for corrupting their girl child. They wanted to separate us. They wanted to be sure no one would ever see Julie with me. The idea that her daughter could be a lesbian was more than she could think. I think she thought that if I weren't there, Julie would revert to her normal self."

She said *normal* with a lot of bite in it.

"It wasn't anything to do with your books?" Susan said.

"Maybe it was, too," Rachel said. "Especially the man. I think he was more comfortable with the kidnaping if it was for a cause. He called it a political act."

"And what did they plan to do with you?" I said.

"I don't know. I don't think they knew. I think the one that actually took me, the big one that works for them . . ."

"Mingo," I said. "Mingo Mulready."

"I think he wanted to kill me."

"Sure," I said. "You'd make a damaging witness if you survived."

Rachel nodded. "And they didn't conceal their identities. I saw them all, and they told me they were Julie's people."

"Did they treat you badly?" Susan said.

324

Rachel looked down at her plate. It was empty.

I said, "Would you like more?"

She shook her head. "No. It's very good, but I'm full, thank you."

"More bourbon?" I said.

"You know, that's the thing you've said to me most, since I got here? You must have great faith in its restorative powers."

"It's a way of being solicitous," I said.

"I know," Rachel said. "And yes, I'll have another. I, too, have great faith in its restorative powers."

I got her the bourbon.

"I wonder why they didn't kill me," she said. "I was afraid they would. I'd lie up there in the dark, and each time they came I'd wonder if they had come to kill me."

"Probably didn't have the balls," I said. "Probably would have had to find a way to maneuver themselves into having Mingo do it."

"Like what?" Rachel said.

"Oh, get up some kind of ultimatum and present it to the cops. An ultimatum that couldn't be met. Then they could say it wasn't their fault. They'd been left no choice, and they'd had to do it to stop your poison because the officials were duped by the Antichrist, or the commies, or Gore Vidal, or whoever."

"The mother would have wanted to most," Rachel said. She looked at Susan. "They didn't mistreat me in the sense of torture or anything. I wasn't tied up or beaten. But the mother wanted to humiliate me. And the son. Julie's brother."

"Lawrence," I said.

"Yes, Lawrence." She shivered.

"What did Lawrence do?" Susan said. Her voice was quite soft.

"He used to come up with my food and sit beside me on the bed and ask me about my relations with Julie. He wanted explicit detail. And he would touch me."

I said, "Jesus Christ."

"I think he got excited by the talk of my lovemaking

325

with Julie. And he would say in his position he rarely had the opportunity to be with a woman, how he had to be careful, that he was in an exposed position and couldn't risk being compromised by a woman. And then he would touch me." She stopped.

Susan said, very quietly, "Did he rape you?"

"Not in the traditional sense," Rachel said. "He—" She paused, looking for the right way to say it. "He couldn't in the traditional sense. He seemed unable to erect."

"His mom probably told him not to," I said.

Susan frowned at me a little.

"And," Rachel went on, looking into the glass half-full of bourbon, "I would try not to talk about Julie and lovemaking because I knew how he would get. But if I didn't tell him, he would threaten me. 'You are entirely under my control,' he would say. 'I can do anything to you I want to, so you better do what I say.' And he was right. I was. I had to do what he said. It was kind of a paradigm of the situation of men and women—the situation which I have so long opposed and tried to change."

"Not only Lawrence but his mother," Susan said.

"Yes. She, too. The matriarch. Trying to prevent the world from changing and making what she had always been seem unimportant, or even worse, silly."

"I wonder how conscious they were of that," I said.

Susan shrugged.

Rachel said, "Not conscious, I think. But subconscious. It was a kind of dramatization of the way they wanted the world to be."

"Who took your clothes?" Susan said.

"The mother. I assume she wanted to demean me. She had Lawrence and the other one that worked for them strip me when they took me to that room."

"I wonder if that might have been for Lawrence, too," Susan said.

Rachel drank some more bourbon. She held some in her mouth while she looked at Susan. "Perhaps. I hadn't thought of that. But perhaps she had some sense that he was not sexually ordinary. Maybe she thought the chance for a nice uncomplicated rape would help him along." She finished the bourbon. I poured her some more without asking.

Susan said, "You haven't said anything very much about how you felt about all this. You've told us what happened. But maybe it would be good to get some feelings out."

"I don't know," Rachel said. "I have learned to keep my feelings under very strong control. Maybe not so different from himself here." She nodded at me. "I have had to, doing what I do. I'll write about the feelings. I write better than I speak. I do know that being a captive is a humiliating, a debasing experience. To be in someone else's hands. To be without control of yourself is terribly destructive of personality and terribly frightening and terribly . . . I don't know quite what I want to say. Terribly . . ."

"It ruins your self-respect," Susan said.

"Yes," Rachel said. "You feel worthless. That's just right. You feel contemptible, almost as if you deserve the mistreatment. As if you're somehow at fault for being where you are."

"And the sexual mistreatment merely intensifies the feeling, I should think."

Rachel nodded. I opened another beer and drank most of it. I had little to offer in this conversation. I gestured the beer bottle at Susan. She shook her head.

Rachel turned and looked at me. She sipped some bourbon and held the glass toward me. "And you," she said. For the first time there was just a faint blurring in her speech. "There are things I need to say to you. And they are not easy to say. While I lay back in your bathtub and tried to soak some of the filthiness of this all away, I thought about what I should say to you and how." She looked at Susan. "You are invited," Rachel said to Susan, "to help me with this. Maybe you have some sense of where my problems lie."

Susan smiled. "I'll pitch in as needed," she said. "I suspect you won't need me."

"There are a lot of things that don't need to be said," I said.

327

"But these things do," Rachel said. "I always knew that if someone found me, it would be you. Somehow whenever I fantasized being rescued, it was never the police, it was always you."

"I had more reason," I said.

"Yes, or you would see yourself as having more reason, because you would perceive yourself as responsible for me."

I didn't say anything. The beer was gone. I got up and got another bottle and opened it and came back and sat down.

"And you did it the way I expected you would. You bashed in the door and shot two people and picked me up and took me away. Tarzan of the Apes," she said.

"My brain is small. I have to compensate," I said.

"No. Your brain is not small. If it were, you wouldn't have found me. And having found me, you probably had to do what you did. And it's what you could do. You couldn't remain passive when they wanted to eject me from the insurance company. Because it compromised your sense of maleness. I found that, and I do find that, unfortunate and limiting. But you couldn't let these people kidnap me. That, too, compromised your sense of maleness. So what I disapproved of, and do disapprove of, is responsible in this instance for my safety. Perhaps my life."

She stopped. I didn't say anything. Susan was sitting with her heels caught over the bottom rung of the chair, her knees together, leaning forward, her chin on her left fist, looking at Rachel. Her interest in people was emanating. One could almost feel it.

Rachel drank some more bourbon. "What I am trying to do," she said, "is to thank you. And to say it as genuinely as I can. I do thank you. I will remember as long as I live when you came into the room and got me, and I will always remember when you killed them, and I was glad, and you came and we put our arms around each other. And I will always remember that you cried."

"What'll you charge not to tell?" I said. "Makes a mess of my image."

She went on without pausing. "And I shall in a way

always love you for those moments." Her glass was empty. I filled it. "But I am a lesbian and a feminist. You still embody much that I must continue to disparage." She had trouble with *disparage*. "I still disapprove of you."

"Rachel," I said, "how could I respect anyone who didn't disapprove of me?"

She got up from the dinner table and walked softly and carefully around to my side and kissed me, holding my face in her hands. Then she turned and went to my bedroom and went to sleep on my bed.

We just got the table cleared when the cops came.

CHAPTER THIRTY-TWO

THEY WERE WITH us a long time: the chief of the Belmont force and two other Belmont cops; a man from the Middlesex DA's office; Cronin, the twerp from the Suffolk DA's office; Quirk and Belson.

Cronin wanted to roust Rachel out of bed, and I told him if he did, I would put him in the hospital. He told Quirk to arrest me, and Quirk told him if he couldn't be quiet, he'd have to wait in the car. Cronin's face turned the color of a Christmas poinsettia, and he started to say something, and Quirk looked at him for a minute, and he shut up.

We agreed that I could give them a statement and that they would wait until morning to take a statement from Rachel Wallace. It was late when they left. Cronin gave me a hard look and said he'd remember me. I suggested that his mind wasn't that good. Susan said she was very pleased to have met everyone and hoped they'd have a Merry Christmas. Quirk gave her hand a small squeeze, Belson blew smoke at me, and everyone left.

In the living room Susan and I sat on the couch. The fire was barely alive, a few coals glowing in the gray ash.

"We've spent a lot of time here the last few days," Susan said.

"There are worse places," I said.

"In fact," Susan said, "there aren't too many better."

"We may spend a lot more time here, because she's in our bed."

"The final sacrifice," Susan said.

"We could think of ways to make the best of it," I said.

"You had to kill two people today," Susan said.

"Yeah."

"Bother you?"

"Yeah."

"Want to talk about it?"

"No."

"Sometimes people need to get feelings out," Susan said.

"Perhaps I could express them sexually," I said.

"Well, since it's for therapy," Susan said. "But you'll have to be very quiet. We don't want to wake Rachel up."

"With half a quart of bourbon in her?" I said.

"Well, it would be embarrassing."

"Okay, you'll have to control your tendency to break out with cries of *atta boy,* then."

"I'll do my best," she said. "Merry Christmas."

Much later we heard Rachel cry out in her sleep, and I got off the couch and went in and sat on the bed beside her, and she took my hand and held it until nearly dawn.

EARLY AUTUMN

For David Parker and Daniel Parker,
with the respect and admiration of their father
who grew up with them.

CHAPTER ONE

THE URBAN RENEWERS had struck again. They'd evicted me, a fortune-teller, and a bookie from the corner of Mass. Ave. and Boylston, moved in with sandblasters and bleached oak and plant hangers, and last I looked appeared to be turning the place into a Marin County whorehouse. I moved down Boylston Street to the corner of Berkeley, second floor. I was half a block from Brooks Brothers and right over a bank. I felt at home. In the bank they did the same kind of stuff the fortune-teller and the bookie had done. But they dressed better.

I was standing in the window of my office looking out at a soft rainy January day with the temperature in the high fifties and no sign of snow. To the right across Boylston I could see Bonwit Teller. To the left Police Headquarters. In Bonwit's windows there were mannequins wearing tight leather clothes and chains. Police headquarters leaned more to Dacron. In the window bay of the advertising agency across the street a young black-haired woman in high-waisted gray trousers leaned over a drawing board. Her back was toward the window.

"My compliments to your tailor," I said out loud. My voice sounded odd in the empty room. The black-haired woman went away and I sat at my desk and looked at the picture of Susan Silverman. It was the blowup of a color picture taken last summer in her backyard. Her tanned face and pink blouse were bright against the dark green of the muted trees. I was still looking at Susan's face when my office door opened and a client came in carrying a belted poplin raincoat over one arm.

She said, "Mr. Spenser?"

I said, "I knew my clientele would upgrade when I moved in over a bank."

She smiled wonderfully at me. She had blond hair that contrasted handsomely with her black eyes and dark eyebrows. She was small and very trim and elegant. She had on a tailored black suit and vest, white shirt, black bow tie with long ends like Brett Maverick used to wear, and black boots with very high narrow heels. She was wearing gold and it looked real: gold earrings, gold watch, gold chains around the neck, gold chain bracelets, a wide gold wedding band, and a large diamond in a gold setting. I was optimistic about my fee.

She said, "You are Mr. Spenser?"

I said, "Yes," and stood up and held a chair for her. She had a precise walk and a very nicely integrated figure and she sat erect in the chair. I went around behind my desk again and sat down and smiled. Time was they started to undress when I smiled, but I guess the smile had lost a step. The black eyes looked at me very carefully. The hands folded still in the lap. Ankles crossed, face serious. She looked at my face, both shoulders, my chest, and as much of my stomach as showed behind the desk.

I said, "I have a puckered scar on the back of my right, ah, thigh where a man shot me about three years ago."

She nodded.

"My eyes look maybe a little funny because I used to be a fighter. That's scar tissue."

"Apparently people hit you in the nose quite often too," she said.

"Yes," I said.

She looked at me some more. At my arms, at my hands. Would I seem forward if I offered to drop trou? Probably.

I said, "Got all my teeth though. See." I bared them.

"Mr. Spenser," she said. "Tell me why I should employ you."

"Because if you don't you'll have wasted all this sizing up," I said. "You'll have spent all this time impressing me with your no-nonsense elegance and your perfect control and gone away empty."

She studied my forehead.

"And I look very dashing in a deer stalker and a trench coat."

She looked directly at me and shook her head slightly.

"And I have a gun," I said. I took it off my hip and showed it to her.

She turned her head away and looked out my window, where it had gotten dark and shiny with the lights glistening off the rain.

I put the gun away and clasped my hands and rested my elbows on the arms of my chair and propped my chin. I let the chair tip back on its spring and I sat and waited.

"Mr. Spenser, do you have time to waste like this," she said.

"Yes, I do," I said.

"Well, I do not," she said and I lip-synched the words with her as she said them. That annoyed her.

"Don't you want the job?" she said.

"I don't know," I said. "I don't know what the job is."

"Well, I want some evidence of your qualifications before I discuss it with you."

"Hell, lady, I showed you my scar tissue and my gun. What else do you need?"

"This is a sensitive job. It is not a matter of guns. It involves a child."

"Maybe you should get hold of Dr. Spock."

Silence. She looked at my hands where my chin was resting.

"Your hands are very strong-looking," she said.

"Want to see me crack a walnut?" I said.

"Are you married?" she said.

"No."

She smiled again. It was a good one. Hundred, hundred-fifty watt. But I'd seen better. Susan could have smiled her right into the woodwork. She moved her body slightly in the chair. She remained trim and upright, but somehow a wiggle came through.

I said, "If you bat your eyes at me I'm calling a policewoman."

She wiggled again, without moving. *How the hell does she do that?*

"I've got to trust you," she said. "I have no one else. I must turn to you."

"Hard," I said. "Hard for a woman alone, I'll bet."

Wiggle. Smile. Sigh. "Yes, I've got to find someone to help me. Will it be you?" She leaned forward slightly. She moistened her lower lip. "Will you help me?"

"I would gather stars," I said, "out of the blue."

"Don't make fun of me," she said. "I'm desperate."

"What are you desperate about?"

"My son. His father has taken him."

"And what would you like me to do?"

"Bring him back."

"Are you divorced?"

"Yes."

"Do you have custody?"

"Yes, of course. I'm his mother."

"Does his father have visitation privileges?"

"Yes, but this isn't a visit. He's taken Paul and he won't bring him back."

"And the court?"

"There's a hearing, and Mel's being subpoenaed but they can't find him."

"Is Mel your husband?"

"Yes. So I've spoken to the police and they said if they could find him they'd serve him a summons. But you know they aren't going to look for him."

"Probably not. They are sometimes busy," I said.

"And so I want you to find him and bring my Paul back."

"How's the boy feel about all this?"

"Naturally he wants to be with his mother, but he's only fifteen. He has no say. His father has simply taken him and hidden him."

"Mel misses Paul that much?"

"He doesn't miss him. He doesn't care about Paul one way or the other. It's merely his way of getting at me. He doesn't want me to have Paul."

"So he took him."

"Yes."

"Good deal for the kid," I said.

"Mel doesn't care about that. He wants to hurt me. And he's not going to."

There was no wiggle when she said the last sentence. "I want you to bring that kid back to me, away from his father. Paul is legally mine."

I was silent.

"I can pay any reasonable fee," she said. "I got an excellent alimony settlement." She was quite brisk and business-suity again.

I took in some air and let it out through my nose. I looked at her.

She looked back.

"What's the matter," she said.

I shook my head. "It does not sound like a real good time," I said.

"Mr. Spenser," the lower lip moistened again, mouth open a little, tip of the tongue running along the inner edge of the lip. "Please. I have no one else. Please."

"There's a question whether you need anyone else," I said, "but I'll take a whack at it on one condition."

"What?"

"You tell me your name so I'll know where the bill gets sent."

She smiled. "Giacomin," she said, "Patty Giacomin."

"Like the old Ranger's goalie," I said.

"I'm sorry?"

"Gentleman of the same name used to be a hockey player."

"Oh. I'm afraid I don't follow sports much."

"No shame to it," I said. "Matter of not being raised properly. Not your fault at all."

She smiled again, although this time it was a little unsure, as if now that she had me she wasn't certain she wanted me. It's a look I've seen a lot.

"Okay," I said. "Tell me everything you can think of about where old Mel might be."

I pulled a lined white pad closer, picked up a pencil, and listened.

CHAPTER TWO

AT 120,000 MILES my 1968 Chevy convertible had bought the farm. There's just so much you can do with duct tape. With some of Huge Dixon's bounty money I had bought Susan's maroon MGB with whitewalls and a chrome luggage rack on the trunk lid, and at ten fifteen the next morning I was sitting in it outside an apartment building on Hammond Pond Parkway in Chestnut Hill. According to Patty Giacomin her husband's girl friend lived there. She knew that because she had once followed her husband out here and seen him go in and come out with a woman from his office named Elaine Brooks.

I'd asked how she knew it was a girl friend and not just business and Patty Giacomin had given me a look of such withering scorn that I'd let it go. Patty didn't know where her husband lived. She couldn't reach him through his office. They didn't know where he was. The girl friend was all we could think of.

"He'll show up there," Patty had said, "unless he's got a new one. He's always got to have a little honey."

So I sat with the motor idling and the heater on. The temperature had dropped forty-two degrees since yesterday and January in Boston was back to normal. I turned on the radio. A disc jockey with a voice like rancid lard was describing how much he liked the new record by Neil Diamond. Then Neil began to sing his new record. I shut it off.

A lot of cars went by heading under Route 9 for the Chestnut Hill Mall. There were two Bloomingdale's in Chestnut Hill Mall. Susan and I had come shopping there two weeks before Christmas, but she'd complained of sensory overload and we'd had to leave.

A jogger went by with a watch cap pulled over his ears and a blue jacket on that said TENNESSEE TECH STAFF. Even in the cold his stride had an easy spring to it. I'd done the same thing along the Charles three hours earlier and the wind off the river had been hard as the Puritan God. I looked at my watch. Ten forty-five. I turned on the radio again and fished around until I found Tony Cennamo's jazz show. He was doing a segment on Sonny Rollins. I listened.

At eleven the show was over and I shut the radio off again. I opened my businesslike manila folder and looked at my page and a half of notes. Mel Giacomin was forty. He ran an insurance agency in Reading and until his divorce he had lived on Emerson Road in Lexington. His wife lived there still with their fifteen-year-old son, Paul. As far as his wife knew, the agency did well. He also ran a real estate business out of the same office and owned several apartment houses, mostly in Boston. The marriage had been troubled from the start, in dissolution for the last five years, and husband and wife had separated a year and a half ago. He'd moved out. She never knew where. The divorce proceedings had been bitter, and the decree had become final only three months ago.

Giacomin was, in his wife's phrase, "a whoremonger" and, his wife said, was very active among the younger women in his office and elsewhere. I looked at his picture. Long nose, small eyes, big droopy mustache. Hair worn medium length

over the ears. On the back I read his wife's description: 6'1",
210-225 (weight varied depending on how much he was drinking and exercising and dieting). Had been a football player at
Furman and still showed signs of it.

I had a picture of the boy too. He had his father's nose
and small eyes. His face was narrow and sullen. His dark hair
was long. His mouth was small and the upper lip formed a
cupid's bow.

I looked again at my watch. Eleven thirty. He probably
wasn't into morning sex. I didn't know what she looked like.
There was no picture available and Patty Giacomin's description was sketchy. Blond hair in a curly perm, medium height,
good figure. "Busty," Patty had said. I'd called Giacomin's office at nine, nine thirty, and ten of ten and she'd not been in.
Neither had he. No one knew when to expect either. I looked
at my watch again. Eleven thirty-five. I was sick of sitting. I
pulled the MG up around the corner onto Heath Street and
parked and walked back down to the apartment building. On
the directory inside the outer doors Elaine Brooks was listed
on the third floor, apartment 315. I pushed the buzzer. Nothing happened. I pushed it again and held it. After nearly a
minute a thick female voice said hello through the intercom.
The voice had been sleeping one minute prior.

I said, "Harry?"

She said, "What?"

I said, "Harry. It's me, Herb."

She said, "There's no goddamned Harry here."

I said, "What?"

She said. "You pushed the wrong button, you asshole."

I said, "Oh, sorry." The intercom went dead.

She was in there and I'd wakened her. She wouldn't be
going right out. I went back and got into my car and drove the
two or three hundred yards to Bloomingdale's and bought a
big silver wine bucket for a hundred bucks. It left me two
dollars for lunch. If I got a chance for lunch. I was hungry. But
I was used to that. I was always hungry. I had the wine
bucket gift wrapped and went back to the apartment building.
I parked out front this time and went into the foyer and rang

Elaine Brooks again. She answered the first buzz and her voice had freshened up some.

"Package for Ms. Brooks," I said.

"Just leave it in the foyer," she said. "I'll get it in a while."

"Mr. Giacomin said deliver it personal, ma'am. He said don't leave it in the hall or nothing. He said give it right to you."

"Okay," she said, "bring it up."

I said, "Yes, ma'am." The door buzzed and I went in. I was wearing off-white straight-legged Levi's cords, and moccasins and a blue wool shirt and a beige poplin jacket with a sheepskin lining and collar. A little slick for a cabbie maybe—if she noticed how much the shirt cost, but she probably wouldn't.

I took the elevator to the third floor and counted numbers to 15. I knocked. There was silence while I assume she peeped out through the little spyglass. Then the door opened on a safety chain and a narrow segment of face and one eye looked out at me. I'd figured on that. That's why I'd bought the bucket. In the box it was much too big to fit through a safety chain opening. I held the box up and looked at the small opening.

She said, "Okay, just a minute," and closed the door. I heard the chain slide off and then the door opened. The Bloomingdale's wrapper does it every time. Maybe I should rely on that more and on my smile less.

The door opened. She was as described only better looking. And she was busty. So is Dolly Parton. She'd done her hair and face, but hadn't dressed yet. She wore a long brown robe with white piping and a narrow white belt tied in front. Her feet were bare. Her toenails were painted. It didn't help much. Never saw a toenail I liked.

"Here you go, ma'am," I said.

She took the package. "Any message?"

"Not to me, ma'am. Maybe inside. All Mr. Giacomin told me was see that I put it right in your hands.'

"Well, thank you," she said.

"Okay." I didn't move.

She looked at me. "Oh," she said. "Wait a minute." She closed the door and was gone maybe a minute and then the door opened and she gave me half a buck. I looked at it sort of glumly.

"Thanks," I said.

She closed the door without comment and I went on back down to the car. I pulled out of the turn-around in front of the apartment and parked up the road a little so I could see in the rearview mirror. And I waited.

I'd accomplished a couple of things maybe. One, for certain, I knew what she looked like so if she left I could follow; otherwise, I had to wait for old Mel to show up. The second thing, maybe, was she'd call to thank him for the gift and he'd say he never sent it and that would stir them up and one would go to the other. Or it would make them especially careful and I wouldn't be able to find him through her. The odds were with me though. And if his wife was right, he was too randy to stay away from her forever.

Over the years I'd found that stirring things up was better than not. When things got into motion I accomplished more. Or I seemed to.

CHAPTER THREE

WHEN SHE CAME out I almost missed her. I was watching the front door and just caught a glimpse of her as she cruised out from behind the apartment building in a black Buick Regal. I got in behind her, separated by one car as she swung up onto Route 9 and headed west. She had no reason to be looking for a tail and I had no reason to be tricky about it. I stayed a car or two behind her all the way onto 128 North and up Route 93 and onto Route 125 in Andover. Route 125 was harder. It was nearly deserted, running through the Harold Parker State Forest. Staying too close to her might make her notice. I hung a long way back and almost missed her again when she turned off just before Route 114 and went down Chestnut Street in Andover. What saved me was the red light. The car that had been ahead of her was stopped at it, and she wasn't there. She must have taken the left just before it. I yanked the MG around and accelerated down Chestnut Street. It was a winding back road at this end and the MG did much better time than the Buick. I caught sight of her in about two hundred yards. I slowed and let her pull ahead again. A mile or so farther and she stopped on the right-hand side. I turned right a block behind her and stopped out of sight and got out and walked back. Her car was there and she was disappearing into a big white house on the right.

I walked down. The house she was parked in front of was a two-family, up and down. The front hall door was unlocked and inside were two other doors. The one on the right obviously led to the downstairs apartment. The one directly ahead to the upstairs. I put my ear against the downstairs door. I could hear a TV set and the sound of a baby crying. That wouldn't be Giacomin. If she was visiting Giacomin. For all I knew she was here to play Parcheesi with an elderly aunt.

I tried the knob of the upstairs door. It turned but the door didn't open. Above it was the round key side of a spring bolt. They were easy, if the jamb wasn't tight. I took a thin plastic shim from my coat pocket and tried it. The jamb wasn't tight. I popped the bolt back and opened the door. The stairs rose straight up ahead of me to a landing and then they turned right. I went up them. At the top was another door. I put my ear against it. I could hear a radio and the low sound of conversation.

I put my hand on the knob and turned it quietly. The door was not locked. I opened it silently and stepped into a kind of foyer. Ahead was a dining room. To my right a living room through an archway. In the living room Elaine Brooks sat in a red plush armchair leaning forward, talking with a big man with a long nose and small eyes and a droopy mustache. *Elementary, my dear Watson, elementary.*

She didn't see me, her back was toward me. But he did. He was standing with a drink in his hand while she talked to him, and when I opened the door we looked right at each other. I had never figured the drill on a situation like this. Did I say "Ah, hah" vigorously, or just stare accusingly. He was quicker than I. He knew just the right thing to say.

He said, "What the hell do you want?"

"Perfect," I said. "The very phrase."

Elaine Brooks turned and looked at me. Her eyes widened.

"That's him, Mel," she said. "That's the guy brought the package from you."

Giacomin was wearing a gold Ban-Lon turtleneck and green polyester pants with no belt loops and one of those little flaps that buttons across in front instead of a belt. On the little finger of his right hand was a silver ring in the form of a snake biting its tail. On the little finger of his left hand was a silver ring with an amethyst set in it. The Ban-Lon shirt was not flattering to his body. He was fat around the middle. He said, "I asked you a question. I want an answer and I want it now."

I said, "You shouldn't wear a Ban-Lon shirt like that if you're going to scare people. It's a loser. Cary Grant wouldn't look good in Ban-Lon, you know."

"What did you bring her a present for? What the hell you doing trying to sneak into my house?"

I noticed he had sucked up his gut a little, but there's not a lot you can do with beer wings. I said, "My name is Spenser. I know it sounds corny, but I'm a private detective. Your wife hired me to find her son."

"My ex-wife," he said. "She offered to screw you yet?"

"No. I was surprised. Most women do at once." I looked at Elaine Brooks. "Am I starting to show my age, you think? I'm zero for two today."

Giacomin said, "Listen, Jack, I've heard all I'm going to hear from you. Move out."

346

I shook my head. "Nope. I need to stay and talk a little about your kid. Let's start over. Pretend I haven't snuck in here. Pretend you haven't yelled at me. Pretend I haven't been a wise guy. It's a bad habit, I know, but sometimes I can't resist."

"The kid ain't here. Now get the hell out of here or I'm going to throw you down the stairs."

"Now I told you, we have to talk. I am very stubborn. Maybe I've lost my sex appeal, but I'm still stubborn. I'm going to find that kid and I'm pretty sure you can help."

Giacomin was looking at me. He was a big guy and he'd played football, and he was probably used to being tough. But he probably also knew something about physical potential from his old football days and I think he had a suspicion that he couldn't throw me down the stairs.

"I don't know where he is," Giacomin said.

"Are you worried at all about the fact that his mother doesn't know either?" I said.

"She tell you that?" he said.

"Not exactly. She told me he was with you."

"Well, I told you before he's not. Now are you going to leave or am I going to call the cops?"

"You're going to call the cops," I said.

"You think I won't?"

"I think you won't," I said.

"You think you can stop me?"

"I don't need to. I don't want to. I enjoy meeting policemen. Sometimes if you're good they let you play with their handcuffs."

He looked at me. Elaine Brooks looked at me. If there'd been a mirror, I would have looked at me. But there wasn't. So I looked at them. In the quiet I could hear a television playing. It didn't seem to be from downstairs.

"Look, Jack, I'm getting pretty tired of you," he said. "What is it you want?"

"I want to take your kid back to his mother," I said. "I told you that already."

"And I told you he ain't here."

"Why don't I look around and prove it to myself," I said.

"You got a search warrant?"

"A search warrant? You gotta stop watching *Starsky and Hutch,*" I said. "I'm not a cop. I don't get search warrants."

"You can't just walk in here and search my house," he said.

"Why not?"

We looked at each other some more. I was pretty sure the kid was there. If he wasn't, why not call the cops? All I had to do was stay there. They'd bend. They wouldn't be able to think of anything else to do.

Giacomin stopped looking at me long enough to look at his girl friend. She didn't have anything to offer. He looked back at me.

"All right," he said. "I've had enough. Either you walk out of here now or I kick your ass out."

"Don't do that," I said. "You're out of shape. I'll hurt you."

Giacomin looked at me and looked away. I knew he wasn't going to.

"The hell with it," he said with a small push-away hand gesture. "It's not worth a fight. Take him. He's down the hall." Giacomin gestured with his head. He didn't look at me or Elaine Brooks.

But the boy wasn't down the hall. He was right around the corner in the dining room. He stepped into sight around the archway.

"Swell fight you put up for me, Daddy dear," he said.

He was a short thin kid and his voice had a soft whine to it. He was wearing a short-sleeved vertically striped dress shirt that gapped open near his navel, and maroon corduroy pants and Top-Siders with the rawhide lacing gone from one.

Giacomin said, "You remember who you're talking to, kid."

The kid smiled without humor. "I know," he said. "I know who I'm talking to, Dads."

Giacomin turned away from him and was silent.

I said, "My name is Spenser. Your mother sent me to bring you back to her."

The kid shrugged elaborately. I noticed that the pants were too big for him. The crotch sagged.

"You want to go?" I said.

He shrugged again.

"Would you rather stay here?"

"With him?" The kid's soft whine was full of distaste.

"With him," I said. "Or would you prefer to live with your mother?"

"I don't care."

"How about you?" I said to Giacomin. "You care?"

"The bitch got everything else," he said. "She can have him too. For now."

I said, "Okay, Paul. You got any stuff to pack?"

He shrugged. The all-purpose gesture. Maybe I should work on mine.

"He's got nothing to pack," Giacomin said. "Everything here is mine. She isn't getting any of it."

"Smart," I said. "Smart. I like a man gets out of a marriage gracefully."

"What the hell's that supposed to mean?" Giacomin said.

"You wouldn't know," I said. "The kid got a coat? It's about nineteen degrees out. I'll see that she sends it back if you want."

Giacomin said to his son, "Get your coat."

The boy went to the front hall closet and took out a navy pea coat. It was wrinkled, as if it had been crumpled on the floor rather than hanging. He put it on and left it unbuttoned. I opened the door to the stairs and he walked through it and started down the stairs. I looked at Giacomin.

"You've gotten yourself in a lot of trouble over this, Jack, and don't you forget it," he said.

I said, "Name's Spenser with an S, like the poet. I'm in

the Boston book." I stepped through the door and closed it. Then I opened it again and stuck my head back into the hall. "Under Tough," I said. And closed the door, and walked out.

CHAPTER FOUR

THE KID SAT in the front seat beside me and stared out the window. His hands fidgeted on his lap. His fingernails were chewed short. He had hangnails. I turned left at the foot of Chestnut Street and drove south past the Academy.

I said, "Who would you rather live with, your mother or your father?"

The kid shrugged.

"Does that mean you don't know or you don't care?" I said.

"I don't know."

"Does that mean you don't know the answer to my question or you don't know who you'd rather live with?" I said.

The kid shrugged again. "Can I turn on the radio?" he said.

I said, "No. We're talking."

He shrugged.

"Would you rather be adopted?"

This time he didn't shrug.

"A ward of the state?"

Nothing.

"Join a gang of pickpockets and live in the slums of London?"

He looked at me as if I were crazy.

"Run off and join the circus? Make a raft and float down the Mississippi? Stow away on a pirate ship?"

"You're not funny," he said.

"Lot of people tell me that," I said. "Who would you rather live with, your mother or your father?"

"What'll you do if I won't say?" he said.

"Ride around and be funny at you till you plead for mercy."

He didn't say anything. But he didn't shrug. And he did look at me. Briefly.

"Want me to turn around and take you back to your father?"

"What difference does it make?" the kid said. "What do you care? It's not your business. Whyn't you leave me alone?"

"Because right now you're in my keeping and I'm trying to decide what's best to do with you."

"I thought my mother hired you. Whyn't you do what she tells you?"

"I might not approve of what she wants me to do."

"But she hired you," he said.

"She gave me a hundred bucks, one day's pay. If you don't want me to take you to her, I'll take you back to your old man, give her back her hundred."

"I bet you wouldn't," he said. He was staring out the window when he said it.

"Convince me you should be with him and I will."

"Okay, I'd rather be with him," the kid said. His face was still turned to the window.

"Why?" I said.

"See. I knew you wouldn't," he said. He turned his face toward me and he looked as if he'd won something.

"I didn't say I wouldn't," I said. "I asked for reasons. This is important stuff, choosing a parent. I'm not going to have you do it to win a bet."

He stared out the window again. We were in North Reading, still going south.

"See, Paul, what I'm trying to do is get you to decide what you'd like best to do. Are the questions too hard for you? You want to try watching my lips move?"

With his face still turned to the window the kid said, "I

don't care who I live with. They both suck. It doesn't make any difference. They're both awful. I hate them."

The soft whine was a little shaky. As if he might cry.

"Son of a bitch," I said. "I hadn't thought of that."

Again he looked at me in an odd sort of triumph. "So now what are you going to do?"

I wanted to shrug and look out the window. I said, "I'll probably take you back to your mother and keep the hundred dollars."

"That's what I thought," the kid said.

"Would you rather I did something else?" I said.

He shrugged. We were through Reading Square almost to 128. "Can I turn on the radio now?" he said.

"No," I said. I knew I was being churlish, but the kid annoyed me. In his whiny, stubborn desperation he irritated the hell out of me. Mr. Warm. There's no such thing as a bad boy.

The kid almost smirked.

"You want to know why I'm taking you to your mother?" I said.

"To get the hundred bucks."

"Yeah. But it's more than a hundred bucks. It's a way of thinking about things."

The kid shrugged. If he did it enough, I would stop the car and bang his head on the pavement. "When all your options are lousy," I said, "you try to choose the least lousy. Apparently you're equally bad off with your mother or your father. Apparently you don't care which place you're unhappy. If I take you back to your father you're unhappy and I get nothing. If I take you back to your mother you're unhappy and I get a hundred bucks. So I'm taking you back to your mother. You understand?"

"Sure, you want the hundred."

"It would be the same if it were a dime. It's a way to think about things. It's a way not to get shoved around by circumstances."

"And Mommy will give you money," he said. "Maybe

you can fuck her." He checked me carefully, looking sideways at me as he said it, to see how shocked I'd be.

"Your father suggested the same thing," I said. "Your mom into sex, is she?"

The kid said, "I dunno."

"Or you figure I'm so irresistible that it's inevitable."

The kid shrugged. I figured I could take maybe two more shrugs before I stopped the car. "I don't want to talk about it," he said.

"Then you shouldn't have brought it up," I said.

He was silent.

I turned off of Route 28 onto Route 128 South, toward Lexington.

"I also think it's bad form to talk about your mother that way to a stranger."

"Why?"

"It's not done," I said.

The kid shrugged and stared out the window. He had one shrug left.

"If my father had started to fight with you, what would you do?"

"I'd have subdued him."

"How?"

"Depends how tough he is."

"He used to be a football player and he still lifts weights at the health club."

I shrugged. It was catching.

"Do you think you could beat him up?" he said.

"Oh, sure," I said. "He's a big strong guy, I guess, but I do this for a living. And I'm in better shape."

"Big deal," the kid said.

"I didn't bring it up," I said.

"I don't care about muscles," the kid said.

"Okay," I said.

"I suppose you think you're a big man, having muscles," the kid said.

"I think they are useful to me in what I do," I said.

"Well, I think they're ugly."

I took my hands off the wheel long enough to turn my palms up.

"How come you're a detective?" he said.

"Like the man said, because I can't sing or dance."

"It's an awful gross job to me," he said.

I made the same palms-up gesture. We were passing the Burlington Mall. "What exit do I take?" I said.

"Four and two-twenty-five toward Bedford," he said. "How come you want to do a gross job?"

"It lets me live life on my own terms," I said. "You sure you mean toward Bedford?"

"Yes. I'll show you," he said. And he did. We turned off toward Bedford, turned right, and right again and over an overpass back toward Lexington. Emerson Road was not far off the highway, a community of similar homes with a lot of wood and glass and some stone and brick. It was contemporary, but it worked okay in Lexington. I parked in the driveway out front and we got out. It was late afternoon and the wind had picked up. We leaned into it as we walked to his back door.

He opened it and went in without knocking and without any announcement.

CHAPTER FIVE

I RANG THE DOORBELL a long blast and followed him in. It was a downstairs hall. There were two white hollow core doors on the left and a short stairway to the right. On the wall before the stairway was a big Mondrian print in a chrome frame. Four steps up was the living room. As I went up the stairs behind the kid his mother came to the head of the stairs.

The kid said, "Here's a big treat, I'm home."

Patty Giacomin said, "Oh, Paul, I didn't expect you so soon."

She was wearing a pink silk outfit—tapered pants with a loose-fitting top. The top hung outside the pants and was gathered at the waist by a gold belt.

I was standing two steps down behind Paul on the stairs. There was a moment of silence. Then Patty Giacomin said, "Well, come up, Mr. Spenser. Have a drink. Paul, let Mr. Spenser get by."

I stepped into the living room. There were two glasses and a pitcher that looked like martini on the low glass coffee table in front of the couch. There was a fire in the fireplace. There was Boursin cheese on a small tray and a plate of crackers that looked like little shredded-wheat biscuits. And on his feet, politely, in front of the couch was the very embodiment of contemporary elegance. He was probably my height and slim as a weasel. He wore a subdued gray herringbone coat and vest with charcoal pants, a narrow pink tie, a pin collar, and black Gucci loafers. A pink-and-charcoal hankie spilled out of the breast pocket of his jacket. His hair was cut short and off the ears and he had a close-cropped beard and a mustache. Whether to see or be seen I had no way to tell, but he was also sporting a pair of pink-tinted aviator glasses with very thin black rims. The pink tie was shiny.

Patty Giacomin said, "Paul, you know Stephen. Stephen, this is Mr. Spenser. Stephen Court."

Stephen put out his hand. It was manicured and tanned. St. Thomas, no doubt. His handshake was firm without being strong. "Good to see you," he said.

He didn't say anything to Paul and Paul didn't look at him. Patty said, "Would you join us for a drink, Mr. Spenser?"

"Sure," I said. "Have any beer?"

"Oh, dear, I'm not sure," she said, "Paul, go look in the refrigerator and see if there's any beer."

Paul hadn't taken his coat off. He went over to the TV set in the bookcase and turned it on, set no channel, and sat down in a black Naugahyde armchair. The set warmed up and a *Brady Bunch* rerun came on. It was loud.

355

Patty Giacomin said, "Paul, for God's sake," and low-ered the volume. While she did that I went into the kitchen on my right and found a can of Schlitz in the refrigerator. There were two more with it, and not much else. I went back into the living room with my beer. Stephen was sitting again, sipping his martini, his legs arranged so as not to ruin the crease in his pants. Patty was standing with her martini in hand.

"Did you have much trouble finding Paul, Mr. Spen-ser?"

"No," I said. "It was easy."

"Did you have trouble with his father?"

"No."

"Have some cheese and a cracker," she said. I took some. Boursin on a Triscuit isn't my favorite, but it had been a long time since breakfast. I washed it down with the beer. There was silence except for a now softened *Brady Bunch*.

Stephen took a small sip of his martini, leaned back slightly, brushed a tiny fleck of something from his left lapel, and said, "Tell me, Mr. Spenser, what do you do?" I heard an overtone of disdain, but I'm probably too sensitive.

"I'm a disc jockey at Régine's," I said. "Haven't I seen you there?"

Patty Giacomin spoke very quickly. "Mr. Spenser," she said, "could I ask you a really large favor?"

I nodded.

"I, well, I know you've already done so much bringing Paul back, but, well, it's just that it happened much sooner than I thought it would and Stephen and I have a dinner reservation. . . . Could you take Paul out maybe to McDon-ald's or someplace? I'll pay of course."

I looked at Paul. He was sitting, still with his coat on, staring at *The Brady Bunch*. Stephen said, "There's a rather decent Chinese restaurant in town, Szechuan and Mandarin cooking."

Patty Giacomin had taken her purse off the mantel and was rummaging in it. "Yes," she said. "The Yangtze River. Paul can show you. That's a good idea. Paul always likes to eat there." She took a twenty out of her purse and handed it to me. "Here," she said. "That should be enough. It's not very expensive."

I didn't take the twenty. I said to Paul, "You want to go?" and then I shrugged at the same time he did.

"What are you doing?" he said.

"Practicing my timing," I said. "Your shrug is so expressive I'm trying to develop one just like it. You want to go get something to eat?"

He started to shrug, stopped, and said, "I don't care."

"Well, I do," I said. "Come on. I'm starving."

Patty Giacomin still held the twenty out. I shook my head.

"You asked for a favor," I said. "You didn't offer to hire me. My treat."

"Oh, Spenser," she said, "don't be silly."

"Come on kid," I said to Paul. "Let's go. I'll dazzle you with my knowledge of Oriental lore."

The kid shifted slightly. "Come on," I said. "I'm hungry as hell."

He got up. "What's the latest you'll be home," he said to his mother.

"I'll be home before twelve," she said.

Stephen said, "Good meeting you, Spenser. Good seeing you Paul."

"Likewise I'm sure," I said. We went out.

When we were in the car again Paul said, "Why'd you do it?"

"What, agree to take you to dinner?"

"Yes."

"I felt bad for you," I said.

"How come?"

"Because you came home after being missing and no one seemed glad."

"I don't care."

"That's probably wise," I said. "If you can pull it off." I turned out of Emerson Road. "Which way?" I said.

"Left," he said.

"I don't think I could pull it off," I said.

"What?"

"Not caring," I said. "I think if I got sent off to eat with a stranger my first night home I'd be down about it."

"Well, I'm not," he said.

"Good," I said. "You want to eat in this Chinese place?"

"I don't care," he said.

We came to a cross street. "Which way?" I said.

"Left," he said.

"That the way to the Chinese restaurant?" I said.

"Yes."

"Good, we'll eat there."

We drove through Lexington, along dark streets that were mostly empty. It was a cold night. People were staying in. Lexington looks like you think it would. A lot of white colonial houses, many of them original. A lot of green shutters. A lot of bull's-eye glass and small, paned windows. We came into the center of town, the green on the right. The statue of the Minuteman motionless in the cold. No one was taking a picture of it.

"It's over there," Paul said, "around that square."

In the restaurant Paul said, "How come you wouldn't let her pay for it?"

"It didn't seem the right thing to do," I said.

"Why not? Why should you pay? She's got plenty of money."

"If we order careful," I said, "I can afford this."

The waiter came. I ordered a Beck's beer for me and a Coke for Paul. We looked at the menu.

"What can I have?" Paul said.

"Anything you want," I said. "I'm very successful."

We looked at the menu some more. The waiter brought the beer and the Coke. He stood with his pencil and paper poised. "You order?" he said.

"No," I said. "We're not ready."

"Okay," he said, and went away.

Paul said, "I don't know what to have."

I said, "What do you like?"

He said, "I don't know."

I nodded. "Yeah," I said, "somehow I had a sense you might say that."

He stared at the menu.

I said, "How about I order for both of us?"

"What if you order something I don't like?"

"Don't eat it."

"But I'm hungry."

"Then decide what you want."

He stared at the menu some more. The waiter wandered back. "You order?" he said.

I said, "Yes. We'll have two orders of Peking ravioli, the duck with plum sauce, the moo shu pork, and two bowls of white rice. And I'll have another beer and he'll have another Coke."

The waiter said, "Okay." He picked up the menus and went away.

Paul said, "I don't know if I'll like that stuff."

"We'll find out soon," I said.

"You gonna send my mother a bill?"

"For the meal?"

"Yes."

"No."

"I still don't see why you want to pay for my dinner."

"I'm not sure," I said. "It has to do with propriety."

The waiter came and plunked the ravioli on the table and two bottles of spiced oil.

"What's propriety?" Paul said.

"Appropriateness. Doing things right."

He looked at me without any expression.

"You want some raviolis?" I said.

"Just one," he said, "to try. They look gross."

"I thought you liked to eat here."

"My mother just said that. I never been here."

"Put some of the oil on it," I said. "Not much. It's sort of hot."

He cut his ravioli in two and ate half. He didn't say anything but he ate the other half. The waiter brought the rest of the food. We each ate four of the raviolis.

359

"You put the moo shu in one of these little pancakes, see, like this. Then you roll it up, like this. And you eat it."

"The pancake doesn't look like it's cooked," Paul said.

I ate some moo shu pork. He took a pancake and did as I'd showed him.

I said, "You want another Coke?"

He shook his head. I ordered another beer.

"You drink a lot?"

"No," I said. "Not as much as I'd like."

He speared a piece of duck with his fork and was trying to cut it on his plate.

"That's finger food," I said. "You don't have to use your knife and fork."

He kept on with the knife and fork. He didn't say anything. I didn't say anything. We finished eating at seven fifteen. We arrived back at his house at seven thirty. I parked and got out of the car with him.

"I'm not afraid to go in alone," he said.

"Me either," I said. "But it's never any fun going into an empty house. I'll walk in with you."

"You don't need to," he said. "I'm alone a lot."

"Me too," I said.

We walked to the house together.

CHAPTER SIX

IT WAS FRIDAY night, and Susan Silverman and I were at the Garden watching the Celtics and the Phoenix Suns play basketball. I was eating peanuts and drinking beer and explaining to Susan the fine points of going back door. I was having quite a good time. She was bored.

"You owe me for this," she said. She had barely sipped

at a paper cup of beer in one hand. There was a lipstick half moon on the rim.

"They don't sell champagne by the paper cup here," I said.

"How about a Graves?"

"You want me to get beat up," I said. "Go up and ask if they sell a saucy little white Bordeaux?"

"Why is everyone cheering?" she said.

"Westphal just stuffed the ball backward over his head, didn't you see?"

"He's not even on the Celtics."

"No, but the fans appreciate the shot. Besides, he used to be."

"This is very boring," she said.

I offered my peanuts to her. She took two.

"Afterwards I'll let you kiss me," I said.

"I'm thinking better of the game," she said.

Cowens hit an outside shot.

"How come most of the players are black?" Susan said.

"Black man's game," I said. "Hawk says it's heritage. Says there were a lot of schoolyards in the jungle."

She smiled and sipped at the beer. She made a face. "How can you drink so much of this stuff?" she said.

"Practice," I said. "Years of practice."

Walter Davis hit a jump shot.

"What were you saying before about that boy you found Wednesday? What's his name?"

"Paul Giacomin," I said.

"Yes," Susan said. "You said you wanted to talk about him."

"But not while I'm watching the ball game."

"Can't you watch and talk at the same time? If you can't, go buy me something to read."

I shelled a peanut. "I don't know," I said. "It's just that I keep thinking about him. I feel bad for him."

"There's a surprise."

"That I feel bad for him?"

"You'd feel bad for Wile E. Coyote," Susan said.

Westphal hit a left-handed scoop shot. The Celtics were losing ground.

"The kid's a mess," I said. "He's skinny. He seems to have no capacity to decide anything. His only firm conviction is that both his parents suck."

"That's not so unusual a conviction for a fifteen-year-old kid," Susan said. She took another peanut.

"Yes, but in this case the kid may be right."

"Now you don't know that," Susan said. "You haven't had enough time with them to make any real judgment."

The Suns had scored eight straight points. The Celtics called time out.

"Better than you," I said. "I been with the kid. His clothes aren't right and they don't fit right. He doesn't know what to do in a restaurant. No one's ever taught him anything."

"Well, how important is it to know how to behave in a restaurant?" Susan said.

"By itself it's not important," I said. "It's just an instance, you know? I mean no one has taken any time with him. No one has told him anything, even easy stuff about dressing and eating out. He's been neglected. No one's told him how to act."

The Celtics put the ball in play from midcourt. Phoenix stole it and scored. I shook my head. Maybe if Cousy came out of retirement.

Susan said, "I haven't met this kid, but I have met a lot of kids. It is, after all, my line of work. You'd be surprised at how recalcitrant kids this age are about taking guidance from parents. They are working through the Oedipal phase, among other things, often they look and act as if they haven't had any care, even when they have. It's a way to rebel."

The Celtics threw the ball away. The Suns scored.

I said, "Are you familiar with the term blowout?"

"Is it like a burnout?" she said.

"No, I mean the game. You are witnessing a blowout," I said.

"Are the Celtics losing?"

"Yes."

"Want to leave?"

"No. It's not just who wins. I like to watch the way they play."

She said, "Mmm."

I got another bag of peanuts and another beer. With five minutes left the score was 114 to 90. I looked up at the rafters where the retired numbers hung.

"You should have seen it," I said to Susan.

"What?" She brushed a peanut shell from her lap. She was wearing blue jeans from France tucked into the tops of black boots.

"Cousy and Sharman, and Heinsohn and Lostcutoff and Russell. Havlicek, Sanders, Ramsey, Sam Jones, and K. C. Jones, Paul Silas and Don Nelson. And the war they'd have with the Knicks with Al McGuire on Cousy. And Russell against Chamberlain. You should have seen Bill Russell."

She said, "Yawn." The sleeves of her black wool turtleneck were pushed up on her forearms and the skin of her forearms was smooth and white in contrast. On a gold chain around her neck was a small diamond. She'd removed her engagement ring when she'd gotten divorced and had the stone reset. She'd had her hair permed into a very contemporary bunch of small Afro-looking curls. Her mouth was wide and her big dark eyes hinted at clandestine laughter.

"On the other hand," I said, "Russell ought to see you."

"Gimme a peanut," she said.

The final score was 130 to 101 and the Garden was nearly empty when the buzzer sounded. It was nine twenty-five. We put on our coats and moved toward the exits. It was easy. No pushing. No shoving. Most people had left a long time ago. In fact most people hadn't come at all.

"It's a fine thing that Walter Brown's not around to see this," I said. "In the Russell years you had to fight to get in and out."

"That sounds like a good time," Susan said. "Sorry I missed it."

On Causeway Street, under the elevated, it was very

cold. I said, "You want to walk up to The Market? Or shall we go home?"

"It's cold," Susan said. "Let's go home to my house and I'll make us a goodie." She had the collar of her raccoon coat turned up so that her face was barely visible inside it.

The heater in my MG took hold on Route 93 and we were able to unbutton before we got to Medford. "The thing about that kid," I said, "is that he's like a hostage. His mother and father hate each other and use him to get even with each other."

Susan shook her head. "God, Spenser, how old are you? Of course they do that. Even parents who don't hate each other do that. Usually the kids survive it."

"This kid isn't going to survive it," I said. "He's too alone."

Susan was quiet.

"He hasn't got any strengths," I said. "He's not smart or strong or good-looking or funny or tough. All he's got is a kind of ratty meanness. It's not enough."

"So what do you think you'll do about it?" Susan said.

"Well, I'm not going to adopt him."

"How about a state agency. The Office for Children, say, or some such."

"They got enough trouble fighting for their share of federal funds. I wouldn't want to burden them with a kid."

"I know people who work in human services for the state," Susan said. "Some are very dedicated."

"And competent?"

"Some."

"You want to give me a percentage?"

"That are dedicated and competent?"

"Yeah."

"You win," she said.

We turned onto Route 128. "So what do you propose," Susan said.

"I propose to let him go down the tube," I said. "I can't think of anything to do about it."

"But it bothers you."

364

"Sure, it bothers me. But I'm used to that too. The world is full of people I can't save. I get used to that. I got used to it on the cops. Any cop does. You have to or you go down the tube too."

"I know," Susan said.

"On the other hand I may see the kid again."

"Professionally?"

"Yeah. The old man will take him again. She'll try to get him back. They're too stupid and too lousy to let this go. I wouldn't be surprised if she called me again."

"You'd be smart to say no if she does. You won't feel any better by getting into it again."

"I know," I said.

We were quiet. I turned off of Route 128 at the Smithfield Center exit and drove to Susan's house.

"I've got a bottle of new Beaujolais," Susan said in the kitchen. "How about I make us a couple of cheeseburgers and we can eat them and drink the Beaujolais?"

"Will you toast my hamburger roll?" I said.

"I certainly will," Susan said. "And who knows, maybe later I'll light your fire too, big fella."

"Oh, honeylips," I said. "You really know how to talk to a guy."

She handed me the bottle of wine. "You know where the corkscrew is," she said. "Open it and let it breathe a little, while I do the cheeseburgers."

I did.

CHAPTER SEVEN

PATTY GIACOMIN CALLED me in April on a Tuesday afternoon at four o'clock. I hadn't heard from her in three months.

"Could you come to the house right now," she said.

I had been sitting in my office with my feet up on the desk and the window open sniffing the spring air and reading *A Distant Mirror* by Barbara Tuchman. I kept my finger in my place while I talked on the phone.

"I'm fairly busy," I said.

"You have to come," she said. "Please."

"Your husband got the kid again?"

"No. He's not my husband anymore. No. But Paul was almost hurt. Please, they might come back. Please, come now."

"You in danger?"

"No. I don't know. Maybe. You've got to come."

"Okay," I said. "If there's any danger, call the cops. I'll be there in half an hour."

I hung up and put my book down and headed for Lexington.

When I got there Patty Giacomin was standing in the front doorway looking out. She had on a white headband and a green silk shirt, a beige plaid skirt and tan Frye boots. Around her waist was a wide brown belt and her lipstick was glossy and nearly brown. Probably just got through scrubbing the tub.

I said, "The kid okay?"

She nodded. "Come in," she said. "Thank you for coming."

We went into the hall and up the three steps to the living room. Outside the picture window at the far end of the living room things were beginning to bloom.

"Would you like a drink?" she said.

"Same as last time," I said. "I'll take a beer if you have one."

She went to the kitchen and brought me back a can of Budweiser and a beer mug.

"I don't need the mug," I said. "I'd just as soon drink from the can."

Somewhere in the house there was a television set playing. It meant Paul was probably in residence.

Patty poured herself a glass of sherry. "Sit down," she said.

I sat on the couch. She sat across from me in an armchair and arranged her legs. I looked at her knees. She sipped her sherry. I drank some beer.

She said, "Was the traffic bad?"

I said, "Mrs. Giacomin, I galloped out here to your rescue. Don't sit around and talk at me about traffic conditions."

"I'm sorry. It's just that, well, now that you're here, I feel a little foolish. Maybe I overreacted." She sipped some more of her sherry. "But, dammit, someone did try to take Paul again."

"Your husband?"

"It wasn't him, but I'm sure he was behind it."

"What happened?"

"A strange man stopped Paul on his way home from school and told him that his father wanted to see him. Paul wouldn't go with him, so the man got out of the car and started after him, but there was a policeman at the school crossing and when Paul ran back toward him the man got back into his car and drove away."

"And Paul came home."

"Yes."

"He didn't say anything to the cop."

"No."

"He didn't—I know it's corny, but I used to be a cop—get a license number, did he?"

"I don't think so. He didn't say anything about it."

"And he didn't know the man."

"No."

We were quiet. I finished the beer. She sipped some more sherry. I looked at her knees.

"Have you told the cops?" I said.

"No."

"You figure he had some friend of his try to pick the kid up? And the friend was overzealous?"

"I don't know," she said. There was a little thigh beginning to show along with the knees. "He knows some terrible people. In his business he knew some very thuggy-looking people. I'm sure it was one of them."

"Wide lapels? Dark shirts? White ties? Big hats?"

"I'm serious," she said. "I think he knew some people on the wrong side of the law. Maybe he was on the wrong side sometimes himself."

"Why do you think so?"

"Oh, I don't know, just a sense. The kind of people he was with. How secretive he sometimes was." She spread her hands. "Just a sense. Would you like another beer?"

"Sure."

She went to the kitchen and got me one and popped the top for me and brought it to me. Then she poured herself another glass of sherry.

"Do you have a plan?" I said.

She was standing now with her legs apart and one hand on her hip looking at me. *Vogue* magazine.

"A plan?"

"You know, for me. What do you want me to do?"

"I want you to stay here with us," she said.

"Damn," I said. "You're the fifth beautiful woman today to ask me that."

"I want you to guard Paul and, the truth, me too. I don't know what Mel might do."

"Are you suggesting that he's capable of anything?"

"Yes. He is. I know you're laughing at me, but you don't know him. I'm afraid."

She sat on the edge of the chair, her knees pressed

together, her hands, one of them holding the sherry, were pressed together on top of her knees. She leaned forward toward me and moistened her bottom lip with the tip of her tongue. Vulnerable.

"You want me to move right in here and spend the night and all?"

She lowered her eyes. "Yes," she said.

"That's quite expensive. That means you pay me twenty-four hours a day."

"That's all right, I have money. I don't care. I need someone here."

"For how long?" I said.

She looked startled. "I don't know. I haven't thought about it."

"I can't stay here till the boy's twenty-one. Guarding is a temporary measure, you know. You'll have to find a better solution in the long run."

"I will," she said. "I will. But just for a little while. I'm frightened. Paul is frightened. We need a man here."

I looked past her and at the head of the stairs, in shadow, Paul stood listening. We looked at each other. Then he turned and disappeared. I looked back at his mother.

She raised her eyes. "Will you stay?" she said.

"Sure. I'll have to go home and pack a bag."

"We'll come with you," she said. She was smiling. "Paul and I will ride along. I'd love to see where you live anyway."

"Well, I've got a sports car. There's only room for two in it."

"We'll take my car," she said. "That way we'll be safe with you. And we can stop and get dinner on the way back. Or would you like a home-cooked meal? Poor man, you probably eat out all the time. Are you married? No, you're not, are you. I think I knew that." She called up the stairs. "Paul. Paul, come down. Mr. Spenser is going to stay with us." She drank the rest of her sherry.

"We can get a sandwich or something on the way," I said.

"No. When we get back I'll cook supper for you. No

argument . . . Paul, come on, we're going to get some of Mr. Spenser's things so he can stay."

Paul came down the few steps from his bedroom to the living room. He had on a long-sleeved shirt with pastel flowers all over it, black corduroy pants, and the Top-Sider moccasins. If anything, he'd gotten thinner since January.

I nodded at him. He didn't say anything. His mother said, "Get your coat, we're going to drive Mr. Spenser home to get his suitcase."

Paul put on the same pea coat he'd had in January. There were two buttons missing. But it was too warm to button it anyway. We climbed into Patty Giacomin's stick-shift Audi Fox and cruised into Boston. We went into my apartment, where Paul sat down with his hands in the pockets of his pea coat and put on my television. His mother told me the apartment was beautiful and referred to it as a bachelor pad. She looked at Susan's picture on the bookcase and asked about her. She remarked that the kitchen was spotless. I put some extra clothes and a shaving kit and a box of .38 ammunition in my suitcase and said I was ready. Patty asked if I didn't get lonely living alone. I said sometimes I did. Paul stared at a rerun of *My Three Sons*. She said she supposed it was easier for a man, living alone. I said I wasn't sure that it was, but that I had friends and I was often busy. I didn't try to explain about Susan.

On the way back to Lexington we stopped at a Star Market and Patty Giacomin cashed a check at the courtesy booth and bought some groceries. Then we went back to her house and she cooked us dinner. Steak, peas, and baked potato, and a bottle of Portuguese rosé. Innovative.

After dinner Paul returned to the tube and Patty Giacomin cleared the table. I offered to help.

"Oh, no," she said. "You sit right there. It's a pleasure to wait on a man again."

I looked at my watch. It wasn't ten o'clock yet.

CHAPTER EIGHT

THE GIACOMIN HOUSE was on three levels. I had a room on the first. There was a lavatory with a shower across the hall from me. There was a family room with a Ping-Pong table next to me, and next to the lavatory across the hall was an office where Mel Giacomin had worked out of his house occasionally when he'd lived there. The next level was living room with a dining ell and kitchen. The third level was a bathroom and three more bedrooms. Patty Giacomin slept up there and so did Paul.

The next morning I drove Paul to school at seven twenty-five. He didn't eat any breakfast. When we left, his mother was in the bathroom with the door closed. I delivered him right to the school door.

When he got out, I said, "What time does school get over?"

He said, "Five after two, I guess. I don't know exactly."

I said, "When it gets out, I'll be right here at this door. Don't come out another one. Don't go anywhere with anyone but me."

He nodded and walked into the school. I noticed his hair wasn't combed. I sat in the car and watched him until he was out of sight, then I turned and drove back to Emerson Road. Patty Giacomin was out of the bathroom, bathed and powdered and shiny with makeup. She had on a red apron with yellow flowers and underneath it a maroon silk blouse, white tapered pants, and white sandals. There was polish on her toenails. Coffee was perking in an electric pot, bacon was frying. Toast was in the toaster. The dining room table was set for two and the orange juice was all poured. There was jam out and butter on a plate.

"Sit down," she said. "Breakfast is almost ready."

"Paul doesn't know what he's missing, going off to school like that," I said.

"Oh, he never eats breakfast. Hates it. I'm glad actually. He's such a grouch in the morning. How do you like your eggs?"

"Over easy."

"Sit," she said. "It's almost ready."

I sat.

"Drink your orange juice," she said. "Don't wait. I'll sit right down in a minute."

I drank my orange juice. Frozen. The toast popped. Patty Giacomin put the four slices on a plate, put four more pieces of bread in to toast, and put the plate on the table.

I said, "You want me to butter it?"

"Yes, thank you."

I buttered the toast. Patty put four strips of bacon and two eggs, over easy, on my plate and put my plate in front of me. She served herself one egg and two strips of bacon. Then she sat down and drank her orange juice.

"This is very nice," I said.

"Well, if you're going to be stuck here with a woman and a kid, I felt you should at least be treated right."

I poured some coffee first into her cup and then mine.

"You men will have to rough it this weekend though," she said.

I ate a piece of bacon and a bite of egg.

"I'll be going away for the weekend," she said.

I nodded.

"I'm going to New York to visit friends."

I nodded again, and ate some more.

"I go down every month, go to the theater, to a museum exhibit. It's very stimulating."

"Yeah," I said. I finished up my eggs.

She ate a small bite of her egg. "Do you know New York, Mr. Spenser?"

"I know what everyone means when they say that. I know midtown Manhattan."

"Yes, I suppose that's true, isn't it. That is what we mean by New York when we go to visit." She drank some coffee.

"Who stayed with Paul before when you'd go? Pinkerton man?"

She smiled at me, "No, I hired a woman, Mrs. Travitz, normally. Sometimes Sally Washburn would come in. I always got someone."

"You think Paul will mind staying alone with me?" I said.

She looked a little startled, as if I'd asked a dumb question.

"Oh, no. Paul likes you. He understands that I have to get away. That I must find some fulfillment of my own. He realizes I can't just be a mother, as I couldn't just be a wife."

"Of course," I said.

"It's remarkable, I think, how long it took women to realize the value and need of self-actualization," she said.

"Isn't that amazing," I said. "How long it took."

"Yes, New York is my safety valve in a sense."

"Get a chance to shop while you're there," I said.

She nodded. "Yes, usually I spend a day on Fifth Avenue."

"Ever take Paul?"

"Oh, God, no. He wouldn't have any fun and he'd just drag along. No, he'd spoil it. You don't have children, do you?"

"Nope."

She made a little snorting laugh. "You're lucky," she said. "Twice lucky, you're a man and you have no children."

"What about self-actualization and stuff?" I said.

"I meant it. I struggle for that. But what good is it for a single woman?"

"Why is being married so important?" I said.

"Because that's where the bucks are," she said. "And you know it."

"I'm not sure I know that, but I've never been married."

"You know what I mean. Men have the money. A woman needs a man to get it."

"I wonder if Gloria Steinem makes house calls," I said.

"Oh, that's crap," Patty Giacomin said. Her color was high. "You probably mouth the liberal line like everyone else around here, but you know what's reality all right. Men have the money and the power and if a woman wants some, she better get hold of a man."

I shrugged. I was beginning to see where Patty had picked up the habit.

"I know some folks who might argue with you," I said. "But I'm not one of them. I'm too busy counting my money and consolidating my power."

She smiled. "You do look quite powerful," she said. "Do you lift weights?"

"Sometimes," I said.

"I thought so. My husband, my ex-husband, used to."

"Not enough," I said.

"That's right, you've seen him, haven't you. He's gotten fat. But when we met he was really quite good-looking."

"You really think he'll make another try for Paul," I said.

"Absolutely," she said. "He's, he's . . ." She groped for words. "I don't know, he's like that. He has to get even. He can't stand to lose."

"Capture the flag," I said.

"Excuse me?"

I shook my head. "Just musing aloud."

"No, please tell me. You said something. Do you disapprove of me?"

"It's not my business to approve or disapprove," I said. "It's my business to see that your kid is okay."

"But you said something before. Please tell me."

"I said capture the flag. The kid's like a trophy you two are fighting for."

"Well, that son of a bitch is not going to get him," she said.

"That's right," I said.

"Why don't you take your coffee into the living room and read the paper," she said. "I'll clean up here."

I did.

She bustled about in her flowered apron and put the dishes away in the dishwasher and swept the floor. When my breakfast had settled and I'd finished the paper I went to my room and changed and went out to run.

The winter was over. The weather was good and somewhere the voice of the turtle was probably being heard. What I heard were mostly sparrows. I jogged toward the center of town, feeling the spring sun press on my back. There was still an edge to the air. It had not yet softened into summer. But by a mile I had a pleasant sweat working and my legs felt strong and my muscles felt loose. There were other joggers out, mostly women this time of day. Probably looking for a man to grab so they could cut in on the money and power. Probably why Susan had latched on to me. Poor old Patty. She'd read all the stuff in *Cosmopolitan* and knew all the language of self-actualization, but all she really wanted was to get a man with money and power.

Ahead of me a young woman was jogging. She had on the top of a beige-and-blue warmup suit and blue shorts cut high. I slowed down to stay behind her and appraise her stride in the high-cut shorts. Women looked realer in the spring. Like this one. She hadn't had a chance to get this year's tan yet and her legs were white and vulnerable-looking. Good legs though. I wondered if I offered her money and power if she'd jog with me. She might. On the other hand she might accelerate and run off and I wouldn't be able to catch her. That would be humiliating. I picked up the pace and went past her. She had big gold hoop earrings on and she smiled a good-fellowship smile at me as I went past. I tried to look powerful and rich, but she didn't hurry to catch me.

I cruised down through Lexington Center past the Minuteman and looped back in a wide circle to Emerson Road. It took about an hour and a quarter, which meant I'd done seven or eight miles. Patty's car was gone. I did some stretching, took a shower, and dressed. I heard Patty's car pull in.

And when I went out, she was just breezing into the kitchen with some groceries.

"Hi," she said. "Want some lunch?"

"Are you after my money and power?" I said.

She looked quickly sideways at me. "Maybe," she said.

CHAPTER NINE

ON THE WEEKEND Paul improved his TV viewing average. Patty Giacomin had departed to self-actualize in New York. I had the living room and Paul stuck to his bedroom except to make a periodic trip to the kitchen to stare, often for minutes, into the refrigerator. He rarely ate anything. Looking into the refrigerator seemed merely something to do.

I had to stick with him, so I couldn't run or build some cabinets in Susan's house like I'd promised I would. I read most of the day about Enguerrand de Coucy and life in the fourteenth century. Saturday afternoon I watched a ball game on the tube. About six o'clock Saturday afternoon I yelled up the stairs to him.

"You want some supper?"

He didn't answer. I yelled again. He came to his bedroom door and said, "What?"

I said, "Do you want some supper?"

He said, "I don't care."

I said, "Well, I'll make some, I'm hungry. If you want some, let me know."

He went back into his room. I could hear the sounds of an old movie playing.

I went to the kitchen and investigated. There were some pork chops. I looked into the cupboard. There was rice. I found some pignolia nuts and some canned pineapple, and some garlic and a can of mandarin oranges. I checked the refrigerator again. There was some all-purpose cream. Heavy would have been better, but one makes do. There were also twelve cans of Schlitz that Patty Giacomin had laid in before she left. She hadn't asked. If she'd asked, I'd have ordered Beck's. But one makes do. I opened a can. I drank some. Perky with a nice finish, no trace of tannin.

I cut the eyes out of the pork chops and trimmed them. I threw the rest away. Patty Giacomin appeared not to have a mallet, so I pounded the pork medallions with the back of a butcher knife. I put a little oil into the skillet and heated it and put the pork in to brown. I drank the rest of my Schlitz and opened another can. When the meat was browned, I added a garlic clove. When that had softened, I added some juice from the pineapple and covered the pan. I made rice with chicken broth and pignolia nuts, thyme, parsley, and a bay leaf and cooked it in the oven. After about five minutes I took the top off the frying pan, let the pineapple juice cook down, added some cream, and let that cook down a little. Then I put in some pineapple chunks and a few mandarin orange segments, shut off the heat, and covered the pan to keep it warm. Then I set the kitchen table for two. I was on my fourth Schlitz when the rice was finished. I made a salad out of half a head of Bibb lettuce I found in the refrigerator and a dressing of oil and vinegar with mustard added and two cloves of garlic chopped up.

I put out two plates, served the pork and rice on each of them, poured a glass of milk for Paul, and carrying my beer can, went to the foot of the stairs.

I yelled, "Dinner," loud. Then I went back and sat down to eat.

I was halfway through dinner when Paul appeared. He didn't say anything. He pulled out the chair opposite me and sat down at the place I'd set.

"What's this?" he said.

"Pork, sauce, rice, salad," I said. I took a bite of meat and washed it down with a sip of beer. "And milk."

Paul nudged at the pork medallion with his fork. I ate

some rice. He picked up a lettuce leaf from the salad bowl with his fingers and ate it.

I said, "What were you watching?"

He said, "Television."

I nodded. He nudged at the pork medallion again. Then he took a small forkful of rice and ate it.

I said, "What were you watching on the television?"

"Movie." He cut a piece off the pork and ate it.

I said, "What movie?"

"Charlie Chan in Panama."

"Warner Oland or Sidney Toler?" I said.

"Sidney Toler." He reached into the salad bowl and took a forkful of salad and stuffed it into his mouth. I didn't say anything. He ate some pork and rice.

"You cook this?" he said.

"Yes."

"How'd you know how to do that?"

"I taught myself."

"Where'd you get the recipe?"

"I made it up."

He looked at me blankly.

"Well, I sort of made it up. I've eaten an awful lot of meals and some of them were in places where they serve food with sauces. I sort of figured out about sauces and things from that."

"You have this at a restaurant?"

"No. I made this up."

"I don't know how you can do that," he said.

"It's easy once you know that sauces are made in only a few different ways. One way is to reduce a liquid till it's syrupy and then add the cream. What you get is essentially pineapple-flavored cream, or wine-flavored cream, or beer-flavored cream, or whatever. Hell, you could do it with Coke, but who'd want to."

"My father never cooked," Paul said.

"Mine did," I said.

"He said girls cook."

"He was half right," I said.

"Huh?"

"Girls cook, so do boys. So do women, so do men. You know. He was only half right."

"Oh, yeah."

"What did you do for supper when your mother wasn't home?"

"The lady who took care of me cooked it."

"Your father ever take care of you?"

"No."

We were through eating. I cleared the table and put the dishes into the dishwasher. I'd already cleaned up the preparation dishes.

"Any dessert?" Paul said.

"No. You want to go out and get ice cream or something?"

"Okay."

"Where should we go," I said.

"Baskin-Robbins," he said. "It's downtown. Near where we ate that time."

"Okay," I said. "Let's go."

Paul had a large cone of Pralines 'n Cream. I had nothing.

On the ride home Paul said, "How come you didn't have any ice cream?"

"It's a trade-off I make," I said. "If I drink beer I don't eat dessert."

"Don't you ever do both?"

"No."

"Never?"

I deepened my voice and swelled up my chest as I drove. I said, "Man's gotta do what he's gotta do, boy."

It was dark, and I couldn't see well. I thought he almost smiled.

CHAPTER TEN

IT WAS ALMOST the first day of May and I was still there. Every morning Patty Giacomin made me breakfast, every noon she made me lunch, every evening she made dinner. At first Paul ate dinner with us, but the last week he'd taken a tray to his room and Patty and I had been eating alone. Patty's idea of fancy was to put Cheez Whiz on the broccoli. I didn't mind that. I used to like the food in the army. What I minded was the growing sense of intimacy. Lately at dinner there was always wine. The wine was appropriate to the food: Blue Nun; Riunite, red, white, and rosé; a bottle of cold duck. I'd eat the eye of the round roast and sip the Lambrusco, and she'd chatter at me about her day, and talk about television, and repeat a joke she'd heard. I had begun to envy Paul. Nothing wrong with a tray in your room.

It was warm enough for the top down when I dropped Paul off at school on a Thursday morning and headed back to Emerson Road. The sun was strong, the wind was soft, I had a Sarah Vaughan tape on at top volume. She was singing "Thanks for the Memories" and I should have been feeling like a brass band. I didn't, I felt like a nightingale without a song to sing. It wasn't spring fever. It was captivity.

While I could get in my miles every morning, I hadn't been to a gym in more than two weeks. I hadn't seen Susan in that time. I hadn't been thirty-five feet from a Giacomin since I'd come out to Lexington. I needed to punch a bag, I needed to bench press a barbell, I needed very much to see Susan. I felt cramped and irritable and scratchy with annoyance as I pulled into the driveway.

There were flowers on the kitchen table, and places set for two, with a glass of orange juice poured at each place. And the percolator working on the counter. But Patty Giacomin wasn't in the kitchen. No eggs were cooking. No bacon. Good. My cholesterol count was probably being measured in light-years by now. I picked up one of the glasses of orange juice and drank it. I put the empty glass into the dishwasher.

Patty Giacomin called from the living room, "Is that you?"

"Yes, it is," I said.

"Come in here," she said. "I want your opinion on something."

I went into the living room. She was standing at the far end, in front of the big picture window that opened out onto her backyard. The morning sun spilled through it and backlit her sort of dramatically.

"What do you think?" she said.

She was wearing a metallic blue peignoir and was standing in a model's pose, one foot turned out at right angles, her knees slightly forward, her shoulders back so her breasts stuck out. The sunlight was bright enough and the robe was thin enough so that I was pretty sure she had nothing on under it.

I said, "Jesus Christ."

She said, "You like?"

I said, "You need a rose in your teeth."

She frowned. "Don't you like my robe," she said. Her lower lip pushed out slightly. She turned as she talked and faced me, her legs apart, her hands on her hips, the bright sun silhouetting her through the cloth.

"Yeah. The robe's nice," I said. I felt a little feverish. I cleared my throat.

"Why don't you come over and take a closer look?" she said.

"I can see an awful lot from here," I said.

"Wouldn't you like to see more," she said.

I shook my head.

She smiled carefully, and let the robe fall open. It hung straight and framed her naked body. The blue went nicely with her skin color.

"Are you sure you wouldn't like a closer look?" she said.

I said, "Jesus Christ, who writes your dialogue."

Her face flattened out.

"What?"

"This is how it would happen on *The Dating Game,* if they were allowed to film it."

She blushed. The robe hanging open made her seem less sexy than vulnerable.

"You don't want me," she said in a loud whisper.

"Sure, I want you. I want every good-looking woman I ever see. And when they point their pubic bone at me I get positively turbulent. But this ain't the way, babe."

Her face stayed flushed. Her voice stayed in the whisper, though it sounded hoarser and less stagey now.

"Why?" she said. "Why isn't it?"

"Well, for one thing, it's contrived."

"Contrived?"

"Yeah, like you read *The Total Woman* and took notes."

Her eyes had begun to fill. She had let her hands drop to her sides.

"And there's other things. There's Paul, for instance. And a woman I know."

"Paul? What the hell has Paul go to do with it?" She wasn't whispering now. Her voice was harsh. "I have to get Paul's permission to fuck?"

"It's not a matter of permission. Paul wouldn't like it if he found out."

"What do you know about my son?" she said. "What do you think he cares? Do you think he'd think less of me than he does now?"

"No," I said. "He'd think less of me."

She stood without movement for maybe five seconds. Then she deliberately took hold of her robe and shrugged it back over her shoulders and let it drop to the floor. She was naked except for a pair of sling-back pumps made of, apparently, transparent plastic. "You saw most of it already," she said. "Want to see it all?" She turned slowly around, 360

382

degrees, her arms out from her sides. "What do you like best?"
she said. Her voice was very harsh now and there were tears
on her cheeks. "You want to pay me?" She walked over to me.
"You figure I'm a whore, maybe you'll pay me. Twenty bucks,
mister? I'll give you a good time."

"Stop it," I said.

"Who'd tell Paul that you fucked his whorey mother?
How would he find out you'd been dirty?"

Her voice was shaking and clogged. She was crying.

"You'd tell him when there was a good occasion. Or
you'd tell his father and his father would tell him. And besides
there's this woman I know."

Patty Giacomin pressed against me. Her shoulders
were heaving, she was crying outright. "Please," she said.
"Please. I've been good. I've cooked. I pay you. Please, don't do
this."

I put my arms around her and patted her bare back.
She buried her face against my chest and with both hands
straight at her sides, stark naked except for her transparent
shoes, she sobbed without control for a long time. I patted her
back and tried to think of other things. *Carl Hubbell struck
out Cronin, Ruth, Gehrig, Simmons, and Jimmy Foxx* in an
all-star game. Was it 1934? The crying seemed to feed on
itself. It seemed to build. I rested my chin on the top of her
head. *Who played with Cousy at Holy Cross? Kaftan. Joe Mul-
laney? Dermie O'Connell. Frank Oftring.* Her body pressed at
me. I thought harder: *All-time all-star team players I'd seen.
Musial; Jackie Robinson; Reese; and Brooks Robinson. Wil-
liams; DiMaggio; Mays; Roy Campanella; Sandy Koufax, left-
hand pitcher; Bob Gibson, right-hand pitcher; Joe Page in the
bullpen.* She was crying easier now.

"Come on," I said. "You get dressed, I'll take a cold
shower, and we'll have some breakfast."

She didn't move, but the crying stopped. I stopped patting. She stepped away and squatted gracefully to pick up the
peignoir. She didn't put it on. She didn't look at me. She
walked away toward her bedroom.

I went into the kitchen and stood at the open back door

383

and took in a lot of late April air. Then I poured a cup of coffee and drank some and scalded my tongue a little. The principal of counterirritant.

It was maybe fifteen minutes before she came out of the bedroom. In the meantime I rummaged around in the kitchen and got together a potato-and-onion omelet. It was cooking when she came into the kitchen. Her makeup was good and her hair was neat, but her face still had the red, ugly look faces have after crying.

"Sit down," I said. "My treat this morning." I poured her coffee.

She sat and sipped at the coffee.

I said, "This is awkward, but it doesn't have to be too awkward. I'm flattered that you offered. You should not consider it a negative on you that I declined."

She sipped more coffee, shook her head slightly, didn't talk.

"Look," I said. "You've been through a lousy divorce. For sixteen years or more you've been a housewife and now all of a sudden there's no man in the house. You're a little lost. And then I move in. You start cooking for me. Putting flowers on the table. Pretty soon you're a housewife again. This morning had to happen. You had to prove your housewifery, you know? It would have been a kind of confirmation. And it would have confirmed a status that I don't want, and you don't really want. I'm committed to another woman. I'm committed to protecting your son. Screwing his mom, pleasant as that would be, is not productive."

"Why not?" She looked up when she said it and straight at me.

"For one thing it might eventually raise the question of whether I was being paid for protecting Paul or screwing you, of being your husband substitute."

"Gigolo?"

"You ought to stop doing that. Classifying things under some kind of neat title. You're a whore, I'm a gigolo, that sort of thing."

"Well, what was I if I wasn't a whore?"

384

"A good-looking woman, with a need to be loved, expressing that need. It's not your fault that you expressed it to the wrong guy."

"Well. I'm sorry for it. It was embarrassing. I was like some uneducated ginzo."

"I don't know that the lower classes do that sort of thing much more often than we upper-class types. But it wasn't simply embarrassing. It was also in some ways very nice. I mean I'm very glad to have seen you with your clothes off. That's a pleasure."

"I need men," she said.

I nodded. "That's where the bucks are," I said.

"That's still true," she said. "But it's more than that."

I nodded again.

"Women are so goddamned boring," she said. She stretched out the *or* in boring.

"Sometime I'll put you in touch with a woman I know named Rachel Wallace," I said.

"The writer?"

"Yeah."

"You know her? The feminist writer? Well, that's all right in theory. But we both know the reality."

"Which is?"

"That we get a lot further batting our eyes and wiggling our butts."

"Yeah," I said. "Look where it got you."

With a quick sweep of her right hand she knocked the half-full cup of coffee and its saucer off the table and onto the floor. In the same motion she got up out of her chair and left the kitchen. I heard her go up the short stairs to her bedroom and slam the door. She never did try my potato-and-onion omelet. I threw it away.

CHAPTER ELEVEN

IT WAS TWO DAYS after the peignoir that they came for the kid. It was in the evening. After supper. Patty Giacomin answered the doorbell and they came in, pushing her backward as they came. Paul was in his room watching television. I was reading *A Distant Mirror,* chapter seven. I stood up.

There were two of them and neither was Mel Giacomin. The one doing the shoving was short and dumpy and barrel-bodied. He was wearing the ugliest wig I've ever seen. It looked like an auburn Dynel ski cap that he'd pulled down over his ears. His partner was taller and not as bulky. He had a boot camp crew cut and a navy watch cap rolled up so that it looked like a sloppy yarmulke.

The short one said, "Where's the kid?"

The tall one looked at me and said, "Spenser. Nobody told me about you in this."

I said, "How are you, Buddy?"

The short one said, "Who's he?"

Buddy said, "He's a private cop. Name's Spenser. You working, Spenser?"

I said, "Yes."

"They didn't tell me you'd be here."

"Mel didn't know, Buddy. It's not Mel's fault."

"I didn't say anything about no Mel," Buddy said.

"Aw, come on, Buddy, don't be a jerk. Who the hell else would send you for the kid?"

The short one said, "Never mind all the crap. Parade the fucking kid out here."

I said to Buddy, "Who's your friend with his head in a bag?"

Buddy made a very small smile.

The short one said, "What the hell's that remark supposed to mean, douchebag?"

"It means you look like you're wearing an Astroturf bathing cap for a rug. Funniest looking rug I've ever seen."

"Keep running your mouth, douchebag, and we'll see how funny you are."

Buddy said, "Be cool, Harold." To me he said, "We come to take the kid back to his old man. We didn't know you'd be here, but that don't change the plan."

I said, "No."

"No, we can't take him back? Or no, it don't change the plan," Buddy said.

"No, you can't take him back," I said.

Harold pulled a black woven leather sap from his hip pocket and tapped it gently against the palm of his hand.

"I'll enjoy this," he said. And I hit him a stiff left jab on his nose, turning my body sideways as I threw the punch to get all of me into it and to make a smaller target. The blood spurted out of Harold's nose and he staggered three steps backward, flailing his arms for balance. The blackjack hit a table lamp and smashed it. Harold got his balance. He held one hand against the blood coming from his nose and shook his head once as if there were a fly in his ear.

Buddy shrugged a little sadly. Harold came back at me and I hit him the same jab, same place, a little harder. It sat him down. Blood was all over his face and shirt.

"Jesus Christ, Buddy," he said. "Jump in. He can't take two of us."

"Yeah, he can," Buddy said. Harold started to get up. His legs were wobbly. Buddy said, "Leave it alone, Harold. He'll kill you if you try again."

Harold was on his feet, trying to keep his nose from bleeding. He still held the blackjack in his right hand, but he didn't seem to remember that. He looked confused.

I said, "That's what you brought for muscle, Buddy?"

Buddy shrugged. "He'd have been all right for the broad," he said. "He does good with barbers and car salesmen that get a little behind on the vig." Buddy spread his hands.

"How come Mel didn't come himself?"

"I don't know no Mel."

"Come on, Buddy. You want to discuss unlawful entry and assault with the Lexington cops?"

"What are they going to do, beat the shit out of me with a Minuteman?"

"Jail is jail is jail, babe. Don't matter who put you there. How long since you and Harold summered at Walpole?"

"How about we just walk out of here," Harold said. His voice was thick. He had a handkerchief wadded against his nose.

I reached around and took my gun out of its hip holster. I showed it to both of them. I smiled.

Buddy said, "So we know Mel. We thought we'd do him a favor. He heard that his old lady had hired some private cop to be a bodyguard. We figured we come get the kid for him. We didn't know it was you. We figured it would be some stiff that used to be a bank guard. Hell, we didn't even bring a piece."

"How you happen to know Mel, Buddy?"

Buddy shrugged again. "Seen him around, you know. Just trying to do him a favor."

"What did he pay you?"

"A C each."

"Big league," I said.

"See you again," Buddy said. "Come on, Harold. We're walking."

Harold looked at the gun. He looked at Buddy. Buddy said, "Come on," and turned toward the front door. Harold looked at me again. Then he turned after Buddy.

Patty said, "Spenser."

I shook my head and put the gun away. "Tell Mel that if he keeps sending people down to annoy us I'm going to get mad," I said. Buddy nodded and went down the three stairs to the front hall. Harold followed him.

"The next people he sends won't walk out," I said.

Buddy paused and looked back. "You never were a shooter," he said. "It's what's wrong with you." Then he went out the front door and Harold went after him. I heard it close behind them.

Patty Giacomin stood where she'd stood throughout. "Why did you let them go?" she said.

"We had a deal," I said. "If they told me what I asked I wouldn't turn them in."

"You didn't say that," she said.

"Yeah, but Buddy and I both knew it."

"How do you know him? Who are they?"

"I don't know Harold. Buddy I've run into over the years. He works on the docks, and he grifts. He unloads ships when there's work. When there isn't, he steals. He's an errand boy. You want your warehouse burned for insurance, you give Buddy a couple of bucks and he torches it. You want a Mercedes sedan, you pay Buddy and he steals you one. Some grocery clerk owes you money and he won't pay and Buddy goes over and collects. Nothing heavy. Nothing complicated."

"He belongs in jail," Patty said.

"Yeah, I suppose so. He's been there. He'll be there again. He's not that bad a guy."

"Well, I think he's pretty bad," she said. "He broke into my house, manhandled me, tried to kidnap my son. I think he is very bad."

"Yeah, I suppose you would. But that's because you don't know any people who are in fact very bad."

"And you do?"

"Oh, my, yes," I said.

"Well, I'm glad I don't. I hope Paul didn't see this."

"Oh, he saw it," I said. I nodded at the stairs. In the shadows of the upper hall, three stairs up from the living room, Paul was standing looking down.

"Paul," she said. "How long have you been there?"

He didn't say anything.

I said, "Since Buddy and Harold came in."

"Don't be scared, Paul," she said. "It's okay, Mr. Spenser has made them go away. He won't let them bother us."

Paul came down the stairs and stood on the middle step.

"How come you didn't shoot them?" he said.

"I didn't need to," I said.

"Were you scared to?"

Patty Giacomin said, "Paul."

"Were you?"

"No."

"The guy said that there was something wrong with you. That you weren't a shooter."

"True."

"What'd he mean?"

Patty said, "Paul, that's enough. I mean it. You're being very rude."

I shook my head. "No. This all revolves around him. He has a right to ask questions."

"What did he mean?" Paul said.

"He meant that if I was quicker to kill people, my threat would work better."

"Would it?"

"Probably."

"Why don't you?"

"Something to do with the sanctity of life. That kind of stuff."

"Have you ever killed someone?"

Patty said, "Paul!"

"Yes."

"So?"

"I had to. I don't if I don't have to. Nothing's absolute."

"What do you mean?" He stepped down to the living room level into the light.

"I mean you make rules for yourself and know that you'll have to break them because they won't always work."

Patty said, "I don't know what either one of you is talking about, but I want you to stop. I don't want any more talking about killing and I don't want to talk about either of those men again. I mean it. I want it stopped." She clapped her hands when she said the last sentence. Paul looked at her as if she were a cockroach and turned and went back up to his room.

"I think I need a drink," Patty said. "Could you put one together for me?"

"Sure," I said. "What'll it be?"

CHAPTER TWELVE

THE NEXT TIME they tried, it was meaner. Patty Giacomin was food shopping when I went to pick up Paul at school. When I came back into the house with Paul, the phone was ringing. Paul answered and then handed it to me.

"It's for you," he said.

I took the phone and Paul lingered in the doorway between the kitchen and the living room to see who it was. It was a voice I didn't know.

It said, "Spenser?"

I said, "Yeah."

It said, "There's someone here wants to talk with you."

I said, "Okay." Repartee is my game.

There was a shuffling at the other end, then Patty Giacomin's voice came on. It sounded shaky.

"Spenser. That man Buddy and some other men have me. They said if you don't give Paul to them they won't let me go."

I said, "Okay, put Buddy on. We'll work something out."

She said, "Spenser . . ." and then Buddy's voice came on.

"You there?"

I said, "Yeah."

Buddy said, "Here's the plan. You bring the kid to the Boston end of the Mass. Ave. Bridge. We'll bring Momma to

391

the Cambridge end. When we see you start the kid we'll start Momma the other way. Get the idea?"

"Yeah. Shall we do it now?"

"One hour. We'll be there in one hour."

"Okay."

"Spenser?"

"Yeah?"

"Don't fuck this up. I got people with me that ain't Harold, you understand?"

"Yeah."

Buddy hung up.

I broke the connection and dialed information.

"Harbour Health Club in Boston," I said to the operator. I looked at my watch. Two twenty-five. The operator gave me the number. I punched it out on the push-button phone. It rang. A woman answered.

I said, "Henry Cimoli, please."

The woman said, "One minute." She sounded like she was chewing gum.

Henry said, "Hello."

I said, "Spenser. I need Hawk. You know where he is?"

Henry said, "I'm looking at him." Sometimes it's better to be lucky than good.

I said, "Put him on."

In a moment Hawk said, "Umm," into the phone.

I said, "You know Buddy Hartman?"

Hawk said, "Umm-hmm."

I said, "He and several others have a woman. They want to exchange her for a boy that I have. At three twenty-five they are going to be at the Cambridge end of the Mass. Ave. Bridge. I'm going to be at the Boston end. We're going to start them together. When they meet, halfway across, I want you to discourage Buddy and his pals while I drive out onto the bridge and pick up both of them, the woman and the kid."

Hawk said, "It's five minutes' work, but I gotta drive there and go home again. Cost you a deuce."

"Yeah, I haven't got time to haggle fee with you. I'm on my way."

"I be there," Hawk said. We hung up.

Paul was staring at me.

I said, "Come on, we gotta go get your mother."

"You going to give me to them?"

"No."

"What if they try to shoot me?"

"They won't. Come on. We'll talk in the car."

In the car I said, "You heard what I said on the phone to Hawk?"

Paul said, "Who's Hawk?"

"Friend of mine, doesn't matter. You heard what I said?"

"Yes."

"Okay. I can't believe we're talking a lot of danger here. But here's what I want you to do. When I tell you to go, you start walking along the Mass. Ave. Bridge toward Cambridge."

"Where's the Mass. Ave. Bridge?"

"Across the Charles, by MIT. You'll see. When your mother reaches you, say to her, 'Lie flat on the ground, Spenser's coming,' and then you drop flat down on the pavement. If she doesn't get down, tell her to. I'll drive out onto the bridge and I'll get out of the car. Tell her to get in the driver's side. You get in the other side."

"What about that Buddy?"

"Hawk will look after him till I get there."

"But what if he doesn't?"

I smiled. "You say that because you don't know Hawk. Hawk will take care of the Cambridge end." I wrote Susan's address on a piece of paper. "Have your mother drive you there."

The kid was nervous. He yawned repeatedly. I could hear him swallow. His face looked tight and without color. "What if she's not there?" he said.

"No reason she shouldn't be," I said.

"What if this doesn't work?"

"I'll make it work," I said. "I'm good at this. Trust me."

"What would they do if they got me?"

"Take you to your father. You wouldn't be any worse off than now. Relax. You got nothing to lose here. Your father wouldn't hurt you."

"He might," Paul said. "He doesn't like me. He just wants to get even with my mother."

I said, "Look, kid, there's just so much value to thinking about things you can't control. It's time to stop now. You've had a tough life and it doesn't seem to be looking up. It's time to start growing up. It's time to stop talking and start being ready. You know?"

"Ready for what?"

"For whatever comes along. Your way out of a lousy family life is to grow up early and you may as well start now."

"What am I supposed to do?"

"What I tell you. And do it with as little whining as you can. That would be a start."

"But I'm scared," Paul said. There was outrage in his voice.

"That's a normal condition," I said. "But it doesn't change anything."

He was silent. We passed Mount Auburn Hospital and crossed the Charles onto Soldier's Field Road. To the right Harvard Stadium looked like it was supposed to, round and looming with arches and ivy on the walls. The Harvard athletic plant sprawled for acres around it. Soldier's Field Road became Storrow Drive and I went off Storrow by BU, and made the complicated loop turn till I was heading inbound on Commonwealth. At Mass. Ave. there was an underpass. I stayed to the right of it and turned onto Mass. Ave. and drove past the up ramp from Storrow and parked on the bridge with my emergency lights blinking. It was three twenty. Beside me Paul's stomach rolled. He belched softly.

"You see them?" he said.

"No."

A car behind me blew its horn at me, and the driver glared as he went by. Two kids in a Buick pulled around the car. The one in the driver's seat gave me the finger. The passenger called me an asshole through his rolled-down window. I kept my eyes fixed on the Cambridge side of the bridge.

At three twenty-five I said to Paul, "Okay. It's time for you to walk. Tell me what you're going to do."

"I'm going to walk to the middle and when my mother gets to me I'm going to tell her lie down, that you're coming, and then I will lie down too."

"And if she doesn't hit the sidewalk?" I said.

"I'll tell her again."

"And when I show up what happens?"

"I get in one side. She gets in the other. We drive to that address."

"Good. Okay, walk across the street. They'll start her on their side."

He sat for a moment. Belched again. Yawned. Then he opened the door of the MG and stepped out onto the sidewalk. He crossed and began to walk slowly toward the Cambridge side. He went about ten feet and looked back at me. I grinned at him and made a V with my fingers. He kept going. At the far end of the bridge I saw his mother get out of a black Oldsmobile and start toward us.

The Mass. Ave. Bridge is open. It rests on arches that rest on pilings. There's no superstructure. On a summer evening it is particularly pleasant for strolling across. It is said that some MIT students once measured it by repeatedly placing an undergraduate named Smoot on the ground and marking off his length. Every six feet or so there is still the indication of one smoot, two smoots, painted on the pavement. I could never remember how many smoots long the bridge was.

He was almost to his mother. Then they met. Across the bridge the Oldsmobile began to move, slowly. The boy dropped to the pavement. His mother hesitated and then crouched down beside him, tucking her skirt under her. *Flat,* I muttered, *flat, goddammit.*

I slammed the MG into gear and headed for Paul and his mother. Across the way the Olds began to pick up speed. A Ford station wagon swung around the corner from Memorial Drive, looped out into the wrong lane with a lot of squealing rubber and blaring horns, and rammed the Olds from the side, bouncing it against the high curb and pinning it. Before the cars had stopped, Hawk rolled out of the driver's side with a handgun the size of a hockey stick and took aim over the hood of the wagon. I cut across the traffic and rolled the MG up beside the sidewalk between the Olds and the two Giacomins. From down the bridge I heard gunfire. I jerked up the emergency, slapped the car into neutral, and scrambled out of the MG.

"Patty, get in, take Paul and drive to Smithfield, Paul's got the address. Explain who you are and wait for me there. Move."

There was another gunshot from five smoots away. I had my gun out and was running toward the Olds when I heard the MG take off with its tires squealing. I was almost at the Olds when I saw Hawk go over the hood of the wagon, reach into the driver's side of the Olds and pull somebody out through the window with his left hand. With the barrel of his gun he chopped the pistol out of the other man's hand, shifted his weight slightly, put his right hand, gun and all, into the man's crotch and pitched him over the railing and into the Charles River.

A big guy with a tweed cap got out of the back seat of the Olds as I came around behind it. I turned sideways on my left foot and kicked him in the small of the back with my right. He sprawled forward and a gun that looked like a Beretta clattered on the pavement ahead of him as he sprawled. It skittered between the risers of the railing and into the river. I looked into the car and saw Buddy crouched down on the passenger's side of the front floorboards, huddled under the dash. Hawk looked in at the other window, the enormous handgun leveled. We saw Buddy at the same time.

Hawk said, "Shit," stringing out the vowel the way he did. From the Boston side of the bridge I heard a siren. So did Hawk. He put the bazooka away inside his coat.

"Let's split," I said.

He nodded. We ran down Mass. Ave. and into one of the MIT buildings.

We moved through a crowded corridor lined with ship models in glass cases.

"Try and look like an upwardly mobile nineteen-year-old scientist," I said.

"I am, bawse. I got a doctor of scuffle degree."

Hawk was wearing skintight unfaded jeans tucked into his black boots. He had on a black silk shirt unbuttoned nearly to his waist, and the handgun was hidden under a white leather vest with a high collar that Hawk wore turned up. His head was shaven and gleamed like black porcelain. He was my height, maybe a hair taller, and there was no flesh on his body, only muscle over bone, in hard planes. The black eyes over the high cheekbones were humorous and without mercy.

We went out a side door at the end of the corridor. Behind us there were still sirens. We strolled across the MIT campus away from Mass. Ave.

"Sorry about your car," I said.

"Ain't my car, man," Hawk said.

"You boosted it?" I said.

"'Course. Ain't gonna fuck up my own wheels, man."

"'Course not," I said. "I wonder if they've fished that guy out of the Charles yet."

Hawk grinned. "Damn," he said. "Wish the fuzz had been a little slower. I was gonna throw 'em all in."

CHAPTER THIRTEEN

WE WANDERED in a mazy motion through the MIT complex down to Kendall Square and caught the subway to Park Street. We walked up across the Common to Beacon, where Hawk's car was parked in front of the State House by a sign that said RESERVED FOR MEMBERS OF THE GENERAL COURT. It was a silver-gray Jaguar XJ 12.

Hawk said, "You owe me two bills, babe."

I said, "Gimme a ride to Susan's house."

"Smithfield?"

"Yeah."

"That's the woods, man. That's your fucking forest primeval out there."

"Hawk, it's thirteen miles north. We could run it in about two hours."

"Dinner," Hawk said. "Dinner and some champagne, I buy the champagne. They sell champagne out in the woods, babe?"

"We can stop at the trading post," I said. "Cost plenty wampum, though."

We got in and Hawk put the Jag in gear and we purred north over the Mystic Bridge. Hawk put an Olatunji tape on and the car trembled with percussion all the way to Saugus, where Hawk pulled into a Martignetti's off Route 1 and bought three bottles of Taittinger Blanc de Blancs. At forty-five bucks a bottle it was cutting a lot of profit off the two hundred I was paying him. He also brought out two six-packs of Beck's beer.

"No point wasting the champagne on you," he said. "You born beer, you gonna die beer. There's a bottle opener in the glove compartment."

Hawk peeled the foil off the neck of one bottle of Taittinger and twisted the cork out with a pop. I opened a bottle of beer. Hawk drank from the neck of his forty-five-dollar champagne bottle as he tooled the Jaguar up Route 1. I drank some Beck's.

"Difference between you and me, babe," Hawk said, "right here." He drank some more champagne.

"As long as there is one," I said. "Any difference will do."

Hawk laughed quietly and turned his Olatunji tape up louder. It was a quarter to six when we pulled into Susan's driveway. My MG was there beside the car Susan had bought

398

to replace the MG. It was a big red Ford Bronco with a white roof and four-wheel drive and heavy-duty this and that, and big tires with raised white letters.

Hawk looked at it and said, "What the fuck is that?"

I said, "That's Suze's new vehicle. For Christmas I'm getting her some foxtails and a pair of big rubber dice."

"That's a big ten-four momma," Hawk said.

We went in. Susan was the only person I've ever seen that Hawk seemed to have any feeling about. He grinned when he saw her. She said, "Hawk," and came over and kissed him. He gave her the two unopened bottles of champagne.

"Brought us a present," he said. "Spenser promised supper."

She looked at me. "What am I, Howard Johnson's," she said.

"You're a real looker when you're angry," I said.

She took the champagne and went toward the kitchen, "Goddamn host of the goddamn highway," she said.

"You forgot to take my beer," I said.

She kept going. Hawk and I went into the living room. Paul was watching a bowling show on television. Patty was sipping what looked like bourbon on the rocks.

"This is Hawk," I said. "Patty Giacomin and her son, Paul."

Paul looked at Hawk and then looked back at the bowling show. Patty smiled and started to get up and changed her mind and stayed seated.

"Are you the other one?" she said.

Hawk said, "Yes." He drank some champagne from the bottle.

Susan came back into the room with another bottle of champagne in a bucket and four fluted champagne glasses on a tole serving tray.

"Perhaps you'd care to try a glass," she said to Hawk.

"'Spect ah might, Missy Susan," Hawk said.

Susan said to Patty, "May Paul have a glass?"

Patty said, "Oh, sure."

Susan said, "Would you care for a glass, Paul?"

Paul said, "Okay."

Patty Giacomin said to Hawk, "I'd like to thank you for what you did today."

Hawk said, "You're welcome."

"I really mean it," Patty said. "It was so brave, I was so terrified. You were wonderful to help."

"Spenser gave me two hundred dollars," Hawk said. "I figure it'll show up in his expense voucher."

"Are you a detective too?" Patty said.

Hawk smiled. "No," he said. "No, I am not." His face was bright with mirth.

I said, "I'm going to put this beer away," and went into the kitchen. Susan came out behind me.

"Just what in hell do you think we're going to feed these people?" Susan said.

"Got any cake?" I said.

"I'm serious. I don't have anything in the house to serve five people."

"I'll go get something," I said.

"And let me entertain your guests?"

"Your choice," I said. "I don't care to have a fight though."

"Well, don't do this to me. I don't simply sit around here waiting for your problems to drop by."

"Love me, love my problems," I said.

"Sometimes I wonder if that's a worthwhile trade-off."

"There you go," I said, "taking that education management jargon again."

She was looking in the refrigerator. "If I want to say trade-off, goddammit, I'll say trade-off. I've got some of that Williamsburg bacon. We could make up a bunch of BLTs."

"Toasted," I said. "And on the side, some of those home-made bread-and-butter pickles we did last fall."

"And cut flowers in a vase, and the Meyer Davis Orchestra? You better go back in and help out on the conversation. Hawk must be ready to jump out of his skin."

"Not Hawk," I said. "He doesn't mind silence. He

doesn't want to talk. He won't talk. He doesn't sweat small talk much."

"He doesn't sweat anything too much," Susan said, "does he?"

"Nope. He's completely inside. Come on in and talk a bit, then we'll all transfer to the kitchen and make sandwiches and eat. There's some cheese too, and a couple of apples. It'll be a feast." I patted her lightly on the backside. "Besides, we need your advice."

"My advice to you, big fella, is to keep your hands to yourself," she said.

I opened another beer and we went back into the living room. Hawk was stretched out in a wing chair near the fireplace, feet straight out in front of him, body slumped easily in the chair. When we came in, he took a small sip from his champagne glass and put it back on the end table near him. Patty and Paul were watching the six o'clock news. No one was talking.

I sat in a Boston rocker on the opposite side of the fireplace from Hawk.

I said, "Paul, you did good today."

He nodded.

"Patty," I said, "tell me what happened."

"I came out of the supermarket and three men with guns made me get into the car. That one that came to our house was one of them."

"Buddy?" I said.

"Yes. He sat in front with the driver and the other man sat in back with me and we drove to a pay phone in Boston. Then we drove to the bridge and they told me to get out and start walking. Other than that they didn't talk to me at all or say anything."

"You recognize any of them, Hawk?"

"Dude I threw in the river is Richie Vega. He used to shake down massage parlors."

Patty said, "My God, how would Mel find people like that to hire?"

Hawk raised his head slightly and looked at me. I shrugged. Hawk let his chin settle back onto his chest.

Patty Giacomin said to Hawk, "Do you know my husband?"

Hawk said, "No. Not if he go by Mel Giacomin."

"Well, that's his name."

Hawk nodded.

Patty said, "Do you know what this is all about?"

Hawk said, "No."

"You got in a fight with three men and they had guns, and you threw one into the river, and you don't even know why?"

Hawk said, "Yeah, that's right."

"And you're not a detective or anything?"

"Nope."

Paul was watching and listening. We had distracted him from the tube.

"A strong-arm man?" he said.

"Yeah, something like that," I said.

The newscasters joked painfully with the weather forecaster on television.

I said to Susan, "I don't know how much Patty's told you since she arrived, but for your benefit and Hawk's I'll run through it very quickly."

I did.

When I got through, there was silence. Hawk seemed almost asleep. Only the evening news mewled in one corner.

Susan said, "You can't continue this way. You and your husband will have to negotiate."

"After what he pulled today?" Patty said. "I will not talk to that man."

"What about the law?" Susan said.

"The law has already given me custody."

"But kidnapping," Susan said. "Kidnaping is illegal."

"You mean report him to the police."

"Certainly. You can identify at least two of the men. Hawk and Spenser can testify that they had indeed kidnaped you. Surely the police could trace it back to your husband."

Susan looked at me. I nodded. Hawk sipped champagne and put the glass back gently on the end table. He was nearly prone in the chair, his feet stretched out and crossed at the ankles.

"He'd kill me," Patty said.

"You mean you're afraid to tell the police because of what your husband would do?"

"Yes. He'd be furious. He'd . . . I can't do that."

"But he's already had you kidnaped. Aren't you already afraid of him?"

"But he wouldn't try to hurt me. If I told, he'd . . . I can't. I can't do that."

"So do you plan to employ me permanently?" I said.

"I can't. I can't keep paying you. I'm . . . running out of money."

Hawk smiled to himself. I looked at Susan.

She said, "What about Paul? How can he grow up like this?"

Patty Giacomin shook her head.

We were all quiet. Paul was watching the television again. The network news was on now. Authoritative.

Patty said, "It isn't me he wants. It's Paul. If I told on him . . ."

"The heat would be on you," I said. "Instead of on Paul."

Susan said, "That's it, isn't it?"

Patty shook her head. "I don't know," she said. "What difference does it make? I'm not going to the police. I'm not." Her voice was shaky. "I've still got money. We'll do something."

I said, "What?"

She said, "You take Paul."

"Take him where?" I said.

"I don't know. Anywhere. I'll pay you," she said.

"I hide Paul out so your husband can't find him?"

"Yes. I'll pay you."

"Why won't they just try the same swap again that they tried today?"

"I'll go live with a friend. Mel won't find me."

"So why not take Paul too," I said. "Much cheaper."

"He won't let me bring Paul."

"Your friend?"

"Yes."

"That wouldn't be old disco Stephen, would it? The one I met when I first brought Paul home?"

She nodded.

I said, "Probably afraid if it got too crowded, his cashmere sweaters would wrinkle."

"He's not like that. You don't know him," she said.

"Well, a friend in need . . ." I said.

"Will you take Paul?" Patty said.

I looked at him. He was staring hard at the network news. His shoulders were stiff and awkward. He was concentrating on ignoring us.

"Sure," I said. "It would be a pleasure."

Susan looked at me with her eyes widened. Hawk made a sound under his breath like a soft hog call.

"He ain't heavy," I said at large. "He's my brother."

Susan shook her head.

CHAPTER FOURTEEN

WE ATE OUR BLTs and drank champagne in the kitchen without much talk.

For an extra fifty dollars Hawk said he'd take Paul and his mother home and stay there till I arrived. Neither of the Giacomins looked very happy with that, but they went.

"Don't be scared," Hawk said as they left. "Some of my best friends are honkies."

Patty Giacomin looked at me.

"It's okay," I said. "He's nearly as good as I am. In the dark maybe better. You'll be fine."

Paul looked at me. "When am I going to stay with you?" he said.

"Tomorrow. I'll be home later tonight and tomorrow we'll pack up and go."

"He be around, kid," Hawk said. "One thing about old Spenser, he predictable. He say he going to do something. He do it." Hawk shook his head. "Dumb," he said.

They went out. Susan and I stood in the doorway and watched them. Susan waved. Then Hawk's Jag murmured into gear and they were gone. I closed the door and turned and picked Susan up in my arms.

"Couch or bed, little lady," I said.

"God, you're masterful," she said.

"Maybe you could kick your little feet and pound prettily on my chest with your little fists?" I said.

"Be happy I don't apply heel to groin," she said, "after all the goddamned unannounced company."

"You mean I'm going to have to force my attentions upon you?" I said.

"Yes," she said. "But you may as well force them in the bedroom. It's more comfortable."

I walked toward the hall with her. "You smell good," I said.

"I know," she said. "Halston."

The bedroom door was ajar. I pushed it open with my foot and walked in.

"You better kiss me," she said. "Stifle my screams."

I sat on the edge of the bed and kissed her. I kept my eyes open. In the light from the hall I could see that she closed hers. She moved her head away and opened her eyes and looked up at my face.

I said, "Lipwise you've still got it, baby."

Her face was serious and still, but her eyes glittered. "You ain't seen nothing yet," she said.

It was late when we were through. Most of our clothing was scattered about and the bedspread was badly wrinkled. I lay on my back with my heart pounding and my chest heaving in air. Susan lay beside me. She held my hand.

"Have you overexerted?" she said.

"Your resistance was fierce," I said.

"Umm," she said.

From the living room there was the faint sound of the television, which Paul had left on. The image of it gesticulating to an empty room pleased me.

"Just what do you plan to do with that boy, cookie?" Susan said.

"I thought we might want to talk that out," I said.

"We?"

"You know about kids."

"I know about guidance," Susan said. "There's a difference."

"I'll need help."

"You'll need more than that. The boy is bound to be difficult. Even without knowing him one could predict that. My God, he's chattel in a divorce settlement. What do you know about the needs of a neurotic adolescent?"

"I thought I'd ask you," I said.

"Based on my experience with you?" she said.

"I'm not neurotic," I said.

Susan turned her face toward me. In the half-light she was smiling. She squeezed my hand. "No," she said, "you aren't. You're complicated, but you are not even a little bit neurotic."

"The kid needs to get away from his parents," I said.

"That's not the conventional wisdom, except in cases more extreme than this."

"Maybe the conventional wisdom is right," I said, "if the choice is to get into the welfare-youth services—foster-home system."

"But not if he's going to be with you?"

"Not if he's going to be with me," I said.

"You think you can make life better for him?"

"Yes."

"How long do you plan to keep him?"

"I don't know."

"It's hard enough to raise children you love," Susan said. "I've seen it from the failure end, over and over, parents whose kids are just a goddamned mess. Parents who love them and have presided over the complete botching of their lives. I think your eyes are bigger than your stomach on this one, dear heart."

"How about that property in Maine," I said.

Susan propped up on one elbow. "Fryeburg?" she said.

"Yeah. I told you I'd build a house on it."

"When you got a chance, you said."

"This is the chance."

"You and Paul?"

"Yes."

She was quiet, lying naked beside me, on her right side with her head propped on her right elbow. Her lipstick was smeared. The intelligence in her face was like energy. It seemed almost to shimmer. That she was beautiful was only the first thing you noticed.

"Work release," she said.

"The kid's never been taught how to act," I said. "He doesn't know anything. He's got no pride. He's got nothing he's good at. He's got nothing but the tube."

"And you plan to teach him."

"I'll teach him what I know. I know how to do carpentry. I know how to cook. I know how to punch. I know how to act."

"You're not so bad in the rack either, big fella."

I grinned. "We'll let him work that out on his own, maybe."

She shook her head. "You make it sound simple. It's not. You don't teach people unless they want to learn. It's not just an intellectual exercise. It's a matter of emotion, of psychology. I mean the boy may be positively pathological."

"He's got nothing to lose," I said. "Compared to an afternoon of game shows on TV, anything is up. For crissake, the kid watches soap operas," I said.

"So do I," Susan said.

"Well, your degeneracy is already established," I said. "Besides you do others things."

"Only with you, sweet potato."

"You want to get in on this?" I said.

"The salvation of Paul Giacomin?"

"Yeah."

"I'm willing to consult," she said. "But I don't want to see you overinvested in this. The chances of success are slight. What happens if next week his mother runs out of money?"

"We'll worry about that when it happens."

"It'll happen soon," Susan said.

"Woman's intuition?"

"Believe me," Susan said. "It'll be soon."

I shrugged.

"You'll keep him anyway," she said.

I didn't say anything.

"You will," she said, "you big goddamned sap. You know you will."

"He needs to grow up quick," I said. "He needs to get autonomous. It's the only hope he's got. For him he's gotta stop being a kid at fifteen. His parents are shit. He can't depend on them anymore, He's gotta get autonomous."

"And you're going to show him how?"

"Yes."

"Well, no one better. You're the most autonomous human being I've ever seen. It's a grim prospect for a fifteen-year-old boy though."

"How do you like his prospects if he doesn't grow up quick?"

Susan was quiet, looking down at me. "Spring will be a little late this year," she said.

"For Paul? Yeah." I laughed with no pleasure. "Spring is gone. It's early autumn for Paul. If I can do it."

"And if he can," Susan said.

CHAPTER FIFTEEN

IT WAS EARLY MAY and the sun was thick and warm. The forsythias had begun. The birds were about and the joggers were out of their sweat pants, legs gleaming white in the spring sun. Paul Giacomin came out of his house with a big green plaid suitcase and a white drawstring laundry bag. He was still wearing his pea coat. He needed a haircut. His corduroy pants were too short. He was straining to carry the two bags.

I was driving Susan's Bronco. I got out and took the suitcase from Paul and put it in the back. He stuck the laundry bag in beside it and left the drawstring hanging out over the tailgate. I flipped the string inside and put the power window up with the key. Patty Giacomin came out and stood by the Bronco. Pale green slacks, lavender shirt, white blazer. Big sunglasses, bright lipstick. Stephen was with her. He was as beautiful as she—jeans with a Pierre Cardin patch on them, Frye boots, a half-buttoned tailored collarless shirt in vertical blue-on-blue stripes, a gray sharkskin vest, unbuttoned. His dark maroon Pontiac Firebird was parked in the Giacomin driveway.

"The Firebird's not right," I said. "It doesn't go with the rest of the look."

"Oh, really," Stephen said. "What would you suggest?"

"A Z maybe, or a Porsche. Extend that clean sophisticated continental look, you know?"

Stephen smiled. "Perhaps," he said.

Patty said to her son, "I'll write you a letter."

He nodded. She made an awkward gesture of hugging him. But she didn't seem able to carry through and ended up putting one arm across his shoulders for a moment and patting him slightly on the back. He stood silently while this happened. Then he got into the Bronco. The high step into the front seat was difficult and he had to struggle, and finally squirm up onto the seat. I got in the driver's side.

Patty said, "Bye."

Paul said, "Bye," and we drove off. As we turned off Emerson Road I saw tears fill Paul's eyes. I kept watching the road. He didn't cry. We took Route 3 to 495, 495 to 95 and went north on 95 to the Portsmouth Circle. In that time Paul didn't say anything. He sat and stared out the window at the unvarying landscaping along the highways. I plugged a Johnny Hartman tape into the stereo on the assumption that it was never too soon to start his education. He paid no attention. At the Portsmouth Circle we took the Spaulding Turnpike and then Route 16. We were in rural New England now. An hour from Boston cows grazed. There were barns and feed stores and towns with a mill that no longer milled at the center.

We got to North Conway, New Hampshire, about one thirty in the afternoon. I stopped at a restaurant called Horsefeathers opposite the green in the center of town. There was a softball diamond on the green and some kids were playing a game without umpires.

I said, "Let's eat."

He said nothing, but got out of the car and went into the restaurant with me. We'd been in rural New England. Now we were in rural chic. North Conway is a major ski resort in the winter, and summer homes abound around it in New Hampshire and across the border in Maine. Horsefeathers had brass and hanging plants and looked just like restaurants in San Francisco.

The food was good and at two twenty we were in the car again heading for Fryeburg. At a quarter to three we were parked at the edge of Kimball Lake. The land Susan had gotten from her husband as part of the divorce settlement was nearly three quarters of an acre at the end of a dirt road with woods all around. There were cabins along the lake close enough to keep you from feeling like Henry Thoreau, but it was secluded. Susan's ex-husband had used the place for hunting and fishing. At one edge of the property he'd built a small cabin with running lake water for showering, a well for drinking water, electricity, and a flush toilet, but no central heat. There was a free-standing fireplace in the living room, a small electric stove and an old electric refrigerator in the galleylike kitchen, and two small bedrooms with metal bunk beds in them, and no closets. Susan and I came up occasionally to cook steaks over a wood fire, swim in the lake, and stroll in the woods until the bugs closed in.

Paul said, "We're gonna stay here?"

"Yes. We'll live in that cabin and tomorrow we'll start building a new and better one."

Paul said, "What do you mean?"

I said, "We're going to build a house. You and me."

"We can't do that."

"Yeah, we can. I know how. I'll teach you."

"How do you know how to build a house?"

"My father was a carpenter."

The kid just looked at me. It never occurred to him that houses were built by people. Sometimes they were built by construction companies and sometimes they probably just generated spontaneously.

"Come on, unload. We're going to be very busy up here. There's a lot to do."

"I don't want to build a house," Paul said.

"I'll need help. I can't do it alone. It'll be good to work with your hands. You'll like it."

"I won't."

I shrugged. "We'll see," I said. "Help me unload."

The back seat of the Bronco folded forward, leaving a lot of cargo space. The cargo space was full. There was the big old tool chest that had been my father's. And there was a radial arm saw I'd bought last year and used in Susan's cellar sometimes. There was also a set of barbells, a weight bench, a heavy bag, a speed bag, my suitcase, a large green cooler with perishables in it, a big carton with other food, a pump-action Ithaca shotgun, ammunition, some fishing equipment, two sleeping bags, some boots, a five-cell flashlight, an ax, some books, a machete, a carton of records, two shovels, a mattock, and one hundred feet of rope.

I unlocked the cabin and opened all the windows. We started to carry and stow. A lot of the things were too heavy for Paul and everything he carried he seemed to handle badly. He picked things up only with the tips of his fingers. When I told him to take the shotgun in, he carried it awkwardly by the butt rather than where it balanced. He carried one of the shovels by its blade. When we were through, there was sweat on his face and he seemed red and hot. He still wore his pea coat.

It was after five when we finished. The bugs were out and it was getting cool. Last fall Susan and I had bought a cheap stereo and put it in the cabin. I put on the Benny Goodman 1938 jazz concert while I made a fire. I had a beer while I started supper. Paul came in from looking at the lake and got a Coke out of the refrigerator. He went into the living room. In a minute he was back.

"Didn't you bring a television?" he said.

"No," I said.

He snorted angrily and went back in the living room. I figured he'd stare at the record player. Anything in a pinch.

I opened a large can of beans and put them in a pan to heat. While they heated I put out some pickles and rye bread, ketchup, plates, and utensils. Then I panfried two steaks. We ate at a table in the living room, the kitchen was too small, listening to the Goodman band, watching the fire move, and smelling the wood smoke. Paul still wore the pea coat although the room was warm from the fire.

After supper I got out my book and started to read. Paul picked up the record albums and looked at them and put them back in disgust. He looked out the window. He went outside to look around but came back in almost at once. The bugs were out as it got dark.

"You shoulda brought a TV," he said once.

"Read," I said. "There's books there."

"I don't like to read."

"It's better than looking at the lamp fixtures till bed-time, isn't it?"

"No."

I kept reading.

Paul said, "What's that book?"

"*A Distant Mirror*," I said.

"What's it about?"

"The fourteenth century."

He was quiet. Sap oozed out of the end of a log and sputtered onto the hot ash beneath it.

"What do you want to read about the fourteen hun-dreds for?" Paul said.

"Thirteen hundreds," I said. "Just like the nineteen hundreds are the twentieth century."

Paul shrugged. "So why do you want to read about it?"

I put the book down. "I like to know what life was like for them," I said. "I like the sense of connection over six hun-dred years that I can get."

"I think it's boring," Paul said.

"Compared to what?" I said.

He shrugged.

"I think it's boring compared to taking Susan Silver-man to Paris," I said. "Things are relative."

He didn't say anything.

"I know more about being human when I know more about their lives. I get a certain amount of perspective. The time was full of people that killed, tortured, suffered, strug-gled, and agonized for things that seemed worth anything to them. Now they've been dead for six hundred years. What's it all about, Ozymandias?"

"Huh?"

"'Ozymandias'? It's a poem. Here, I'll show you." I got up and found a book in the box I hadn't unpacked yet.

"Listen," I said. I read the poem to him. Deliberately in the firelit room. It was about his level.

He said, "She your girl friend?"

I said, "What?"

He said, "Susan Silverman. She your girl friend?"

"Yes," I said.

"You going to get married?"

"I don't know."

"You love her?"

"Yes."

"How about her?" he said.

"Does she love me?"

He nodded.

"Yes," I said.

"Then why don't you get married?"

"I'm not sure. Mostly it's a question of how we'd affect each other, I suppose. Would I interfere with her work? Would she interfere with mine? That sort of thing."

"Wouldn't she quit work?"

"No."

"Why not? I would. I wouldn't work if I didn't have to."

"She likes her work. Makes her feel good about herself. Me too. If you just did it for money, of course you'd want to quit. But if you do it because you like to . . ." I gestured with my hand. "What do you like to do?"

He shrugged. "That guy Hawk your friend?"

"Sort of."

"You like him?"

"Sort of. I can count on him."

"He seems scary to me."

"Well, he is. He's not good. But he's a good man. You know the difference?"

"No."

"You will," I said. "It's a difference I'm going to help you learn."

CHAPTER SIXTEEN

THE NEXT MORNING I woke Paul up at seven.

"Why do I have to get up?" he said. "There's no school."

"We got a lot to do," I said.

"I don't want to get up."

"Well, you have to. I'm going to make breakfast. Anything special you want?"

"I don't want any."

"Okay," I said. "But there's nothing to eat till lunch."

He stared at me, squinting, and not entirely awake.

I went out to the kitchen and mixed up some batter for corn bread. While the bread was baking and the coffee perking, I took a shower and dressed, took the corn bread out, and went into Paul's room. He had gone back to sleep. I shook him awake.

"Come on, kid," I said. "I know you don't want to, but you have to. You'll get used to the schedule. Eventually you'll even like it."

Paul pushed his head deeper into the sleeping bag and shook his head.

"Yeah," I said. "You gotta. Once you're up and showered you'll feel fine. Don't make me get tough."

"What'll you do if I don't," Paul muttered into the sleeping bag.

"Pull you out," I said. "Hold you under the shower. Dry you, dress you, Et cetera."

"I won't get up," he said.

I pulled him out, undressed him, and held him under the shower, It took about a half an hour. It's not easy to control someone, even a kid, if you don't want to hurt them. I shampooed his hair and held him under to rinse, then I pulled him out and handed him a towel.

"You want me to dress you?" I said.

He shook his head, and wrapped the towel around himself, and went to his room. I went to the kitchen and put out the corn bread and strawberry jam and a bowl of assorted fruit. While I waited for him I ate an orange and a banana. I poured a cup of coffee. I sipped a little of it. I had not warned him against going back to bed. Somehow I'd had a sense that would be insulting. I wanted him to come out on his own. If he didn't I had lost some ground. I sipped some more coffee. The corn bread was cooling. I looked at his bedroom door. I didn't like cool corn bread.

The bedroom door opened and he came out. He had on jeans that had obviously been shortened and then let down again, his worn Top-Siders, and a green polo shirt with a penguin on the left breast.

"You want coffee or milk?" I said.

"Coffee."

I poured some. "What do you take in it?" I said.

"I don't know," he said. "I never had it before."

"May as well start with cream and sugar," I said. "Calories aren't your problem."

"You think I'm skinny?"

"Yes. There's corn bread, jam, fruit, and coffee. Help yourself."

"I don't want anything."

I said, "Okay," and started on the corn bread. Paul sipped at the coffee. He didn't look like he liked it. After breakfast I cleaned up the dishes and said to Paul, "You got any sneakers?"

"No."

"Okay, first thing we'll do is go over to North Conway and buy you some."

"I don't need any," he said.

"Yes, you do," I said. "We'll pick up a newspaper too."

"How you know they sell them over there?"

"North Conway? They probably got more flashy running shoes than aspirin," I said. "We'll find some."

On the ride to North Conway Paul said, "How come you made me get up like that?"

"Two reasons," I said. "One, you need some structure in your life, some scheduling, to give you a sense of order. Two, I was going to have to do it sometime. I figured I might as well get it over with."

"You wouldn't have to do it if you let me sleep."

"It would've been something. You'd push me until you found out how far I'd go. You have to test me, so you can trust me."

"What are you, a child psychologist?"

"No. Susan told me that."

"Well, she's crazy."

"I know you don't know any better, but that's against the rules."

"What?"

"Speaking badly of another person's beloved, you know? I don't want you to speak ill of her." We were in Fryeburg Center.

"Sorry."

"Okay."

We were quiet as we drove through the small open town with its pleasant buildings. It was maybe fifteen minutes to North Conway. We bought Paul a pair of Nike LDVs just like mine except size 7, and a pair of sweat pants.

"You got a jock?" I said.

Paul looked embarrassed. He shook his head. We bought one of them and two pairs of white sweat socks. I paid and we drove back to Fryeburg. It was ten when we got to the cabin. I handed him his bag of stuff.

"Go put this stuff on and we'll have a run," I said.

"A run?"

"Yeah."

"I can't run," he said.

"You can learn," I said.

"I don't want to."

"I know, but we'll take it easy. We won't go far. We'll

run a little, walk a little. Do a little more each day. You'll feel good."

"You going to make me?" Paul said.

"Yes."

He went very slowly into the cabin. I went in with him. He went into his room. I went into mine. In about twenty minutes he came out with the new jogging shoes looking ridiculously yellow and the new sweat pants slightly too big for his thin legs, and his scrawny upper body pale and shivery-looking in the spring sun. I was dressed the same, but my stuff wasn't new.

"We'll stretch," I said. "Bend your knees until you can touch the ground with both hands easily. Like this. Good. Now without taking your hands from the ground, try to straighten your knees. Don't strain, just steady pressure. We'll hold it thirty seconds."

"What's that for?" he said.

"Loosen up the lower back and the hamstring muscles in the back of your thighs. Now squat, like this, let your butt hang down toward the ground and hold that for thirty seconds. It does somewhat the same thing."

I showed him how to stretch the calf muscles and loosen up the quadriceps. He did everything very awkwardly and tentatively as if he wanted to prove he couldn't. I didn't comment on that. I was figuring out how to run with a gun. I normally didn't. But I wasn't normally looking after anyone but me when I ran.

"Okay," I said. "We're ready for a short slow run. Wait till I get something in the house." I went in and got my gun. It was a short Smith & Wesson .38. I took it from its holster, checked the load, and went out carrying it in my hand.

"You going to run with that?" Paul said.

"Best I could think of," I said. "I'll just carry it in my hand." I held it by the cylinder and trigger guard, not by the handle. It was not conspicuous.

"You afraid they'll find us?"

"No, but no harm to be safe. When you can, it's better to deal with possibilities than likelihoods."

"Huh?"

"Come on, we'll jog. I'll explain while we run."

We started at a slow pace. Paul looked as if he might never have run before. His movements seemed unsynchronized, and he took each step as if he had to think about it first.

"Say when you need to walk," I said. "There's no hurry."

He nodded.

I said, "When you're thinking about something important, like if your father might try to kidnap you again, it's better to think of what the best thing would be to do if he tried, rather than trying to decide how likely he was to try. You can't decide if he'll try, that's up to him. You decide what to do if he does. That's up to you. Understand?"

He nodded. Already I could see he was too winded to talk.

"A way of living better is to make the decisions you need to make based on what you can control. When you can."

We were jogging up a dirt road that led from the cabin to a larger dirt road. It was maybe half a mile long. On either side there were dogberry bushes and small birch and maple saplings under the tall white pines and maples that hovered above us. There were raspberry bushes too, just starting to bud. It was cool under the dappling of the trees, but not cold.

"We'll hang a right here," I said, "and head along this road a ways. No need to push. Stop when you feel the need and we'll walk a ways." He nodded again. The road was larger now. It circled the lake, side roads spoking off to cabins every hundred yards. The names of the cabin owners were painted on hokey rustic signs and nailed to a tree at the head of each side road. We had gone maybe a mile when Paul stopped running. He bent over holding his side.

"Stitch?"

He nodded.

"Don't bend forward," I said. "Bend backward. As far back as you can. It'll stretch it out."

He did what I told him. I hadn't thought he would. An old logging road ran up to our left. We turned up it. Paul walking with his back arched.

"How far did we run?"

"About a mile," I said. "Damn good for the first time out."

"How far can you run?"

"Ten, fifteen miles, I don't know for sure."

Walking on a felled log, we crossed a small ravine where the spring melt was still surging down toward the lake. In a month it would be dry and dusty in there.

"Let's head back," I said. "Maybe when we get back to the road you can run a little more."

Paul didn't say anything. A redheaded woodpecker rattled against a tree beside us. When we got back to the road I moved into a slow jog again. Paul walked a few more feet and then he cranked into a jerky slow run behind me. We went maybe half a mile to the side road leading to our cabin. I stopped the jog and began to walk. Paul stopped running the moment I did.

When we were back to the cabin, I said, "Put on a sweat shirt or a light jacket or something. Then we'll set up some equipment."

I put on a blue sweat shirt with the sleeves cut off. Paul put on a gray long-sleeved sweat shirt with a New England Patriots emblem on the front. The sleeves were too long.

We brought out the weight bench, the heavy bag, the speed bag and its strike board, and the tool chest. Paul carried one end of the tool chest and one end of the weight bench.

"We'll hang the heavy bag off this tree branch," I said. "And we'll fasten the speed bag to the trunk."

Paul nodded.

"And we'll put the weight bench here under the tree out of the way of the heavy bag. If it rains we'll toss a tarp over it."

Paul nodded.

"And when we get it set up, I'll show you how to use it."

Paul nodded again. I didn't know if I was making progress or not. I seemed to have broken his spirit.

"How's that sound, kid?" I said.

He shrugged. Maybe I hadn't broken his spirit.

CHAPTER SEVENTEEN

IT TOOK ABOUT an hour to set up. Most of that time was spent getting the speed bag mounted. I finally nailed through the strike board into two thick branches that veered out at about the right height. For me. For Paul we'd have to get a box to stand on. It took three trips in and out for me to get the weights out. Paul carried some of the small dumbbells. I carried the bar with as many plates as I could on either end, and then went back and carried out the rest of the plates in a couple of trips.

"Now, after lunch," I said, "we'll work out for a couple of hours and then knock off for the day. Normally we'd do this in the morning and build the house in the afternoon, but we got a late start today because we had to get you outfitted, so we'll start the house tomorrow afternoon."

For lunch we had feta cheese and Syrian bread with pickles, olives, cherry tomatoes, and cucumber wedges. Paul had milk. I had beer. Paul said the cheese smelled bad. There were a couple of camp chairs outside the cabin, and after lunch we went out and sat in them. It was one thirty. I turned on the portable radio. The Sox were playing the Tigers.

Paul said, "I don't like baseball."

"Don't listen."

"But I can't help it if it's on."

"Okay, a bargain. I like the ball game. You like what?"

"I don't care."

"Okay. I'll listen to the ball game when it's on. You can listen to whatever you want to any other time. Fair?"

Paul shrugged. On the lake a loon made its funny sound.

"That's a loon," I said. Paul nodded.

"I don't want to lift weights," Paul said. "I don't want to learn to hit the punching bags. I don't like that stuff."

"What would you rather do?" I said.

"I don't know."

"We'll only do it on weekdays. We'll take Saturday and Sunday off and do other stuff."

"What?"

"Anything you want. We'll go look at things. We'll fish, shoot, go to museums, swim when the weather's warmer, see a ball game in case you learn to like them, eat out, see a movie, go to a play, go down to Boston and hang around. Have I hit anything you like yet?"

Paul shrugged. I nodded. By two thirty the Sox were three runs ahead behind Eckersley and our lunch had settled.

"Let's get to it," I said. "We'll do three sets of each exercise to start with. We'll do bench presses, curls, pullovers, flyes, some shrugs, some sit-ups. We'll work out combinations on the heavy bag and I'll show you how to work the speed bag."

I hung a big canteen of water on one of the tree branches. It was covered with red-striped blanket material and it always made me feel like Kit Carson to drink from it.

"Drink all the water you want. Rest in between times. No hurry. We got the rest of the day."

"I don't know how to do any of those things."

"I know. I'll show you. First we'll see how much you can work with. We'll start with bench presses."

I put the big York bar on the bench rests with no weight on it.

"Try that," I said.

"Without any weights?"

"It's heavy enough. Try it for starters. If it's too light we can add poundage."

"What do I do?"

"I'll show you." I lay on my back on the bench, took the barbell in a medium-wide grip, lifted it off the rack, lowered it to my chest, and pushed it straight up to arms' length. Then I lowered it to my chest and pushed it up again. "Like so," I said. "Try to do it ten times if you can."

I put the bar back on the rack and got up. Paul lay on the bench.

"Where do I hold it?"

"Spread your hands a little, like that. That's good. Keep your thumbs in, like this, so if it's too heavy it won't break your thumbs. I'll spot you here."

"What's spot?"

"I'll have a hand on it to be sure you don't drop it on yourself."

Paul wrestled it off the rack. It was too heavy for him. His thin arms shook with the strain as he lowered it to his narrow chest. I had a hand lightly at the midpoint of the bar.

"Okay," I said. "Good. Good. Now push it up. Breathe in, now blow out and shove the bar up, shove, blow, shove." I did some cheerleading.

Paul arched his back and struggled. His arms shook more. I put a little pressure under the bar and helped him. He got it extended.

"Now onto the rack," I said. I helped him guide it over and set it in its place. His face was very red.

"Good," I said. "Next time we'll do two."

"I can't even do it," he said.

"Sure you can. You just did it."

"You helped me."

"Just a bit. One of the things about weights is you make progress fast at first. It's encouraging."

"I can't even lift it without the weights," he said.

"In a couple of months you'll be pressing more than your own weight," I said. "Come on. We'll do another one."

He tried again. This time I had to help him more.

"I'm getting worse," he said.

"Naturally, you're getting tired. The third try will be

423

even harder. That's the point. You work the muscle when it's tired and it breaks down faster and new muscle builds up quicker." I was beginning to sound like Arnold Schwarzenegger. Paul lay red-faced and silent on the bench. There were fine blue veins under the near-translucent skin of his chest. The collarbone, the ribs, and the sternum were all clearly defined against the tight skin. He didn't weigh a hundred pounds.

"Last try," I said. He took the bar off its rest and this time I had to keep it from dropping on him. "Up now," I said, "blow it up. This is the one that counts most. Come on, come on, up, up, up. Good. Good."

We set the bar back on the bench. Paul sat up. His arms were still trembling slightly.

"You do some," he said.

I nodded. I put two fifty-pound plates on each end of the bar and lay on the bench. I lifted the weight off the cradle and brought it to my chest.

"Watch which muscles move," I said to Paul, "that way you learn which exercise does what for you." I pressed the bar up, let it down, pressed it up. I breathed out each time. I did ten repetitions and set the bar back on the rack. A faint sweat had started on my forehead. Above us in the maple tree a grosbeak with a rose-colored breast fluttered in and sat. I did another set. The sweat began to film on my chest. The mild breeze cooled it.

Paul said, "How much can you lift?"

I said, "I don't know exactly. It's sort of a good idea not to worry about that. You do better to exercise with what you can handle and not be looking to see who can lift more and who can't and how much you can lift. I can lift more than this."

"How much is that?"

"Two hundred forty-five pounds."

"Does Hawk lift weights?"

"Some."

"Can he lift as much as you?"

"Probably."

I did a third set. When I got through I was puffing a little, and the sweat was trickling down my chest.

"Now we do some curls," I said. I showed him how. We couldn't find a dumbbell light enough for him to curl with one hand, so he used both hands on one dumbbell.

After two hours Paul sat on the weight bench with his head hanging, forearms on his thighs, puffing as if he'd run a long way. I sat beside him. We had finished the weights. I handed Paul the canteen. He drank a little and handed it back to me. I drank and hung it back up.

"How you feel?" I said.

Paul just shook his head without looking up.

"That good, huh? Well, you'll be stiff tomorrow. Come on. We'll play with the bags a little."

"I don't want to do any more."

"I know, but another half hour and you'll have done it all. This will be fun. We won't have to work hard."

"Why don't you just let me alone?"

I sat back down beside him. "Because everybody has left you alone all your life and you are, now, as a result, in a mess. I'm going to get you out of it."

"Whaddya mean?"

"I mean you don't have anything to care about. You don't have anything to be proud of. You don't have anything to know. You are almost completely neutral because nobody took the time to teach you or show you and because what you saw of the people who brought you up didn't offer anything you wanted to copy."

"It's not my fault."

"No, not yet. But if you lay back and let oblivion roll over you, it will be your fault. You're old enough now to start becoming a person. And you're old enough now so that you'll have to start taking some kind of responsibility for your life. And I'm going to help you."

"What's lifting weights got to do with that stuff?"

"What you're good at is less important than being good at something. You got nothing. You care about nothing. So I'm going to have you be strong, be in shape, be able to run ten miles, and be able to lift more than you weigh and be able to box. I'm going to have you know how to build and cook and to work hard and to push yourself and control yourself. Maybe we can get to reading and looking at art and listening to something besides situation comedies later on. But right now I'm working on your body because it's easier to start there."

"So what," Paul said. "In a little while I'm going back. What difference does it make?"

I looked at him, white and narrow and cramped, almost birdlike, with his shoulders hunched and his head down. He needed a haircut. He had hangnails. *What an unlovely little bastard.*

"That's probably so," I said. "And that's why, kid, before you go back, you are going to have to get autonomous."

"Huh?"

"Autonomous. Dependent on yourself. Not influenced unduly by things outside yourself. You're not old enough. It's too early to ask a kid like you to be autonomous. But you got no choice. Your parents are no help to you. If anything, they hurt. You can't depend on them. They got you to where you are. They won't get better. You have to."

His shoulders started to shake.

"You have to, kid," I said.

He was crying.

"We can do that. You can get some pride, some things you like about yourself. I can help you. We can."

He cried with his head down and his shoulders hunched and the slight sweat drying on his knobby shoulders. I sat beside him without anything else to say. I didn't touch him. "Crying's okay," I said. "I do it sometimes."

In about five minutes he stopped crying. I stood up. There were two pairs of speed gloves on top of the light bag strike board. I picked them up and offered one pair to Paul.

"Come on," I said. "Time to hit the bag."

He kept his head down.

"Come on, kid," I said. "You only got up to go. Let me show you how to punch."

Without looking up he took the gloves.

426

CHAPTER EIGHTEEN

WE WERE DIGGING the last hole for the foundation tubes. It was hot, the going was slow through rocks and the usual root web. I was working with a mattock and Paul had a shovel. We also had use for an ax, a crowbar, and a long-handled branch cutter, which we used on some of the roots.

Paul was dressed like I was: jeans and work boots. Mine were bigger. The sweat shone on his thin body as he dug at the dirt I loosened.

"What are these holes for again?" he said.

"See the big round cardboard tubes over there? We put them in these holes and get them level and fill them with reinforced concrete. Then we put a sill on them and the cabin rests on them. It's easier than digging a cellar hole, though a cellar's better."

"Why?" He dug the shovel blade into the dirt and picked it up. He was holding the shovel too far up the handle and the dirt flipped as he pried it up and most of it fell back in the hole.

"Cellar gives you place for a furnace, makes the floors warmer, gives you storage. This way the house sits above ground. Colder in the winter. But a lot less trouble."

Paul shifted his grip a little on the shovel and took another stab at the dirt. He got most of it this time. "Don't they have machines to do this?"

"Yes." I swung the mattock again. It bit into the soil pleasingly. We were getting down a layer, where the roots and rocks weren't a problem. "But there's no satisfaction in it. Get a gasoline post-hole digger and rattle away at this like a guy making radiators. Gas fumes, noise. No sense that you're doing it."

"I should think it would be easier."

"Maybe you're right," I said. I swung the mattock again, the wide blade buried in the earth to the haft. I levered it forward and the earth spilled loose. Paul shoveled it out. He still held the shovel too high on the handle and he still moved too tentatively. But he cleared the hole.

"We'll use some power tools later on. Circular saws, that sort of stuff. But I wanted to start with our backs."

Paul looked at me as if I were strange and made a silent gesture with his mouth.

"It's not crazy," I said. "We're not doing this just to get it done."

He shrugged, leaning on the shovel.

"We do it to get the pleasure of making something. Otherwise we could hire someone. That would be the easiest way of all."

"But this is cheaper," Paul said.

"Yeah, we save money. But that's just a point that keeps it from being a hobby, like making ships in a bottle. Only when love and need are one, you know?"

"What's that mean?" he said.

"It's a poem, I'll let you read it after supper."

We finished the last hole and set the last tube into it. We drove reinforcing rods into the ground in each tube and then backfilled the holes around the tubes. I went around with a mason's level and got each tube upright and Paul then shoveled the earth in around it while I kept adjusting it to level. It took us the rest of the afternoon. When the last one was leveled and packed I said, "Okay, time to quit."

It was still warm and the sun was still well up in the western sky when I got a beer from the refrigerator and a Coke for Paul.

"Can I have a beer?" he said.

"Sure." I put the Coke back and got a beer.

We sat in the camp chairs with the sweat drying on our backs in the warm breeze. When the sun went down it would get cold, but now it was still the yellow-green spring of the almost deserted forest, and no human sounds but the ones we made.

"In the summer," I said, "it's much noisier. The other cabins open up and there's always people sounds."

"You like it up here?"

"Not really," I said. "Not for long. I like cities. I like to look at people and buildings."

"Aren't trees and stuff prettier?"

"I don't know. I like artifacts, things people make. I like architecture. When I go to Chicago I like to look at the buildings. It's like a history of American architecture."

Paul shrugged.

"You ever seen the Chrysler Building in New York?" I said. "Or the Woolworth Building downtown?"

"I never been to New York."

"Well, we'll go sometime," I said.

One squirrel chased another up one side of a tree and down the other and across a patch of open ground and up another tree.

"Red squirrel," I said. "Usually you see gray ones."

"What's the difference?" Paul said.

"Aside from color, gray ones are bigger," I said.

Paul was silent. Somewhere on the lake a fish broke. A monarch butterfly bobbed toward us and settled on the barrel of the shotgun that leaned against the steps to the cabin.

Paul said, "I been thinking of that stuff you said that time, about being, ah, you know, about not depending on other people."

"Autonomous," I said.

"Well, what's that got to do with building houses and lifting weights? I mean, I know what you said, but . . ." He shrugged.

"Well, in part," I said, "it's what I can teach you. I can't teach you to write poetry or play the piano or paint or do differential equations."

I finished the beer and opened another one. Paul still sipped his. We were drinking Heinekens in dark green cans. I couldn't get Amstel, and Beck's was only available in bottles.

For a cabin in the woods, cans seemed more appropriate. Paul finished his beer and went and got another one. He looked at me out of the corner of one eye while he opened the new can.

"What are we going to do tomorrow?" he said.

"Anything you'd like to do?" I said. "It's Saturday."

He shrugged. If he did enough weight lifting maybe I could get him too muscle-bound to do that. "Like what?" he said.

"If you could do whatever you wanted to do, what would it be?"

"I don't know."

"When you are twenty-five, what do you imagine yourself doing?"

"I don't know."

"Is there anyplace you've always wanted to go? That no one would take you, or you were afraid to ask?"

He sipped at the beer. "I liked the movie *The Red Shoes*," he said.

"Want to go to the ballet?" I said.

He sipped at the beer again. "Okay," he said.

CHAPTER NINETEEN

IT WAS SATURDAY morning.

I put on a blue suit and a white shirt from Brooks Brothers, all cotton, with a button-down collar. I had a blue tie with red stripes on it, and I looked very stylish with my black shoes and my handsome Smith & Wesson in my right hip pocket. The blue steel of the barrel was nicely coordinated with my understated socks.

Paul broke out a tan corduroy jacket and brown pants and a powder blue polyester shirt with dark blue pocket flaps.

He wore his decrepit Top-Siders and no tie. His socks were black.

"That is about the ugliest goddamned getup I've seen since I came home from Korea," I said.

"I don't look okay?"

"You look like the runner-up in a Mortimer Snerd look-alike contest."

"I don't have any other stuff."

"Okay, that's what we'll do this afternoon," I said. "We'll get you some clothes."

"What will I do with these?"

"Wear them," I said. "When we get new ones you can throw those away."

"Who's Mortimer Snerd?"

"A famous ventriloquist's dummy from my youth," I said. "Edgar Bergen. He died."

"I saw him in an old movie on TV."

The ride to Boston took three and a half hours. Most of the way down Paul fiddled with the radio, switching from one contemporary music station to another as we went in and out of range of their signal. I let him. I figured I owed him for the near daily baseball games he'd listened to while we worked. We got to Boston around a quarter to twelve.

I parked Susan's Bronco on Boylston Street in front of Louis'.

"We'll go here," I said.

"Do you buy your clothes here?" he said.

"No. I don't have the build for it," I said. "They tend to the leaner pinched-waist types."

"You're not fat."

"No, but I'm sort of misshapen. My upper body is too big. I'm like a knockwurst on a canapé tray in there. The lapels don't fall right. The sleeves are too tight. Guy that's lean like you, they'll look terrific."

"You mean skinny."

"No. You were skinny. You're beginning to tend toward lean. Come on."

We went into Louis'. A slim, elegant salesman picked us up at the door.

"Yes, sir?"

He was wearing a pale gray-beige double-breasted suit with the jacket unbuttoned and the collar up, a round-collared shirt open at the neck with the blue paisley tie carefully loosened, Gucci loafers, and a lot of blue silk handkerchief showing at the breast pocket. He had a neat goatee. I decided not to kiss him.

"I'd like a suit for the kid," I said.

"Yes, sir," he said. "Come with me." If Louis' were a New York restaurant, it would be the Tavern-on-the-Green. If it were a municipality, it would be Beverly Hills. Lots of brass and oak and indirect lighting and stylish display, and thick carpet. As we got into the elevator I said softly to Paul, "I always have the impulse to whiz in the corner when I come in here. But I never do."

Paul looked startled.

"I got too much class," I said.

We bought Paul a charcoal three-piece suit of European cut, black loafers with tassels, nearly as nice as mine, two white shirts, a red-and-gray striped tie, a gray-and-red-silk pocket handkerchief, two pairs of gray over-the-calf socks, and a black leather belt. We also bought some light gray slacks and a blue blazer with brass buttons, a blue tie with white polka dots, and a blue-and-gray-silk pocket handkerchief. Under pressure they agreed to get the pants shortened for the evening. The jackets fit him decently off the rack. I offered the elegant salesman a check for seven hundred fifty dollars. He shook his head and took me to the front desk. A far less elegant young woman handled the money. The salesmen were too dignified.

"We'll have those trousers ready at five o'clock, sir."

I said thank you, and the salesman left me to the clerical ministrations of the young woman.

"I'll need two pieces of identification," she said. She was chewing gum. Juicy Fruit, from the scent. I gave her my

driver's license and my gumshoe permit. She read the gumshoe permit twice. We got out of the store at three ten.

"Ever been to the Museum of Fine Arts?" I said.

"No."

"We'll take a look," I said.

At the museum I offended a group being taken through
by a guide. I was telling Paul something about a painting of
the Hudson River School when one of the ladies in the group
told us to shush.

"You're disturbing us," she said.

"Actually you're disturbing me," I said. "But I'm too
well-bred to complain."

The guide looked uncomfortable. I said to Paul, "It's
like a Cooper novel. The wilderness is lovely and clean. It's
romantic, you know?"

The whole party glared at me in concert. Paul whispered, "I never read any novels by that guy."

"You will," I said. "And when you do, you'll think of
some of these paintings."

He looked at the painting again.

"Come on," I said. "I can't hear myself think in here."

At five o'clock we picked up Paul's clothes at Louis'.
The elegant salesman glided by as we did so and nodded at us
democratically. We drove over to my apartment so he could
change.

"Change in my bedroom," I said. "And when you get
through, bring that crap out here."

"My old clothes?"

"Yes."

"Which outfit should I wear?"

"Your choice."

"I don't know what goes with what."

"The hell you don't," I said. "We picked it all out at
Louis'."

"But I forgot."

"Get in there and get dressed," I said. "This is a decision you can make. I won't do it for you."

He went in and took twenty minutes to change. When

433

he came out he was wearing the gray suit and a white shirt. He carried the red-and-gray tie. "I can't tie it," he said.

"Turn around," I said. "I have to do it backwards on you."

We stood in front of the mirror in my bathroom and I tied his tie.

"All right," I said when I ran the tie up and helped him button the collar. "You are looking good. Maybe a haircut, but for the ballet it's probably the right length."

He looked at himself in the mirror. His face was sun- and windburned, and looked even more colorful against the white shirt.

"Come on," I said. "We gotta meet Susan at Casa Romero at six."

"She's coming?"

"Yeah."

"Why does she have to come?"

"Because I love her and I haven't seen her in a couple of weeks."

He nodded.

Susan was standing on the corner of Gloucester and Newbury when we walked up. She had on a pale gray skirt and a blue blazer with brass buttons and a white oxford shirt open at the throat and black boots with very high heels. I saw her before she saw me. Her hair looked glossy in the afternoon sun. She was wearing huge sunglasses. I stopped and looked at her. She was looking for us up Newbury and we were on Gloucester.

Paul said, "What are we stopping for?"

"I like to look at her," I said. "I like to see her sometimes as if we were strangers and watch her before she sees me."

"Why?"

"My ancestors are Irish," I said.

Paul shook his head. I whistled through my teeth at Susan. "Hey, cutie," I yelled. "Looking for a good time?"

She turned toward us. "I prefer sailors," she said.

As we walked down the little alley to the entrance I

gave Susan a quick pat on the backside. She smiled, but rather briefly.

It was early. There was plenty of room in the restaurant. I held Susan's chair and she sat down opposite Paul and me. The room was attractive and Aztecky with a lot of tile and, as far as I could see, absolutely no Mexicans.

We ate beans and rice and chicken *mole* and *cabrito* and flour tortillas. Paul ate a surprising amount, although he was careful to poke at each item with his fork tines first, as if to see that it was dead, and he sampled very tiny bits to make sure it wasn't poisonous. Susan had a margarita and I had several Carta Blanca beers. There wasn't much conversation. Paul ate staring into his plate. Susan responded to me mostly in short answers and while there was no anger in her voice I sensed no pleasure either.

"Suze," I said over coffee, "since I'm spending the rest of the evening at ballet. I was hoping this would be the high point."

"Did you really," she said. "Am I to gather you're disappointed?"

Paul was eating pineapple ice cream for dessert. He stared down into it as he ate. I looked at him then at Susan.

"Well, you seemed a little quiet."

"Oh?"

"I think I will pursue this, if at all, another time," I said.

"Fine," she said.

"Would you care to join us at ballet?" I said.

"I think I will not," she said. "I don't really enjoy ballet."

The waiter presented the check. I paid it.

"May we drop you somewhere?" I said.

"No, thank you. My car is just down Newbury Street."

I looked at my watch, "Well, we've got a curtain to make. Nice to have seen you."

Susan nodded and sipped her coffee. I got up and Paul got up and we left.

CHAPTER TWENTY

I HAD NEVER been to a ballet before, and while I was interested in the remarkable things the dancers could do with their bodies, I wasn't looking forward to the next time. Paul obviously was. He sat motionless and intent beside me throughout the program.

Driving back to Maine I said to him, "Ever been to a ballet before?"

"No. My dad said it was for girls."

"He's half right again," I said. "Just like the cooking."

Paul was quiet.

"Would you like to do ballet?"

"You mean be a dancer?"

"Yeah."

"They'd never let me. They think it's . . . they wouldn't let me."

"Yeah, but if they would, would you want to?"

"Take lessons and stuff?"

"Yeah."

He nodded. Very slightly. In the dark car, trying to keep an eye on the road, I barely caught the nod. It was the first unequivocal commitment I'd seen him make, and however slight the nod, it was a nod. It wasn't a shrug.

We were quiet. He hadn't turned the radio on when he got in the car, as he almost always did. So I didn't either. Past the Portsmouth Circle, on the Spaulding Turnpike, an hour north of Boston, he said without looking at me, "Lots of men dance ballet."

"Yes," I said.

"My father says they're fags."

"What's your mother say?"

436

"She says that too."

"Well," I said, "I don't know about their sex life. What I can say is, they are very fine athletes. I don't know enough about dance to go much further than that, but people who do know seem to feel that they are also often gifted artists. That ain't a bad combination, fine athlete, gifted artist. It puts them two up on most people and one up on practically everybody except Bernie Casey."

"Who's Bernie Casey?"

"Used to be a wide receiver with the Rams. Now he's a painter and an actor."

There were a few streetlights and not many towns now. The Bronco moved through the night's tunnel as if it were alone.

"Why do they say that?" Paul said.

"Say what?"

"That dancing's for girls. That guys that do it are fags. They say that about everything. Cooking, books, everything, movies. Why do they say that?"

"Your parents?"

"Yes."

We went through a small town with streetlights. Past an empty brick school, past a cannon with cannonballs pyramided beside it, past a small store with a Pepsi sign out front. Then we were back in darkness on the highway.

I let some air out of my lungs. "Because they don't know any better," I said. "Because they don't know what they are, or how to find out, or what a good person is, or how to find out. So they rely on categories."

"What do you mean?"

"I mean your father probably isn't sure of whether he's a good man or not, and he suspects he might not be, and he doesn't want anyone to find out if he isn't. But he doesn't really know how to be a good man, so he goes for the simple rules that someone else told him. It's easier than thinking, and safer. The other way you have to decide for yourself. You have to come to some conclusions about your own behavior and then you might find that you couldn't live up to it. So why not go the safe way. Just plug yourself into the acceptable circuitry."

"I can't follow all that," Paul said.

"I don't blame you," I said. "Let me try another way. If your father goes around saying he likes ballet, or that you like ballet, then he runs the risk of someone else saying men don't do that. If that happens, then he has to consider what makes a man, that is, a good man, and he doesn't know. That scares the shit out of him. Same for your mother. So they stick to the tried and true, the conventions that avoid the question, and whether it makes them happy, it doesn't make them look over the edge. It doesn't scare them to death."

"They don't seem scared. They seem positive."

"That's a clue. Too much positive is either scared or stupid or both. Reality is uncertain. Lot of people need certainty. They look around for the way it's supposed to be. They get a television-commercial view of the world. Businessmen learn the way businessmen are supposed to be. Professors learn the way professors are supposed to be. Construction workers learn how construction workers are supposed to be. They spend their lives trying to be what they're supposed to be and being scared they aren't. Quiet desperation."

We passed a white clapboard roadside vegetable stand with last year's signs still up and the empty display tables dour in the momentary headlights. NATIVE CORN. BEANS. And then pine woods along the road as the headlight cone moved ahead of us.

"You're not like that."

"No. Susan says sometimes in fact I'm too much the other way."

"Like what?"

"Like I work too hard to thwart people's expectations."

"I don't get it," Paul said.

"Doesn't matter," I said. "The point is not to get hung up on being what you're supposed to be. If you can, it's good to do what pleases you."

"Do you?"

"Yeah."
"Even now?"
"Yeah."

CHAPTER TWENTY-ONE

WE RAN FIVE MILES in the late May warmth and both of us glistened with sweat when we got back to the cabin. The new cabin was on the verge of beginning to look like something. The concrete pilings had cured. The sills and floor joists were down. The big plywood squares that formed the subflooring were down and trimmed. The composting toilet was in, the stool perched flagrantly on the unadorned subfloor.

"We don't lift today," Paul said. His breath was easy.

"No," I said. I took two pairs of speed gloves off the top of the speed bag strike board and gave one pair to Paul. We went first to the heavy bag. "Go ahead," I said.

Paul began to hit the bag. He still pushed his punches.

"No," I said. "Snap the punch. Try to punch through the bag." Paul punched again. "More shoulder," I said. "Turn your body and get your shoulder into it more. Turn. Turn. No, don't loop. You're hitting with the inside of your clenched hand now, on the upper parts of your fingers. Look."

I punched the bag. Jab. Jab. Hook. Jab. Jab. Hook. "Try twisting your hand as you hit. Like this, see, and extend." The bag popped and hopped as I hit it. "Like this. Punch. Extend. Twist. Extend. You try it."

Paul hit the bag again. "Okay. Now keep your feet apart like I told you. Move around it. Shuffle. Don't walk, shuffle. Feet always the same distance apart. Punch. Left. Left. Right. Right again. Left. Left. Left. Right."

Paul was gasping for breath. "Okay," I said. "Take a break." I moved in on the heavy bag and worked combinations for five minutes. Left jab, left hook, overhand right. Left jab, left jab, right hook. Then in close and I dug at the body of the bag. Short punches, trying to drive a hole through the bag, keeping the punches no more than six inches. When I stopped I was gasping for breath and my body was slick with perspiration. Paul was just getting his breath back.

"Imagine if the bag punched back," I said. "Or dodged. Or leaned on you." I said. "Imagine how tired you'd be then."

Paul nodded. "The speed bag," I said, "is easy. And showy. You look good hitting it. It's useful. But the heavy bag is where the work gets done." I hit the speed bag, making the bag dance against the backboard. I varied the rhythm, making it sound like dance steps. I whistled the "Garryowen" and hit the bag in concert with it.

"Try it," I said. "Here. You'll need this box." I put a wooden box that tenpenny nails had come in upside-down under the bag. Paul stepped up. "Hit it with the front of your fist, then the side, then the front of the other fist, then the side. Like this. I'll do it slow." I did. "Now you do it. Slow."

Paul had little success. He hit the backboard and bent over red-faced, sucking on the sore knuckles. The box wobbled as he shifted his weight and he stepped down and kicked it, still holding his knuckles to his mouth, making a wet spot on the glove.

"You'll probably hit the swivel at least once too," I said. "That really smarts."

"I can't hit it," he said.

"It's easy to pick up. You'll be able to make it bounce pretty good in about a half hour."

It took more than a half hour, but the bag was showing signs of rhythm when it was time for lunch. We showered first. And, still damp, we sat out on the steps of the cabin and had cheddar cheese with Granny Smith apples, Bartlett pears, some seedless green grapes, and an unsliced loaf of

440

pumpernickel bread. I had beer and so did Paul. Neither of us wore shirts. Both of us were starting to tan and signs of pectoral muscles were beginning to appear on Paul's chest. He seemed a little taller to me. Did they grow that fast?

"Were you a good fighter?" Paul said.

"Yes."

"Could you have been champion?"

"No."

"How come?"

"They're a different league. I was a good fighter, like I'm a good thinker. But I'm not a genius. Guys like Marciano, Ali, they're like geniuses. It's a different category."

"You ever fight them?"

"No. Best I ever fought was Joe Walcott."

"Did you win?"

"No."

"That why you stopped?"

"No. I stopped because it wasn't fun anymore. Too much graft, too much exploitation. Too many guys like Beau Jack who make millions fighting and end up shining shoes someplace."

"Could you beat Joe Walcott in a regular fight?"

"You mean not in the ring?"

"Yes."

"Maybe."

"Could you beat Hawk?"

"Maybe."

I drank some beer. Paul had another piece of cheese and some grapes.

"The thing is," I said, "anybody can beat anybody in a regular fight, a fight without rules. It matters only what you're willing to do. I got a gun and Walcott doesn't and poof. No contest. It doesn't make too much sense worrying about who can beat who. Too much depends on other factors."

"I mean a fair fight," Paul said.

"In a ring with gloves and rules, my fight with Walcott wasn't fair. He was much better. He had to carry me a few rounds to keep the customers from feeling cheated."

441

"You know what I mean," Paul said.

"Yes, but I'm trying to point out that the concept of a fair fight is meaningless. To make the match fair between me and Walcott I should have had a baseball bat. In a regular fight you do what you have to to win. If you're not willing to, you probably shouldn't fight."

Paul finished his beer. I finished mine.

"Let's start on the framing," I said.

"You can turn on the ball game if you want," Paul said.

CHAPTER TWENTY-TWO

"You want the studs to be sixteen inches on center," I said, "so that four-by-eight sheeting and stuff will fall right. You'll see when we get the walls up."

We were building the wall frames on the ground. "When we get them built we'll set them up on the platform and tie them together," I said.

"How do you know they'll fit right?" Paul said.

"I measured."

"How can you be sure your measurement is right?"

"It usually is. You learn to trust it, why wouldn't it be right?"

Paul shrugged; a gesture from the past. He began to drive a nail into one of the two-by-four studs. He held the hammer midway up the middle. His index finger was pointed along the handle toward the head. He took small strokes.

"Don't choke up on the handle," I said. "Hold it at the end. Don't stick your finger out. Take a full swing."

"I can't hit the nail that way," he said.

"You'll learn. Just like you did with the speed bag. But you won't learn if you do it that way."

He took a full swing and missed the nail altogether.

"See," he said.

"Doesn't matter. Keep at it. In a while it'll be easy. That way you let the hammer do the work."

By midafternoon we had three walls studded in. I showed Paul how to cut a length of two-by-four the proper size for a sixteen-inch on-center spacing so he didn't have to measure each time.

"What about windows?" he said as we started on the fourth wall.

"When we get the walls up, we'll frame them in, and the doors."

We were finishing up the fourth wall and getting ready to raise them when Patty Giacomin's Audi bumped in from the road and parked beside the Bronco.

When Paul saw her he stopped and stared at the car. He was wearing a hammer holster on his belt and a nailing apron tied around his waist. His bare upper body was sweaty and speckled with sawdust. There was sawdust in his hair too. As his mother got out of the car he put the hammer in its holster.

Patty Giacomin walked from her car toward us. She was awkward walking in slingback high-heeled shoes over the uncivilized ground.

"Paul," she said. "It's time to come home."

Paul looked at me. There was no expression on his face.

"Hello," she said to me. "I've come to take Paul home." To Paul she said, "Boy, don't you look grown-up with your hammer and everything."

I said, "Things straightened out between you and your husband, are they?"

"Yes," she said. "Yes, we've worked out a good compromise, I think."

Paul took his hammer out of the holster, turned, knelt

443

beside the wall we were studding, and began to drive a nail into the next stud.

"Paul," his mother said, "get your things. I want to get back. Spenser, if you'll bill me, I'll send you a check."

I said, "What kind of arrangement have you worked out?"

"With Mel? Oh, I've agreed to let Paul stay with him for a while."

I raised my eyebrows. She smiled. "I know, it seems like such an about-face, doesn't it?" she said. "But a boy needs a father. If it were a daughter, well, that's different."

Paul hammered at the studs, holding four or five nails in his teeth, apparently concentrating entirely on the job.

"Surprising you just thought of that," I said.

"I suppose I've been selfish," she said.

I folded my arms on my chest and pursed my lips and looked at her face.

"Paul," she said, "for heaven's sake stop that damned hammering and get your stuff."

Paul didn't look up. I looked at her face some more.

"Paul." She was impatient.

I said, "Patty. This needs some discussion."

Her head snapped around, "Now just one minute, mister. I hired you to look out for Paul, that's all. I don't need to explain things to you."

"Clever rhyme," I said.

"Rhyme?"

"Paul and *all.* Cute."

She shook her head shortly. I kept looking at her with my arms folded.

She said, "Why are you doing that?"

I said. "There's a credibility problem here. I'm trying to figure it out."

"You mean you don't believe me?"

"That's right," I said. "You been living with Stevie Elegant?"

"I've been staying with Stephen, yes."

"You running out of money to pay me?"

"I'll pay you what I owe you. Just send me a bill."

"But you can't afford to keep paying me."

"Not forever, of course not, who could?"

"Would you like to keep staying with the disco prince?"

"I don't see why you have to talk about Stephen that way."

"Would you?"

"I'm very fond of Stephen, and he cares for me. Yes. I'd like to share his life."

I nodded. "You want to move in with the spiffy one on a permanent basis. But he won't take the kid. You can't keep paying me to baby-sit, so you're going to ship him off to the old man."

"It's not the way you make it sound."

"So in effect your ex-husband is being asked to do you a favor. Does he know that?"

"I don't see . . ."

"He doesn't, does he? He thinks you've just been beaten down and have given up."

She shrugged.

"What do you suppose he'll do when he finds out he's doing you a favor?"

"What do you mean?"

"I mean he's spent the last six months trying to get the kid away from you because he thought you wanted to keep him and you've spent the last six months trying to keep him from getting the kid because you thought he wanted him. But he doesn't and you don't. When he finds out that you're glad he's got the kid he'll want to give him back. You'll spend the next six months trying to give him to each other."

"For God's sake, Spenser, not in front of Paul."

"Why not? You do it in front of Paul. Why shouldn't I talk about it in front of him. Neither one of you is interested in the goddamned kid. Neither one of you wants him. And both of you are so hateful that you'll use the kid in whatever way is available to hurt the other."

"That is simply not true," Patty said. Her voice sounded a little shaky. "You have no right to talk that way to

445

me. Paul is my son and I'll decide what's best for him. He's coming home with me now and he's going to live with his father."

Paul had stopped nailing and was kneeling, his head turned toward us, listening. I looked at him. "What do you think, kid?" I said.

He shook his head.

"You want to go?" I said.

"No."

I looked back at Patty Giacomin.

"Kid doesn't want to go," I said.

"Well, he'll just have to," she said.

"No," I said.

"What do you mean?" Patty said.

"No," I said. "He's not going. He's staying here."

Patty opened her mouth and closed it. A big, fuzzy, yellow-and-black bumblebee moved in a lazy circle near my head and then planed off in a big looping arch down toward the lake.

"That's illegal," Patty said.

I didn't say anything.

"You can't take a child away from its parents."

The bee found no sustenance near the lake and buzzed back, circling around Patty Giacomin, fixing on her perfume. She shrank away from it. I batted it lightly with my open hand and it bounced in the air, staggered, stabilized, and zipped off into the trees.

"I'll have the police come and get him."

"We get into a court custody procedure and it will be a mess. I'll try to prove both of you unfit," I said. "I bet I can."

"That's ridiculous."

I didn't say anything. She looked at Paul.

"Will you come?" she said.

He shook his head. She looked at me. "Don't expect a cent of money from me," she said. Then she turned and marched back across the uneven leaf mold, wobbling slightly on her inapt shoes, stumbling once as a heel sank into soft earth. She got into the car, started up, yanked it around, and spun the wheels on the dirt road as she drove away.

Paul said, "We only got three studs to go and the last wall is finished."

"Okay," I said. "We'll do it. Then we'll knock off for supper."

He nodded and began to drive a tenpenny nail into a new white two-by-four. The sound of his mother's car disappeared. Ours was the only human noise left.

When the last wall was studded we leaned it against its end of the foundation and went and got two beers and sat down on the steps of the old cabin to drink them. The clearing smelled strongly of sawdust and fresh lumber, with a quieter sense of the lake and the forest lurking behind the big smells. Paul sipped at his beer. Some starlings hopped in the clearing near the new foundation. Two squirrels spiraled up the trunk of a tree, one chasing the other. The distance between them remained the same as if one didn't want to get away and the other didn't want to catch it.

" 'Ever will thou love and she be fair,' " I said.

"What?"

I shook my head. "It's a line from Keats. Those two squirrels made me think of it."

"What two squirrels?"

"Never mind. It's pointless if you didn't see the squirrels."

I finished my beer. Paul got me another one. He didn't get one for himself. He still sipped at his first can. The starlings found nothing but sawdust by the foundation. They flew away. Some mourning doves came and sat on the tree limb just above the speed bag. Something plopped in the lake. There was a locust hum like background music.

"What's going to happen?" Paul said.

"I don't know," I said.

"Can they make me come back?"

"They can try."

"Could you get in trouble?"

"I have refused to give a fifteen-year-old boy back to

his mother and father. There are people who would call that kidnaping."

"I'm almost sixteen."

I nodded.

"I want to stay with you," he said.

I nodded again.

"Can I?" he said.

"Yes," I said. I got up from the steps and walked down toward the lake. The wind had died as the sun settled and the lake was nearly motionless. In the middle of it the loon made his noise again.

I gestured toward him with my beer can.

"Right on, brother," I said to the loon.

CHAPTER TWENTY-THREE

"WELL, FATHER FLANAGAN," Susan said when she opened her door. "Where's the little tyke?"

"He's with Henry Cimoli," I said. "I need to talk."

"Oh, really. I thought perhaps you'd been celibate too long and stopped by to get your ashes hauled."

I shook my head. "Knock off the bullshit, Suze. I got to talk."

"Well, that's what's important, isn't it," she said, and stepped away from the door. "Coffee?" she said. "A drink? A quick feel? I know how busy you are. I don't want to keep you."

"Coffee," I said, and sat at her kitchen table by the bay window and looked out at her yard. Susan put the water on. It was Saturday. She was wearing faded jeans and a plaid shirt and no socks and Top-Siders.

"I have some cinnamon doughnuts," she said. "Do you want some?"

"Yes."

She put a blue-figured plate out and took four cinnamon doughnuts out of the box and put them on the plate. Then she put instant coffee into two blue-figured mugs and added boiling water. She put one cup in front of me and sat down across the table from me and sipped from the other cup.

"You always drink it too soon," I said. "Instant coffee's better if it sits a minute."

She broke a doughnut in half and took a bite of one half. "Go ahead," she said, "talk."

I told her about Paul and his mother. "The kid's making real progress," I said. "I couldn't let her take him."

Susan shook her head slowly. Her mouth was clamped into thin disapproval.

"What a mess," she said.

"Agreed."

"Are you ready to be a father?"

"No."

"And where does this leave us?" she said.

"Same place we've always been."

"Oh? Last time we went out to dinner it was a fun threesome."

"It wouldn't be that way all the time."

"Really? Who would guard him when we were being a twosome? Do you plan to employ Hawk as a baby-sitter?"

I ate a doughnut. I drank some coffee. "I don't know," I said.

"Wonderful," Susan said. "That's really wonderful. So what do I do while you're playing *Captains Courageous?* Should I maybe join a bridge club? Take dancing lessons? Thumb through *The Total Woman?*"

"I don't know. I don't know what you should do, or I should do. I know only what I won't do. I won't turn the kid back to them and let them play marital Ping-Pong with him some more. That's what I know. The rest has to be figured out. That's what I wanted to talk with you about."

"Oh, lucky me," Susan said.

"I did not want to talk about how you're in a funk because I'm paying more attention to him than to you," I said.

"Perhaps what you want to talk about isn't terribly important," she said.

"Yes, it is. What we have to say to each other is always important, because we love each other and we belong to each other. And will forever."

"Including what you refer to as my funk?"

"Yes."

She was silent.

"Don't be ordinary, Suze," I said. "We're not ordinary. No one else is like us."

She sat with her hands folded on the edge of the table-top, looking at them. A small wisp of steam drifted up past her face from her coffee cup, a fleck of cinnamon sugar marred her lower lip near the corner of her mouth.

The kitchen clock ticked. I could hear a dog bark some-where outside.

Susan put one hand out toward me and turned it slowly palm up. I took it and held it.

"There's no such thing as a bad boy," she said. "Though you do test the hypothesis."

I held her hand still and said, "First the kid wants to be a ballet dancer."

"And?"

"And I have no idea how he should go about that."

"And you think I do?"

"No, but I think you can find out."

"Aren't you supposed to be the detective?"

"Yeah, but I've got other things to find out. Can you get a handle on ballet instruction for me?"

She said, "If you'll let go of my hand I'll make some more coffee."

I did. She did. I said, "Can you?"

She said, "Yes."

I raised my coffee cup at her and said, "Good hunting." I sipped some coffee.

She said, "Assuming you can keep him despite the best efforts of both parents and the law, which rarely awards children to strangers over the wishes of the parents. But assuming that you can keep him, are you prepared to support him through college? Are you prepared to share your apartment with him? Go to P.T.A. meetings? Maybe be a Boy Scout leader?"

"No."

"No to which?"

"No to all of the above," I said.

"So?"

"So, we need a plan."

"I would say so," Susan said.

"First, I'm not sure how much the parents will want to get tangled up in legal action at the moment. Neither one wants the kid. They only wanted him to annoy each other. If they had to get into a court action to get him away from me, I'd try to prove them unfit and I might dig up things that would embarrass them. I don't know. They may each, or both, get so mad that I wouldn't give the kid up that they'll go to court, or the old man may call out his leg breakers again. Although I would think after the first two debacles they might be getting discouraged."

"Even parents who dislike their children resent giving them up," Susan said. "The children are possessions. In some cases the parents' only possession. I don't think they'll give him up."

"They don't want him," I said.

"That's not the point," Susan said. "It's a shock to the most fundamental human condition. The sense that no one can tell me what to do with my child. I see it over and over in parents at school. Kids who are physically abused by parents who were abused when they were children. Yet the parents will fight like animals to keep the kid from being taken away. It's got to do with identity."

I nodded. "So you think they'll try to get him back."

451

"Absolutely."

"That'll complicate things."

"And the courts will give him back. They may not be good parents, but they aren't physically abusive. You haven't got a case."

"I know," I said.

"If they go to the courts. As you say, the father seems to have access to leg breakers."

"Yeah. I think about that. I wonder why."

"Why what?"

"Why he has access to leg breakers. Your average suburban real estate broker doesn't hang out with a guy like Buddy Hartman. He wouldn't know what rock to look under."

"So?"

"So what kind of work has Mel Giacomin been involved in that he would know Buddy Hartman?"

"Maybe he sold him real estate, or insurance."

I shook my head. "No. Nothing Buddy's involved in is legitimate. Buddy'd find a way to steal his insurance."

"What are you thinking?"

"I'm thinking if I can get something on Mel, and maybe something on Patty too, I'd have some leverage to bargain with on the kid."

Susan smiled at me for the first time in some days. "Mr. Chips," she said. "Are you speaking of blackmail?"

"The very word," I said.

CHAPTER TWENTY-FOUR

I PICKED PAUL up at the Harbour Health Club. "He benched one-oh-five today on the Universal," Henry said.

"Not bad," I said.

Paul nodded. "The Universal is easier," he said.

"One-oh-five is one-oh-five," I said.

We walked up to the Faneuil Hall Market area and ate in Quincy Market, moving among the food stalls and collecting a large selection of food and sitting in the rotunda to eat.

"I have a plan," I said.

Paul ate part of a taco. He nodded.

"I am going to try to find out things about your parents that will let me blackmail them."

Paul swallowed. "Blackmail?"

"Not for money. Or at least not for money for me. I want to have some leverage so that I can get them off your back and off mine and maybe get you their support in what you want."

"How can you do that?"

"Well, your father knows some ugly people. I thought I might look into how come."

"Will he go to jail?"

"Would you mind if he did?"

Paul shook his head.

"Do you feel anything for him?" I said.

"I don't like him," Paul said.

"'Course it's not that simple," I said. "You're bound to care something about his opinions, his expectations. You couldn't avoid it."

"I don't like him," Paul said.

"It's something we'll need to talk about, probably with Susan. But we don't have to do it right now." I ate some avocado-and-cheese sandwich. Paul started on his lobster roll.

"You want to help me look into this?" I said.

"About my father?"

"Yes. And your mother. We may find out things that you won't like to know."

"I don't care."

"If you help?"

"No. I don't care if I hear things about my mother and father."

"Okay. We'll do it. But remember, you probably will care. It probably will hurt. It's okay for it to hurt. It's very sensible that it should hurt."

"I don't like them," Paul said. He finished off his lobster roll.

"All right," I said. "Let's get to it."

I was parked in a slot behind the Customs House Tower by a sign that said U.S. GOVT. EMPLOYEES ONLY. As we walked to the car Paul was a few steps ahead. He'd gotten taller since I'd had him. And he was starting to fill out. He wore jeans and a dark blue T-shirt that said ADIDAS on it. His shoes were green Nikes with a blue swoosh. The hint of definition showed in his triceps at the back of his arms. And there was, I thought, a small broadening of his back as the *latissimus dorsi* developed. He walked straighter and there was some spring. He had a lot of color, reddish more than tan, as he was fair-skinned.

"You look good," I said as we got into the car.

He didn't say anything. I drove down Atlantic Avenue, across the Charlestown Bridge, and pulled up near a bar off City Square, not far from the Navy Yard. The front of the bar was done in imitation fieldstone. There was a plate glass window to the left of the doorway. In it a neon sign said PABST BLUE RIBBON. Across the window behind the neon was a dirty chintz curtain. Paul and I went in. Bar along the right, tables and chairs to the left. A color TV on a high shelf braced with

454

two-by-fours. The Sox game was on. They were playing Milwaukee. I slid onto a barstool and nodded Paul onto the one next to me. The bartender came down the bar. He had white hair and tattoos on both forearms.

"Kid ain't supposed to sit at the bar," he said.

"He's a midget," I said, "and he wants a Coke. I'll have a draft."

The bartender shrugged and moved down the bar. He poured some Coke from a quart bottle into a glass, drew a small draft beer from the tap, and set them in front of us.

"I don't care," he said. "But it's a state law, you know."

I put a five-dollar bill on the bar. "Buddy Hartman around," I said.

"I don't know him," the bartender said.

"Sure you do," I said. "He hangs out here. He hangs out here and he hangs out at Farrell's on Rutherford Avenue."

"So?"

"So I want to give him some business." I put another five on top of the first one without looking at it. Like I'd seen Bogie do once in a movie. The bartender took the top five, rang it up, brought me the change. He put it on the bar on top of the first five.

"He don't usually come in here till about three," he said. "Sleeps late. And he comes in here and has a fried egg sandwich, ya know." It was two twenty-five.

"We'll wait," I said.

"Sure, but the kid can't sit at the bar. Whyn't you take that table over there."

I nodded and Paul and I went to a table in the back of the bar near the door to the washroom. I left the change on the bar. The bartender pocketed it.

Paul paid no attention to the ball game, but he looked at the barroom carefully.

At two fifty Buddy Hartman strolled in, smoking a cigarette and carrying a folded newspaper. He sat on a barstool. The bartender came down the bar and said, "Guy looking for you over there. Says he's got some business."

Hartman nodded. He said, "Gimme a fried egg

sandwich and a draft, will ya, Bernie?" Then he looked casually over toward me. The cigarette in his mouth drooped and sent smoke up past his left eye. He squinted his left eye against it. Then he recognized me.

He spun off the stool and headed for the door.

I said to Paul, "Come on," and went out of the barroom after him. Buddy was cutting across the expressway entry ramps, heading for Main Street.

"Watch the traffic," I said to Paul, and shifted up a gear as we crossed the ramps. Paul stayed behind me. We were both running easily. We were up to five miles a day in Maine, and I knew we'd catch Buddy all right. He was ahead, near the big pseudo-Gothic church, running erratically. He wouldn't last long. He didn't. I caught him by the church steps with Paul close behind me. I got hold of his collar and yanked him backward and slammed his face first up against the church wall to the left of the steps. I patted him down quickly. If he had a weapon he had it well concealed.

Buddy was gasping. I let him go. He turned, coughed, and spit. His chest heaved.

"Dynamite shape, Bud," I said. "Like to see a man keep himself fit."

Buddy spit again. "Whaddya want?" he said.

"I came over to train with you, Bud. Learn some of your physical conditioning secrets."

Buddy stuck a cigarette in his mouth and lit it. He inhaled, coughed, inhaled again. "Don't fuck around with me, man. Whaddya want?"

He was in the angle between the church steps and the church wall. I had him penned so he couldn't run. His eyes kept moving past me to either side.

"I want to know how you happen to know Mel Giacomin," I said.

"Who?"

I slapped him across the face with my left hand. The cigarette flew out of his mouth in a flurry of sparks.

He said, "Hey, come on."

I said, "How do you know Mel Giacomin?"

"I seen him around, you know. I just ran into him around."

I slapped him with my right hand. His head rocked back against the wall. Buddy said, "Jesus Christ. Come on. Stop it."

"How do you know Mel Giacomin?" I said.

"He's a friend of a guy I know."

"Who's the guy?"

Buddy shook his head.

"I'm going to close my fist," I said.

"I can't tell you. He'll kill me," Buddy said.

I hit him a left hook in the side, under the last rib. He grunted and twisted.

"Him later. Me now," I said. "Whose friend is he?"

"Gimme a break," Buddy said.

I feinted another left hook and hit him in the stomach. He started to slide down the wall. I caught him and pulled him upright. He looked past me, but there was no one there. If anyone saw us, they were not getting involved.

"Who?"

"Cotton."

"Harry Cotton?"

Buddy nodded.

"How's he know Cotton?" I said.

"I don't know. Harry just told me he was a friend and wanted a favor. I don't know nothing else, honest to God."

"You doing much work for Harry?"

"Some."

"Torch?"

Buddy shook his head and flinched. "Nothing queer, Spenser, just errands." He covered his middle with his arms.

"I won't tell Harry you mentioned his name to me," I said. "I wouldn't think you'd want to either."

"I won't say nothing," Buddy said. "If he finds out, he'll have somebody burn me. Honest to God he will. You know Harry."

"Yeah. He still got that car lot on Commonwealth?"

Buddy nodded.

I turned and made a come-along gesture to Paul. We walked down Main Street toward our car. Paul looked back once to see where Buddy was, but I didn't bother.

In the car I said to Paul, "How do you feel about that scene?"

"It scared me."

"I don't blame you. If you're not used to it, it's disturbing," I said. "In fact it's sort of disturbing even if you are used to it."

Paul was looking out the window.

"You change your mind," I said. "You want to stay with Susan for a while till I get this straightened out?"

"No. I want to go with you."

"Susan wouldn't mind," I said.

"Yes, she would," Paul said.

I didn't say anything. We went out Rutherford Avenue, across the Prison Point Bridge, and out onto Memorial Drive on the Cambridge side of the river. There were joggers on the riverbank and racing shells on the river, and a rich mix of students and old people walking along the drive. Past the Hyatt Regency I went around the circle and up onto the BU Bridge.

"Where we going?" Paul said.

"To see Harry Cotton," I said.

"He's the man Buddy said."

"Yes. He's a bad man."

"Is he a crook?"

"Yes. He's a major league crook. If your father knew him, your father was in deep."

"Are you going to do the same to him?"

"As Buddy?"

"Yes."

"I don't know. I just go along and see what happens. He's a lot harder piece of material than Buddy. You sure you want to come?"

He nodded. "There isn't anybody else," he said.

"I'm telling you, Susan . . ."

"She doesn't like me," he said. "I want to stay with you."

I nodded. "We're stuck with each other, I guess."

CHAPTER TWENTY-FIVE

HARRY COTTON'S CAR lot was up Commonwealth Avenue, near the old Braves Field, in an old gas station that no longer sold gas. There were colored lights strung around the perimeter of the lot and around the useless gas pumps. The overhead door to the repair bay was down. It had been painted with various paints in the glass panes. There was no sign to identify the business, just eight or ten lousy-looking cars without license plates jammed into the lot. There was no one on the lot. But the door to the office side of the gas station was open. I went in. Paul came in behind me.

In the office there was an old walnut desk, a wooden swivel chair, a phone, and an overhead light with a dozen dead flies inside the globe. There was an ashtray in the shape of a rubber tire full of cigarette butts on the desk. In one corner of the room a Chow with snarled hair and a gray muzzle raised his head and looked at me as I came in.

At the desk talking on the phone was Harry Cotton. Harry went with the office. He was scrawny and potbellied, with long dirty fingernails and yellow teeth. His hair was about the color of a Norway rat and parted just above his left ear. It was a lot thinner than a Norway rat's and while he tried to swoop it up and over, it didn't make it very well, and a lot of pale scalp showed through. He was smoking a menthol cigarette, which he held between the tips of his first two fingers. Apparently he always held his cigarette that way because the two fingers were stained brown from the top joint to the tip. To the right of the Chow a door opened into the maintenance bay. It was empty except for a metal barrel and three folding chairs. Three men sat on the folding chairs around the barrel playing blackjack. They were drinking Four Roses out of paper cups.

Harry hung up the phone and looked at me. He needed a shave. The stubble that showed was gray. He was wearing a red flannel shirt and over it a long-sleeved gray sweat shirt tucked into black sharkskin pants with shiny knees. His belt was too long and an extended length of it stuck out from his belt loop like a black tongue. He wore black high-top sneakers. With his feet up on the desk, his white shins showing above sagging black socks, he looked like a central casting version of Fagin and he was worth maybe three and a half million dollars.

"What do you want?" he said. The dog stood and growled. Paul moved a little more behind me.

I said, "I'm in the market for a rat farm. Everyone says you're the man to see."

"Are you trying to kid me," he said. His voice was shrill and flat.

"Me?" I said. "Kid you? A big shot like you? Not me. The boy here just asked me to define *class* and I thought it would be easier to bring him over here and show him."

The three card players in the garage looked up. One of them got up and moved to the office door. I wasn't sure he could fit through it.

"You want to get your ass kicked," Harry said, "you come to the right place. Ain't he, Shelley? Ain't he come to the right place?"

From the doorway Shelley said, "That's right. He come to the right place." Shelley looked about the same size and strength as a hippopotamus. Probably not as smart, and certainly not as good-looking. His hair was blond and wispy and hung over his ears. He wore a flowered shirt with short sleeves and his arms were smooth and completely hairless. He burped quietly and said, "Fucking anchovies."

"I'm trying to locate a guy named Mel Giacomin," I said.

"You see him here?" Harry said.

"No."

"Then buzz off."

"I heard you'd know where he is."

"You heard wrong."

"Listen up, Paul," I said. "You want to learn repartee. You're in the presence of a master."

Shelley frowned. He looked at Harry.

Harry said, "Do I know you?"

"Name's Spenser," I said.

Harry nodded. "Yeah. I know you. You're the one cleaned out Buddy Hartman and that woodchuck he brought with him a while ago."

"That's me," I said. "The woodchuck's name was Harold, I think. He had a blackjack."

Harry nodded. He was looking at me while he dragged hard on the short cigarette, making a long glowing coal reach almost to his fingers. He dropped the butt on the floor and let it smolder. He exhaled slowly, letting the smoke seep out of each corner of his mouth.

"I'm one of the guys that threw one of your people in the river off the Mass. Ave. Bridge too," I said.

Shelley was chewing tobacco. He spit tobacco juice on the floor behind him.

"What makes you think it was one of mine?" Cotton said.

"Aw, come on, Harry. We both know they were yours. We both know you're tight with Mel Giacomin and you were doing him a favor."

Harry looked at Paul. "Who's the kid?"

"He's a vice cop, undercover," I said.

"That Giacomin's kid?"

I put my hands in my hip pockets. I said, "What's your connection with Giacomin, Harry?"

"I got no connection with Giacomin," Harry said. "And I don't want you sticking your nose into my business. You unnerstand?"

"Understand, Harry. With a *D*. Un-*der*-stand. Watch my lips."

Harry's voice got a little shriller. It sounded like chalk on a blackboard.

"Shut your fucking mouth," he said. "And keep your fucking snoop nose out of my fucking business or I'll fucking bury you right here, right out front here in the fucking yard I'll bury you."

"Five," I said. "Five *fuck*'s in one sentence, Paul. That's colorful. You don't see color like that much anymore."

The other two card players were standing behind Shelley. They weren't Shelley, but they didn't look like tourists. Harry took out his handkerchief and blew his nose. He examined the results, then folded the handkerchief up and stuffed it back in his right pants pocket. Then he looked at me.

"Shelley," he said. "Throw the bum the fuck out, and make it hurt." There was a faint touch of pink on his cheeks.

Shelley spit another batch of tobacco juice on the cement floor behind him and took a step toward me. I took my gun out of its hip holster and pointed it at him.

"Stay right there, Shelley. If I put a hole in you, the shit will seep out and you'll weigh about ninety-eight pounds."

Behind me I heard Paul breathe in.

"Harry," I said. "I can see you out of the corner of my eye. If your hands go out of sight under the desk, I'll shoot you through the bridge of your nose. I'm very good with this thing."

Everyone was still. I said, "Now what was your connection with Giacomin, Harry?"

"Go fuck yourself," Harry said.

"How about I shoot off one of your earlobes?"

"Go ahead."

"Or maybe one of your kneecaps?"

"Go ahead."

We were all quiet. The Chow had stopped growling and

462

was sitting on his haunches with his jaw hanging and his purple tongue out. He was panting quietly.

"Paul," I said. "You see before you an example of the law of compensation. The little weasel is ugly and stupid and mean and he smells bad. But he's tough."

"You'll find fucking out how tough I am," Harry said. "You may as well stick that thing in your mouth and pull the trigger. 'Cause you're a dead man. You unnerstand that. I'm looking at a dead fucking man."

"On the other hand," I said to Paul. "I am handsome, good, intelligent, and sweet-smelling. And much tougher than Harry. Let's go."

Paul went out the door. I backed out after him. The Bronco was right in front of the station. "Go around," I said, "and go fast. Get in the other side and crouch down."

He did what I told him and I followed, backing, my gun steady at the open door. Then we were in the car and out of the lot, and heading toward Brighton on Commonwealth Avenue.

Beside me Paul was very white. He swallowed several times, audibly.

"Scary," I said.

He nodded.

"Scared me too," I said.

"Did it really?" he said.

"Sure. Still does. But there's nothing to be done about it. Best just to go ahead with your program. Being scared is normal, but it shouldn't change anything."

"You didn't seem scared."

"Best not to," I said.

"Why would he let you shoot him? If he's doing something with my father, he must really want to keep it quiet."

"Maybe. Or maybe he's just stubborn. Won't be pushed. He didn't get to be as big a deal in this town as he is by being a piece of angel cake. Even garbage has pride sometimes. Maybe you need to have more if you're garbage."

I U-turned where Commonwealth curves off toward BU and headed back downtown.

"What did you get out of that?" Paul asked.

"Found out a little," I said.

"What?"

"Found out that your father's connection to Harry Cotton is worth covering up."

"Maybe that other guy was lying," Paul said.

"Buddy? No. If he lied, it wouldn't be like that. If Cotton ever heard that Buddy had fingered him, he'd have Buddy killed. Buddy would lie to get out of trouble. But not that way."

"If that guy Cotton is so rich and everything," Paul said, "why is he so junky?"

"I suppose he figures it doesn't attract attention," I said. "Maybe he's just thrifty. I don't know. But don't let it fool you."

"What are we going to do now?"

"Your father have an office set up at his apartment?"

"Yes."

"We're going to burgle it."

CHAPTER TWENTY-SIX

PAUL AND I spent the night in my apartment in Boston. And the next morning about ten thirty we broke into his father's apartment in Andover. There was no one home. Like all the other good suburban business types, Mel Giacomin was out laying nose to grindstone.

"His office is in back where I slept when I was here," Paul said.

Through the dining room with the kitchen opening to the right and down a very short hall there were two bedrooms and a bath. Mel wasn't a neat guy. The breakfast dishes were still laying around the kitchen. Coffee for one, I noticed, and a Rice Krispies box. A health food addict. Mel's bed in the right-hand bedroom was unmade and there were dirty clothes on the floor. There were wet towels on the bathroom floor. The other door was closed and locked with a padlock. I stepped as far back as the narrow hall would let me, raised my right foot, and kicked the door with the flat of my foot. The padlock hasp tore loose from the wood. We went in. The office was neat. There was a studio couch. A table that once functioned in a kitchen, a straight chair, and a two-drawer metal file with a lock. On the table were a phone, a lamp, a beer mug holding pencils and pens, and a card file. The card file was locked too. There was a small Oriental rug on the floor, an air conditioner in the room's one window, and nothing else.

"Let's just take the files," I said. "Simpler than breaking them open and going through them here."

"But won't he know?"

"He'll already know I kicked in his door. I don't care if he knows that someone took his files. If he thinks it's me, fine. If there's things in here to make him nervous, maybe he'll make a move. If he does, things will happen. That's a plus. You take the card file."

And out we went. Paul with the card file, and me wrestling the bigger file. "It's not heavy," I said. "It's just awkward."

"Sure," Paul said. "That's what they all say."

We loaded the files in the back of the Bronco and drove away. No one yelled at us. No policemen blew their whistles. I'd learned over the years that if you're not wearing a mask you can walk in and out of almost anywhere and carry away almost anything and people assume you're supposed to.

I parked in the alley in back of my office and Paul and I carried the files up. It had been a while since I'd been in my office. There was a batch of mail on the floor below the mail slot. A spider had made a web in one corner of my window. Since it didn't interfere with my view of the ad agency across the street, I left it alone.

I put the big file down next to my desk. Paul put the card file on top of it. I opened the window and picked up my mail and sat at my desk to read it. Most of it went right to the wastebasket unopened. What was left was a copy of a book autographed by the woman who'd written it, a woman I'd done some work for awhile ago, and an invitation to attend the wedding of Brenda Loring to someone named Maurice Kerkorian. Reception following the ceremony at the Copley Plaza Hotel. I looked at the invitation for a long time.

"What are we going to do with these files?" Paul said.

I put the mail down. "After we get them open we'll look and see what's there."

"What are we looking for?"

"Don't know. We'll see what's there."

"What did you mean it would be good if my father knew you'd taken the files?" Paul said.

I got a pinch bar out of the coat closet in the corner of the office and began to pry the file drawers open.

"Gets him moving. The worst thing that can happen if you're trying to find out about people is to have them hunker down and stay put. If they simply sit on whatever it is and do nothing, then nothing happens. They don't commit themselves, don't give you a chance to counterpunch, don't make mistakes, don't open themselves up, if you follow."

"What do you think my father might do?"

"He might try to get the files back."

"And what if he does?"

"We'll see."

"But you don't know?"

The last file drawer snapped open under the pressure of the bar. "No, I don't know. But if you'll excuse the phrase, it's the way life is. You don't know what's going to happen. People whose lives work best are the ones who recognize that and, having done what they can, are ready for what comes. Like the man said, 'Readiness is all.'"

"What man?"

"Hamlet."

"That's what you did with Harry."

"Yeah, partly. You go from handle to handle. I tried Buddy, and then Harry, and now your father. It's like walking down a long corridor with a bunch of doors. You keep trying them to see which one opens. You don't know what's behind the doors, but if you don't open any, you don't get out of the corridor."

"All that's in this card file are a bunch of names," Paul said.

I took a card and looked at it. It said *Richard Tilson. 43 Concord Avenue. Waltham. Whole Life. 9/16/73. Prudential #3750916.* "Client file, I guess," I said. I looked at some other cards. Same setup. "Run through them," I said. "Make a note of any names you know. Make sure it's all client information."

"Why do you want me to list people I know?"

"Why not? Might matter. It's a thing to do with the file. Maybe a pattern will crop up. You won't know till you've done it."

I gave Paul a pad and pencil from my desk and he sat in my client's chair with the file on his side of my desk and began to go through it. I turned on the portable radio to a contemporary sound station for Paul and began to go through the contents of the big file on my side of the desk. It was slow. There was correspondence to be read, all of it couched in the clotted, illiterate jargon of economic enterprise. After ten minutes I was getting cerebral gas pains. The music wasn't helping. "If Andy Warhol were a musician, he'd sound like this," I said.

Paul said, "Who's Andy Warhol?"

"It's better you should not know," I said.

At one thirty I tuned to the ball game. Relief. At two I said to Paul, "You hungry?"

"Yeah."

"Why don't you walk over to that sandwich shop on Newbury and get us some food."

"Where is it?"

"Just a block down and around the corner. Right across from Brooks Brothers."

"Okay."

I gave him some money. "Get whatever looks good," I said.

"What do you want?"

"Use your own judgment," I said.

467

"Okay."

He went out and I kept at the files. Paul came back with turkey sandwiches on oatmeal and roast beef sandwiches on rye and two lemon turnovers and a carton of milk. I had coffee from the coffee pot. By three Paul had finished with his file. He said, "I'm going to walk around."

I said, "You need any money?"

He said, "No. I still got change from what you gave me before."

At five Paul came back. He'd bought a book on ballet at the Booksmith up Boylston.

He read his book while I worked on the files. It got dark. I turned on the lights in the office. At eight fifteen I said, "Enough. Come on, I'll buy you dinner."

We went up to Café L'Ananas and ate. I got a bottle of wine and Paul had some. Then we walked back to my apartment. "What about your car?" Paul said.

"We'll leave it there. It's only a four-block walk to my office."

"We going back tomorrow?"

"Yeah, I'm not through."

"I only found three people on the list."

"More than I've found so far."

We went upstairs and went to bed.

CHAPTER TWENTY-SEVEN

IT WAS NEARLY noon the next day before I found anything. It wasn't a bloody dagger or even an Egyptian dung beetle sculptured from gold. It was a list of addresses. It wasn't much, but it was all there was. It was on a single sheet of paper by itself in an unlabeled file folder in the back of the bottom file drawer.

"What's important about that?" Paul said.

"I don't know, but it's the only thing that doesn't have a simple explanation."

I got a city directory out of the bottom drawer of my desk and thumbed through it, looking up the names of the people at the addresses. The fourth one I looked up was Elaine Brooks.

"Isn't Elaine Brooks your father's girl friend?"

"Yes."

"This isn't where she lives."

Paul said, "I don't know where she lives."

"I do. I followed her to you, remember?"

"Maybe she used to live there."

"Maybe."

"She's on my list," he said.

"From the card file?"

"Yes."

"Let me see this list."

He gave it to me. There were two other names besides Elaine Brooks. I consulted the city directory. Both the names were listed in the city directory as owning property at one or another address on the list. Elaine Brooks owned two addresses.

"The card file alphabetical?"

Paul said, "Yes."

"Okay. I'm going to read you some names. You look them up and see if they are in your file. If they are, pull the card and give me the address."

I went through the whole list of addresses, looking each up in the city directory and giving Paul the name I found. All of them were in the file. None of them were listed on the cards at the address in the city directory. "What kind of insurance is listed?" I said when we were through and all the cards were pulled.

"This one says casualty."

"Yeah?"

"This one says homeowner's."

"Any of them say life?"

Paul ruffled through the cards. "No," he said.

I took the cards and made a master list of names and both addresses and the kinds of insurance each had. All had casualty. Everyone was insured with a different company. When I was through, I said to Paul, "Let's go take a look at this property."

The first address was on Chandler Street in the south end. The south end was once rather elegant redbrick town houses. Then it fell into slum wino. Now it was coming back. A lot of upper-middle-class types were moving in and sandblasting the bricks and buying Dobermans and installing alarm systems and keeping the winos at bay. It was an interesting mix: black street kids; winos of many races; white women in tapered pants and spike heels; middle-aged men, black and white, in Lacoste shirts. Our address was between a soul-food takeout and a package store. It was burned out.

" 'Bare ruined choirs,' " I said, " 'Where late the sweet birds sang.' "

"Frost?" Paul said.

"Shakespeare," I said. "Why'd you think it was Frost?"

"'Cause you always quote Frost or Shakespeare."

"Sometimes I quote Peter Gammons," I said.

"Who's he?"

"The *Globe* baseball writer."

We drove to the next address on Symphony Road in the Back Bay. Symphony Road was students and what the school board called Hispanics. The address was a charred pile of rubble.

"Bare ruined church," Paul said.

"Choirs," I said. "Do we sense a pattern developing?"

"You think they'll all be burned?"

"Sample's a little small," I said, "but the indices are strong."

The third address was on Blue Hill Avenue in

Mattapan. It was between a boarded-up store and a boarded-up store. It had burned.

"Where are we?" Paul said.

"Mattapan."

"Is that part of Boston?"

"Yes."

"God, it's awful."

"Like a slice of the South Bronx," I said. "Life is hard here."

"They're all going to be burned," Paul said.

"Yeah, but we gotta look."

And we did. We looked in Roxbury and Dorchester and Allston and Charlestown. In Hyde Park and Jamaica Plain and Brighton. The addresses were always obscure so that we sometimes crisscrossed the same neighborhoods several times, following our list. All the addresses were in unpretentious neighborhoods. All had been burned. It was dark when we got through, and a little rain was starting to streak my office windows.

I put my feet up on my desk and shrugged my shoulders, trying to loosen the back muscles that eight hours of city driving had cramped. "Your daddy," I said, "appears to be an arsonist."

"Why would he burn all those buildings down?"

"I don't know that he burned them. He may have just insured them. But either way it would be for money. Buy it, burn it, collect the insurance. That's his connection to Cotton. Your old man's business was real estate and insurance. Cotton's is money and being bad. Put them together and what have you got?"

"Bibbity-bobbity-boo," Paul said.

"Oh, you know the song. How the hell could you?"

"I had it on a record when I was little."

"Well, it fits. And then when your father needed a little cheap sinew to deal with his divorce situation, Cotton sent him Buddy Hartman and Hartman brought Harold and his musical blackjack."

"What will you do now?" Paul said.

471

"Tomorrow I'm going to call up all these insurance companies and find out if your father was in fact the broker on these fire losses, and if they paid off."

"The ones in the card file?"

"Yeah."

"How will you know who to call?"

"I've done a lot of work for insurance companies. I know people in most of the claims departments."

"Then what will you do?"

"Then I'll file all of what I know for the moment and see what I can get on your mother."

Paul was quiet.

"How do you feel?" I said.

"Okay."

"This is awful hard."

"It's okay."

"You're helping me put the screws to your father and mother."

"I know."

"You know it's for you?"

"Yes."

"Can you do it?"

"Help you?"

"All of it. Be autonomous, be free of them, depend on yourself. Grow up at fifteen."

"I'll be sixteen in September."

"You'll be older than that," I said. "Let's get something to eat and go to bed."

CHAPTER
TWENTY-EIGHT

IT WAS RAINING hard in the morning when Paul and I ran along the Charles River. It rained all day. I sat in my office and called insurance companies. Paul had finished his book on ballet. He went out and, at my suggestion, walked up to the Boston Public Library and used my card to take out a copy of *Catcher in the Rye*. Five minutes after he was back, Susan called.

"The line's been busy for an hour," she said.

"Broads," I said. "Word's out that I'm back in town and the broads have been calling since yesterday."

"Paul with you?"

"Yes."

"Let me speak to him, please."

I held the phone out to Paul. "For you," I said. "Susan."

Paul took the phone and said, "Hello."

Then he was quiet.

Then he said, "Okay."

Then he was quiet.

Then he said, "Okay," and hung up.

"She says there's a prep school out in Grafton that specializes in drama, music, and dance," he said. "She says she'll take me out to look at it this afternoon if I want to go."

"You want to go?"

"I guess so."

"Good. You should. Is it a boarding school?"

"You mean live there?"

"Yes."

"She didn't say. Would I have to live there?"

"Maybe."

"You don't want me to live with you?"

"Eventually you'll have to move on. Autonomy means self-reliance, not changing your reliance from your mother and father to me. I'm what they call in politics a transition coordinator."

"I don't think I want to go away to school."

"Wait, see, take a look at the place. We'll talk. I won't make you do what you genuinely can't stand to do. But keep open. Keep in mind that sometimes I go to unpleasant places and people shoot at me. There are drawbacks to living with me."

"I don't mind."

"Some of the drawbacks might be mine," I said.

"Oh."

"Don't make more of that than it is. If one of us starts fearing that honesty will hurt the other's feelings, we've slid back some. I'm trying to work this out so it's best for all of us, me as well as you. Susan too."

He nodded.

"I've taken you this far. I won't push you out of the nest until we both know you can fly. You understand that?"

"Yes."

"You can trust me to do what I say. Do you know that?"

"Yes."

"Okay. Willing to make another trip out in the rain?"

"Yes."

"I'm in a Dunkin' Donut frenzy," I said. "If you went up Boylston Street and bought some, and coffee to go, and hurried back before the coffee got cold, I might be able to make it until afternoon."

He grinned. "Since I've known you you've been a health food freak."

I gave him five dollars. He put on the yellow slicker jacket I'd bought him and left.

I called a guy in Chicago named Flaherty at Colton Insurance Company of Illinois. He told me that they had insured property in the name of Elaine Brooks, that six months

474

later the building burned, and that while everyone guessed it was arson, no one could prove it and they paid and privately agreed not to insure Elaine again.

"Thing is," he said, "if it was arson, it was also murder. Two winos were apparently cooping up in there and never got out. What they found was mostly charred bones and a muscatel bottle that had half melted."

I said, "Thanks, Jack," and noted the information on my master list.

He said, "You got anything I should know about on this thing, Spenser?"

"No, I'm into something else, this is just collateral, you know."

"Well, don't hold out on us. I throw a lot of investigative work your way."

"Yeah, and it's real exciting too," I said.

"Don't knock it, money's good."

"Money's not everything, Jack," I said.

"Maybe not, but you ever try spending sex?"

"There's something wrong with that argument," I said, "but I can't think what right now. I may call you later with my comeback."

"Keep in touch," Flaherty said.

We hung up. Murder, two counts. Better and better. Or worse and worse, depending on where you stood. From where I stood it looked like enough to keep Mel Giacomin in line.

Paul came back with coffee and doughnuts. Plain for me. Two Boston creams for him—disgusting. I made some more of my calls. Everything was clicking in. Giacomin was involved with some kind of arson ring, and there was no doubt, though at the moment, no proof, that Harry Cotton was in it with him.

Susan showed up in the MG at two thirty. She had on a soft felt hat with a big floppy brim and a brass ring on the hatband. She also wore a light leather trench coat and high-heeled boots of the same color. I wished I were going to look at ballet schools with her. "This will be the real test," I said to

Susan. "If the instructional staff doesn't attempt to seduce you *en masse* it will prove they're gay."

She wrinkled her nose at me. "I'll tell them how big and tough you are," she said. "Maybe they'll hesitate long enough for us to escape."

Paul said, "What if they attempt to seduce *me?*"

I grinned. "That would be further proof, I think."

They left and I finished up my phone calls. There were no surprises.

I made the final notes on my master sheet and then got out some fresh bond paper and typed it all out neatly and went out to a copy shop and had two copies made and came back and filed the original in my office. I mailed the second one to myself at my apartment and stuck the third copy in my pocket for handy reference. Also maybe for showing to Mel Giacomin along with threats. I looked at my watch. Four twenty. I had to get away from the desk.

I locked up the office, got into the Bronco, and cruised down to the waterfront. Henry Cimoli was sitting behind the office desk in the Harbour Health Club in white pants, sneakers, and a white T-shirt. He looked like the world's toughest jockey. He had in fact been one of the best lightweight fighters around and gone fifteen rounds once and lost a split decision to Willie Pep. His arms bulged against the T-shirt and his short body moved like a compressed spring, a great deal of contained energy.

"Come to try and rescue what's left, kid?" he said.

"Yeah. You think it's too late?"

"Almost."

I went to my locker and changed. In the exercise room there were weight machines, barbells, dumbbells, a heavy bag, two speed bags. The walls were mirrored. I started working on bench presses.

I was almost through my workout when Hawk came in at about seven. He wore silky-looking warmup pants with the bottoms unzipped, and high white boxer's shoes and no shirt. He had a pair of speed gloves in the hip pocket of the warmup pants and he carried a jump rope. Most of the people in the room eyed him covertly. He nodded at me, did a few stretching exercises, and began to jump rope. He jumped rope for a half hour, varying the step and speed, crisscrossing the rope.

As he finished I started on the speed bag. He hung the rope up and came over beside me and started on the other bag. As I began to get a rhythm down on the bag he began to punch in counterpoint. I grinned and started to whistle "Sweet Georgia Brown."

He nodded and picked up the beat. We began to alternate, picking up the pace. Like a battle of two drummers from the forties. Hawk picked up the tempo, I picked it up a little more. Hawk used his elbows and fists. I alternated one hand then the other. People began to group around us and the rhythm of the bag and the sense of competition began to carry me. I concentrated as the bag was a wine-colored blur in time with Hawk's. We did paradiddles and rolls, and some of the men in the exercise room cheered at one or another of us. Then they began to clap in rhythm to the bags and Hawk and I carried them with us until the place was in an uproar and Henry came in from the front desk and yelled at Hawk, "Telephone."

Hawk did shave-and-a-haircut-two-bits on his bag and I responded and we stopped, and Hawk, grinning widely, went to the phone. The rest of the room cheered and clapped. I yelled after him.

"Hey, gee whiz, my dad's got a barn, maybe we can put on a show."

Hawk disappeared around the corner and I went to the heavy bag. When he came back his grin wasn't as wide, but his face had a look of real pleasure.

He leaned on the other side of the bag while I pounded it.

"You going to like this, babe," he said.

"You been drafted," I said.

"You been messing with Harry Cotton, haven't you?"

I dug a hook into the bag. "I spoke with him."

"You got that slick way, you know, how you talk so sweet to people. Harry putting out a hit on you."

477

"He's too sensitive," I said. "Call a guy a weasel and tell him he smells bad and he goes right into a goddamned swivet," I said.

"He do smell bad, that's a fact," Hawk said.

"You know Harry?"

"Oh, yes. Harry's an important person in this town."

"That him on the phone?"

"Yeah. He want me to whack you." Hawk's smile got wider. "He ask me if I know who you are. I say, yeah, I think so."

I did a left jab and an overhand right.

"How much he offering?" I said.

"Five G's."

"That's insulting," I said.

"You'd have been proud of me," Hawk said. "I told him that. I said I wouldn't do it for less than ten. He say lot of people be happy to do it for five. I said that wasn't the point. I said lot of people be happy to do it for nothing, but they can't, 'cause they ain't good enough. I said it's a ten-thousand-dollar job at least. He say no."

"Harry was always cheap," I said.

"So I said no. Guess you safe again."

"From you at least." I did some low body punches into the bag. Hawk held it steady.

"Harry will hire cheap," Hawk said. "He'll hire some bum, don't know no better. You'll bury him and . . ." Hawk spread his hands. "I got nothing going for a while. Maybe I hang around with you some."

"What would the rate for hitting us both be?" I said.

"'Bout one hundred and thirty-two trillion," Hawk said.

"Harry's too cheap for that," I said.

CHAPTER TWENTY-NINE

AT NINE O'CLOCK I was at the Giacomin house in Lexington. I forced the back door and went in and turned on the lights. In Patty Giacomin's bedroom was a small secretary with slender curving legs and gold stenciling. Her picture in a leather frame was on it. I opened the leaf and sat down on the small rush-bottomed stool in front of it and began to go through the contents. When I'd been here I'd seen Patty do her bills here, and there wasn't much else but bill-payment receipts and canceled checks. The only handle I had besides her sweet Stephen was her periodic trips to New York.

In a half hour I found what I wanted: American Express receipts from the New York Hilton dated roughly a month apart going back several years. They were all room charges, she'd paid them all with her American Express card, and she'd kept the receipts. She kept all receipts apparently without discrimination. So there was nothing terribly significant about her keeping these. She probably didn't know what was important, so she kept them all.

I went through everything else in the house and there was nothing else worth looking at. I took all the American Express receipts and Patty's picture, turned off the lights, and closed the door.

The spring night was quiet in Lexington. The rain had stopped. Lights shone in people's houses and there were open windows. Voices drifted out occasionally, and the sounds of television. It was late, but there were still cooking smells in the air. As I went toward my car, a cat slid past me and into the shrubs in the next yard. I thought about Harry Cotton's contract. I touched the gun on my hip. The street, when I got to the car, was empty. In the circle of the streetlights moths flew without apparent purpose. The cat appeared from the shrubs and sat on its haunches under the streetlight and looked up at the moths. It was a yellow-striped cat with white chest and face and paws.

I got into the Bronco and started up and drove away from Emerson Road. The ball game was coming in from Milwaukee and it made the sound it always made, soft crowd murmur in the background, the voices of the announcers in familiar pattern, the occasional sound of the bat hitting the ball, the metallic stilted voice of the P.A. announcer, repeating the hitter's last name. The sound seemed almost eternal.

It was nearly midnight when I got back to my apartment. Susan and Paul were still up watching a movie on television. Susan said, "There's a sub out there if you haven't eaten."

I got the sandwich and a beer and came back into the living room. The movie was *An American in Paris*. "How was the Laurel School?" I said.

"The admissions guy was a feeb," Paul said.

I looked at Susan. She nodded. "Regrettable but true," she said. "Everything you hoped he wouldn't be."

"Effeminate?"

"Effeminate, affected, supercilious," Susan said.

"Susan yelled at him," Paul said. His eyes were bright.

I looked at Susan. "He was a pompous little twerp," she said.

"Is he now aware of that?" I said.

"That's what she told him," Paul said.

"Did he get scared?" I said.

Susan said, "I think so."

"Well," I said. "It can't be the only school in the world."

There was an extended dance scene on the television screen. Paul watched it closely. We were quiet while I finished the sub and the beer. I went to the kitchen and put the can in the wastebasket and the plate in the dishwasher. I washed my hands and face at the kitchen sink and came back into the living room. There was a commercial on the tube.

I said to Paul, "You ever been to New York?"

He said, "No."

"Want to go tomorrow?"

"Okay."

"How about you, sugarplum?" I said to Susan.

"I've been," she said.

"I know," I said. "Want to go again?"

"Yes."

I felt the softening of relief and pleasure in the area of my diaphragm.

"We'll hit the shuttle, bright and early."

"Bright maybe," Susan said, "but not too early. I have to call in sick and I have to pack."

"We'll go when you're ready, my love," I said.

And the next day we did. We got the one o'clock shuttle from Logan to LaGuardia. I had my stuff and Paul's in a single suitcase. Susan had two. As I drove to the airport I noticed Hawk's silver Jag parked outside my house. It followed me to the airport garage and as I turned in, it drove by and headed out the exit road. Neither Susan nor Paul noticed. I didn't remark on it.

We got into New York at about one thirty and into the New York Hilton at about two fifteen. We got adjoining rooms. Paul and me in one, Susan in the other. The New York Hilton is big and conveniently located on Sixth Avenue. It is efficient, flossy, and as charming as an electric razor.

Paul was looking out the window of the hotel, staring down into Fifty-fourth Street far below. I remembered the first time I'd come to New York. I'd come with my father at about Paul's age. My father had brought me to go to ball games and tour Rockefeller Center and eat in an Italian restaurant he knew of. He'd pinned half his money to his undershirt in the hotel room, and put the other half back into his wallet. I remembered his grin when he pinned the money to his undershirt. Always tell a country boy, he'd said. I remembered the smell of the city and the sound of it, and the sense of it boiling at all hours, and almost always the sound of a siren somewhere at the edge of the sound. I had stood as Paul was standing, staring out. I'd never seen anything like it. And since then I never have.

I went through the connecting door into Susan's room. She was carefully hanging her clothes up.

I said, "Have you ever noticed what happens to me when I enter a hotel room?"

She said, "Yes. Actually it seems to happen in the elevator going up to the hotel room. But what are we going to tell Paul?"

"Maybe later," I said. "The little fella has to sleep sometime, doesn't he?"

"Let us hope so," Susan said. "Now that we're here, what are we here for?"

"I want to look into Patty Giacomin. She came here about once a month and stayed overnight. It's all I could find that seemed in any way unusual. I thought I'd ask around."

She looked at her watch. "Do you think Paul would care for a tour of Radio City?"

"I would think so," I said. "Can you stand to take him?"

"Yes."

"Thank you."

She smiled. "You're welcome. If he's very tired tonight, he may go to sleep early."

I nodded.

"Do you suppose they have champagne on the room service menu?" she said.

"They better," I said.

Her clothes were all hung up. She was very careful with them. She checked herself in the mirror, made an unidentifiable adjustment to her hair, went to the other room and said, "Come on, Paul. We'll go for a mystery walk."

"What's that?" Paul said.

"You'll find out," Susan said.

Paul opened the door. Susan paused in it and said to me, "I want the Four Seasons," she said.

"Tonight," I said. "It's yours."

When they were gone I made the reservation and then took Patty's picture and went down to the lobby. There was an assistant manager's desk near the elevator bank. The assistant manager was behind it, in a three-piece black pinstripe suit and a pink shirt with a pin collar. I took my license out and placed it on the desk in front of him. He read it without expression. Then he looked at me. "Yes?" he said.

"Who's your security man and/or woman as the case may be?"

"What can we do for you?"

"Gee," I said. "The sign says assistant manager."

"A harmless euphemism," he said. He had receding hair and a neat mustache and good color. I noticed that his hands were manicured and his fingernails were buffed. "Euphemism?" I said. "What kind of security person says euphemism?"

"I was a cop in this city for twenty-two years, sailor. You want to try me out."

I shook my head. "Not me," I said, "I need to find out about this lady here."

I showed him Patty Giacomin's picture.

"In what context?" the assistant manager said.

Trying to explain what I was doing was too complicated. "She's missing," I said. "Husband's worried. Asked me to come down and look.

"She stayed here overnight about once every month," I said. "Last time was about three weeks ago."

"She's not here now?"

"No." I said, "I already checked."

He looked at me for a moment. His shaving lotion was strong and expensive. "You got somebody to vouch for you?" he said. "I don't like talking hotel business with every jerk that comes in here and waves a license at me."

"I liked you better when you were saying things like *euphemism*," I said.

"I don't care what you like. You got somebody to vouch for you?"

"How about Nicky Hilton?"

He almost smiled. "Best you can do?"

"Look at me in profile," I said. "Could I be anything but trustworthy?"

He heaved a sigh. "Come on," he said. He came out from behind the desk and we walked down the lobby to a cocktail lounge. It was almost empty at three in the afternoon. The bartender was a tall trim black man with a tight Afro and big handlebar mustache. The assistant manager gestured him down the bar with his head.

"What'll it be, Mr. Ritchie," the bartender said.

Assistant Manager Ritchie said, "Jerry, you know this babe?" I held up the picture of Patty Giacomin. Jerry looked at it carefully, his hazel eyes expressionless. He looked at Ritchie.

Ritchie said, "Tell him, Jerry. He's okay."

"Sure," Jerry said, "I know her. She comes in here about once a month, gets fried on Chablis, picks up a guy, and goes out with him. To her room, I assume."

Ritchie nodded. "Yeah, to her room. Next day she checks out, pays her bill, and we don't see her for a month."

"Different guy each time?" I said.

"Yeah. I guess so," Jerry said. "Couldn't swear there was never somebody twice, but if it was, it was an accident. She was in here to get laid. She didn't care who."

"Know any of the guys?" I said.

Jerry looked at Ritchie. Ritchie said, "No."

"And if you did?" I said.

"I wouldn't tell you," Ritchie said.

"Unless I come back with somebody from your old outfit," I said.

"Come back with a New York cop on a missing person's investigation, we'll spill our guts. Otherwise, you have found out all you're going to."

"Maybe enough," I said.

CHAPTER THIRTY

WE HAD DINNER at the Four Seasons, in the pool room, under the high ceiling near a window on the Fifty-third Street side. Paul had pheasant, among other things, and paid very close attention to everything Susan and I did. We had some wine, and the bill came to $182.37. I have bought cars for less. The next day we went to the Metropolitan Museum in the afternoon and in the evening we took Paul up to Riverside Church to see Alvin Ailey and his group dance.

In the cab going back downtown Paul said, "That's not exactly ballet, is it?"

"Program says contemporary dance," I said.

"I like that too."

"There are surely lots of variations," Susan said, "Tap dance too."

Paul nodded. He stared out the cab window as we went down the West Side Highway and off at Fifty-seventh Street. We were alone, the three of us, going up in the hotel elevator and Paul said, "I want to learn. I'm going to learn how to do that. If I have to go away to school or whatever. I'm going to do that."

Sunday we slept late and in the early afternoon went up to Asia House and looked at nineteenth-century photographs of China. The faces looking back at us from 130 years were as remote and unknowable as patterns on another planet, and yet there they were; human and real, maybe feeling at the moment the shutter clicked a rolling of the stomach, a stirring of the loins.

We took a late-afternoon shuttle back to Boston and drove Susan out to her house. It was after six when we got there. I pulled the Bronco in next to my MG and parked and ran the back window down with the lever on the dash. Susan and Paul got out on their side, I got out on mine. As we walked back to get the luggage, I heard a car engine kick in. I looked up and a 1968 Buick was rolling down the street toward us. The barrel of a long gun appeared in the window. I jumped at Paul and Susan, got my arms around both of them, and took them to the ground with me on top, scrambling to get us all behind the car. The long gun made the urgent bubbling sound an automatic weapon makes and slugs ripped into the sheet metal of the Bronco and then passed and the Buick was around the corner and gone before I could even get my gun out.

"Lay still," I said. "They could make a U-turn." I had the gun out now and crouched behind the engine block. The car didn't come back and the street was quiet again. The neighbors didn't even open a door. Probably didn't know what they'd heard. Automatic fire doesn't sound like a gunshot.

"Okay," I said. "Let's unpack."

Susan said, "Jesus Christ," as she got up. The front of her dress was littered with grass blades and small leaves. Paul didn't say anything, but he stayed close to me as we carried the bags into the house.

"What was that about?" Susan said in her kitchen.

"I annoyed a guy," I said. "Probably Harry Cotton, Paul."

Paul nodded.

"Who's Harry Cotton?" Susan said. She was making coffee.

"Guy that Mel Giacomin did business with."

"And why is he shooting at you, and, incidentally, us?"

"I have been looking into the relationship between Harry and Mel Giacomin. And Harry doesn't like it."

"Are we going to call the police?"

"No."

"Why not?"

"It would blow what I'm working on."

"Maybe you'd better tell me in more detail what you're

working on," Susan said. "Since it seems to be getting me shot at."

"Okay," I said. "You know I have been trying for some purchase on Paul's parents so I could get them off his back."

"Blackmail," Susan said.

"Yes. Well, I've got it. I can produce a batch of evidence that Mel Giacomin was involved in a major arson scheme to burn down buildings for the insurance. He was in it with Harry Cotton, who's a big-league bad person in town. I can't prove Harry's part, but if I give what I've got to Marty Quirk, it's only time till the fuzz can. So I got something fairly heavy on Mel. To get it I've had to lean on some people including Harry Cotton and he's mad at me. He put out a contract."

"To kill you?" Susan said.

"Yes, he's employed people to kill me."

"How do you know?" Paul said.

"He tried to hire Hawk," I said.

"Aren't you scared?" Paul said.

"Yes. But like I said, there's nothing to be done about that, so I don't spend much time thinking about it."

"I'm scared," Susan said.

"Me too," Paul said.

"Okay, we all are. They're not after you. You just happened to be there."

Susan said, "One of the things I'm scared for is you." She was cutting celery up into a stainless-steel bowl that already contained white meat tuna fish. I reached across from the kitchen table and patted her hip.

"I got what I needed on Patty Giacomin this past weekend in New York."

Paul said, "What was it?"

I said, "This is tough. She went to New York each month to pick up strange men in the bar at the hotel."

Paul said, "Oh."

"I thought about not telling you that," I said. "But whatever we are doing, it doesn't work well on lying."

Paul nodded. Susan frowned. "There's nothing illegal in that."

"No, but Patty will bend to it. She won't want to look at herself in that light. It wouldn't help in custody or alimony fights, in the future. If any. It's enough ammunition for me."

Susan said, "Poor woman."

"Yeah, it's kind of tough to think about how desperate she was for whatever it was she thought she'd find. I don't assume she found it, that way."

"Promiscuity doesn't have to be a sign of unhappiness in a woman," Susan said.

"Once a month, in a distant city, with strangers, while drunk?"

Susan looked at Paul. "So why don't we call the police about these men shooting at us?" she said.

"It would be hard to explain without bringing in Mel and Harry and such. I don't want Mel in jail. I want him out earning money so he can support his kid and pay for his education and stuff."

"Yes, I see that." Susan mixed some mayonnaise into her tuna salad.

"I'll stay with you tonight, and tomorrow I'll see what I can do to wrap this thing up."

"What are you going to do about the contract?" Paul said.

"I'll probably have to talk with Harry about that," I said.

Susan nodded. "I knew that would come."

"You have a better thought?"

"No, it's just you're so predictable. You're going to talk with him because he shot at us. If it had just been you . . ." She shrugged.

"Well, I need to get him out of my way if we're going to get Paul into dance school."

Susan was putting tuna salad on whole-wheat bread. The coffee had stopped perking. Her shoulders were stiff and angry.

"I cannot let some gorilla shoot at you," I said. "I cannot. It's against the rules."

Paul said, "What rules?"

Susan said, "His. Don't ask him to explain them now. I can't stand it." She put the platter of sandwiches on the table and poured some coffee. "At least take Hawk with you," she said. "Will you do that? At least take Hawk. You have Paul to think of too." She took a carton of milk out of the refrigerator and poured Paul a glass. "And me," she said. Her hand shook slightly as she poured the milk.

" 'I could not love thee, dear, so much,' " I said, " 'loved I not honor more.' "

"Shit," Susan said.

CHAPTER THIRTY-ONE

Susan took Paul with her to work. "He can read in my office waiting room," she said. "Until this is cleared up he won't be safe alone and probably not with you."

"It'll be cleared up quick," I said. "Next week, kid, we'll be back working on the cabin."

He nodded. Susan and Paul drove to the junior high school in her Bronco, the left side pocked with bullet holes. I followed in my MG. When I saw them safely inside, I drove back into Boston to my office. I needed time for sitting and thinking. I parked in my alley and went up the back stairs. When I got there, the door was ajar. I took out my gun and kicked it open.

A voice said, "Don't shoot, babe, it's Hawk." He was sitting in my clients' chair, tipped back against the wall out of the line of fire from the door. Hawk was never careless. I put the gun away.

"Didn't know you had a key," I said.

Hawk said, "Haw."

I went around my desk and sat down. "Cotton raise the ante?"

"Naw, I just come by to hang out with you, you know. I got nothing to do and I get restless. You wasn't at your apartment so I figured you'd come here."

I said, "Somebody tried to hit me at Susan's last night."

"She okay?" he said.

"Yeah, but that's not the gunny's fault."

"We gonna go see Cotton today," Hawk said. His face was impassive but the lines around his mouth seemed a little deeper and his cheekbones seemed a little more prominent.

I looked at him for a minute. "Yeah," I said. "We are."

Hawk stood up. "May as well get an early start," he said. I nodded. I took out my gun, spun the cylinder so there was a slug under the hammer, put a fresh slug in the chamber I usually kept empty under the hammer, and put the gun back on my hip. We went out. I locked the office door, and we went down the back stairs.

In the alley I said, "Where you parked?"

"Down front of your place," Hawk said.

"I'm right here," I said. "We'll take mine."

We got into the MG. Hawk pushed the passenger seat back further. "Cute," he said. We drove down Berkeley and turned west onto Commonwealth. The trees were leafing and brownstone town houses were bright with early flowering.

As we went through Kenmore Square, Hawk said, "You gonna have to kill him."

"Harry?"

"Uh-huh. You can't scare him."

I nodded.

"He near put a hole in Susan," Hawk said.

I nodded. About a block short of Harry's used-car lot I pulled in and parked in a loading zone. We got out.

Hawk said, "I think I might drift around back, case they see you coming."

I said, "You know the place?"

"I been in there," Hawk said.

I nodded. Hawk turned down a side street, and cut through an alley and disappeared. I walked straight up Commonwealth and into Harry's office. Harry was at his desk. Shelley and two others were in the service bay. When I came in the door, Harry reached into the desk drawer for a gun. He got it out and half raised when I reached across the desk and slapped it out of his hand. Then I took him by the shirt front with both hands and yanked him out of his chair and frontward across the desk. Shelley yelled, "Hey," from somewhere to my left and then I got a dark glimpse of Hawk between me and the sound of Shelley's voice. I dragged Harry across the desk and slammed him against the far wall of the cinder-block office. He grunted. I pulled him away from the wall and slammed him back against it. He was kicking and clawing at me but I didn't notice much. I shifted my right hand from his shirt to his throat and jammed him against the wall, holding him up by the throat with his feet off the floor.

"Which one shot at us last night?" I said.

Harry swatted at my face. I ignored it and leaned my hand in against his windpipe. "Which one?"

He pointed at Shelley. I dropped Harry and he slid down the wall and sat gasping on the floor. I turned toward Shelley. "If you can get past me," I said, "Hawk won't shoot. You're out of here free."

Shelley and two others stood motionless against the wall in the repair section. Hawk with his gun steady and relaxed stood in front of them. There were three pistols on the floor. Shelley looked at Hawk. Hawk shrugged. "Okay by me, Shell. You ain't gonna make it by him anyway."

"Yeah, if I win you shoot me."

"You don't try and I shoot you now," Hawk said.

One of the other two men was Buddy Hartman. I said to him, "Buddy, take your pal and beat it. You ever come near me or anyone I know, I'll kill you."

Buddy nodded. His companion was a lean, dark, handsome man with the dark-blue shadow of a recently shaven heavy beard. His companion nodded too and they went past me and out the door of the gas station and down the street, walking fast without looking back. Hawk shook his head. "Should have burned them," he said.

Shelley stared after the two men who had gotten out. Then he lunged toward me, trying for the door. He weighed more than I did and the force of his lunge pushed me back against the door jamb. I got a short uppercut in under his jaw and straightened him up with it slightly. Hawk leaned against the far wall with his arms crossed, the revolver still in his right hand. To my left, Harry Cotton was inching along toward his desk. I hit Shelley again under the jaw, and he stepped back and swung at me. I shrugged my shoulder up and took the punch on it. I hit Shelley four times, three lefts and a right in the face. He stumbled back, blood rushing from his nose. I hit him another flurry. He stumbled, waved an arm at me, and backed into Harry's desk. His hands dropped. I hit him one big left hook and a haymaker right hand and he went backward over the desk and hit the swivel chair. It broke under his weight and he lay still on the floor with one foot still on the desk. Harry was trying to get the gun I'd knocked away from him. It was partly under Shelley's body. I took a step around the desk and kicked Harry in the neck. He fell backward and made a swacking noise. I stood over him.

I said, "Never come near anybody I know. Never send anybody else. You understand me?"

Hawk said, "Ain't good enough. You gotta kill him."

"That right, Harry? Do I? Do I have to kill you?"

Harry shook his head. He made a croaking sound.

"You gotta kill him," Hawk said.

I stepped away from Harry. "Remember what I told you," I said.

Hawk said, "Spenser, you a goddamned fool."

"I can't kill a man lying there on the floor," I said.

Hawk shook his head, spit through the open door into the repair bay, and shot Harry in the middle of the forehead.

"I can," he said.

CHAPTER THIRTY-TWO

MEL GIACOMIN'S OFFICE was on a side street just off Reading Square. It was a private home that had been remodeled as an office. The secretarial pool sat out front in a big open room, and Mel and a couple of other men had private offices down the hall. Past Mel's office was the kitchen, which had been left intact, and there were cups and a box of doughnuts and instant coffee and Cremora on the kitchen table. Mel was in there drinking coffee when I showed up.

"What the hell do you want?" he said.

"Clever repartee," I said.

"What?"

"I want to talk about fire insurance," I said.

"I don't want to sell you any."

"It's about fire insurance you've already sold, like to Elaine Brooks."

Mel looked at me. He opened his mouth and closed it. "I didn't . . ." he started. "I . . ." A woman with red hair in a frizz came into the kitchen. She wore a lime-green sweater and a pair of white pants that had been tight when she was ten pounds lighter.

"Let's talk in your office," I said.

Giacomin nodded and I followed him next door. We went in. He shut the door.

"What do you want?" he said when he got behind his desk. He was wearing a tan glen plaid three-piece suit and a blue-figured tie and a white shirt with light tan-and-blue double stripes in it. The vest gapped two inches at the waist, revealing belt buckle and shirt.

"I'll make it short," I said. "I know the arson scam. And I can prove it."

"What are you talking about?"

I took out the copy of my arson file memo and put it on his desk.

"Read this," I said.

He read it over quickly. I noticed that his lips moved very slightly as he read. Then his lips stopped. He was through reading it, but he kept staring down at the paper. Finally, without looking up, he said, "So?"

"So I got you," I said.

He kept staring at the paper. "You tell the cops?"

"Not yet."

"You tell anybody?"

"Don't even think about that," I said. "You don't have a chance against me, and even if you did, note that you're looking at a copy."

"You want a piece of the action?"

I grinned, "Now you are catching on."

"How much?"

"It'll vary."

He looked up. "What do you mean?"

"It means I want two things. I want you to stay away from your kid, and I want you to pay for his support, his schooling, whatever he needs."

"Stay away?"

"Relinquish, leave alone, get off the back of, fill in your own phrase. I want him free of you."

"And send him money?"

"Yes."

"That's all?"

"Yes."

"Nothing for you?"

"No."

"How much I gotta send him?"

"Tuition, room, board, expenses."

"How much will that be?"

"We'll let you know."

"I mean I'm not made of money, you know?"

I stood up and leaned over the desk. "Listen to me, Rat

Shit, you're talking like you could bargain. You can't. You do what I say or you take a big fall. Two people died in one of those fires. Homicide in the commission of a felony is murder one."

"I didn't . . ."

I hit the desk with the palm of my hand and leaned a little closer so my face was about three inches from his. *"Don't bullshit, you keep saying didn't to me and you'll be down to Walpole doing the jailhouse rock for the rest of your god-damned life. Don't didn't me, creep."* *Not bad, me and Kirk Douglas.* I wondered if the palm slamming was overacting.

It wasn't. He folded like a camp chair. "Okay, okay. Sure. I'll go for it. It's a good deal."

"You bet your ass it's a good deal," I said. "And if you don't stick to your end of it, you'll boogie on down to Walpole faster than you can say first degree murder. And, I may stick my thumb in your eye before you leave."

"Okay," he said. "Okay. How much you want to start?"

"I'll bill you," I said. "And if you think when I leave you can call Harry Cotton and have me taken away, you are going to be disappointed."

"I wasn't thinking that," Giacomin said.

"Bills are due upon receipt," I said.

"Yeah, sure. On receipt."

I straightened up and turned and walked out the door. I closed it behind me. I waited about thirty seconds then I opened it again. Giacomin was on the phone. When I looked in he hung up suddenly.

I nodded. "Rat shit like you is predictable," I said. I leveled a forefinger at him. "Don't mess with this, Melvin. Maybe it won't be Walpole. Capital punishment is regaining favor."

He sat and looked at me and said nothing. I left the door open this time and walked away without looking back.

I drove into Boston. Disco Stephen lived in Charles River Park and I still had Patty Giacomin to talk with. I parked on Blossom Street and walked down.

Patty Giacomin let me in. Stephen was there too in a

faded Levi's shirt and jeans, and artfully broken-in over-the-ankle moccasins with big leather stitching. There was a leather thong tight around his neck. He was sipping from an enormous brandy snifter.

"What do you want?" she said. She was carrying a snifter twin to Stephen's.

"Christ, it must run in the family," I said.

"What?"

"Clever repartee."

"Well, what *do* you want?"

"We need to talk alone."

"I have no secrets from Stephen."

"I bet you do," I said. "I bet you don't share too many of your adventures in the New York Hilton with Old Disco."

Her head lifted a little. "I beg your pardon?" she said.

"Can we speak privately for about five minutes?"

She paused for a long time then she said, "Certainly, if you insist. Stephen? Could you?"

"Certainly," he said. "I'll be in the bedroom if you need me."

I let that pass.

When he was gone, she walked over to the window and looked down at the river. I walked with her. When we were as far as we could get from where Stephen could hear, she said softly, "You rotten bastard, what are you doing to me?"

"I'm telling you I know about how you used to go down to the New York Hilton once a month and screw whatever came by."

"You rotten prick," she said softly.

"Oh," I said. "You've found out."

She didn't speak. Her face was very red. She drank some brandy.

I said, "I've made a deal with your husband on whom I also have the goods. He stays away from Paul and pays his bills, and I keep my mouth shut. I'm offering you an even better deal. You stay away from him and I keep my mouth shut. You don't even have to pay any money."

"What goods have you got on him?"

"Zero in on the important stuff, babe."

"Well, what?"

"That's not your problem. Your problem is whether you do what I ask or I start blabbing to the like of Disco Darling down the hall."

"Don't call him that. His name is Stephen," she said.

"Will you stay away from the kid?"

"My own son?"

"That's him, you've got the right one. Will you?"

"What do you mean, stay away?"

"I mean let him go away to school, let him spend holidays with me, or where he wants to, make no attempt to claim custody or make him live with you or your husband."

"My God, just so you won't tell about one indiscretion?"

"Monthly indiscretions—random, promiscuous. Actually, probably neurotic. If I were you, I'd get some help. Also, if you don't do what I say, you get not another penny from your husband, alimony, nothing."

"How can you . . ."

"Call him," I said. "See what he says."

She looked at the phone.

"So there you'll be," I said. "Alone and broke. Disco Steve will roll you like a buck's worth of nickels if he thinks you're messy."

"It's not neurotic," she said. "If a man did it, you'd say it was normal."

"I wouldn't, but that doesn't matter to me. I want that kid out of the middle and I'll do what needs to be done to get him out. You go along or you're broke and abandoned like they say in the soap operas."

She looked down the hall where Stephen had disappeared. She looked at the phone. She looked down at the river. And she nodded her head.

"Do I hear a yes?" I said.

She nodded again.

"I want to hear it," I said.

"Yes," she said, staring at the river.

497

"Okay," I said. "You and Stephen can go back to watching his jeans fade."

I started for the door. "Spenser?"

"Yeah?"

"What did Mel do?"

I shook my head and went out and closed the door.

CHAPTER THIRTY-THREE

PAUL SAT ASTRIDE the ridge pole of the cabin, nailing the final row of cedar shingles four inches to the weather. He was shirtless and tan and the muscles moved on his torso as he took the wide roofing nails one at a time from his mouth and drove them three to a shingle with the hammer. He wore a nailing apron over his jeans and periodically he took some nails from it and put them in his mouth. I put together the ridge cap on the ground. When he was finished with the final row, I climbed the ladder with the ridge cap and we nailed it in place, working from each end and moving toward the center of the ridge. The early fall sun was warm on our backs. At the center I said, "You drive one on that side and I'll drive one on this."

He nodded, took an eightpenny nail out, tapped it into place, and drove it with three hammer swings. I drove mine. We slipped the hammers into his hammer holster and I put out my hand, palm up. He slapped it once, his face serious. I grinned. He grinned back.

"Done," I said.

"On the outside," he said.

"Okay, half done," I said. "Enclosed."

498

We scrambled down the ladder, me first, Paul after, and sat on the steps of the old cabin. It was late afternoon. The sun slanting along the surface of the lake deflected and shimmered in formless patches when we looked at it.

"I never thought we'd build it," Paul said.

"Never thought you'd run five miles either, did you?"

"No."

"Or bench press a hundred fifty pounds?"

"No."

"Or put on twenty pounds?"

Paul grinned at me. "Okay," he said. "Okay, you were right. I was wrong. You want to have an award ceremony?"

I shook my head. There was very little breeze and the sweat on our bodies dried slowly. On the lake someone water-skied behind a hundred hp outboard. There were bird sounds in the close woods. The area was strong with the smell of sawn wood and the faint burnt odor that a power saw produces when the blade dulls.

I got up and went in the cabin and got a bottle of Moët & Chandon champagne from the refrigerator and two clear plastic cups from the cupboard. I put some ice and water into a cooking pot and stuck the champagne in to keep cold. I brought it and the plastic cups out onto the back steps and set it down.

"What's that?" Paul said.

"Champagne," I said. "Elegantly presented."

"I never had champagne," Paul said, "except that time at Susan's."

"It's time again," I said. I opened the bottle and poured each cup full.

"I thought the cork was supposed to shoot up in the air."

"No need to," I said.

Paul sipped the champagne. He looked at the glass. "I thought it would be sweeter," he said.

"Yeah, I did too when I first tried it. It grows on you though."

We were quiet, sipping the champagne. When Paul's

glass was empty he refilled it. The water skier called it quits and the lake was quiet. Some sparrows moved in the sawdust around the new cabin, heads bobbing and cocking, looking for food, now and then finding it. Grackles with bluish iridescent backs joined them, much bigger, swaggering more than the sparrows, with a funny waddling walk, but peaceable.

"When do we have to leave tomorrow?" Paul said.

"Early," I said. "Eight thirty at the latest. We pick up Susan at eleven."

"How long a ride to the school?"

"Four hours."

"How come Susan's going?"

"After we drop you, we're going to have a couple of days together in the Hudson Valley."

What breeze there was had gone. It was still, the sun was almost set. It wasn't dark yet, but it was softer, the light seemed indirect.

"Do I have to have a roommate?"

"First year," I said.

"When can I come home? Back home? To see you?"

"Any weekend," I said. "But I'd stay around out there for a while. You need to get used to it before you come back. You won't settle in if your only goal is to get out."

Paul nodded. It got darker. The champagne was gone.

"It's better than that place in Grafton."

"Yes."

"Everybody there will know everyone and know how to dance."

"Not everybody," I said. "Some. Some will be ahead of you. You'll have to catch up. But you can. Look what you did in one summer."

"Except I wasn't catching up on anything," Paul said.

"Yeah, you were."

"What?"

"Life."

The woods had coalesced in the darkness now. You couldn't see into them. And the insects picked up the noise level. All around us was a thick chittering cloak of forest. We

500

were alone at its center. The cabin was built and the champagne bottle was empty. Biting insects began to gather and swarm. The darkness was cold.

"Let's go in and eat," I said.

"Okay," he said. His voice was a little shaky. When I opened the door to the cabin I could see in the light from the kitchen that there were tears on his face. He made no attempt to hide them. I put my arm around his shoulder.

"Winter's coming," I said.

About the Author

ROBERT B. PARKER is the author of twenty-three books. Since his first Spenser novel, *The Godwulf Manuscript,* he has had numerous bestsellers, including *Pale Kings and Princes, Crimson Joy, Valediction, A Catskill Eagle* and *Taming a Sea-Horse; Poodle Springs,* his best-selling collaboration with Raymond Chandler; and the more recent *Stardust* and *Playmates.* Mr. Parker currently lives in Boston with his wife, Joan.